Praise for the works of Karin Kallmaker

Because I Said So

Readers looking for a layered romance full of complicated feelings and a perfect ending will want to pick up this one. It might just be my favourite book from Kallmaker and it's one I'll come back to again.
-*The Lesbian Review*

—"*Because I Said So*," was an incredibly fun read with some extra helpings of angst, internal and external, to elevate it to a true romance drama. Plus, I utterly enjoyed Kallmaker's mischievous play with irony when it came to the implications of the "love at first sight" experience! Sneaky!

I recommend it to fans who enjoy a richly portrayed, well-written, well-researched tale of romance with a slightly different, eccentric, exotic and an all-around fun, flavour to it! I, for one, had a blast with it!
-Bugs Cheeky, *NetGalley*

Because I Said So by Karin Kallmaker is a beautiful, though angst-filled love story. As a veteran author with some thirty books to her name, Karin is obviously skilled in writing great stories, and this book is a great example of her work.

This is a character/relationship driven novel, you will not find a lot of action or adventure here. For this kind of story, you really need well-defined characters, and Ms. Kallmaker has provided exactly that. These characters have depth. There is also a great deal of chemistry, especially between Kesa and Shannon. Their attraction crackles with electricity from their first meeting to the last page. Josie and Paz present as first loves with all the youthful enthusiasm you expect from this age, including the flashes of immaturity young adults sometime display. The characters make this story, and I thoroughly enjoyed reading their tale. If you enjoy a good romance with great characters and a fair bit of angst in the story, then this book is for you.
-Betty H., *NetGalley*

My Lady Lipstick

Kallmaker fans and newcomers, both, will delight in this new tale. It has a well-written plot with innovative character drama and a love story that doesn't disappoint. The romance sparkles, the characters are enchanting, and their struggles are fascinating. Don't miss the distinctive pink cover, likely a tongue-in-cheek reference to "Anita's" grumble about her own covers! *My Lady Lipstick* is an intelligent and charming work that's sure to please.

-Lambda Literary Review

My Lady Lipstick is one heck of a ride and I loved every page. There were so many lovely touches that added layers to the story. I especially loved the gaming references, the baking and cooking and the depth of the characters. Both characters are expertly drawn and easy to love. I appreciated that Kallmaker made one a wonderfully complex and relatable butch. We need more butch women who are more than just one-dimensional characters. There is also something particularly special about this book. I can't quite put my finger on what it is, but there is no doubt that this going to be one of my favourites.

-The Lesbian Review

Karin Kallmaker writes exceedingly good romances, and this one is a masterful mixture of a fun tale, delightful characters and her wicked sense of humour. It isn't full of laugh out loud moments, but the more subtle wit that raises a smile at the play on words and the sarcastic banter. Add in Shakespearean character flaws along with the essential growth of our leading ladies and we have a classic. The whole is a perfectly wrapped bundle of enjoyment for anyone who likes a good romance.

-Lesbian Reading Room

With this two likable characters, some great secondary characters and her usual mature writing style, Kallmaker told us a very interesting story of deception, loneliness, vulnerability, broken dreams (and bones), family… and, of course, love. …*My Lady Lipstick* is a well-written story that I really liked and can easily recommend. If you have never read any of Karin Kallmaker's books (she has written nearly thirty novels; what are you waiting for!?), this one can be a good start.

-Pin's Reviews, goodreads

I was also really happy with the pace of the book. I would say the book is slightly longer than average, but it never really lagged for me. I never felt bored, and really enjoyed the actual concept of the book. When it came to the romance, at first I thought maybe the characters had jumped into bed a little fast. But with how the rest of the story unfolded, I was okay with it. There was no rushing to say "I love you." I actually really appreciate that as it seems to happen too often lately in lesfic romances. The romance instead felt like it progressed really organically. Not including the one angsty part, I actually felt the romance was one of the more realistic romances I have read in a while.

This was absolutely the right romance at the right time for me. I enjoyed this read and I hope others do as much as I did. If you are a Kallmaker fan, I believe you will be happy with this read.

-Lex Kent's Reviews, *goodreads*

The Kiss That Counted

For years CJ Roshe has lived with the fear that "The Gathering" would find her and make her pay for turning against them. Constantly looking over her shoulder she has meticulously created a new life with no room for close friends or lovers who might ask too many questions. But her carefully constructed life begins to unravel when she falls in love with the beautiful Karita... Full of suspense and mystery, award-winning Karin Kallmaker pens another page-turner that draws the reader in with her deeply moving characters and storytelling.

-Cecilia Martin, *Lambda Book Report*

The Kiss That Counted is Kallmaker at her finest—a not to be missed romance. She offers us characters with depth and dimension, along with a rich plot, peppered with an air of mystery to keep the reader turning pages long into the night. Read it to see if CJ will be able to take control of her past and if Karita will ever be able to let down her defenses to allow someone in again. Finally, read it to see if the kiss really counted.

-Anna Furtado, *Just About Write*

Kallmaker has used the darkness of Roshe and the glow of Hanssen to tell a story filled with mystery, excitement and danger. *The Kiss That Counted* is a gripping story that will delight Kallmaker fans, and win her many more.

-R. Lynne, *Just About Write*

There is a romance here, but there is also a bit of a mystery as the reader begins to wonder what CJ's secret is and how she will resolve the problem once it is revealed. In the end, *The Kiss That Counted* is also a testimony to friendship and the changes it can cause in a person's life. Kallmaker shows with the skill in this book why she deserves such a large fan following.

-Lynne Pierce, Just About Write

Love by the Numbers

First class rom-com! A wonderful witty romance and a great tale of character development and growth… The romance is sweet and the sex is hot, all in all this had my dopamine, seratonin and oxytocin levels creeping higher and higher.

-The Lesbian Reading Room

The love story is engaging and is filled with just the right amount of tension to make the nerve endings buzz as Nicole and Lily learn to adapt to the inevitable result of their growing passion for one another. The characters are appealing in spite of—or perhaps because of—the secrets each one holds, preventing them from opening their hearts. The story line is appealing and draws the reader in. It's also filled with that tongue-in-cheek, ever-so-sassy humor that Kallmaker does so well… Another win!

-Lambda Literary Review

Engrossing, Romantic and Sexy… Kallmaker's writing is so vivid—she paints the picture so wonderfully it's as if I'm right there with the characters, seeing what they are seeing, smelling the same aromas, tasting the same food. It's wonderful! I've never been to the places Nicole and Lily visit, but that doesn't matter. They are brought to life so beautifully I feel as if I have a scrapbook of my own… *Love by the Numbers* is another of Kallmaker's books that has been added to my "re-read" pile.

-Frivolous Views

Maybe Next Time

No "formula" romance, *Maybe Next Time* is an engrossing, compelling story of redemption, healing and surviving. Kallmaker has explored complicated themes and done so with heart and a touch of humor. In this reader's opinion, it is one of her best novels.

-Midwest Book Review

Maybe Next Time, winner of a Lambda Literary Award for Romance, has everything readers expect from a love story, but with an edge... Filled with angst, sensitivity, intimacy, and joy, *Maybe Next Time* delivers a memorable tale. With flawed but likeable main characters, an intriguing plot with many surprises, award-winning prose and flawless editing, this five-star novel epitomizes great romantic fiction. And in this reader's opinion, Karin Kallmaker tells it beautifully.

-Just About Write

Painted Moon

Painted Moon is a classic that could very well become the next *Curious Wine*.

-Lesbian Review of Books

Painted Moon has what this reader considers classic Kallmaker elements with interesting characters, wry wit and steamy love scenes. (Some of the images of Jackie and Leah have lingered in my mind for years.) If you missed this title the first time around, or if you are new to Kallmaker's novels, pick up a copy of *Painted Moon* and bask its glow.

-Midwest Book Review

Warming Trend

Kallmaker has given us insight into human emotion along with beautiful descriptions of the Alaskan glacial terrain. *Warming Trend* will teach as well as entertain, and the broken relationship between Eve and Ani will have the reader on tenterhooks until the end.

-Anna Furtado, Just About Write

Kallmaker has given her fans a beautifully written novel, complete with breathtaking descriptions of Alaska. Hers is not the Alaska of the cruise lines, but the heart of Alaska, with particular attention to its glaciers, ice, and northern lights... She has told her story with great language, wit, and warmth. She's even included a very large, very lovable dog. If you're a Kallmaker fan, or if you're new to her work, *Warming Trend* is not to be missed.

-R. Lynne Watson, *Just About Write*

Substitute for Love

Kallmaker is a genius. I loved the angst, the drama and the passion... The story construction is fantastic. You get a really personal point of view from both characters. This takes a gifted storyteller, but never fear Kallmaker is here.

-*The Lesbian Review*

What would you do for someone you loved? It's easy to say you'd climb mountains and swim oceans, but when faced with a desperate choice, what would you do? That's the dilemma facing Reyna in Karin Kallmaker's newest, and I think, darkest novel... Kallmaker does a fine job exploring the anguish of Reyna's life, and the second plot, concerning a mathematician, is equally well-developed. Her major and minor characters are credible and spirited, a pleasure to meet and, sometimes, to hate. *Substitute for Love* may just be the best Kallmaker I've read in a long time, and given her extraordinary talent, that's saying something.

-Deborah Pffeifer, *Bay Area Reporter*

I've never been big on reading romance novels, which is why I'm so surprised to come to the revelation that I'm hooked on Karin Kallmaker's books... *Substitute for Love* is no exception. It doesn't seem likely for Holly, who is in a long-term straight relationship, to get involved with Reyna, who writes press releases and articles for a conservative, anti-gay Christian group, but it happens. As the story unfolds, Holly finds out some secrets about her past, while we find out the reason why Reyna has the job she has. This may be one of Karin Kallmaker's best and most engrossing books yet.

-Deborah DiRusso, *Womyn's Words*

Her plots are textured, her characters are engaging, her sex scenes are intense, and her prose style is better than workmanlike—she's the lesbian hybrid of Joyce Carol Oates (if Oates wrote briefer, less bleak books) and Danielle Steele (if Steele wrote well). *Substitute for Love* continues Kallmaker's string of darn good reads... That Kallmaker renders the tortuous travails of Holly and Reyna quite plausible is one of her novel's many charms.

-Richard LaBonte, *Book Marks*

In Karin Kallmaker's *Substitute for Love*, the undisputed Mistress of Romance skillfully weaves a tale of longing, need, and desire, creating a story complete with mystery, good guys, bad guys, tender moments, humor, and raw sexuality. Kallmaker continues her tradition of painstaking research in her latest work. Unlike some romance writers, she again creates new backgrounds and occupations for her heroines, while interweaving this information with their characters, interactions, and the storyline itself.

-Therese Szymanski, *Lambda Book Report*

Simply the Best

Other Bella Books by Karin Kallmaker

When you purchase from the publisher more of your dollars reach the women who write and produce the books you love. Karin thanks you for your support of stories for and about women who love women!

18th & Castro
Above Temptation
All the Wrong Places
Because I Said So
Captain of Industry
Car Pool
Christabel
The Dawning
Embrace in Motion
Finders Keepers
Frosting on the Cake: The Original
Frosting on the Cake: Second Helpings
In Every Port
Just Like That
The Kiss that Counted
Love by the Numbers
Making Up for Lost Time
Maybe Next Time
My Lady Lipstick
Night Vision
One Degree of Separation
Painted Moon
Paperback Romance
Roller Coaster
Stepping Stone
Substitute for Love
Sugar
Touchwood
Unforgettable
Warming Trend
Watermark
Wild Things

About the Author

Karin Kallmaker has been exclusively devoted to lesbian fiction since the publication of her first novel in 1989. As an author published by the storied Naiad Press, she worked with Barbara Grier and Donna McBride and has been fortunate to be mentored by a number of editors, including Katherine V. Forrest.

In addition to multiple Lambda Literary Awards, she has been featured as a Stonewall Library and Archives Distinguished Author. Other accolades include the Ann Bannon Popular Choice and many other awards for her writing, as well as the selection as a Trailblazer by the Golden Crown Literary Society. She is best known for novels such as *Painted Moon, My Lady Lipstick, Captain of Industry, Touchwood,* and *Because I Said So.*

The California native is the mother of two and is grateful to them for their frequent tutorials about what's hip with kids these days. Search for "Kallmaker" on social media—there's only one. That's probably for the best.

Simply the Best

Karin Kallmaker

BELLA
BOOKS
2021

Bella Books, Inc.
P.O. Box 10543
Tallahassee, FL 32302

First Edition - 2021

Editor: Medora MacDougall
Cover Designer: Kayla Mancuso
Author Photo credit: Judy Francesconi Photography

ISBN: 978-1-64247-1-502

Acknowledgments

My most profound thanks to all the readers and colleagues who have participated in auctions this past year for charity. You answer every call and share the love. In particular, Linda, Polly, and MJ, you made a real difference to someone in need, and I thank you for your generosity. Ann, Ann, and Anne, Finnian, Val, Georgi, Patty, Darlene, and Would Like to Remain Anonymous—you all rock like Gibraltar.

After a year of "Namaste, Six Feet Away" and rewriting this particular story several times as the ground shifted under everyone's feet, I am more appreciative than ever of the steady rocks in my life: the dearest of friends and beloved family, including two kids who are just beginning life as adults and are blooming in spite of adversity. As much as I have despaired about the patterns of history that never seem to change, all of you are proof that the circles of love go on.

Dedication

To all those who have lost in the tumult of the past few years and still believe that love is what saves us from ourselves.

For Erica Abbott. I can hear you singing from here.

Thirty is a New Beginning

I have a simple taste, only the best.

-Oscar Wilde

PART ONE

Drowning in History

CHAPTER ONE

Alice Cabot braced herself as her editor tossed his Ticonderoga #2 onto his desk. She was all too familiar with this signal of his exasperation.

The pencil bounced. Hard.

Abruptly aware that she might be in more trouble than she had thought, Alice caught it before it rolled off the edge of his desk and meekly returned it to his No News is Bad News mug-slash-pencil holder.

At least she hoped her expression was meek. These days her inside face was showing on the outside.

Ed Becerra's voice was soaked in irony as he observed, "I would have thought, given your feminist principles, that you wouldn't use a term like 'douchebag.' I thought douches and the bags they came in are tools of the patriarchy that serve no purpose."

Alice spread her hands in acceptance. "You prove my case. The congressman is, quite literally, a douchebag."

His snort might have held agreement, but Ed's vexation wasn't feigned. His remarkable bushy eyebrows were a single line across his untanned, lined forehead as he glanced at his computer monitor. No doubt he was consulting the email he'd received from a power-that-be about the trending #CongressmanDouchebag.

She braced herself for the compulsory lecture. The sooner it was over the sooner she could get back to her own desk and her deadline.

"You're a journalist, Al. Or you used to be. You can't call people names. There are always cell phones pointed at politicians, and those people don't care you were having an off-the-record conversation. You know that."

"He thinks ninety-nine-point-nine percent of all scientists are conspiring to lie about everything from climate change to viral vectors because it's inconvenient to him financially."

"You can't call people douchebags in an interview and claim objectivity."

There were days when she was convinced objectivity was kindling for the planetary inferno. Ed was right, of course. It was not a good mindset for a journalist or a scientist. This discussion wasn't going like all the others, so she mentally stowed her notes for the article due this evening so she could focus on Ed. She'd no sooner logged out of the quantum computing summit than the phone had rung with his summons.

"Objectivity doesn't mean there's no right and wrong. I will never accept that his ignorance deserves the same respect and reporting as actual facts. Calling attention to how his deliberate ignorance hurts everyone else while he lines his own pockets *is* part of my job."

Ed pursed his lips and waited.

She finally muttered, "But name-calling won't happen again."

"You're right, it won't. You're moving to Style."

Alice thought for a moment he'd spoken in Gallifreyan or Elvish. She pushed her glasses back up the bridge of her nose as if that would help. "What?"

"You heard me. *S-t-y-l-e*. You get one last chance to prove you can play well with others and be a journalist."

Her feet thumped on the floor as she sat up straight in the chair. "What the actual fuck, Ed?"

He waved off her outrage with a thick-knuckled hand. "Nobody wants to work with you. The line editors hate you. You have no allies in management. You burn boats to prove you're not afraid of fire." He took a deep breath and lowered his voice. "What do you want from me? Get out of town for a while and get your head right. You're not the only person hurting right now. We're all hurting."

Alice cleared her throat and nodded at the truth of his statement.

"At a minimum, take your potty mouth out of my office. I have better things to do than this."

"It would be great to get out of Manhattan," she retorted. "It's like the inside of a microwave out there, and September isn't going to be any better. Wait—you're sending me somewhere? There's money for that?"

"A very small sum of money. So small that *sum* is an overstatement. I'm hiding you, for all the good it'll do me. There are other people here who want this assignment. You screw it up and there's no point coming back." He pushed a folder at her, good ol' Ed, who still believed in writing on paper. "I want you to do it because if you can't I have no use for you. We've been down this road for the last time and we're only going down this road because there's a journalist under there somewhere."

She started to open the folder, but Ed added, "This isn't negotiable. There's no point looking it over. Yes is your only answer or you can rant into the wind somewhere else. Reality check, Al. Most newspapers don't have a hard science beat anymore. You know how many people we lost and how many never came back from the last furlough. Grow up. You have to earn a place here, every day, regardless of who your mother is."

She glared at him, pissed that he'd brought her mother into it. He knew she hadn't earned this place with nepotism.

He glared back, not a muscle in his face moving an inch.

He meant it. *Damn.*

Closing his office door behind her, she maintained her poker face as she stalked between metal desks, following the gray path worn into the once-yellow 1970s linoleum. With mindless recall she turned left, right, right, left, left, and ended up at her own desk on the other side of the floor without bumping into anything or anyone. She sat down with relief. She'd managed not to look at the chairs that were empty.

Jobs gone forever.

People gone forever.

Funerals never held, memorials en masse—the room was full of ghosts whose names she wouldn't allow herself to remember. At least not sober.

She tried to look busy as she purposely did not open the folder Ed had given her. Her mental notes about the article structure for the quantum computing conference call were jotted. The space limit for tomorrow's article was verified. Social media pings from other journalists wanting a comment on #CongressmanDouchebag were read and ignored. Pencils were sharpened. The sweltering Manhattan street five floors below her was examined—alas, no sign of her favorite kebab vendor.

Finally, there was no choice left but to go out into the blistering, dank, foul-smelling late afternoon. The smell was not improved by the dirty, soapy water spilled across the sidewalk by a worker polishing the letters of "Media Holdings Group" on the side of the building. If she looked closely she could see the faded outline of the newspaper's name, excised nine months ago in favor of the name of the conglomerate. She chose not to confront that particular reality today. She was as stubbornly defiant about it as a sports fan who deemed all attempts to rename ballparks and stadiums as capitulation to evil forces subverting all things good and right in the world.

As usual, she paused just outside the doors to wipe her lenses free of the condensation of fetid air on her air-conditioning chilled glasses. Every day of the humid summer she wished she could wear contacts. She didn't put her glasses back on immediately as she was going to have to wipe them off again. Though the world was blurry, she could make the walk down Eighth Avenue to McGinty's, including navigating around the broken curb at 35th Street. She'd need a drink before she could read up on her assignment with anything like equanimity.

After a block she resorted to a trick learned during the pandemic—peppermint lip balm and a mask. It made the world smell a whole lot better. There were always a few people wearing masks these days. She now kept one handy year-round, but mostly it came out during the smelly summer and whenever her Spidey sense felt something contagious could be incubating in crowded transit hubs—especially the subway. Plus she felt a little bit like QE the First, who'd held orange and clove pomanders to her nose to traverse the sewage-strewn streets of London.

Her humidity-soaked polo shirt had dried out and the barkeep had brought her a second Buchanan's 12-Year by the time she opened the folder where Ed had scrawled "STB" on the tab.

STB—Some Total Bullshit?

One of the managing editors wanted an in-depth series into the corporate success of socialite entrepreneur women's empowerment guru Helene Jolie and her brainchild lifestyle brand, Simply the Best. Deliverable the first week of December.

Holy mother of fuckall.

She wanted to set fire to the folder right then and there. Nevertheless, she had a hefty swallow of her single malt and persisted. The assignment was an in-depth series. The scope should include interviews with top corporate execs on handling whiplash ups and downs in the economy, product developers on market trends that had persisted in spite of pandemics and recessions, and local stakeholders in Los Angeles who had been delighted to lure the Long Island-born Jolie and her Manhattan-birthed company into the glittering landscape of Beverly Hills.

The folder slipped from her nerveless fingers onto the worn finish of the old oak bar. It was a puff series for a part of the paper where a managing editor's daughter-in-law, who'd known Jolie since Wellesley, could suggest such coverage as "upbeat, good people news." It would feature a woman and such series were done for men all the time, after all.

Alice had no problem with that—but it was not the kind of thing a science journalist like her did or wanted to do.

"You're here early."

"Shit, you startled me."

She didn't look at Simon as he slid onto the barstool next to her. The bartender had a gin and tonic in front of him before he'd finished mopping his ruddy brown face with a napkin. She'd wait for him to take a few sips before telling him her bad news. She knew she could count on his sympathy since he was one of the colleagues who hadn't survived the corporate changes. Sports had gone all freelance, and Simon had rebooted himself as a specialist stringer in local sports, particularly baseball.

She tapped her own glass for a top up. "I'm in hell."

"Janet is back?" His deep voice gave her ex's name the same intonation he reserved for pitchers who'd left the Yankees for the Red Sox.

"Much, much worse."

"Really? The only reason I'm still friends with you is that you finally broke up with her."

They toasted each other as testimony to the truth of his statement. Janet had had limited good qualities, all of which were private. It wasn't as if Alice had ever had a lot of friends, but after six months coupled with Janet she'd realized the few friends she had, like Simon, weren't turning up at drinks and were increasingly slow to respond to her messages.

By then she was also not entirely sure what she even saw in Janet, who was foul-mouthed, always sure she was right, and wore cynicism like a badge of honor. And was really good in bed. "We were *way* too much alike."

"True. You're both bitches. You in the good way." Simon's second sip from his glass ended with a low hum of pleasure. "I couldn't handle the two of you at once. You at least make me laugh, so I picked you."

"Thanks. My day is not complete unless I can pick at old scabs with you."

"I live to serve. So, no evil ex—why the extra snarky attitude?"

"I got bumped to Style."

He gave a philosophical grunt as he ran another napkin over his tightly textured hair, still as short as it had been during his long-ago stint in the military. "The video was great, by the way. I grabbed the popcorn and watched six times in a row. 'Douchebag.' So appropriate."

Great, she was more viral than she thought if sports-focused Simon had seen it.

"And I enunciated it so clearly."

"All in all, not the best move when Science and Tech staff are dwindling."

A fact she ought to have remembered before she opened her big mouth. "I know. I think Ed was given the green light to can me, but instead, lucky me, I get to do a Style profile feature. In-depth. Major research."

"It'll be a change. Change is good, usually."

"In Beverly Hills."

He spluttered into his drink. "That's a punishment? You get to go to California and you're complaining?"

"It's not the redwoods, or high country, or even Death Valley. Beverly Hills—where fake meets made-up. And this company…" She pushed aside the top sheet of the papers in front of her to read in a high-pitched whiny tone, "That, like, you know, highlights the attractor in every woman and, like, the perfection of the life ahead of her."

Simon's face scrunched into confusion. "What does that even mean?"

"It means a company worth three hundred million and change. If you take their vitamins, you won't ever miss another day at the beach." A glance at Simon's face in the gilt-edged mirror behind the bar showed a pain in his expression to match her own. "It depresses me that women don't question a claim like that."

"Hey, it's not just women. Change 'day at the beach' to 'night with a supermodel' and a lot of men will pay out big bucks."

"According to this, their beauty bloggers have a morning routine for perfect workday energy. It includes starting the day with an hour's bath and thirty minutes of detox yoga and exactly the right supplements based on the weather."

"The yoga I get. But what if you use the powder for rain and it doesn't rain?"

"That's on you, you loser. Your day goes badly, you didn't push all the buttons in the right order. After having time for a bath and yoga, you blitz your breakfast in the branded special blender and pour it in the branded travel mug—which comes with a detox crystal in it—because you need to save time for your busy day, like getting the kids to school."

"Wait. A woman with school-aged kids has time for a hot bath in the morning?"

"If she doesn't, she needs to do more shopping at Simply the Best."

"And the money rolls in." Simon's phone buzzed and he glanced at the display. "Well, hell. I forgot first pitch is early today."

She watched him finish his G and T in two gulps. "Grab some peanuts or you'll fall over."

He rapidly crunched up an ice cube before lamenting, "What a waste of a good drink. I should have gone right to the park. Same time tomorrow?"

"Until the exile begins."

He gathered his phone and wallet as he got to his feet. "How soon?"

"I'll do as much as I can without being there first. Hopefully never." Maybe Ed would change his mind.

A reprieve seemed unlikely though, she told herself on the A train from Penn Station toward her condo in Chelsea. He'd said her only choice was yes. Since she wasn't willing to quit—yet—then she was going to have to do the assignment. Find the strength somehow to set aside her snark. Do the job.

She wished she'd had another drink as she melted her way through the heat vapors rising off the 14th Street sidewalk. Takeout from Po'Boy Palace sounded good. It was the weirdest fusion sandwich ever—New Orleans-fried crawfish with Korean kimchi slaw on a New York hero roll—but it always satisfied. She would have her sandwich and finish her quantum computing summit piece before the deadline at nine tonight. Ed hadn't said anything about not finishing her existing assignments for Science and Tech.

Now that she thought about it, she had a tickler file with about two weeks' worth of follow-ups on articles she'd published so far this summer. It would be responsible of her to finish them as scheduled—until she was told otherwise. Give Ed a chance to cool off and #CongressmanDouchebag to stop trending. It wouldn't be long until someone else said something stupid.

Air-conditioning on high and a quick shower restored her melted bones. She made short work of the warm, spicy, crunchy sandwich, including licking the drippy hot sauce off her fingers. Her cheap but always reliable friend Jim Beam, along with a splash of ginger ale over ice, joined her at her desk as she logged into the paper's gateway and banged out the eight hundred words she'd been allotted.

Eight hundred words was her limit to fully explain why a computer that held both 0 and 1 in the same bit would lead to advances in artificial intelligence, vastly speed the work of contact tracing when it was needed again, and deliver computation speeds that would make a supercomputer today look like an abacus. She submitted it with thirty minutes to spare.

Expecting to get line edits back in ten minutes, she picked up her phone and tapped the icon for her mother.

"Is it miserable in the city?" Barbara Paul Cabot had never bothered overmuch with social niceties like "Hello."

"It would be a step up to get to 'miserable'."

"Good to know. I have an upcoming ladies-who-lunch thing."

"I'll drink to that." She heard the clink of ice in a cocktail glass and pictured the long salon where her mother had for decades entertained writers, visionaries, athletes, actors, musicians, artists, and many other interesting people. Once upon a time, an invitation to rub shoulders at "Barbara's little place in the Hamptons" meant you were fascinating in ways beyond how you made money. A basketball player had talked Alice's ear off once about mapmaking, a subject that had seemed not all that important to her until he'd connected the historic process to colonialism and narratives of cultural supremacy.

It was one of many surprising conversations that had inspired her to question assumptions presented as facts. Every so often Alice wished she were seventeen again, and hopefully naive about the power of knowledge to transform the world. Instead she was looking at forty in the rearview mirror and painfully aware that too many people preferred a fact-free existence. That even more people didn't want to pay for news and therefore the news they got was worth what they paid for it.

"Did you just file today's story?"

"Waiting on edits."

"I see. You thought you'd call your poor, old, lonely mother to kill some time."

"Not poor, not old, not lonely." Alice actually wasn't sure about the last item. Her mother's salon was quiet these days. She was still asked to conduct interviews with the occasional esoteric personality, but the demand was infrequent. When asked what she was doing with a retirement she had never asked for or announced, her mother said she was in the early planning stages of an outline to encapsulate the notes for the foreword to her memoirs.

"Well, sixty-five is the new thirty, unless you're a woman in the public eye where it's vice versa."

"One reason I've avoided television," Alice pointed out. "Besides, I'm not blond and I will never wear a sleeveless blue dress."

"I'll drink to that. What's otherwise new in your world?"

"You haven't seen the video?"

"What did you say, Al?" The unspoken "this time" hung in the air.

"I may have called someone a name and it got caught by a cell phone camera."

"Was it true?"

"It was as accurate as it was inappropriate. A congressman who thinks science is a plot against his bank account."

Her mother hmphed. "The fact that it was inappropriate doesn't change the reality that it was true. I hope it was at least pithy."

"Pithy enough to get me moved to Style."

After what might have been a gasp of surprise, her mother said, "Not permanently, surely. Style is not your, well, style."

"How long remains to be seen." Alice thought about asking her mother not to call her Shirley, but digressions made Mom cranky. Another thought occurred to Alice and should have sooner. "I truly called simply to say hello, but I've just realized you might know something about my new big assignment that I must do if I want to continue to have a job. Ever heard of Helene Jolie?"

"Of course. Her parents still live out here." With her usual subtle shading that blended innocence with irony, she added, "They are quite proud, to the extent that they're capable of genuine, unfiltered emotion."

"Do tell." She grabbed her notepad, jotted the date and time, wrote "background" and "BPC" at the top of the page.

"It's too late for much detail. Come to dinner Friday and stay the weekend. It'll do you good to get out of the city."

She couldn't argue with that. She would never be too old not to enjoy being fussed over by her mother. What had at first seemed a vexing inconvenience had turned out to be one of the luckiest breaks of her life—she'd been at her mother's when the first lockdown order had hit. The Wi-Fi was good and they'd not run out of toilet paper. Colleagues less fortunate had called trips outside their apartments 'boxing with the Black Death.'

Alice had returned to her apartment two months later with video chat exhaustion, new skills in data compilation from ad hoc reviewing of stats for the Health reporters, and an encyclopedic knowledge of Katherine Hepburn movies.

She struck through her entry in her notepad. "We'll cover it this weekend, then. Can I bring you anything?"

"Vienna roast from Porto Rico's and some of their house-blend Russian tea. I know we can order it, but it's not the same. I like the crinkly plain brown paper bags filled right there in the shop."

"I know just what you mean. I'm happy to make a trip down to that part of the Village. Gives me an excuse to go to Big Gay Ice Cream." Her computer chimed and she checked the notification. "My edits are back."

"See you Friday. Kiss kiss."

"Love you, mean it."

Mindful of Ed's assertion that the line editors hated her, she agreed to the three changes without comment and closed out her workday with a sigh.

Her second bedroom slash home office fell silent, though she could still hear murmurs of conversation next door and the rumbles of cars on the street four floors below her. She effortlessly shut it all out, which made the silence in her own apartment even louder.

The deadline-met good mood faded as she stared at the blank screen.

Beverly Hills.

The congressman was indeed a douchebag, and she regretted losing her cool. Ed hadn't told her she had to apologize, but she would do so in the morning regardless. It didn't matter that an elected official paraded without shame his corrupt and self-serving ignorance. She was a journalist and name-calling was bad. Now that her mother knew there was a video to be found, her mother would find it, and there would be a lecture on Friday over dinner—a lecture she deserved.

Beverly Hills.

La La Land with even more La La.

She'd been to Southern California many times, but Beverly Hills just once, for a small science conference on artificial intelligence. The conference was great, but after a stroll down Rodeo Drive, she'd concluded that "artificial" was an understatement and "intelligence" was questionable. Though she had grown up in the Hamptons and had dated several women who dripped Prada and Chanel, she'd still found the plastic and mirrors galleria glitz complete with $400 ripped jeans pretentious to the point of an alternate reality.

At least there had been a good bar in the hotel.

She was pretty sure it was Beverly Hills where she'd hooked up with that bartender with the purple hair, long legs, and an appetite that had kept them up most of the night. That was before Janet made it onto Alice's List of Huge Mistakes. It turned out being alone was better than feeling alone with someone else.

I'll drink to that, she thought.

She was exiled to make nice-nice with flim-flamsy people who sold bogus New Age nonsense. And the absolute worst part was that she couldn't blame anyone else for it. *Beverly fucking Hills*.

Steeling herself, she went to SimplytheBest.com. Right there on the home page under Creating a Positive Environment—quantum crystals.

They were using *quantum* as if it was a synonym for *shiny*.

How was she going to survive this assignment without calling someone a douchebag? Were frontal lobotomies available at the Botox drive-thru?

Depressed and feeling as if she had every reason to be, Alice recalled the good old days of heading out in search of New York nightlife regardless of the humidity and the eventual hangover. It wasn't even ten o'clock. But she was already on her way to drunk, and the thought of sweating under her leather jacket only to be disdained by chic college girls at the Purple Diva was too much. She poured another drink, stretched out on the sofa, and popped in her noise-canceling earbuds. A couple of clicks later she fell deep into her favorite jazz brass band mix channel.

She'd gotten used to having her own party, just her, a sultry songstress, and the comfort of her dark living room. The inner bitch voice she'd named Sass suggested that a recliner and a half-dozen cats would complete the picture.

Eyes closed, she let the percussion rattle at her ears until the horn section came in, rising like pure light that could save her soul. With every note Beverly Hills went farther and farther away.

CHAPTER TWO

The day was under control until 10:14 a.m.

At 10:16, Pepper Addington ran the length of the second floor of the Simply the Best Laboratory Boutique with her phone in one hand and a clipboard snatched off a maintenance cart in the other. The elevator took longer, but it gave her a chance to finish chewing her belated breakfast and regain her composure before she'd be visible from the guest waiting area.

She smoothed back the tendrils that had escaped from her ponytail and dusted her lips free of crumbs from her aborted snack of an STB Power through Your Morning Bar. Using her reflection in the mirrored elevator doors she smoothed her dress and dabbed on Hint of Sunrise lip gloss. The doors parted and she strode briskly into the reception atrium as she consulted her clipboard.

Clipboards, she had learned, were almost as effective as a lab coat for conveying authority.

The pale stone floor echoed the tap of her kitten-heeled flats as she circled the central seating area. There were two women watching her with annoyed but hopeful expressions. At least it wasn't a larger group. Ann, the Laboratory Boutique receptionist, smiled warmly from behind her curved workstation, but her eyes were screaming, "Save me!"

Using a pen from the holder on Ann's desk, Pepper signed the top sheet on the clipboard with a flourish and handed it off to Ann with an air of finality. "All resolved now."

Ann took charge of the clipboard as if Pepper always gave her such things to deal with. "I'm so sorry you were delayed by having to take care of this."

Pepper gestured at what appeared to be the checklist for sanitizing the public areas. "Would you return this to the right people?" Under her breath she added, "Maintenance cart second floor."

"Certainly. I'll take care of it. No need for you to worry." Ann gestured at the two waiting women as she slipped a piece of paper across the desk to Pepper. "Our Very Important Besties have been very understanding."

Pepper glanced at the information, nodded, pushed the note back to Ann and turned to face Teena and Mary Kessler, owners of River City Gifts and Graces. Ann had also helpfully scrawled, "Soap scents scarves #1 in Iowa."

In unison, the two older women rose to their feet. Their restrained annoyance quickly changed to genuine pleasure as Pepper greeted them.

"You must be Teena and Mary Kessler. I apologize for being late. You're a long way from Iowa City." Pepper didn't mention that her boss was the one who was supposed to do the Very Important Bestie tours, but more and more of them were falling to Pepper. She usually found out Nikki was ghosting a tour when Ann called with the agreed-upon code of "Paperwork was due at 10!"

Nikki Cavanaugh's laser focus was on a vacancy up the corporate ladder. As Nikki's intern, Pepper could only hope that Nikki's success would be shared with her staff. A Personal Assistant job would be much more secure than a series of three-month internships on a $500 stipend. It would give Pepper a chance to show that her MBA made her capable of more than fifty hours a week spent fetching samples, delivering lunch, and ferrying paperwork between buildings.

If there were actual dues which had to paid, she pretty darned well thought she'd paid them in full, twice over. Until that happy day, however, Pepper lived by the Golden Rule: Never, ever let the boss look foolish, lazy, or surprised—even if it was all true.

After introductions and apologies, she swept Mary and Teena into the patter of Simply the Best's corporate philosophies of empowering women's futures by offering them purity and only what they sincerely felt was the best. "We'll start upstairs. Our first stop is the workshop where new scents and designs for our hand-milled soaps are crafted. Which is your favorite?"

Teena was partial to the Jaipur Pomegranate, while Mary couldn't decide between Cotton in Tunisia or Eucalyptus Fog. Pepper made a mental note to be sure one of each was in their end-of-tour swag bags. Teena and Mary's little shop in Iowa City was a top outlet, or they wouldn't have been able to get the insider tour of the Lab. Swag bags, with hundreds of dollars' worth of freebies, were a big part of Creating Satisfaction for the small retail stores in less-traveled areas that carried Simply the Best merchandise. Pepper would deliver the two women later to the main building, where they would briefly meet Helene Jolie herself and be featured in a *Quickly the Best* video clip for social media.

It had been made clear to Pepper that when Helene Jolie met the VIBs, she wanted to hear that her treasured guests had been lavishly rewarded. Nikki thought pampering guests was beneath her pay grade, and maybe it was. Pepper really only resented having to step up without warning and already late. That was no way to treat VIBs, and Pepper would make up for it with extras of everything, including charm.

"These particular soaps, as you both well know, start with pure Grecian olive oil. It's saponified via our patented process." Pepper stepped slowly along the main aisle, gesturing right and left at craftspeople and gleaming equipment. "The olive oil is poured into the laboratory beakers, and Tasmer here—" he returned her wave with a heavily gloved hand "—makes sure the oil is heated to exactly the right temperature before the beakers are transferred to the next stage. I love the way it smells in here, don't you?"

"It's making me crave fresh bread and tapenade," Teena admitted.

"Or a pizza with extra olives." Mary smiled at Teena and Pepper could see all in that one shared glance their mutual, indulgent agreement to make each other's wish come true. *Someday*, Pepper thought, *I'll find someone kind and sweet and caring*. But this was not that day. Or that year. Or that decade.

The thick, heavy scent of olive oil made Pepper's stomach growl. She patted it into silence.

"Didn't you get breakfast, dear?" Teena was all mother hen, which was absolutely adorable.

"I did, thank you, ma'am. It's the aroma. I want flatbread smeared with roasted pepper and olive oil."

Teena patted her arm. "Home cooking is what you need. If you're ever in Iowa City you drop in for some of my peach pie."

"That's so sweet. I'll hold you to that." Her stomach threatened to growl again at the thought of food that wasn't a nutrition bar. "Now that we've settled the important things in life, let's continue, shall we? Over here, as you can see, there's even more protective gear. There's no margin for error working with lye."

Both women nodded knowingly, and they moved on to where a goggled worker was blending the olive oil while dripping in small amounts of lye solution. "Olive oil creates a softer soap, and that has something to do with short triglyceride chains. It emulsifies very quickly but takes a long time to harden and even longer to cure. That gives us plenty of time to add scents and oils and create our unique patterns, and then adapt that to larger-scale production by our approved manufacturers."

Pepper indicated the sign on the door to the next chamber. "Today they're testing a variation on our Madagascar Vanilla Bean."

"I like that one too," Teena said. "It's so delicate."

"It is, isn't it?" Pepper pulled open the door, and they were instantly surrounded by a cloud scented with rich, deep vanilla. Pepper battled her sudden craving for sugar cookies. "It's so delicate that the emulsified olive oil has to be cooled before it's added or it will kill all the scent. Vanillin from orchids is very fragile. We could use vanillin from wood botanical sources. It would be a lot hardier and far less expensive. Most commercially produced soaps use it. But the scent wouldn't be as clear and unmistakable."

"That aroma is divine." Mary sighed fondly, one hand on her heart. "It makes me think of the best crème brûlée I ever had, and that was in Italy."

"That was the best." Teena's twinkling glance suggested there were other fond memories, and Pepper averted her eyes. It wasn't as if she was going to be having "crème brûlée" any time soon.

After watching a technician layer different colors of partially cured soap into narrow stainless-steel pans, they moved on to where another tech was cutting cured slices from the long logs to reveal an intricate mandala pattern. Her guests oohed and aahed and Pepper joined them. She'd seen a lot of soap over the past year, and this swirl of blue, orange, and green truly put the "art" in artisanal.

After the soap lab, they moved into the Parfumerie. The display showing how many stems of lavender it took to create a single ounce of essential oil always drew visitor interest. She shepherded the two women onward to the perfume showcase with sample bottles to smell and add to swag bags.

"I don't mean to hurry you, but the jewelry design studio is even more interesting, and I think you'll both want plenty of time there."

"Lead on, dear." Mary followed in Pepper's wake back to the hallway. "This is all wonderful."

Teena was already at the Best Body Jewelry door. "You're right. This is really what I've been looking forward to."

"The metals and stones used for design are not the real stones that will be in the final pieces, of course," Pepper explained as they entered. "It means the designers can make mistakes and try again for our always inspired jewelry selection. I think it's fascinating."

"That's one of the things we do like about the Simply the Best accessories line," Mary said. "You don't see anything like them elsewhere. But the price point is hard to stock, let alone sell, in our part of the country."

Pepper nodded sympathetically. Her current budget didn't extend to real gemstones and precious metals either. "It makes them a special gift indeed. My parents gave me a necklace last Christmas."

"As we tell our customers," Teena volunteered, "there's Simply the Best items for everyday use, to make every day special. And then there's these beautiful things." She touched a wire and stone necklace set out in pieces, awaiting assembly. It looked as if the final would be thick, tightly woven gold strands with a teardrop centerpiece of a topazy stone. "This is going to be so lovely, I can tell."

From Best Body Jewelry Pepper walked her charges down the stairs and across the atrium. Ann was flirting with the intern from Legal who'd scored high marks last week by dropping in with key lime sugar cookie ice cream sandwiches. No easy achievement on a hot August afternoon. She'd tease Ann later about adding yet another heart to her collection.

"Each of the buildings on campus has a water feature. They're all different, but they all display one of STB's product lines. This one has samples from our cut rock and crystals." She let her guests admire the ceiling-to-floor glass sculpture that began at the top with a long pipette that dripped blue-tinted water into an alembic. Curved copper fittings served as the display shelves for desk and bookshelf carvings of quartz, tourmaline, and the latest addition of labradorite from Madagascar. The alembic emptied into a series of laboratory tubes that flowed into a rock-lined catch basin at the floor. "It's mesmerizing, isn't it? The sound of running water is so soothing."

While the two women took in the fountain, Pepper allowed herself a mental vacation and envisioned her favorite spot on Malibu Beach where, right after it rained, a small waterfall tumbled down rocks before disappearing into the sand.

"My nephew would love this. He's a rockhound."

"Let's take a peek at more of the crystal collection around the corner. Sometimes there are fragments available. Then we'll spend some time in the Textiles Lab."

Textiles always took a while, because guests loved to touch and swoon over fabric bolts and samples from around the world. Some were destined for table runners or scarves, others for future exclusive apparel licensed to specific designers. The two women were thrilled to load up their swag bags with autumn season Fallen Leaf hats, scarves, masks, and gloves that weren't even available to order yet.

Their last stop was the Samples Bar, where they voted for their favorite bite from test flavors of ST-Best nutrition bars for morning, noon, and night. Samples were also free to employees, and Pepper lived on them. It helped make the rent, and she kept her roommate supplied too. She hated asking her parents for money and was currently engaged in a game of seeing how long she could make it totally on her own.

She had liked the Golden Persian Pistachio flavor, until, that is, it had become lunch day after day.

It was 11:22 when she tucked her VIBs safely into one of the golf carts they used to move between the five buildings of the Simply the Best campus. The August day was hot, but tempered by a fresh, lazy ocean breeze blowing over the adjacent fairways and greens of the Beverlywood Country Club. Pepper imagined it was probably heavenly out on the water. After an indirect journey that allowed her to point out the other buildings and some of the campus statuary, she handed her charges off to a personal assistant from Partnership Relations at exactly 11:30. The PA would whisk them Upstairs—the euphemism everyone used to indicate anyone and anything that came from Helene Jolie's office.

She heaved a huge sigh of relief on her way back to the golf cart. Finally able to check her phone, she saw several messages from Nikki. None of them were an apology or thank you for taking the tour. Nikki skipped over such things, especially for interns. The last one was a request for lunch from the Simply the Best Café, and she hopped back in the golf cart to fetch Nikki's kale salad. It was a quarter to noon by the time she was parked at the Lab with lunch and iced coffee doctored exactly the way Nikki liked it.

Ann met her almost at the door. "One of the VIBs left her swag bag somewhere!"

So much for thinking the day had calmed down. "Does she have any idea where? They both had bags when we left Textiles."

"She thought maybe the restroom, but we've looked there."

"Hang on to these for me." She thrust the food into Ann's hands and ran out to the golf cart again. Sure enough, there was one of the ST-Best recycled sailcloth shopping bags, its contents spilled out under the seat where it had slid. Damn—she ought to have noticed it, but she'd been too busy getting Nikki's lunch order done.

She sprinted back inside. "It's in the cart. Tell them I'll be back ASAP."

Ann already had her phone to her ear. "You got it."

She took the stairs to the second floor, dropped off the food on Nikki's desk, grateful that there was no sign of her boss or personal assistant. A new intern Pepper had met only yesterday said she'd pass on the message that Pepper had to take something Upstairs for a VIB.

First they'd kept the Very Important Besties waiting and now this.

Pepper had learned many things on the job. The salient lesson at the moment was that when something went wrong, regardless of her own culpability, Nikki would kick it downhill to where Pepper lived. On sudden inspiration she dashed into the Parfumerie, grabbed a boxed sample from behind the counter while breathlessly exclaiming, "Emergency... for Upstairs..."

She was deeply sorry she'd felt fancy this morning and worn her one silk dress to work because she had dinner plans. She was going to sweat through it at this rate.

She calmed herself by arranging the various soaps, perfume samples, harvest-patterned table square, nutrition bars, and autumn accessories back in the bag. On top she put the perfume she'd just liberated. She buckled it safely in place on the seat next to her and pushed the cart pedal all the way to the metal. She passed two other carts, which were sticking with the campus speed limit of seven miles per hour.

"Watch out," one driver called.

Pepper hoped it wasn't anyone important as she called back, "Sorry, sorry, emergency for Upstairs!"

She realized she didn't know where the VIBs would be waiting for her. It was quicker to go in the back to the elevator if they were still on the second floor. However, if there was a merciful higher power in the universe, the missing bag hadn't been realized until *after* they'd met with Helene Jolie. They would therefore be waiting at main reception on the first floor. She screeched to halt in front, smoothed her hair, and alighted from the cart with what she hoped would be seen as poised alacrity.

The two women were indeed waiting at main reception.

However, there was no merciful higher power, at least not today. Beside them was Helene Jolie herself, and the usually vibrant, charming smile was nowhere in sight as she watched Pepper approach.

VIB Teena was all smiles and thank-yous, though, which helped. "I'm so sorry. I don't know how I forgot it. I'm so sorry you had to come all the way back here after such a wonderful tour. You must be so busy, thank you so much…"

Pepper ignored Ms. Jolie's fixed stare and interrupted the flow of words by pointing at the additional perfume. "I would have been back sooner, but I popped into the Parfumerie again. You took the Femme Salon Number Two, and I remembered that you said you sometimes found resin scents a little heavy. This is the Number Four, which has only a touch of amber. It might be better for summer, when humidity and heat will bloom all the scents and you'd notice the musky notes more. I wouldn't want you to be annoyed with your choice."

"That's so considerate and sweet." Teena held the vial close to her nose and nodded. "You might be right."

"I'm so sorry you had to wait."

"It was worth it—and a good thing I forgot the bag. Now I have another perfume to try."

They took leave of Helene Jolie again and headed out into the hot day in search of more adventures. That left Pepper alone with the chief executive officer of the entire company. Pepper had never formally met her and had only glimpsed her in person a couple of times as the unmistakable figure with flaming red hair had made her way to and from the sleek white Tesla parked in its special designated space adjacent to the building.

Without meeting Jolie's gaze, Pepper murmured, "I'll be getting back to the Lab."

"Who are you?"

The demand was abrupt and imperious, but not unexpected. Stop acting like a scolded puppy, Pepper told herself. She steeled herself to meet the gaze that had stared out at her for more than a year from posters and packages.

Jolie's eyes really were that green. Her hair really was that red, and that tousled, and *that* perfect. Earrings of woven gold nestled against the tangle of hair, complementing the golden tan that had not come from a bottle.

"Pepper Addington. I'm an intern for Nikki Cavanaugh."

"The additional perfume was a nice save and quick thinking."

"Thank you. I know how important our VIBs are."

"How long have you been with us?"

"A little over a year."

"I see." One finely shaped eyebrow lifted slightly.

Pepper knew a year was a long time to be an intern. Interns that Pepper had shown the ropes had been hired permanently while she was still waiting. The last time she'd been overlooked, her roommate, CC, had insisted it was time to start over somewhere else. Taking her MBA to a company that empowered women was her dream job, though. She hadn't been at all interested in the consulting firm her father had preferred. So she'd been trying even harder to score a good recommendation from Nikki—and now she was on the carpet with the boss's boss's boss and feeling as upside-down and choking for breath as the last time she'd wiped out while riding a big wave in competition. She resisted the urge to curl into a ball and protect her head.

Pepper fought down the heat she could feel rising in her cheeks and waited for any indication of what to do next.

She didn't expect the curt, "Come with me."

Jolie was at least a half-foot taller than Pepper's five-five and she moved quickly and confidently with long, even strides. By the time they reached the top of the wide, cantilevered staircase that led from reception to Upstairs, Pepper was slightly out of breath and even more grateful for her low-heeled shoes. They breezed past the elevators, and Jolie seemed oblivious to the two women who scurried out of their way.

Pepper had never been Upstairs. She didn't know quite what she'd expected. Of course the walls were whitewashed knotty pine or covered with cotton and hemp—a hallmark of the ST-Best ethos. Clean, sleek, but not harsh. The use of sustainable, natural materials in their products had been reflected throughout the campus with real wood and glass workstations and stone tiles underfoot.

She only had time to glance down the hallways that led right and left, glimpsing faces she recognized from the staff intranet, including the chief operating officer, who was talking on her cell phone as she disappeared around a corner. They skirted a pendulum that was suspended under a domed skylight of stained glass, its slow arc brushing the surface of a shallow pond below it. Pepper didn't have time to marvel at the cascade of colors shimmering in the rippling water. It was all she could do to keep up without looking flustered as they approached a two-workstation gateway that flanked the entrance to the CEO's office.

Beyond the workstations, double-wide glass doors stood open, and through them Pepper glimpsed an expansive view of pale blue sky and brilliant green grass. One of the workstations was occupied, and Pepper recognized the slender, translucent woman immediately—Clarita Oatley, Jolie's legendary assistant. She was rumored to be the second highest-paid employee and was as fiercely loyal as she was rigorously competent. Oatley recited several messages as Jolie passed her but seemed to take no special note of Pepper.

"I want to talk to Nikki Cavanaugh," Jolie said over her shoulder as she and Pepper continued into her office. Jolie seated herself at a wide glass-topped desk and looked expectantly at the phone, leaving Pepper agonizing over whether she should sit down or wait to be told to do so.

Waiting was better, she decided. Her gaze was drawn to the slowly turning Mobius strip sculpture of burnished brass and aluminum that she recognized from SimplytheBest.com. It was as soothing as the website promised until she realized that where it rested on the clear glass desk meant she was also staring at the CEO's long legs and what looked like the "I Mean Business" black Manolo Blahnik stilettos made exclusively for Simply the Best.

She forced her gaze to the window behind Jolie. She could see across the entirety of their country club neighbor to the rise of the Holmby Hills and the greenbelt that separated Beverly Hills from Bel Air. She distracted herself trying to decide the beeline path from here to Malibu Beach.

The phone chirped and Jolie picked up her handset. "Nikki, there's an issue."

Pepper's heart rate jumped higher. Was she going to get fired? Over a swag bag missing for a few minutes? After a year doing the scut work like nobody's business?

"You're missing an intern. She's here with me. Uh—Penny?"

An inquiring, expectant glance made Pepper prompt her with, "Pepper Addington."

"Pepper. What defect has kept her an intern for a year?"

Jolie looked her up and down as she listened to Nikki's answer, her gaze resting briefly on her shoes. A tiny flick of one eyebrow left Pepper in little doubt what Jolie thought of them. She hoped her dress wasn't damp at the armpits. She knew her hair was coming out of her ponytail like it always did, but she steeled herself not to fuss with it.

Desperately trying not to fidget under the laser focus from those green eyes, she took an interest in the rest of the office as if the conversation on the phone was of no interest to her. On her left was meeting space, dominated by a wall-mounted monitor and what looked like complicated video conferencing equipment. The conference table for six, like Helene Jolie's desk, was clear glass. A dozen blown glass bottles with curving, elongated necks formed a centerpiece of blue and green. The lighting above them merged their shadows into a pool of sea glass green onto the pale stone floor below.

Relieved to see that Jolie had turned her chair to look out the window as she talked, Pepper quickly smoothed her hair and took in the rest of the office. To her right, the wall was lined with the same white pine shelves and cupboards used throughout the campus and in STB pop-up and retail stores. They were stocked with skin care products, essential oils, and soaps, and interspersed with luxurious silk and linen scarves, and even one of the Givenchy summer handbags made exclusively for Simply the Best. A pedestal displayed the glittering gold and sapphire necklace and earrings set that had been featured all summer on the website. It was a one-of-a-kind and would go on auction for the Simply the Best Foundation in just a few days.

Jolie's short, humorless laugh brought Pepper back to the conversation that was likely sealing her fate with ST-Best. "So, what you're telling me is you've held on to her because she's abnormally competent for an intern."

Not sure she could trust what she'd just heard, Pepper managed a hesitant smile.

"Oh, I'm sure." One long-fingered hand was lifting her tempestuous mane of red hair from her neck as she continued to study Pepper as if analyzing what size she wore. "I'll take her off your hands."

Jolie hung up the phone without another word and regarded Pepper with a small, tight smile.

"I don't understand," Pepper finally said. "I'm not interning at the Lab anymore?"

"Clarita!" Jolie relaxed as Clarita joined them more quickly than Pepper would have thought humanly possible. "I've found a new personal assistant. Unlike the last one, she can remember specifics and has a small talent for charming visitors."

"Very good." Clarita didn't even glance in Pepper's direction. "I'll complete the paperwork."

Stunned, Pepper stammered, "I don't know what to say. Th-thank you, Ms. Jolie."

"Goodness, she even says my name correctly." Jolie gave Clarita an amused look before fixing Pepper again with her green, so very green eyes. "Call me Helene."

CHAPTER THREE

After two days of ignoring her impending Beverly Hills exile, Alice was happy to plant herself and her knapsack on the air-conditioned Long Island train. The clack-clackety was soothing and familiar. She was about to text her mother when she'd be arriving at Hampton Bays and thought better of it. The bike shop across from the station would have rentals and it had been too long since she'd been to spin class.

Exercise would open up her lungs. Shake out the cobwebs. Provide endorphins and counteract her mother's housekeeper's excellent cooking. If there was any normalcy remaining in the world, Sophia would make pierogis, and lots of them.

Two minutes into the ride she knew she'd made a rash, reckless decision. There were no ocean breezes, and the thick, liquid air was as bad as in the city. At least it smelled immeasurably better. Shade from old oaks and maples was plentiful at first, but the closer she got to Peconic Bay the fewer trees lined the road. Shade was behind walls around homes with increasingly larger expanses of grass between them and the rest of the world.

The pump of the pedals created a sing-song rhythm in her head: *nit-wit, nit-wit, nit-wit...*

Pausing to catch her breath at the final corner before the familiar curved gravel driveway came into view, she realized she'd forgotten it was uphill all the way to her mother's house from here. After a hearty curse, she attempted to pep talk herself. "Twenty years ago you had no problem with it. It must be the weight of your clothes and all that coffee and tea."

Sass piled on. "*And another fifteen pounds on your ass.*"

Nit-wit, nit-wit, nit-wit. She made it up the hill, through the gate, and finally onto the shady driveway leading to the three-story red brick house. Dripping sweat that was already leaving a salt crust on her skin, she finally parked the bike at the wide, dark-stained oak front door.

The door opened. Her mother—tall and elegant in a royal blue caftan that made her skin look like pure ivory, observed her through thick owlish glasses. "What were you thinking?"

"That I needed exercise." Her wobbly legs managed to get her into the blessedly cooler air of the soaring entrance hall. She admired, as always, the grand staircase. Throughout her childhood, she had swept down the staircase in pretend hoop skirts and tiaras. She'd taken the right-hand side downward if she was attending an imaginary ball and the left for all lesser occasions. Halloweens had included velvet capes, cardboard swords, and storming up the staircase to rescue stuffed animals and liberate their candy.

The prospect of climbing those stairs any time soon was unwelcome. "If I die in the next five minutes, donate my body to science, please."

"As if they'd take it. You need water." Her mother's caftan brushed the cool marble floor as she led the way to the back of the house where the kitchen and sunroom overlooked the tennis court and lawn. "I was just making a smoothie."

Familiar with her mother's fruity boozer-uppers, Alice said, "I would help you drink that." She dropped her knapsack at the foot of the back stairs to carry up later and pulled out the bags of coffee and tea. "Your deliveries, madam, as promised."

Her mother pressed one of the bags of the Vienna roast coffee to her nose and inhaled. "Nectar of the Gods. Thank you. I'll make some after dinner. Sophia is on holiday for the weekend, so we have to fend for ourselves."

"As if that's hard." Alice poured a glass of water from the chilled pitcher in the refrigerator, drank it down, and filled it again. She didn't object when her mother tipped lime-infused vodka into what looked like lemonade, frozen peaches, and ice. "If I know Sophia there's plenty of food."

Over the grind of the blender her mother shouted, "I told her you were coming, and she left pierogi for tonight—"

"—Ambrosia to go with the nectar—"

"—And blintzes for tomorrow. I thought we'd go to the club for dinner tomorrow night."

"Sounds heavenly. We can take my car. Make sure it still runs." Alice pulled two thick steins from the freezer and set them next to the blender. "I hope Sophia made a lot of pierogi. I'm starved now."

"I doubt she has forgotten the size of your appetite." Her mother tasted the contents of the blender by dipping her finger into it. "That'll do." The steins were quickly filled, and her mother handed her one frosty glass. "Cool off. You look like you're going to fall down."

Fifteen minutes later, legs stretched out in front of her, and enjoying the cool air flowing through the sunroom, Alice couldn't decide if she was slightly muzzy due to dehydration or the vodka. She massaged her forehead. "How old does a person have to be to remember about brain freeze?"

"Twelve?"

"I'm behind the curve then."

"Not just about brain freeze."

"Love you, mean it."

Her mother was curled up in her favorite oversized chair. Next to her the side table was crowded with books, notebooks, and a squat crystal vase turned pencil and reading glasses holder. Her head rested on the dusty gold cushions behind her, and her eyes were fixed on the garden where sluggish bees drifted around scarlet and purple verbena. "I watched the video."

Alice tried to forestall the lecture with, "I know, I know."

"The congressman is without a doubt a douchebag."

"I know, I know."

"You're better than that."

"I know, I know."

Her mother's head rolled ever so slightly in Alice's direction. A *New Yorker* caricaturist hadn't been wrong to enlarge her deep brown eyes to fill the lenses completely. Even the mildest glance left Alice feeling as if the microscope was on and she was being examined in minute, exacting detail. "Seriously, Alice, what is wrong?"

"Nothing—what do you mean?"

"Are you burned out?"

Her mouth got ahead of her frozen brain. "Maybe."

"It's been a rough couple of years, if you'll excuse the understatement."

"I can't let go of the feeling that they're not over and might never be over."

Her mother gestured with her glass in a toast of agreement. "What does this all have to do with Helene Jolie and her family?"

"My penance is going to Beverly Hills."

"Ah. To see the new empire. For a Style focus piece?"

Alice laughed at her mother's unerring grasp of the situation. "You know the biz so well."

"It's rather like Edward R. Murrow interviewing Liberace."

"Except I'm not Murrow. Never was, never will be. Nobody is Murrow anymore. Most people I work with don't even know who he was."

"You make yourself sound ancient."

"I feel it sometimes."

"Well, if you're not Murrow, Helene Jolie is definitely not Liberace. She makes no secret of her same sex relationships, for one thing." Her mother closed her eyes in thought for a moment, then refocused on Alice's face. "I suppose she has no reason to hide since she hardly dwells in the real world as it is."

"A point in her favor." Alice hadn't begun deep research, but the cursory glances she'd made showed that Jolie was in her late forties, and her past relationships were with other successful, highly attractive women. Pop stars, golf pros, actresses, and the like. "I would say tell me everything you've heard, but I don't have my notebook, Mom."

"Then I don't have to be diplomatic. Besides, I don't know much about her. Her parents, though…"

Alice smiled to herself. "Deep background, then."

"The deepest. Her father is a snob of the worst kind. Awash in the self-made millionaire origin story that leaves out the trust fund he inherited. I stopped seeing them when Eric Brady Jolie the Third insisted that elitists were ruining the world while holding a glass of thirty-year port in the same hand that sported a Yale class ring. Anything that threatens his money is a conspiracy and it's hard work he does, fending off the barbarians at his gate. In short, he's rich and there is no there, there."

"He hasn't lost the family fortune?"

"Not for want of trying. Several years ago he invested heavily in Ultra-ray."

"What's that?"

"The replacement for Blu-ray."

"Never heard of it."

Her mother arched one eyebrow.

"Point taken."

"What money they've made in venture capital is *Mrs.* Eric Brady Jolie's doing. She also pointed out the lack of women on certain corporate boards and now has several seats that pay very well. Not that she's a feminist, oh no. She'll take whatever advantage she can of gender parity and oppose equal pay measures and family leave— Phyllis Schlafly would be proud."

"Bravely accepts help opening doors for herself and lets them hit the women behind her in the face."

"Exactly. She's selfish, but she's not stupid. Trust me, of the two, Helene gets her brains from her mother."

"So you think she has brains?"

"Of course. She figured out how to take her opinion and turn it into something other people valued." She waved a pale, blue-veined hand heavy with the diamond wedding ring from Alice's father. "That's what I did, you know."

Alice allowed a heartfelt "piff" to underscore her outraged snort at the comparison. "*You* are a journalist. A rare personality. One of a kind."

"Aren't you sweet? Kiss kiss." She sipped from her smoothie with a satisfied sigh. "I sold perspective. She sells—"

"Rocks for women to put up their hoo-hoos."

"Please be joking."

"And quantum atmosphere sanitizers. A.k.a. a pile of crystals you put on your desk."

"Be careful, darling. You're putting a value judgment on the outcome. I'm talking about what she made out of her name."

Alice realized too late that her whiny groan sounded like that of a recalcitrant toddler. "I like science. Facts. I can't help but make a value judgment about selling useless products." Her breath tightened in her chest the way it had when she'd written about silver toothpaste and fish tank tablets being touted as cures for pandemic flus by the vilest of profiteers. Simply the Best didn't sell fake cures, but they weren't selling truth either.

"You've misunderstood what she's selling."

Striving to sound more calm than she felt, Alice heaved a philosophical sigh. "I know, she's selling a brand. An affiliation.

Prestige, status. In the form of a facial roller made of rose quartz that 'wakes up your skin and quiets your face' at the same time. Outcomes that can't be measured and mean nothing. It offends me."

Her mother favored her with a long blink. "With that mindset, you're going to call her a douchebag."

"That's what I'm afraid of." She stared at the bottom of her glass. No wonder she had brain freeze. "I'm tipsy."

"Do you feel as if you have to hold on to the chair?"

"It's not that bad."

"Then I'll make another pitcher."

"Food soon?"

Her mother snorted. "You know where the kitchen is. Make yourself useful."

"Shower first."

* * *

The cool water was heavenly, but the mirror showed patches of red on her cheeks and chin, further highlighting the lines around her mouth that had little to do with laughter. Was that a sunburn? When she was younger it had taken only a few hours in the sun to put a golden glow on her light brown skin and she'd never burned. Those days were apparently over.

"How long has it been since you've been in the sun? A decade?" Her reflection didn't answer. Sunburn was not flattering to what her mother had always lovingly called her "scruffy puppy good looks."

Slathered in cream purloined from her mother's bathroom and with her short, thick brown hair spiked up to dry, Alice returned to the kitchen in the spare denim shorts and old, soft polo shirt she still kept in her dresser for just such occasions. Spare clothes on hand had been very useful when they'd all been in lockdown together. While her mother concocted more frozen deliciousness, Alice dropped Sophia's perfect, puffy, tender, cheese-stuffed pierogi into salted boiling water for a scant two minutes, then moved them into a sizzling, heavily buttered skillet.

There was a covered dish of fresh haricots verts in the fridge that she was sure they were meant to eat as well, because Sophia believed in vegetables, and Sophia was not wrong. A few minutes in the microwave left them crisp and bright green, and she tossed them in the butter left in the pan after she'd lifted the golden-brown pierogi onto their plates.

Unlike at her condo, where the stove was as pristine as the day it had been delivered, she enjoyed cooking at her mother's. There were all the pans, tools, and ingredients a person could want. Usually, Sophia was there to make a suggestion or help decide if something was done, and during lockdown she'd taught Alice a few more tricks. It wasn't her life, but it was certainly always nice to visit it. Especially when someone else had done most of the work.

Dinner led to rewatching *Woman of the Year* and sleeping like a rock for ten hours in her familiar, quiet childhood bedroom. The last thing she saw was her She-Ra and Swiftwind action figures alongside Princess Leia. No He-Man, no Luke. So diagnostic.

She would have lazed in bed Saturday morning, but the promise of blintzes and mimosas lured her to the kitchen. It wasn't until the afternoon that she asked her mother again about the Jolies. This time she had a notebook.

Her mother set aside the book she was reading. "I'm afraid whatever I say will be confirmation bias for you. I don't like them, but then I don't like hypocrites, and that's what they both are, in their own way. I've only met Helene once, and that was… Goodness."

Alice smiled at the absent-minded way her mother tugged at her ear lobe as she sifted through her memory.

Finally, her mother went on, "I think you weren't even in kindergarten yet. Which means she was eleven? Twelve? Very pretty, very clever, talked to me in French about her clothes, which was both preciously precocious and predictably pretentious."

"Say that three time fast." Her mother opened her mouth to try, but Alice forestalled her with, "They spent a lot of time in France?"

"Yes, he had his father's business interests to squander."

Alice's laugh turned into a sigh. "The worst thing about this assignment is not being sure I can set aside my presumptions. Like I thought the accent was an affectation when I heard it online."

"Who says it originally wasn't? One that became permanent?" Her mother ran a hand through her short hair, a sign that she was about to give advice. "Dear, go back to basics."

Alice recited from another maternal lecture from long ago. "Explore what information the reader needs so they can draw their own conclusions?"

Her mother nodded. "If your name is on the piece, that's what you do." She favored Alice with a sympathetic smile. "Your editor could not have designed a better torture. You've never wanted to interpret or intuit. You favor facts over perception or philosophy. You want to discover, research, and know."

Alice gave voice to a thought she'd kept to herself for a long while, but today's concoction of strawberries and coconut rum had left her mellow. "How is it we have the same profession and do it completely differently?"

"That's easy. You're a hybrid. Doing your father's work but in my job."

It was an answer she should have thought of. Her father had been a physicist and deep into studies of light and luminescence at MIT when he'd died in a commuter train derailment. Alice had only been three. She glanced at the snapshot on the table in front of the window with the three of them posed in their Easter best in front of a house Alice didn't remember. Her father's round, handsome brown face was softened by an indulgent smile as he steadied a wobbly Alice in a puffy pink dress and white shoes. Her mother was looking at him in the kind of complete adoration that Alice had never felt for Janet or any of her predecessors. "Science is in the blood?"

"That and a lot of rum at the moment."

"True that."

"Shall I make more?"

Alice gave herself a little shake to avoid dozing off. Too much rum. "I think I'll call a break until dinner."

"Probably a good idea. Anyway, the Jolies are like too many people—wealthy and living in a state of constant terror that someone will take a penny from them."

"Have you heard that the daughter is the same way?" Alice could almost hear the wheels turning as her mother pondered how to answer, so she had another sip of her drink and waited.

"No. Only that she's clever and driven. I do recall that her company has had a couple of major turning points forced by litigation and social pressure."

"False health claims. I saw that one. What's the social pressure point?"

"Product sourcing in countries with no child labor laws. Shoes, purses, clothes made by children for pennies a day. Jolie changed their process in response. From that I deduced that she can feel shame."

"Or feared loss of income. That's not the same thing." Alice took off her glasses to rub the perpetual sore spot on the bridge of her nose.

A slightly more acerbic tone was accompanied by a hard stare. "There are plenty of people who haven't responded to shaming about their use of sweatshops. Or any unethical practices—they can't be shamed about anything. They say exploitation is on those people in that other country. They've committed no crime, so it's nothing to do with them as they pocket the proceeds."

Alice grunted agreement. "Again, you speak truth."

"Jolie changed her business structure. I don't believe she had to."

"Okay, so maybe she's not a spoiled rich elite, upcharging for a logo."

"She could be all that, you know, and still have a moral philosophy and ethics. She's been around long enough to develop them." Her mother set aside her glass with a thoughtful sigh. "I used to believe integrity was an absolute. You had it or you didn't. Take it from an old woman with no fracks to give. Very few people are all bad or all good."

"I get that. It's undeniable she began high up in life, and she has made a lot of herself on top of that. Like starting between second and third base, and she's sliding into home at the World Series." Simon would be so proud of her for that analogy. She put her glasses back on to jot it down before she forgot it. "Have you heard of any charity backing she's done personally, on the quiet?"

"Nothing below the radar, though I'm not sure I would know if she had. There was an invitation-only gala for the Met before she moved herself and her company to California."

"How did folks feel about that out here?"

"I would guess the same way people on Fifth Avenue felt. The way a devotee of the serious *theatuh* feels when a rising star heads off to the ephemera of Hollywood." Her mother frowned and closed her eyes. "There's never a shortage of judgment when a woman, any woman, makes a decision."

"There is so much truth from you today."

That earned her a glare from the owl eyes. "Ungrateful child. I give you the wealth of hard-earned wisdom and you snark."

"I wonder where I learned that?"

Her mother's glare continued for several moments before changing to a moue of distaste. "Does she really sell rocks for women to put up their hoo-hoos?"

Alice sighed. "Yes. And I still have to go to Beverly Hills."

PART TWO

More Bounce in California

CHAPTER FOUR

"Don't you dare cancel!" Pepper upped the volume on the car's speaker as the signal broke up. Or perhaps CC was feigning poor signal. "I know you can hear me—don't you even dare."

Her roommate's voice was laden with ennui. "Dearest darling friend, I can't face it."

"I sure can't face it alone. And I even have fantastic, amazing news."

"Oh, you dreamer." CC didn't bother to cover her microphone as she shouted at someone, "My shift's over. No, you shut up!"

"You better be there."

"We're all going to have the kale bowl. And blond Belgian ale. It's the same every time."

"So what? You have something else to do on a Friday night? They're our oldest friends, CC." Pepper turned her elderly Prius onto Beverly Glen Boulevard and began the climb through hillside neighborhoods. Progress was slow, but no more so than the 405 would be, and at least this route was shady in most places and lined with bougainvillea. Once she reached Mulholland the view was spectacular, even on a hot, smoggy late August afternoon. "They took us in the very first day of high school."

"Just because they weren't the mean bitches that the rest of the girls were doesn't mean we have to endure a lifetime of kale bowl dinners."

"We went a year and a half without any at all, and once we could indoor dine again we said we'd go back to making it monthly. Now it's been months since the last one. The call is going to drop around the next corner. I'll pick you up in about forty minutes."

The background noise in CC's call changed. It sounded like she was outside now and probably walking home from her brunch-to-early dinner shift at Bistro Baby. "Aren't you going to come up to change? I have to shower today's special out of my hair. Calamari and garlic over squid ink noodles. I smell like the inside of a vampire-infested aquarium."

"I'm already in a silk dress." She wasn't turning up for a casual meal with the gang at the Bounty Bowl in less.

"So that's what all that banging about was this morning."

"I'll ping when I'm two minutes out. Don't make me circle the block."

CC's colorfully worded response was cut off when the call dropped. The mobile dead zone was the other reason Pepper took this route. It meant a blissful half hour out of touch with the entire world, in a space all to herself. The quiet hum of the car or her choice of music allowed her to picture rolling ocean waves that washed her mind free of work and stress.

It didn't succeed so well today, not with her head spinning with a whirlwind of details. She'd gone back to clean out her cubbyhole in Nikki's office suite and returned to report to Clarita as instructed. From there she'd been sent to Human Resources to fill out paperwork and returned Upstairs to be given an immediate project of printing specific contact information sheets that Clarita then put in an orange envelope on Helene's desk.

After that, Pepper went back to her old digs to gather samples to restock the selection in Helene's office. Maintaining the supply was now her job. The list of tasks she was responsible for got longer as the afternoon went on and she'd started texting herself reminders. She needed a better tracking system.

She was also starving. A break for lunch had never materialized and she'd had to gobble down nutrition bar samples to shut up her stomach. She never wanted to taste Golden Pomegranate *anything* ever, ever again.

Giving up on calming her mind with quiet, she picked the next best thing—Lizzo followed by Joan Jett and Superchick, all turned up loud enough to make the old speakers buzz.

She was so engrossed crooning along to a Beyoncé ballad, she forgot to text her arrival, but she'd no sooner pulled into the loading zone in front of their building than a message arrived from CC, saying, "Down in a min turn it down have a headache."

CC was such a hothouse flower, but Pepper dutifully turned off the music so there'd be no excuse for CC to back out. Her brain kept track of her time in the loading zone while she watched for the parking patrol. The pizza takeout owner would come out to yell at her in another twenty seconds. He liked their rent on the small apartment over the business but saw everything else about their presence as an interference to his income—unless they were having his pizza for dinner. Which they did, all too often.

The parking monitor's scooter turned the corner down the street. About to curse CC, she jumped at a bang on the passenger window. A flapping crow stood there—CC, black sweater, black jeans, black eyeliner, navy blue lipstick, and her short red hair in wild spikes.

"It's hot out here, unlock the door!"

Pepper complied and flinched at the wave of heat as CC got in. "You could have worn something other than wool."

"Nothing else was clean." CC waved cheerily at Mr. Huan, who had come to the door of his shop gesticulating with both gnarled arms at their malingering in "his" loading zone.

"The A/C is on max. Give it a minute."

CC's settling in and buckling up didn't stop the flow of complaints. "We're never going to find parking. I'm melting. Would it hurt any of them to come toward us?"

Pepper wasn't about to tell her usually trendsetterish best friend that the choice of red hair and navy blue lipstick, combined with her natural pallor, gave her a leftover Fourth of July vibe. But it was also true she didn't look like a bland bot-clone Southern California blond. Pepper carefully didn't look at herself in the rearview mirror as she pulled the tie off her ponytail. "Maybe we'll get lucky. I really don't want to pay to valet it."

"You and me both. I flamed out of the opening round of the tournament last night, so no prize money this week."

"I'm sorry, that sucks." CC's gaming was good enough to cover groceries and her student loans. It had been a godsend during the bouts of unemployment during the pandemic.

"It's my new Zowie. Still getting used to the side button placement and I didn't trigger a couple of buffs fast enough. So, what's this big news you can't wait to share?"

Gratified that CC had remembered from their earlier call, Pepper recapped the news of her day, finishing with, "It's a done deal. I have a desk and assignments."

CC bounced in her seat as she drummed on the dashboard. "Finally! An actual job with actual wages and actual benefits?"

"Quit that! You'll set off the airbag. I can't wait to tell my parents."

"Don't screw it up."

Pepper took her gaze off the taillights in front of her long enough to skewer CC with laser side-eye. "Thanks for the vote of confidence."

CC didn't seem the least bit fazed. "I know you can do that job. You have a phenomenal memory. You seem to know in advance when shit could go sideways—all those class events you organized and not one single blip. Plus you're not hard to look at."

"Thanks. I think." She slammed on the brakes as traffic stopped again, then zipped into the next lane to join the queue to turn onto Victory Boulevard. CC wasn't wrong about the chore of driving to the Promenade. The rest of the gang lived in Woodland Hills and had only a short drive. She and CC were the commuters, coming from the much lower rent Encino flatlands.

"You know what I mean. It's not like they've treated you fairly so far. A year with a shitty stipend for working fifty hours a week. They don't want to pay overtime, so they didn't pay you at all."

It was a sore subject. CC's dreams of working her way into television production had collapsed under the weight of a series of "learning opportunities" and "exposure" that had paid nothing, but in which she was expected to provide her own high-end laptop with its own high-speed Internet, a car suitable for driving A-listers around, and the gas to do so, and frequently was not paid back money she advanced getting last-minute goodies for paid talent. Complaining had gotten her work as a waiter and time to devote to professional gaming.

"It's over now, I hope. H-Helene is intimidating but realized I had potential."

"You get to call the big boss *Heh-heh-heh-leeeeeene?*"

Pepper gritted her teeth. Once CC came up with an attitude about something she was unlikely to stop when asked. "She told me to. I'm getting used to it."

"What's she like?"

"Gorgeous. You know how you said that meeting performers they always seem slightly unreal. Like they're a different species?"

"Yeah. It's focus on appearance as a required part of the job. Anybody can be one of the beautiful people if they've got the time and money."

"It's like that, except some of it is natural energy."

CC pointed at a black sports car cutting lanes as if LA rush hour traffic was a *Fast and Furious* movie. "Watch out for that idiot."

"I see him."

"Energy—that's the thing that's hard to fake. When I laid eyes on Meryl Streep the first time she was fifty feet away and I could feel it. I kind of fell in love with her right then and there."

"Helene's like that," Pepper said. "Well, I didn't fall in love."

The blended snort of skepticism combined with promise to later say "I told you so" was one of CC's signature and most annoying habits. "We'll see. That energy thing is potent mojo. That's all I'm saying."

"Thanks for the warning." Pepper reminded herself that for all her show of jaded heartlessness, CC was soft and mushy inside. She hadn't complained about her own treatment on her last TV job. It had been another intern's unpaid coffee runs she'd protested. The reward of doing a good job with some people was them taking even more advantage of it.

Pepper opened her mouth to say she'd found out she'd been kept an intern because Nikki Cavanaugh hadn't wanted to give Pepper up for a promotion, but telling CC that would make her sad and angry, and then Pepper would be sad and angry, and that wasn't productive. There was no need to pile on when it was all behind her now.

"I'm buying a round of beers to celebrate."

"You bet you will."

She circled around to the back of the Promenade, hoping to find an empty space in the lot's remote corners. From high school onward, the Promenade had been part of her life. It was where Westlake High students went to see and be seen, buy designer anything, and drink milkshakes called smoothies for their health. Those not yet able to drive waited there for parental pick up.

Not being gifted with generous allowances or prepaid debit cards, Pepper and CC had nursed diet sodas in the food court and split up their homework. Pepper masterminded English and history papers while CC tackled science and art projects. That division of labor had been working for them since the fourth grade.

Sometimes she'd gazed at the glittering lights and soft, inviting colors of the rest of the Promenade, inhaled the tantalizing aromas of salty, fried yummy things, and yearned to be one of the glittery, carelessly rich girls, if only for an hour or two, once a week. Well, now she was working for the goddess of rich girls and surrounded by a beautiful workplace full of creativity that was all about empowering women. For a paycheck, even.

"Taillights just came on up there." CC pointed and Pepper raced up the long aisle to claim it. A few minutes later they were on the curved escalator that took them up to where the lime green door, white tables, and colorful murals of Bounty Bowl beckoned.

"Maybe none of them will show."

"Our best friends, CC."

"Once upon a time, when we were all captives. It's Stockholm syndrome."

Pepper saw Valerie first, then Beth and Jasmine. It was hard to tear her gaze from Valerie, though, who was sporting a brand-new undercut with long dark bangs. Valerie had long declared her large clear brown eyes to be her only beauty, and the wisps of bangs made them all the more beguiling. Plus, she had lashes Pepper had always envied.

"Oh my gosh, Valerie! I love your hair," she exclaimed as they approached. "What a change! How long have you had it this way?"

Valerie ducked her head in her usual modest way. "Last week. It was time."

"Copycat," CC snarked as she hugged Valerie. "Admit it, it was my daring fashion-forward trends that inspired you to chop off that thin, weedy ponytail."

Valerie had a wonderfully dismissive eyebrow lift that Pepper had never been able to copy and she used it to perfect effect now. "Tell yourself whatever you have to."

It felt just like old times to have CC and Valerie trading barbs. Pepper hugged Beth, who gave everything she did, including hugs, the full 100 percent. The prolonged squeeze left her slightly breathless and immensely restored.

Jasmine shared shoulder-touching hugs with Pepper and CC as she said, "I think it suits you, Valerie. You need a dab of lip color, that is, if you're still determined not to do anything else for your skin."

Beth turned to gesture at the host. "Looks like our table is ready."

"It should be. I made the reservation personally. Of course, in my phone it's under the old name. I still don't know why they changed it."

CC spread her arms in an it's-obvious-to-everyone-but-you shrug. "Because Krishna Dishna was being cutesy with someone else's deity?"

Jasmine waved a dismissive hand as she led the way into the restaurant, giving Pepper enough distance to admire her long, silky duster in a tealish-aqua blue that put even more honey in Jasmine's blond French braid. "You'll have actual paychecks now," she reminded herself. She could make cautious improvements to her wardrobe. And probably should, she thought, remembering Helene Jolie's glance at her presentable but hardly noteworthy shoes.

The cool, green tea-scented air inside the Bounty Bowl was welcome, as were the soothing tones of hang music that would still allow them to hear each other. Happily, the host led them to Pepper's favorite table. She loved it because the poured acrylic was embedded with a photograph looking down into an aquarium full of clown and angel fish plus coral in blue, orange, and the brightest of greens. The overhead light was tinted blue and rotated slowly, creating the impression that the water was sparkling and moving. It reminded her of snorkeling in Hawaii. As they were seated, she sent a mental hello to the little swimming Nemos as she always did.

As they started to open their menus, Pepper couldn't hold in her news any longer. "You'll never guess what happened today at work."

"You've finally given up toiling at Simply the Best?" Beth's natural afro bounced as she nodded a yes to the host's question about a carafe of water for the table.

"Not at all—but I'm going to get paid for it now." She couldn't restrain a head-to-toe wiggle of glee. "I'm Helene Jolie's new personal assistant."

"Congratulations!" Jasmine, next to Pepper, gave her a hearty high five. "Tell me everything about her. I watch her every week on Simply Hot Insta. She's amazing—you'd never know she was almost *fifty*."

"I caught a glimpse of the miniature studio she uses to make those videos. I'll learn more about it, I suppose." Pepper was gratified by Jasmine's open awe. Of all of them, Jasmine was the one most tuned into what was hot and what was not. Looking back, she was all too aware that Jasmine's trust fund cachet had been a shield for the rest of them from the ridicule of the Mean Girls. Like the time Pepper had over-plucked her eyebrows. Jasmine had declared it Retro Cheap Sunglasses week. By Tuesday sunglasses were in, even among the more chic of their teachers, and on Thursday the lunch DJ devoted the hour to "Cheap Sunglasses" with covers and the original ZZ Top song.

As Pepper finished describing her whole crazy day their server arrived to take their drink orders. The distraction gave Pepper a chance to reach into her purse for sample bottles of the Fallen Leaves-scented hand lotion. "Coming out next week. It's really delicate. Kind of earthy and restful. It's meant to be unisex."

Jasmine sniffed, then dabbed it on her hands, carefully avoiding her shiny diamond engagement ring that never failed to catch the light. "I was wondering about it. Thank you. It's a little musky for me, but I wouldn't mind if Jared used this scent."

Pepper basked in the approval while saying to Valerie, "Sorry, there's no hypoallergenic version in the sample size."

"I like the scent, it's foresty without being pine. I'll test it in an inconspicuous place. Thanks for remembering."

"That's why Pepper is going to be so awesome at this job," Beth said. "She remembers everything."

"Oh stop," Pepper said, back of her hand pressed to her forehead. "Don't tell me more about how wonderful I am."

"Please don't," CC said. "She's hard enough to live with as it is."

Their server arrived to take their food order, and as CC had predicted, it was kale bowls all around. Pepper kicked CC under the table when she ordered one as well, but CC only gave her an innocent, sunny smile as she chose Szechwan grilled tofu for the protein. When their ales were delivered, they toasted Pepper's brilliant news with a clank of frosty pilsner glasses. CC nodded at her as if to say, "Okay, I get why you insisted."

They chattered and laughed as they enjoyed their meals. Jasmine's wedding planning was a nightmare since it was impossible to convince her mother and her mother's wedding planner about anything. Beth's showing at a Beverly Hills gallery was on schedule for the middle of October.

"I expect to get an email every day saying they've reconsidered, but not so far." The same overhead light that turned Pepper's skin an insipid blue rendered Beth a glowing dark bronze that radiated vitality. "I need to finish the last two pieces."

Jasmine waved her phone. "I have the opening all programmed. We'll be back from our honeymoon by then. We finally settled on Bora Bora."

"You all have to show up," Beth pleaded. "What if people hate it? Or nobody shows up?"

Beth's quiet confidence and unshakable dignity had always been a rock in Pepper's world. If Beth admitted to being nervous, it was serious. "I absolutely promise. I'll dress up and act rich."

Valerie finished the last of her beer. "I will be there to cheer you on, though I just got moved to a new department and there's some travel involved. I hope I don't miss the opening because of it."

"That sounds exciting," CC commented.

"Kinda." Valerie gave a non-committal shrug and smiled in her reserved way. "Not quite a promotion but more responsibility and another aspect of the company to round out my pharmaceuticals marketing experience. I won't be able to score any high-end swag like Pepper, though."

"Hand lotion is nothing. You're in drugs. You can do better than that," Pepper protested.

Valerie brushed her hair out of her eyes. "Yeah, maybe not. The new gig is in all things rectal."

"Okay, then. You can keep it all for yourself."

"Eww." Jasmine wrinkled her nose. "How am I supposed to talk about wedding canapés now?"

"Sorry," Valerie said.

"Can I call you Ass Master?" CC burst out laughing at Jasmine's horrified expression.

Beth seized her napkin and wiped the front of her dress. "You made me spew!"

"No, you can't call me that," Valerie said firmly. "But speaking of what you can call me, I have some news. Well, not news. An update. Not news to me. It's new to you all."

"You're babbling as usual," CC said, then evaded Pepper's mock attempt to slug her in the shoulder.

"I know." Valerie looked longingly at her now empty glass of beer. "So okay. From here on out I'm going by Val, not Valerie. And my pronouns are they and them."

"Oh!" Pepper blinked in surprise. "Is the new hair cut a celebration?"

Val nodded. Their light brown complexion had gone gray, and they looked like a scared fourteen-year-old.

Aware too that Jasmine had gone rigid, Pepper said quickly, "I hope you'll cut me slack for a while. If I slip, it's just my brain being slower than my intentions."

Val's nervous smile pulled to one side. "I've been getting used to it for like five years, so I get it—plenty of slack." Voice trembling, they added, "I know where your heart is."

"I promise it won't be five years. I can retrain my brain."

"It's cool that you're taking control of it. It can't be easy," CC said. "Or it wouldn't have been so hard for you to tell us. Even if you're still the biggest loser I know."

"Bitch," Val said sweetly.

Beth leaned into the table to say directly to Val, "Can you talk about it a little more? I mean—you have lady bits. We had P.E. together."

Val smiled as if it was a question they'd anticipated. "Now that I'm not in P.E. class, I really don't want to talk about my pleasure parts with anyone who isn't going to see them. They work and I'm keeping them."

Jasmine lifted her chin. "Then what's the point?"

"The point is that I thought the world had two tents and only two tents. When I realized there were a lot more tents I found where I'm comfortable. I don't *have* to go on squeezing into one where I don't feel like I belong. Like I shouldn't be there, and sometimes I have to pretend to be something I'm not quite. Which is lying to other people and myself. I can't anymore."

Jasmine wagged a finger in Val's direction. "And your pleasure parts aren't female anymore?"

"I never said that."

"Then I don't get it."

"Unless you're actually interacting with my private bits, their functionality is none of your business. And they shouldn't have anything to do with how you treat me."

"Or how much you get paid," CC added dryly.

"For real," Val agreed.

Her chin jutted out in challenge, Jasmine asked, "Would a baby call you Mommy or Daddy?"

"You know perfectly well that in Korean it's Appa or Umma. Of course, there's also a word for 'parent,' just like in English."

"You could invent a word," Pepper suggested, earning her a warning glare from Jasmine she shrugged off. "Something mellifluous but strong."

Jasmine was frowning so hard her eyebrows were almost touching. "Sure. Parenting is all about making it up as you go along."

Beth laughed outright. "That's what mine did. Which made life pretty fun."

"Jas," Val pleaded in a shaky voice, "I'm trying to make my brain, and heart, and body row the same direction instead of always having to filter and adjust because I'm non-binary. I want to look in the mirror and see the person I know I am. I'm sorry if it's hard for you."

"Oh, shut up," CC snapped. "Sorry. I mean stop apologizing for wanting your friends to treat you like you want to be treated. Everybody gets to do that, and frankly, any friend who doesn't want to do that work isn't a friend." Her gaze flicked to the silent, stone-faced Jasmine before she added, "I draw the line, however, at 'Val Who Must Be Obeyed, My Sovereign Forever,' so that's out."

"Right out. Not saying it," Pepper chimed in as Beth laughed.

Val feigned outrage. "Really? I can't get a little unquestioning adulation on bended knee after all this time? Lazy asshats."

Jasmine, her gaze fixed on her salad, said, "You know, I come to our dinners to relax and have fun, not to talk about politics."

Pepper opened her mouth, but she was slower than CC, as usual.

"Exactly how is Valer—*Val*—asking us to call her—*them*—words that make them comfortable in any way political?"

"It's distracting," Jasmine muttered. "And feels like I'm being told what to do regardless of what I believe."

Val's voice steadied. "Your beliefs don't define me."

"Yours don't define me," Jasmine fired back.

"I'm not defining you in any way. You do you. I'm asking you to let me be me by changing a few words in how you talk to me and about me when I can hear you."

Jasmine stuck out her chin. "I'm saying no."

"What?" Pepper set down the fork that had been frozen halfway to her mouth. "Asking was a courtesy. She—sorry! *They* don't need our permission for anything."

"I never asked any of you to call me CC instead of Colleen." CC's voice wobbled with indignation. "I told you, and because we're friends you did it. If you hadn't, I'd have probably found new friends."

"Come on, Jas," Beth chided. "Remember how we all hated on the teachers who insisted Colleen on the school roster and meant Colleen forever?" In an excessively nasal whine, she mimicked, "What if she changes her mind? What if all the students had nicknames? What if they picked rude ones? It would be a slippery slope to anarchy."

"You've ruined everything! I don't know why I keep wasting my time on any of you." Jasmine snatched up her belongings and pushed away from the table. The angry, rapid click of her heels was lost in the quiet music that filled the ensuing silence.

"Buh-bye bay-bee." CC lifted her beer with an exaggerated, casual toast in Jasmine's direction before sipping from it. "Does she think we'll follow her?"

"She's always hated change she wasn't in charge of." Beth's sigh was heartfelt. "I think our wedding invitations are going to get lost in the mail."

"So be it." Val pushed aside the sweep of bangs, and Pepper could see that their eyes were shimmering with tears. "I'm sorry—" CC bristled, and they rushed on, "I'm sorry if I derailed celebrating Pepper's new job. It's worth celebrating, really."

"It's okay. I've just realized that it was Jasmine I wanted to impress. Like I'm still fifteen and she's our Heather alpha." Pepper rubbed her cheeks to ease away a heavy frown. "She's the one with the great life and lots of travel and fun. Marrying a rich guy and on her way to His and Hers Mercedes. And hair that holds a braid."

"And a big hole in her heart," Beth muttered.

"Shit," CC said. "We're paying for her dinner now."

"I'll pay for it," Pepper said. "New job. And I think I have to buy new shoes before I leave here tonight."

"Shoe shopping?" Beth perked up. "I am so on it."

CC put her fingertip to her temple. "Kill me now."

Val sniffed one last time and made a valiant attempt at a sunny expression. "Why don't you and I go over to the arcade in Agoura Hills? Pepper can pick you up there after she and Beth have their shoe orgy."

"You love the arcade," Pepper reminded CC. "Got hand sanitizer? I have a Simply the Best spritzer."

"Of course." CC went back to eating her dinner as she nodded at Val. "I'm going to so kick your ass at Space Invaders. Again."

"All talk, as usual."

The mood at the table settled, especially after the server cleared away Jasmine's plates. Color came back into Val's cheeks, and CC seemed especially intent on making sure Val was at ease.

Shoe shopping with Beth was hedonistic, fun, and exactly what Pepper needed. She left the Promenade swinging a silver shopping bag and nursing a huge hole in her wallet. The black patent pumps with zebra-striped heels were worth it. As she put the pretty, so pretty shoes on her dresser to admire and plan what to wear for her first real day as Helene Jolie's personal assistant, she reminded herself that future indulgences would have to be at resale shops. Personal assistant wages would put an end to asking her parents for cash infusions every couple of months, but they weren't going to support shopping at the Promenade.

She couldn't wait to tell her folks that their patience had paid off, and she was finally on her way inside Simply the Best. There had never been quite enough cash to match the lifestyle of most of their neighbors, but her folks weren't reckless like CC's parents, whose go-big-or-go-home stock market bets had crashed into bankruptcy twice, the second time forcing CC to scramble for student loans or be forced to leave college three years in. She had nothing but admiration for the fact that CC was financially independent.

At the same time, she had nothing but gratitude that her own parents could help her out when things got desperate so she could survive her intern gigs, and the double whammy when being laid off from an internship hadn't let her qualify for unemployment during the pandemic. Her parents were generous to her, though it came with large doses of her mother's coulda-shoulda-woulda hindsights. Eventually, her goal was to repay them for their faith in her by succeeding at something useful, even notable.

That is, if she could meet Helene Jolie's standards and keep the job.

She surveyed her pointy chin and thin eyebrows that had never recovered from the plucking incident. Extra care with makeup. More gel in her hair to help it stay in a sleek ponytail. Extra liner to make something out of her plain brown eyes. She recalled Jolie's piercing gaze, demanding standards, and the casual elegance that had probably been natural to her from birth.

I'm in over my head.

"Stop that," she told her reflection. "A year invested in scut work making the boss look good paid off." She narrowed her eyes at her reflection and made the face that CC lovingly termed Fury Road. "You may be in over your head, but you know how to swim. Just don't take a board to the head."

CHAPTER FIVE

Alice could hear Ed's disapproval through the phone. "You've dragged this out as long as possible."

"I've made progress." She swiveled her chair to put her back to the rest of the floor, even though there was virtually no one there to overhear her being chewed out. "I've requested corporate media packages. Been to our archives and read every possible article about the company. I'm nearly done with all the ones that include her name. I'm about to start tackling all the gossip sites and red carpet video iterations of 'how does it feel to be here tonight' questions." She was due hazard pay for that, but now seemed the wrong time to snark about it.

"The ground rules have been finalized. I sent them to you four days ago. Go to California and get it done."

Alice didn't want to admit that she'd not read them yet. She was going to have to, since it was now perfectly clear Ed wasn't going to put her back in Science, not even after one of the political reporters had been caught pants-less on department-wide video chat during a work meeting. Calling a congressman a douchebag paled by comparison, didn't it? "I've been trading emails with their media relations head. I've been moved along to a personal assistant for appointments and scheduling. I'll be contacting them next."

"I pity them."

She bit her tongue to hold back, "I quit," and said instead, "I'm on it."

"That's better. Stop chapping my ass, Cabot."

True to her word, she sent the ground rules memo to the nearby printer, collected the dozen or so pages and stapled them all together, and returned to her desk. With her heels up on the old radiator, she dated and initialed the first page and kept her pencil at the ready to make notes.

Six article series in print edition, check. Run dates the Wednesday, Friday, and Sunday of the first two weeks of December, check. Two additional articles in digital edition only, check. Run date digital article one the Sunday prior to the first print article as teaser, check. Run date digital article two, Thursday after the sixth print article as follow-up—wait.

Not only follow-up. To also tie in to the gala benefit December 15 at the official opening of a new Simply the Best showcase on Fifth Avenue the following day. The entire series was a run-up to a big holiday charity gala combined with a grand opening.

Her inner journalist recognized the newsworthy aspects of a large, big-name tenant opening a shop on Fifth Avenue. The core of Manhattan business had been gutted and a highly visible investment by an industry leader in its retail prospects was a hopeful sign.

But fuckall crapbiscuits, did it have to be for Simply the Best? A company that sold rocks for women to put up their hoo-hoos?

Her feet thumped to the floor. Breathe, she told herself. *You don't have enough points here to waste on a temper tantrum.* She glared across the floor at the closed door to Ed's office, wishing, not for the first time, her eyes were equipped with directed-energy particle beams.

Blood rushing in her ears, she gently put the memo into the folder Ed had originally given her and the folder into her messenger bag. She was early to meet up with Simon, but she had to get outside. There were so many empty desks. Today they were all a reminder of how much somebody else would love to have her job and/or the very real possibility that her job would disappear like all the others.

She was aware more than ever that something in the world was breaking.

Not breaking. Already broken.

The dank air on the street choked her for a moment. The predicted cooler temps of mid-September hadn't materialized, but at least the heat and smell weren't as bad as August. Dang it, she was going to probably miss the best weather of the year in New York City—the first two weeks of October. Shirt-sleeve days, fresh air, long twilight hours, midnights cool and breezy. Sleeping with the windows open and watching for the first signs of turning leaves in Central Park.

It was inconceivable that Los Angeles, with its one year-round season, had anything that could compete.

Nevertheless, she was going to fly off to La La Land to provide an interesting, "balanced" look into the foremost lifestyle and wellness brand for women. Champions of empowering women to be their very best.

So what if the "Simply the Best Things to Know" daily blogs offered many ways various natural, soothing, healing products helped with modern life while ignoring anything they didn't sell? Like the one about switching to and from daylight savings. It had touted daily vitamins in individual packets hand lettered with the days of the month by artisans of southern France. There was also a special lamp using Kathmandu glass, no doubt crafted lovingly by Nepali monks, plus luxurious sheets woven under a full Tahitian moon by holistically trained turtles.

So what if it didn't mention that sunshine, which was free, could also be helpful in the fall-back-spring-forward transitions? It was a simple thing, but to her mind, lost opportunities to bolster their authority with their customers. But it had nothing to do with the assignment.

"Lady, if you ain't buying, keep walking."

Startled, Alice realized she'd been standing in the middle of the sidewalk for several minutes. The cranky voice had come from a street vendor with a scattering of handbags and makeup palettes on a dingy square of fabric. She muttered an apology as she resumed the well-known walk to McGinty's. Peanuts and whiskey, just what the doctor ordered.

Give up criticizing their methods until you do the research, she told herself. *You are not their target customer*. She caught a glimpse of herself in a shop window and actually laughed. She chose her clothes for utility. Her hair was short because it was easy. Her jeans were worn and faded because they were old. Simply the Best would go on making gobs of money without Alice Paul Cabot's patronage.

Crossing the threshold into McGinty's oiled oak and amber light immediately lifted her spirits. She found her usual place at the bar and watched the bartender pour her Buchanan's. With the arrival of her favorite gift from the Scots imminent, she told herself to consider the good things about Simply the Best. The patently false claims had stopped, after all. Their board of directors was almost completely female. The brand was going to be opening a showpiece of a store in a space vacated by a big-name fashion label that hadn't survived the chaos of the last few years.

Jolie's pre-pandemic decision to pack up her corporate offices and head for Southern California sunshine and to make Rodeo Drive the site of the company's first and flagship retail store had been roundly criticized at the time. A lot of business and social pundits had predicted she'd rue the day. A few short years later, with nothing but rising sales, STB boasted a dozen stores in cities around the world where the rich liked to play and the continuing success of pop-ups at upscale festivals like Cannes and Coachella. They probably sold a vitamin and supplement blend that would help the naysayers eat their crow now. With extra antioxidants.

She thanked the barkeep for her drink and the bowl of peanuts. She rolled the first sip of liquid gold across her tongue and let her mind travel to a cool, quiet place until she swallowed. The smoothest of fires warmed her throat and all the ghosts of the messed-up world melted into the glow.

She had hoped to share her misery with Simon when he arrived. Simon, however, had no misery to share.

He tinked his gin and tonic to her Buchanan's with a broad, happy smile. "Guess who's covering the National League playoffs?"

"Is it someone I know?"

"Smartass."

She aerated a sip of Buchanan's across her tongue to fill her head with the caramel oak aroma. Keep your candles made by virgins during harmonic convergences. *This* was her kind of aromatherapy. "That's great, really. Who's paying you?"

"AP. The Yankees' press office recommended me from the local pool of talent."

"That's amazing. Dues paid and reward received." She toasted him again. "Where is it being held?"

Simon stared at her for a very long moment. "Does your mother know you're ignorant? We're two games from clinching with twelve to go."

"Made you tell me."

He popped several peanuts into his mouth while giving her major side-eye. "When are you going to the Land of Make Believe, cupcake?"

"Okay, I deserved that. About the same time you go wherever the playoffs are, give or take."

"At least you won't be here, drinking alone."

"No, I'll be in Beverly freaking Hills, drinking alone. Do you know how much money Simply the Best Incorporated makes on its annual conference alone? Sorry, excuse me. Its Composium?

"What's a composium?"

"The essence of nature is knowledge."

His dark brow furrowed. "Stop."

"To engage with our best is to be one with our best."

"Stop it."

She gave an evil laugh. "I can do this all day. Because nature is a wellspring of luminosity."

"Stop. It. Now." He made a threatening gesture at her drink, which she moved out of his reach. "Okay, I'll bite. How much do they make?"

"Three hotels. Four days. Two thousand passes sold a day. Going rate for a day pass—two thousand bucks."

He whistled. "We are in the wrong business."

"That's not all. It's another thousand for the closing night champagne and chocolate gala encrusted with celebrities—all the big names in Insta and TikTok and an armload of Hollywood big names. Not to mention what vendors paid for access to attendees with their own services, like meditation, massage, life coaching, and all the rest. I'm guessing last year they grossed twenty-five million and netted half that."

"That's a lot of rich women."

Alice finished her whisky and signaled for another. "Depends on what you call rich. An ST-Bester—"

Simon spluttered into his gin and tonic. "Stop it! Please, I'm begging you."

"I'm not making that up, champ. And you're kind of judgy for someone who says phrases like Bleacher Creatures and the Red Sux." She gestured at him with a tip of her glass. "According to a bank branch manager in Dallas, the company is her ST-Bestie. She scored a designer clutch that she put on eBay and recouped half her one-day ticket. All those vendors that pay for access also give away piles of pricey swag. Cosmetics and perfumes, clothing. There are drawings for custom-made evening gowns, handmade boots—it goes on and on. Their target market is any woman with disposable income and a need to feel better about herself."

Simon blinked. "So any woman with disposable income."

Alice sighed. "It's all so subtle. They post a daily blog, sometimes two, on a particular topic, always with crucially relevant product recommendations."

He shrugged his broad shoulders. "Typical e-commerce."

"Yep, and they're really, I mean *really*, good at it. The posts all start off the same way. Super sympathetic." She dropped into a soothing monotone. "Simon, life is stressful. So stressful. You are perfect. So many people are counting on you. You're beautiful exactly the way you are. Stress takes a toll on your vitality. Stress shows in skin and hair and confidence. It robs you of radiance. You need radiance. Everyone expects so much from you, and we have radiance. Right here in this bottle. Have a good day making all the people who count on you happy, you amazing, radiant woman you."

"Sounds genius."

"It is," she agreed. "Simultaneously sympathizing with the unrealistic expectations the world puts on women and still making her feel insecure. If you take all of their recommended morning products that fix stress, weather, disappointment, demanding bosses, and needy family, you've spent fifteen bucks before breakfast."

"Are the products any good?"

"Clothes, jewelry, what's to complain about? Supplements and crystals, though, they had some rocky claims in the past, but they have cleaned up their act. They no longer claim that the water bottles with crystals in them purify toxins from either the water or you. They still sell them, but they're all about adding 'natural essence'— unquantifiable and undefined by regulators—to your day."

His smile over the top of his glass was wicked. "The mastermind behind it sounds like she could be fascinating."

"Might be." She glanced at her watch. "Don't you have a game to cover?"

"Televised, so starting an hour later than usual. But I should head out."

"Congrats again on the playoffs gig. That's awesome. And thanks for listening to me gripe."

He downed the rest of his drink and gave her a sympathetic shoulder squeeze in parting.

She spent a few minutes trying to decide if she should have another drink to put off the deep dive she had to do on entertainment media or if she should go home now and get it all over with. With Simon gone, she realized the bar had gotten crowded and someone had immediately grabbed his empty stool. She'd drink more to drown out the noise and still end up with a headache from it. She relinquished her barstool to a younger woman who had been hovering hopefully for several minutes.

They changed places, with the other woman making no effort to avoid brushing against Alice. "Are you running away?"

Alice's brain ran through the invitation and the evening it would lead to in her head. More drinks, probably making out, ending up in bed. It was tempting. "Yes."

She nearly gave in when the eyelashes fluttered along with a sound of profound regret. "Now I'm sad."

"Sorry, I have a date with a pile of work." She cursed herself for being a fool, but she was cranky and feeling sorry for herself. She didn't feel up to the negotiations of stranger contact. It would take a lot of booze to change her mind and she'd learned a long time ago that sex when she was that drunk rarely felt good later.

A wind had come up while she was in the bar, and now the mid-September afternoon had a hint of coolness in the air, enough that she decided to walk home instead of enduring the stale air and too-close quarters of the subway. She popped in her earbuds and zigzagged streets and avenues so that her path would go by her favorite spot for eggs Indian style. Two feathery light dosa wrapped around silky curried eggs later, she was foot-weary but stomach-happy.

Restored by a cool shower, she settled down to the mind-numbing task of reading entertainment sites and blogs for news about Helene Jolie. She'd already read the corporate origin story—"It Began with Pocketless Pants"—but knew well enough that unflattering details were never included in such things. She didn't deal in gossip, but she accepted that seeds of truths useful to her series might be found in such.

Her mind steeled for the task, she logged into the paper's archives to finish reading the articles that had referenced Jolie or Simply the Best. She scrolled with her right hand while taking notes with her left, making good use of her own shorthand to record where photographs of Jolie could be found if wanted later by the layout folks.

The Pocketless Pants Scandal had been Jolie's earliest Internet presence, written on her Wellesley's sorority "web-log," and had led to a promise to feature and recommend the best clothing designers who gave women pockets. By the time Jolie left Wellesley, she had a mailing list of ten thousand who wanted to know what Helene Jolie thought was the best *anything*. When social media came into existence, Jolie and Simply the Best, Inc., never hesitated. While some people claimed 140 characters wasn't enough space to communicate anything, Simply the Best found it more than ample for motivational quips and product recommendations to empower women.

The rest was corporate history. Fast forward to today and her personal curation of "the best" had made her an influencer before they called it that. The lifestyle brand wasn't about the merchandise, it was about being, deserving, and owning the best. "Best" being defined in any number of extremely profitable ways.

Alice had to admit that it was a fascinating look at hard work and risk taking. Sure, Jolie had never found it hard to raise capital along the way. She was connected. She'd had a trust fund. The company's IPO had moved Jolie into the bona fide One Percenters. Her influence was lauded and powerful enough that top tier designers made exclusives for Simply the Best.

All of that success hadn't been through licensing her name or ideas while others grew the business. She'd grown the business herself and hired a lot of the right people. Though Alice was no follower of high fashion, she recognized some of the names on the corporate roster as former brand managers hired away from large fashion houses.

They'd left New York with Jolie. Alice wondered how they'd adapted to life on the other coast and made a note to follow that interesting line of inquiry. An infographic about the differences they'd discovered between the two coasts could be entertaining. She could sub-feature comments from managers about their transition from the hard streets of Manhattan to the golden boulevards of Beverly Hills.

Even the pandemic hadn't slowed the profitability. Retail had suffered, but online sales had more than compensated as people in lockdown sought out comfort buys. Jolie had made designer masks fashionable and set the standard for brand promotion with thirty-second "why this is simply the best" video clips when festival cancellations had upended their nimble, profitable pop-up stores. Economic crash? She'd launched "Simply the Basics" clothing and jewelry to focus on "the best building blocks for the woman in progress."

Alice's blood pressure eased as she thought about the assignment using her usual tools of good journalism. She'd ignore the company's New Age word salad as best she could. Helene Jolie was no lucky dilettante. She had worked for her success with more than twenty years of relentless focus, and that was something she could admire.

"Yeah," inner bitch voice Sass answered, *"and that doesn't change the fact that she sells rocks for women to put up their hoo-hoos."*

Sass got louder as Alice switched from news sources to entertainment outlets. Cursing Ed, congressmen, and douchebags in general, she started with *Buzztastic*, the worst for presenting innuendo in the language of fact alongside effusive smirking and measuring popularity based on their assessment of other people's sexual heat. One glance at the site sent her out of her office to the living room where she found a documentary on Viking warrior women to watch. She could tune in and out to take a break from the gossip slime.

Buzztastic had lots and lots and lots of photos of Helene Jolie. Stunning, radiant, sophisticated, heavenly. Her red hair a fiery jewel, her green eyes a luscious mystery. Her tall, so slender figure the perfection of the feminine ideal. Helene, Helene, and more Helene, on the red carpet for the Met Gala, opening night at Cannes, opining on new trends during Paris fashion week. Helene with a tennis pro or charity CEO billed as a current "gal pal," and on and on.

Alice frowned as she failed to find anything more in depth than short passing quips. Now that she thought about it, she hadn't found a single in-depth interview with any outlet, print or digital. That was surprising because Simply the Best knew how to use media attention to its advantage. The answer came in an unguarded moment with a fashion reporter at a Met Gala. "I don't mind talking to you," she'd told the reporter in her odd, not-quite French accent in the clip. "It's the *serious* journalists who are out to get me and my empowerment of women."

Well, that's just great, she thought. It was *serious* journalists who'd tracked and reported on fraudulent claims, and Helene Jolie had trust issues. Write a positive, extensive series with a reluctant interviewee at its core.

Great.

She poured herself two fingers of Glenlivet and inhaled the smoky aroma, but it failed to comfort. She had to make a hotel reservation, arrange a flight. She hadn't even begun contacting local officials, vendors, and other stakeholders for their comments.

Her mother was right—Ed could not have chosen a more appropriate torture. Her shower held three products: shampoo, soap, and a washcloth. Her beauty regimen consisted of being clean, an occasional reestablishing of a space between her dense eyebrows, and just enough hair gel to keep her brushed-up dusty brown spikes from taking on a life of their own in the humidity. "Presentable and tidy" was always her goal—made easier, she knew, because she'd gotten good genes from both parents to start with.

Halfway down a second pour of Glenlivet, she scrolled idly through photo gallery after photo gallery. Jolie in this slender gown or that gender-bending suit, Jolie rocking this retro hat or those fashion-forward shoes. In the background there was almost always a young woman holding a notebook or tablet. She counted twelve to fifteen different amanuenses over the last ten years, and all of them had similar silhouettes: long-haired and long-legged, slender, and glistening with vitality, sporting French braids and flawless skin. Impeccably groomed watchdogs guarding their Alpha. Like Jolie herself, they were walking billboards for Simply the Best style and products.

The media relations head had referred Alice to a personal assistant who would be the point of contact for inquiries, appointments, referrals, and all the rest. No doubt the PA would be another of the protective watchdog clones. She reopened the email from p.addington@ simplythebest.com: Pepper Addington, Personal Assistant to Helene Jolie herself.

Out of curiosity, she searched the web for the name—how many could there be? A lot of Addingtons in the area, but only one Pepper. It was easy to pick out the right LinkedIn profile featuring a pretty twenty-something with a rich California tan and a blond ponytail. MBA, Pepperdine, so she had a brain, no surprise there. Alice doubted Helene Jolie had any patience for stupidity. P. Addington's interests included ecology, art—and surfing.

Beach Boys tunes began playing in her head, all at once. Her California Bingo card was complete.

"Siri, play 'Valley Girl' by Moon Zappa." She laughed when the chant and grinding bass drove the surfer drums and reverb guitar out of her head. "Beverly Hills. Bel Air. Oh mah gawd, gag me with a spoon."

So this was the watchdog who would be protecting Helene Jolie from the big bad journalist? A devoted member of the cult under the perfect California tan? And it was a perfect tan, as revealed in a five-year old photo of Ms. Addington carrying her board into the Malibu surf. With perfect muscles and perfect curves. So much California home-grown beach blond perfection. Another perfect walking billboard for Simply the Best.

This assignment was going to put her through her journalist paces to gather information without hating—alienating the subject. She was her mother's daughter, after all. It would be good practice. Or at least that's what she told herself.

Beverly Hills. Hollywood. California glitz. Sure, it was all for practice. She reached for the whiskey again, welcoming its mute promise of comfortable distance from her troubles. There was no escaping them now.

CHAPTER SIX

"Clarita?"

Pepper glanced over at Clarita's empty desk. In the three weeks she'd survived so far, Clarita had always been there when Helene called for her. As she'd seen Clarita do multiple times a day, she quickly got up and went to the office door. "Clarita isn't at her desk. Is there something I can do?"

Helene's quick frown made Pepper feel as if she was personally responsible for Clarita's absence. "The proposal for the Your Best Beauty Winter rollout was due to me fifteen minutes ago."

"I'll inquire about it immediately."

"No, you'll connect me with Halley Beecher."

Pepper swallowed hard. "Right away."

"After that I want to speak with Gail Monteif about that reporter from New York."

Pepper retreated to her desk and cringed at every second she lost looking up Halley Beecher in the corporate directory. She knew Beecher was the Director of Your Best Beauty Marketing, but she didn't yet know the extensions by heart. Should she go through Beecher's personal assistant? No, she decided. She was calling not for herself, but for Helene, and Helene did not go through assistants when she wanted to talk to anyone.

Thankfully, Beecher picked up. "I have Helene Jolie for you."

"Would you tell her that the packet will be on the way in five minutes?"

Not on your life. Pepper said firmly, "She wants to speak to you." Not waiting for an answer, she forwarded the call to ring at Helene's desk and hung up her handset with a shaking hand.

You have to get a grip on your nerves, she scolded herself. After a steadying breath she looked up Gail Monteif's extension and then listened to the rise and fall of Helene's voice. The call sounded like it was wrapping up, so she went ahead and dialed Monteif. It felt like a major victory that the moment Helene disconnected Beecher, Pepper buzzed in, announced Gail Monteif was on hold, and then hung up.

She was queasy. Two little phone calls and her adrenaline was off the charts. She'd been less nervous paddling out to her first big waves off Laniakea. *Riding a big curl took practice, remember?* The problem with her job was there was no do-over after wiping out.

The vivid recollection of fine sand between her toes, golden sun on her shoulders, and the deep, heavy sound of waves rolling ashore steadied her nerves. It was still a huge relief when Clarita returned to her desk.

"Helene is talking to Gail Monteif right now about a reporter. The packet from Halley Beecher isn't here yet, and Helene has spoken to her directly about it."

Clarita nodded and dropped into her seat with uncharacteristic relief. Her normally still, pale face was flushed.

"Are you okay?"

"Something I ate at lunch."

"Would you like a Pellegrino from the fridge?" Pepper was gratified to get what was almost a genuine smile.

Clarita very nearly met her gaze as she said, "Thank you, yes. I think that would help."

The woman was an acquired taste, Pepper mused, as she fetched a bottle of the sparkling water. Clarita was not a warm and fuzzy person, and that was okay. It would be nice to work with someone who gave positive feedback, but Pepper was learning that lack of criticism meant "good job." Or at least that's what she told herself, desperately hoping it was true.

She handed the chilled bottle to Clarita as she said, "There are only a few bottles left now and none in the cupboard, so I'll stock up."

"You have the code to charge?"

"Of course." Pepper had quickly learned that having Helene's code meant she could order anything she wanted at the café, request valuable items from the Boutique, where she used to work, or have products from the catalog delivered to her desk. Clarita got a daily report on its use, so it wasn't as if those who had it could help themselves to new boots or a handbag, which made total sense as a safeguard. It also allowed her to temporarily requisition some of the most expensive jewelry when Helene wanted to show it off at an event. She always heaved a sigh of relief when she returned them to the secure storage.

The best news so far was that she wore the same size shoe Helene did, and Helene got a lot of prototype shoes and samples to examine and possibly wear. Most were rejected as too similar to others or in need of a change before being added to the catalog. Pepper was currently wearing a pair of Garavani red patent sandals with T-strap ankle wraps that lacked a dangling tassel the finalized shoe would have.

She admired the sandals as she drove across the campus from Building One to the café nestled into the bottom floor of Building Four. Free loot was definitely a hidden upside of the job. Samples for all sorts of things, from art prints to workout socks, came into Helene's office. Some were still secret designs, and Pepper now knew what "secure waste disposal" meant as a protocol. Getting caught putting pre-production samples of anything up for sale online was an instant termination offense.

The more ordinary items were left to Clarita to decide where they should go. Some were sent to distributors or back to the source, but many very nice things came to Pepper to offer to the staff. She had so far made a lot of new friends eager to help out if she had a question or needed something at light speed for Upstairs.

The day was hot and lacked even a hint of a breeze. The sky had an almost metallic glitter. Even the open golf cart seemed to cut the air rather than stir it. Visions of offshore winds whipping white foam across Malibu Beach filled her head as she made her first stop at her old building. Receptionist Ann wasn't at her desk, so Pepper left a pair of prototype earrings Helene had approved with some minor modifications to add to the catalog for the holidays. The swirling red and white cloisonne intermingled with drops of gold stars was exactly the sort of thing Ann would wear, and there was no reason all the loot had to be offered first to those who worked Upstairs. She went to the second floor to gather items to refresh Helene's shelves and then headed for the café.

Back in the golf cart she crossed the long narrow campus again. Even on a miserable day the trees and hedges were a welcome sight. The Oval, where many employees went to relax, snack, or have lunch, provided welcome shade. Not that she ever had time to enjoy it, but it was, nevertheless, a feast for the eyes.

At the café she signed for two cases of Pellegrino, some organic canned soft drinks, and a new supply of coffee pods. Halfway back she got a text from Clarita saying Helene was asking for fresh iced tea. She U-turned, scored a tall bottle of freshly made cold brew, and returned to the main building. She commandeered one of the elevators for her supplies and thanked the security guard for his help carrying it all.

She had no sooner carried the first case of Pellegrino to the kitchen when a greenish Clarita scurried toward the restrooms again. That meant she couldn't get out of earshot of the phone. She punched up the number for Linda, over in the CFO's office.

"I wouldn't normally ask, but could you move the supplies in the hallway to Helene's kitchen? I can't leave my desk to finish it up."

Linda was one of the friendlier people Upstairs and immediately agreed. "It's in front of the elevators?"

"Yes please, and thanks. I owe you."

"If a pair of those lined leather gloves comes around?"

"They're yours."

All the while listening for the phone, Pepper pulled a tall glass from the cupboard, made sure it was spotless, and filled it most of the way with ice. Setting it on a small tray with an aluminum straw and the tall bottle of tea, she carried it into Helene's office, set it on the corner of the desk, and left again without being acknowledged. As she did so she couldn't help but hear what Gail Monteif and Helene were discussing with a good measure of passion on both sides. Apparently, the earlier phone call hadn't settled anything.

"Helene, you're being stubborn. This will be utterly free, reputable publicity for the Fifth Avenue opening. A lot of people in New York are still remarkably angry that we left."

Pepper didn't have to see it know that Helene had waved one hand to dismiss the entirety of anyone's displeasure. "And we took a five-year lease on a vacant swath of retail space, expanded our warehouse in Queens, and spent plenty of money supporting the messaging for *New York is Back*. What more do they—"

"You know perfectly well what they want."

"I'm not going to bend the knee."

Gail's sigh was the last thing Pepper heard. She waved her thanks at Linda for stowing the supplies and delayed two calls as the two women continued to talk, all the while increasingly concerned that Clarita hadn't returned. Any minute, Helene would—

"Clarita?"

Pepper went immediately to the doorway. "I'm sorry, she's not at her desk."

Helene's eyebrows went up along with a flicker of concern. "No matter, it's you I wanted. Gail, just so you know, when you sent this journalist my personal assistant's name, this is who you're counting on to keep a New York reporter in check."

Gail, after a glance at the mute, immobilized Pepper, said, "It's way below Clarita's pay grade to give a reporter a campus tour and make appointments and introductions."

"One of your own people with more experience—"

"Would not be able to convey access to you directly—"

"That's my whole concern! I don't want to give a reporter access."

Mortified and angry, Pepper burst out, "I'm perfectly capable of setting boundaries for this Alice Cabot person. I read the ground rules memo carefully."

Helene's mockery was just below the surface as she said, "Really?"

"I have an MBA. I've kept my cool in sporting competitions, and I know how to get people to back off without alienating them. If I *want* to alienate them, they'll know it." She gulped to a halt, feeling faint.

"What sport would that be?"

Pepper lifted her chin. "Surfing."

"Did you win?"

"Enough to make my father proud of me for the rest of my life, but not nearly as often as I wanted to."

"What a shame."

Pepper was pretty sure that Helene had just doubled the number of words she'd spoken to Pepper in the weeks since she'd been hired.

Gail had a tiny smile as her gaze went back and forth between Pepper and Helene as if she was at a tennis match.

After what felt like an hour, but was probably fifteen seconds, during which Helene looked Pepper up and down several times, Helene said, "Perhaps I was too hasty. You may have all the right qualities to play host." She waved a hand. "That's all."

Pepper glanced at Gail Monteif, admiring her poise in the face of the boss's ire, and returned to her desk. A few moments later, Gail emerged from the office as well.

She paused at Pepper's desk, her dark, oval face a mixture of concern and admiration. "She likes it when people speak their mind. Until she doesn't."

Pepper nodded, hoping that her hammering heart wasn't apparent. "I can do this."

"It's a tightrope. It's essential the reporter feel we're not hiding anything. That she has complete access to all but proprietary secrets."

"I need to listen carefully. Offer what's available and help to find it. Try to say yes as often as possible."

She got a brisk nod. "You've got it."

"I learned kind, but firm, customer service skills watching the librarians at the university. Even when they had to say no I still loved them for it."

Gail's smile was heartening. "I think you're going to be fine. If there is any question or dispute about the ground rules, call me directly."

"Thank you."

"Clarita?"

Pepper went to Helene's doorway as Gail left with a wave.

"I'm sorry, she's not back."

"I'm concerned." The mid-afternoon sun was just beginning to shine directly into the office. The natural sunlight turned Helene's red hair into a halo of fiery color.

"It was something she ate, Clarita said." Pepper was surprised when Helene waved her forward, and she ended up halfway to Helene's desk, knees locked like a soldier at attention.

"When she comes back, tell her I said she is to go home immediately and keep her stubborn self at home until she's better." Helene's lips twitched. "You don't have to say stubborn."

"Of course."

Helene gave her a sharp look as she waved a hand at the chairs facing her desk. "Sit down, please."

It was a simple request. Should she take the chair on the left or the right? Should she cross her legs or perch on the edge in preparation to stand up again when their short talk ended? No way could she sit back with the same kind of confidence Gail had shown. She finally settled somewhere in between and did her best to meet Helene's dark-lashed gaze.

She was struck again by the sheer force of Helene's personality. What had CC called it? Energy? The power of glamour and allure? It was almost impossible not to notice her lips, the curve of high cheekbones, the long arms, and graceful, evocative hands. Pepper knew Helene was forty-eight, but in person she looked closer to thirty-five than fifty. That could be the result of a consistent beauty regimen and flawlessly applied makeup—and it was a great advertisement for their products.

Bangle bracelets jangled as Helene made a helpless, defeated gesture at papers on her desk. "Gail insists this interview and series has to happen."

The safest course of action seemed to be nodding in agreement.

"Journalists have agendas. I don't trust any of them." Helene fixed her intense gaze on Pepper, and a frown creased her forehead.

Unsuccessfully squelching a quaver in her voice, she asked, "Are there instructions you'd like to give me about Alice Cabot?"

Helene's gaze swung to Pepper's face as if she'd forgotten Pepper was even there. "Don't volunteer anything. Confirm if what you're being asked about is for background, off the record, or on the record. I learned that the hard way." Her lips twisted in a rueful smile as she finally seemed to relax. "I have scars from previous interviews."

"Did you leave a few in return?" *Oh holy crap, I said that out loud!*

Helene's entire face lit up, and she suddenly looked exactly like the woman in the videos from Fashion Week and Coachella. "I certainly did." After a gusty sigh of acceptance, she went on, "Gail says this is a good thing, and we need good press in New York to make up for the not so good press when we left."

"Of course. I understand." Finally able to keep her voice steady, she said, "About Alice Cabot. Her bio at the paper says she's a seasoned reporter. So I was thinking…" She paused, hoping for some sign that Helene had any interest in her thoughts.

"Does that sentence have an end?"

Note to self—timidity gets you nowhere. "I think that the more information we openly and quickly share with her, the less inclination she'll have to look to a source that isn't us. But if we starve her or make her ask for everything one item at a time, she might, and we can't control that."

"Gail's been talking to you, hasn't she?" Helene didn't seem to want an answer. "It's a matter of trust. I don't like doing business with people I can't trust." She swept her hair up with one hand, twisting it into a ponytail. "Scratch that. I don't *like* people I can't trust, and I tend not to trust people who think they have a direct line to the truth. I haven't met a reporter yet who didn't think they knew everything." She let go of her hair and the lush curls and ringlets spiraled around her shoulders, again catching the sun.

Dazzled and trying not to show it, Pepper managed to say, "I know what you mean, Ms. Jolie. I mean Helene."

"That's right. I remember now. You say my name correctly. *Parlez-vous français?*"

"I wish. No, I listened to videos where you said your name." Wouldn't anyone do that to avoid flubbing the CEO's name?

"How sensible." Helene moved one shoulder so slightly it couldn't rightly be called a shrug. "Most people don't use *zh* for the *J*. One enthusiastic ST-Bester from the South called me Ms. Joe-leen the entire conversation."

Pepper laughed. "There are worse things to be called than after a Dolly Parton song." She realized she was squeezing her hands together in her lap so hard her knuckles were white.

"Remind me why you wished to work for me?"

Pepper wasn't sure if that meant Helene had forgotten she hired Pepper on a whim. She saw no reason to remind her. "It's a privilege to work in such beauty and elegance." *Great. The world's most vapid answer.*

Helene's lips turned down ever so slightly. "Really? Because it's pretty here?"

What had Helene said in that *Buzztastic* interview? "I don't underestimate the power of beauty. Isn't that one of the goals of art, to uplift through beauty? You've built a culture here that is both businesslike and..." She searched for the right words. "And feels nurturing, positive."

The piercing green gaze hadn't left her face. "Thank you. It was my goal."

"I know this is an unparalleled opportunity to learn from someone so successful."

One finely sculpted eyebrow lifted slightly. "Aren't you going to say I am 'simply the best'?"

"I have no doubt that you are, but I'm sure you hear that all the time." Pepper lifted an eyebrow in return, even though she inwardly knew she was so out of her league.

To her surprise, Helene's lush lips curved into a genuine smile. "I've heard it so often in interviews—reporters, and style editors, and employees. Everyone thinks I can't have possibly heard it before."

Pepper hoped the expression on her face was a smile—she was too numb to tell. "I don't think being unoriginal will help me do this job. Or succeed in life, for that matter."

"If only more people valued originality. You wear the Garavanis well, by the way."

Don't blush, don't blush, don't blush. "Th-Thank you. I wouldn't want to be an embarrassment."

"Good." Helene waved her hand and returned her attention to the papers on her desk.

Pepper hurried back to her desk, flustered and pleased. She thought maybe she hadn't completely made a fool of herself. She might even have held her own a couple of times. *Practice helps, remember?*

Speak of the very devil, she thought as she checked her inbox. An email with the subject "Interview and Orientation" from sender CabotAliceP was waiting for her. It was short and to the point.

"Ms. Addington," Pepper read. "Gail Monteif has forwarded me your name as my primary contact for arranging interviews, review of corporate archives and practices, and general orientation to the Simply the Best headquarters. Using Ms. Jolie's availability as the anchor, what other personnel could be available and what activities arranged to maximize my visit to the area?"

Seriously? It was one thing to cooperate in arranging for anything requested and to suggest logical, simple avenues for Cabot's research, but come up with a blanket list of every possible thing Cabot could do in the time frame? That wasn't her job.

Clarita returned to her desk looking marginally better. "I think the worst is over."

"Helene said you should go home and stay there until you feel better."

"I feel better now."

"Clarita?"

Pepper watched Clarita move more slowly than usual into Helene's office. There was a low exchange of voices and then the truly unexpected sound of both women laughing. Old friends, most assuredly.

After checking Helene's calendar for openings of at least an hour, Pepper began her reply to the reporter's request. She offered a tour of the campus on October 1st and time in the corporate archives. The following day would be the interview with Helene, in a one-hour afternoon slot. In between there could interviews with other staff. She also proposed a trip to the Rodeo Drive store, with the tidbit that the Fifth Avenue store would be following much the same design aesthetic. Follow-up interviews and other items could be accommodated as requested. She concluded by offering to recommend dining and suggesting the nearby Beverly Hills Grand for lodging.

She put a hold on Helene's calendar for the times she offered in case she didn't hear back from the reporter today. When Clarita returned to her desk, Pepper put away the supplies in the kitchen. As she finished her phone vibrated with a text message. It was from

Alice Cabot. Pepper had logged out of her workstation as usual upon leaving her desk, and the system had forwarded the email to her text. That was a setting she'd see about changing. She didn't want to get 24/7 direct messages from anyone who had her work email address. Clarita using her personal number was one thing, but some stuffy reporter from New York was entirely another.

She tapped open the converted email. "Would it be possible to receive these documents?" A list followed. A long list, starting with an organizational chart.

She was still scanning the list when a second missive arrived. "First choice of accommodations booked. Second choice is in Santa Monica. Is that too far to commute?"

To be fair, she had offered to give recommendations, but Pepper was still irked. Since it was an easy answer, she quickly replied, "Santa Monica is about a half hour and a very scenic drive."

A moment later she got a direct text back with a thank-you and her phone informed her that CabotAliceP had been added as a direct message contact. *Damn it.*

When she returned to her desk Pepper thought Clarita still looked green around the edges. "You're not going to go home, are you?"

"No, I'm getting better. Thank you for your help earlier."

"You're entirely welcome. I'm getting the arrival of the reporter from New York sorted out now."

"Good. Helene is anxious about it."

"We talked." Pepper changed the calendar dates she'd held for Alice Cabot from pending to confirmed. She knew it would ping Helene to accept and so wasn't surprised when—

"Pepper?"

She went to the doorway. "I hope those dates are fine."

"Yes. I'm glad it will be over quickly."

"The reporter will be out of our hair by the middle of the month."

Helene pulled her masses of red hair to one side and pretended to examine the perfect, silky ends. "We might need a keratin treatment to recover."

"It's a good thing we know where to acquire a good one."

Helene dismissed her with a tiny smile and a wave. Back at her desk Pepper took several steadying breaths. *Get on with your job*, she scolded herself, while part of her was considering what her hair would look like loose and kind of tangled and mussed and red.

There were five more messages from Alice Cabot. Seriously, the woman was on some kind of power trip, Pepper told herself crossly.

Clicking through the emails one by one, she supplied—in the order requested—the org chart, senior staff directory, board member bios, and annual report with supplemental financial reports. She also sent the June 30 quarterly results, which had become public yesterday, just for good measure.

She sent the last email only to see one more had arrived. It was nearly seven in New York now. Didn't the woman have an off switch? She opened the latest email warily.

It was short and read, "Amazing! That was a lot really quickly. Thank you. Is everyone at ST-Best so competent?"

What kind of question was that? Without hesitation she sent back, "Yes."

CHAPTER SEVEN

"It's hot out there today." The rental car clerk stated the obvious with such cheer that Alice contemplated the pleasure of throat punching him. Then she contemplated the probable incarceration and towed her suitcases outside.

For the first ten seconds the heat felt therapeutic. Cleansing. Her muscles relaxed, her bones and joints lost their airplane-seat ache. The sun shone yellow in a pale blue sky, beneficent and healing.

The initial purely physical pleasure in the warmth faded as she dodged a shuttle bus hell-bent on flattening pedestrians. A sleek jet screamed overhead as it gained altitude, while another roared as it slowed for landing. Fuel vapor made the burnt air smell even worse.

"Airports are the same everywhere," she muttered.

After tornado warnings had rerouted her nonstop flight into Dallas, the day had drifted into traveler's non-time, where every TV seemed to be playing the same endless news interview, and there was little to do but mark the passage of time by the level of airport lounge whiskey in her glass. She used to enjoy air travel because it gave her time to read, but lately reading seemed like too much effort. Her brain was overrun with all things Simply the Best. Marketing slogans, lawsuits, sales projections, stock performance, partnerships with designers, and endless speculations about celebrity endorsements and speakers at the next Composium. Simply the Best hadn't just engendered their own business, they had also spawned an industry of followers jockeying for click revenue.

Instead of landing at noon, she'd arrived at nearly four, and she was starving. She'd left her apartment at three a.m., after opting to simply stay up rather than be miserably groggy on two hours sleep. Though she always lied to herself that it would be sufficient, the snatched sleep on the airplane had not been the least bit restful. Her body was clamoring for dinner and bed. Just one errand to complete before heading for her temporary new digs—if there was still time.

Grateful for her transition lenses that protected her eyes from the UV glare, Alice came to a stop at the space with her assigned car.

A convertible. A cherry red, white-topped two-seater convertible.

"My lord, could *anything* be more LA.?" She was no longer in New York, Kansas, or any other place rooted in reality.

And a hearty "fuck you" to the designer who'd thought a black interior was the way to go and to whomever thought it was more thrilling to leave the top down in the sun on a 90-degree-plus day. No amount of air-conditioning was going to take the burn off the seats, let alone the dash. First purchase—a white beach towel. At least the white top would bounce heat as well.

Her suitcases almost didn't fit in the trunk because the storage and mechanism for the hard top took up half the space. She hadn't asked for this and didn't want it, but it was too hot and she was too tired to wrangle about it now.

It took a minute to figure out which buttons to push and in what order to get the top up. Once it locked into place, she backed out of the parking space. She had intended to drop in to see Pepper Addington in advance of their scheduled meeting tomorrow. Her traffic app said it was forty minutes to get to the ST-Best headquarters from here. She might make it in time if she put off getting a bite to eat.

It would be worth the effort, she told herself, as she followed the signs to exit the rental car center. Pepper Addington's emails had been brisk and to the point. Despite Alice's mentioning more than once that she was happy to be flexible and follow the flow, her itinerary was tightly scripted for the next two days, right through Friday afternoon, as if they expected that to be the end of her visit. She considered it only the beginning.

By showing up unannounced, just to say hello and nothing more, Alice hoped to diffuse some of the formality. It was a technique she'd learned from her mother ahead of interviews. A quick, no agenda, whites-of-the-eyes introduction was often thirty seconds well spent. The first official meeting began then on a note of familiarity, since greetings and awkward pauses were over with. It was easier to get down to business in a more trusting tone.

She let the built-in GPS guide her through a maze of exits onto freeways six lanes wide in each direction, filled with vehicles all traveling at breathtaking speeds one minute and slamming on brakes the next. All the freeways were numbers, 405, 90, 187, 10—nothing to hang her tired brain on. The closer she got to Beverlywood, the gateway to Beverly Hills, which was the gateway to Hollywood Hills, the more palm trees stretched toward the soft blue sky. Bright murals of musicians and movie posters lined her exit onto the cutthroat boulevards where just merging over to a turn pocket was a blood sport. Signs encouraged her to turn on the Avenue of the Stars or bear right to Rodeo Drive. That's when she realized her GPS was sending her to the store, not the corporate office.

"It's Beverly Hills. We just take whichever Mercedes is closest," she quipped as she navigated reorienting herself. "Turn at the big country club, what a surprise."

It shouldn't have surprised her that the drive became even more surreal at that point. A broad, rolling vista of green grass opened up, with fairways lined by hundred-year-old palm trees. She had to navigate around the club's entrance, where a limo, Tesla, and Mercedes were angling to be the next to enter. A block further on, finally, a Simply the Best visitors sign pointed her toward a snug parking lot. Behind a white wrought iron fence was another lot for employees. To one side, along the building inviting visitors to enter and register, was a single parking space. A white Tesla glistened in the prime spot, with the license plate "STB=001."

It was easy to guess who that belonged to.

Feeling rumpled and cross, she nevertheless presented herself at the reception desk. Might as well also learn how to register tomorrow and how long that would take. Her question having been answered efficiently by the slender, blue-suited brunette, she then asked for Pepper Addington.

In a soft lilting accent that spoke of Jamaican roots, the receptionist told her, "Ms. Addington is out of the building. Would you like her number to leave a message?"

"I have it. She's not expecting me, but I thought I'd say hello in advance of our meeting tomorrow."

"I don't know how long she'll be."

Recalling the Tesla parked almost at the door, she took a chance though she knew what the answer would be. "How about Ms. Jolie?"

"She's also out of the building." The receptionist seemed to realize Alice had likely seen the car outside, because she added, "We have five buildings across the campus, and she left a bit ago. With Ms. Addington."

Drats. Alice thanked the woman for her help and returned to the warm afternoon air. She stood for a moment looking toward the rest of the campus. Two-story buildings, scattered, not all in a row, connected with wide, gently curving pathways and a variety of landscaping in between—white rock, succulents, and trees she recognized as drought resistant. A fountain of stacked white stone sparkled in the central nexus, where picnic tables were shaded by trees and white canopies.

When she saw a golf cart zip along between buildings she nearly laughed. What kind of reality show was this? It was all so clean, so pure—like a movie set. Any moment now employees would burst out of the doors to spontaneously launch into song and dance numbers from *La La Land.*

All part of the brand.

The scent from nearby rosemary bushes and a musky jacaranda tree made her nose twitch. The sun, drooping lower in the sky now, increased the growing ache behind her eyes. She almost turned back to ask the receptionist if she knew of a nearby place with authentic south-of-the-border cuisine. Probably a waste of time. It wasn't as if authenticity was a big priority here.

Dispirited and dreading the drive to her rental apartment, she walked to the fountain to get a feel for the place. It was farther than it looked, and she supposed she understood the use of golf carts for some distances. It was probably a six- to seven-minute walk between the most northerly and southerly buildings.

As she contemplated the distance, another golf cart began its journey across the campus, heading toward the nexus where she stood. There was no worry of collision—the pathways were wide and she'd seen several signs encouraging pedestrians on the right, carts always on the left. The white top of the cart disappeared momentarily behind a rolling rise in the path, then popped into view.

She saw the passenger's red hair first, lifted in the breeze. One stiletto-shod foot rested on the running board as Helene Jolie turned her face toward the driver. Helene Jolie in the flesh. "Yeah, baby, she's got it," Alice muttered.

Jolie said something in a nonchalant aside and the driver laughed. *Ah*, Alice thought, *that would be P. Addington, watchdog.*

Pepper Addington was exactly what Alice expected. Her blond ponytail bobbed as she talked. Her skin was exquisitely, evenly tanned to gold-bronze perfection, and as they came closer the pert nose and wide smile were all the more evident. She was willing to bet the eyes framed by dark lashes were blue—cornflower or periwinkle. An impossible color for most mere mortals, but not for the embodiment of all things surfer girl.

But she was wrong about that. The eyes that caught her gaze were bright and brown, and they stared at each other as the cart circled the fountain like a highway roundabout and chose the exit heading toward the administration building.

Alice was all at once aware of her rumpled slacks, the greasy blot of barbecue sauce on her sleeve, and her weary, bloodshot eyes. Aware too that, in all this pristine perfection, she was the odd one out.

She didn't move until the cart was parked at the administration building and Jolie was already striding toward the door. Addington turned back to look in Alice's direction. After a moment, she followed her boss inside.

There was nothing left to do but head to her car as a nearby church bell tolled five. A casual drop-in seemed impossible now. Maybe it was hunger or low blood sugar, but Alice felt her shoulders droop as her spirit deflated. A good night's sleep would undoubtedly help.

The overhead solar panels had shaded the car, but the inside was still an oven. Music would be welcome, but as she idled waiting for the A/C to cool the steering wheel a little, she realized the previous renter of the car had liked talk radio. Tomorrow she'd sync her phone— it was too much to contemplate at the moment. She was scanning stations in hopes of finding something better when a knock on her window sent her heart rate through the roof.

"Are you Alice Cabot?" Pepper Addington's voice was low, almost husky.

Flummoxed, she nodded.

"Scoping out the enemy?"

"Are we enemies already?" Alice realized the idiocy of shouting through the window. She killed the engine and got out of the car again.

The very bright brown eyes blinked at her for a moment. "Bad choice of words. Pepper Addington. I recognized you from your picture on your byline."

Alice shook the offered hand, aware of her own rough skin against the firm softness of Pepper's palm. Her rumpled polo shirt and off-the-rack brushed denim trousers had nothing in common with the simple elegance of Pepper's thin silky white blouse and close-fitting black pants. Strappy gold sandals made Alice's loafers look like army boots. Pink painted toenails matched Pepper's manicure, with lipstick several shades darker.

"My byline? Oh, at the paper." Of course she had researched Alice, that was no surprise. Would she have pieced together that this assignment was an anomaly in Alice's career? Had she seen the douchebag video?

There was nothing but polite interest in Pepper's expression as she asked, "Is everything all right with your hotel?"

"I'm sure it will be. I settled on an extended stay rental instead. I haven't been there yet. My flight was delayed. I took a slight detour here first, hoping to simply pop in and say hello, but the receptionist said you weren't available."

"Let's get your credentials now. It won't take but a few moments and will save you time in the morning."

"Aren't you heading home?"

"My day's not quite done," she said lightly. "It will take only a minute or two. There's an event in the community space this evening, so reception is still open."

It seemed there was no other choice but to follow Pepper back inside. Curious, Alice echoed, "Community space?"

"It doubles as a meeting place for large-scale employee meetings, but Ms. Jolie thought there was no reason it couldn't be used by other groups. Tonight it's a local art and theater collective meeting with retailers about a proposed Christmas market and performance space."

Alice digested that information while another part of her brain registered that Pepper was four or five inches shorter than she was and moved quickly and gracefully. The ponytail swayed in hypnotic counterbalance to each step.

The cool of the lobby washed over Alice, drawing a shiver. Pepper had stopped walking and was simply studying her, as if waiting for a reaction.

Alice had been so focused on her errand that she hadn't taken in the design of the building earlier. "So this is the house that Helene Jolie built."

A wall of long-bladed ferns rose behind the receptionist and there was a faint, herbal aroma in the air. The reception atrium soared to a massive skylight of red, blue, and yellow panes of glass. The afternoon sun poured through, throwing long bands of color across the pale tile floor. She studied the colors, surprised to see also purple, green, and orange. Glancing up again, she realized some of the panes were deliberately curved so their shadow would cross into another's, creating secondary colors when the original points of light were all primary colors. A feat by the designer.

"Impressive," she said to Pepper.

Pepper's expression was unreadable. "I feel fortunate to work here."

"It beats the heck out of a ninety-year-old newsroom that smells like cigars from the Nixon administration."

A lopsided smile flashed, but only for a moment. "I have no doubt of that," was all Pepper said as she gestured toward the reception desk. "Shall we?"

As promised, Alice was issued a guest pass that fit into a Simply the Best-branded lanyard. "Please return these at the end of your visit," the receptionist told her. "Everything is recyclable, and we're committed to sustainability."

"Of course," Alice said automatically. She had received a curious look when Pepper told her that Alice was a reporter. Was it the profession or the men's orange polo shirt? Or the loafers Alice always wore through airports? The odd-girl-out feeling, in more ways than one, grew stronger.

"In the morning you can come up to the second floor. Go around the pendulum and that's where you'll find me."

"The pendulum? This I have to see."

Pepper's smile grew infinitesimally more distant. "You do. It's a stained glass, pendulum, and water artwork and very beautiful."

She gestured toward the parking lot, and they turned in unison toward it. Alice dreaded the blast of heat, and it was as bad as she thought it would be as they left the air-conditioning behind. "Is this typical for October first?"

"Heavens no. We're having a heat wave. It will cool off after sundown. It's supposed to break on Friday, and we'll be back in the mid-seventies." Pepper seemed to relax into the heat, as if her body knew not to waste energy fighting it. Perhaps that was why she appeared to have no sweat glands while Alice was drenched. "Are you familiar with our climate?"

"It's hot here."

"Not always, but it is dryer than back east."

"I'll be sure to salt my fries."

The cool facade cracked slightly as Pepper struggled to hide a smile. "Or have the rim salted on your margaritas. I don't think there's a restaurant in all of Southern California that won't offer you one."

Alice laughed. "I'll take that under advisement."

"And water—you can't drink too much of it either."

"What about the ice in the margaritas?"

Pepper stopped at Alice's rental car and turned to regard her with mocking skepticism. "Sure, that's the same thing."

"I'll have to conduct an experiment. For science." She fanned the front of her shirt. The heat in New York was oppressive. This was penetrating. "Care to join me?"

She regretted it the moment she said it—it was a mistake. Pepper was part of the story and had taken great pains to script Alice's interaction. In the frozen moment of wanting to take back the words, she saw that she'd startled Pepper and not in a good way. *Shit-for-brains! Who's the douchebag now?*

"I'm sorry," Alice said immediately. "That was not appropriate. I'm truly sorry. I hereby rescind the invitation." She tried to tack on a smile, but she doubted it was convincing. "I've been up for thirty-six hours except for a doze on the flight. The heat and time change have fried my brain."

"I understand." Pepper's face had settled into a polite mask of not-quite interest that she had no doubt perfected giving creeps the brush-off. "I hope you have a pleasant evening and can catch up on your sleep."

"As do I."

"I'll see you in the morning." Pepper gave a little wave and headed back inside. Alice melted herself back into the rental car. She wanted to pound her forehead on the steering wheel. So much for a casual hello—she'd left Pepper with a skeezy cougar vibe. She had to be at least a dozen years older than P. Addington.

Buckle up, she told herself. *Whatever you do, don't watch her walk away.*

Who's the douchebag now?

PART THREE

Venus Is Her Name

CHAPTER EIGHT

"So that's Alice Cabot," Pepper mused as she made her way back to her desk. Cabot was everything Pepper had expected—a pushy New Yorker who thought she'd seen it all. Calling the stunning lobby "impressive" was damning with faint praise. Pepper was offended and—well, outraged. Outraged and offended.

Presumptuous, too, asking Pepper out for a drink—the nerve.

There was no need to dwell on the fact that she'd nearly said yes. Or that her stomach had sent twisty tingles up and down her spine the moment Alice Cabot had stepped out of the car and studied her through those adorable glasses.

The head shot with her online bio was pleasant enough, with the spiky hair, light brown skin, and those distinctive retro 1950s spectacles. But it didn't convey the deep-seated wit in very dark eyes or the infinitesimal lift to one eyebrow that said she was not "impressed" to any deep level.

Her height had been a surprise—she was probably as tall as Helene. Otherwise, the two women could not be more different. Why was she even comparing them?

Given the past week of daily and then hourly requests for ever more documents and contact information for people in photographs,

Pepper had expected a scowling interrogator. Not a woman who was somehow cocky and shy at the same time. Who asked her out for a drink and took it back the next moment.

What did any of that matter when she had a job to do? Protecting the company and Helene from the overcurious reporter was the job she had told Helene point-blank she was more than capable of handling. It was time to prove this was a wave she could ride.

At her desk she began to collect her things to head home, but the disconnect between her expectations and the reality of Alice Cabot wouldn't stop tickling the back of her brain. It was hard to reconcile the casually dressed woman with remnants of her last meal on her sleeve with a New Yorker who specialized in fashion, entertainment, and lifestyle.

The angular, androgynous look suited her, but it was generic, Pepper thought. Her up-brushed short hair was a fashion statement, but it was an easy one. If she was a successful Style reporter, wouldn't she look more like part of that world? There weren't any designer labels on the shirt or pants and no statement jewelry—not even a neck chain or lone earring.

She was willing to bet that Alice Cabot hadn't been wearing makeup. *Hmph.* Some women got all the thick eyelashes and naturally smoky eyes, leaving Pepper with plain brown. Good ol' serviceable nobody-notices brown.

Even more annoyed that she could so easily picture Alice Cabot's dark eyes, she gave herself a hard mental shake. *Focus—next steps, idiot.* The campus tour with Alice was tomorrow at ten. Helene's interview with Alice was the following afternoon. Helene expected completed, up-to-date memory cards at least twenty-four hours ahead of time. If she stayed a few more minutes now, she could dig into Alice Cabot a little more, and there'd be time tomorrow to relay the information to Helene on schedule.

"Heading home?" Clarita was glaring at her monitor with an expression Pepper had learned meant someone somewhere was late with something and any minute Helene would ask where that something was.

She set her purse down again. "I'm not leaving quite yet—one last thing to see to."

She got a distant nod in reply.

It ended up only taking a few clicks to find a reasonable answer— Alice Cabot's newspaper bio simply said she was assigned to Style and had been with the paper for over a decade. It was when she clicked through to a full bio that Pepper read that Alice's education was an undergrad degree in biochemistry and master's in planetary sciences from MIT, followed by another master's in journalism from Columbia. Another click to see recent articles showed one about quantum computing and another about ice sheets and climate change.

She clicked through to "NASA's Lens on Time" and learned the basics about a telescope-and-mirrors project that skipped light across space like a stone over water to see distant reaches of the galaxy and even within black holes. That somehow meant seeing events both forward and backward in time because of the speed of light. Which was all cool and super interesting but made her brain ache.

The nerdy black-rimmed glasses, the comfort of a polo shirt, casual loafers—Alice Cabot was a techy sciencey type person. She'd done nothing but science articles, the last one posted about a week ago.

With that background, why was she here, doing a feature on Simply the Best? Why did the paper say she was part of the Style staff? Did Media Relations know Alice's specialty was science? Surely they must. Did Helene know?

She went down the rabbit hole of the Internet, looking for articles about Alice Cabot versus ones that she had authored. It was vexing that Google didn't understand the difference. Helene was worried about bias. Someone with a scientific background would naturally be a skeptic, wouldn't they? Pepper herself wasn't convinced that crystals created energy vortexes on your desktop, but she didn't dispute it either. She could easily imagine that a science-minded reporter might, and that was exactly what Helene didn't want in this series.

Her stomach felt like jelly as she considered spending the next week or so defending everything ST-Best stood for and sold to a science reporter. With a helpful smile the whole while.

I don't know if I can do this.

She was in the deep end, exactly where she wanted to be, wasn't she? *Start the eff paddling, surfer girl.* What more could she learn quickly? She clicked off news and onto videos.

She didn't know what she had expected, but it wasn't one of Alice Cabot calling a congressman a douchebag. There was even a popular GIF of Alice's clear enunciation of the word. In slow motion, it was hilarious and she had to stifle a giggle.

Given that Pepper knew the congressman's name from LGBTQ media—and not in a good way—she wanted to applaud. He was an utterly useless waste of time. She pictured Alice standing next to her car, squinting in the sun, blurting out, "Care to join me?" Alice Cabot's mouth got ahead of her brain at times—good to know.

Her eye fell on a tagline for one of the videos giving Alice's full name: Alice Paul Cabot.

"Boo-yah!" Pepper exclaimed. "Sorry," she added, in response to Clarita's sharp glance.

Pepper's mind raced to absorb the implications. Media Relations had completely missed the significance of who Alice Cabot was. A trip to the Columbia School of Journalism alumni page confirmed Alice Cabot's mother was the one and only Barbara Paul Cabot.

Barbara Paul Cabot's heyday conducting TV interviews was in the past, but Pepper's college class on public and media relations included a documentary on interview wins and fails, and several of the samples had been drawn from Cabot's Sunday morning program.

The elder Cabot lived in New York, in the Hamptons. Pepper had overheard Clarita making arrangements for Helene to visit her family there for Thanksgiving. Did that mean Alice and Helene were already acquainted? But the name had meant nothing to Helene, Pepper recalled. Still, the connection might explain why this reporter had been chosen—a friendly mindset? Pals from the old money, posh, waterfront, exclusive 'hood?

What if Helene did know Alice and had simply forgotten? *Never let the boss look foolish, remember?* She knew it was a quick way to get fired.

Though some of Alice Cabot's appearance might be attributed to her interest in science over the fashion world, she hadn't even come close to seeming like someone raised in the real upper crust by a mother who had rubbed shoulders with the rich, famous, and powerful. Pepper knew what some of the super-rich and famous were like, and her parents really wished they were part of that set—

"Oh, crap!"

Clarita sent her a shocked warning look, and Pepper explained. "I forgot I have to go to a party tonight at my parents' place in Westlake Village."

"Then you'd best be on your way."

"Just one more minute." She rapidly typed in this new information and saved it as a draft. Damn Alice Cabot—she'd made Pepper late, and that meant there would be harping on the sin of tardiness. It was bad enough the woman's sleepy-eyed smile was somehow already imprinted on Pepper's brain.

She logged out of her workstation and, once out of sight of Clarita, clattered down the stairs toward her car as quickly as decorum allowed. There was no time to go home and change. Her blouse was only a little wrinkled. Thankfully she was wearing a brand-new pair of Valentino sandals that Helene had found too narrow, and they looked great with her classic black slim-legged ankle pants. The sandals would distract her mother, as would the Mark Jacobs paprika colorblock purse that had clashed with rather than complemented Helene's hair.

The 405 was as clogged as she'd expected, with no lane moving faster than fifteen miles per hour. The gonna-be-late adrenaline burst left her a little shaky, but the A/C blowing right on her face helped. She woke up her phone. "Call Best Friend Forever."

CC answered with a cross, "What?"

"I won't be home for dinner."

"I know. Parental units, required social appearance. I'm going out too."

"Cool. Good. I forgot I told you and didn't want to leave you in the lurch."

"We had this conversation while you were spending your entire evening reading reviews on the Simply the Best website."

Now she vaguely recalled it. "Sorry."

"Remember that I won't be home on Saturday?"

She didn't. "I will remember."

"All work and no play makes Pepper a drone."

"I've learned so much about our customers and products reading them. It's fascinating. Though why I'm defending a deep dive into subject matter to someone who not only knows the actual League of Legends scenarios but also the ones that were discarded—"

"Shut up."

"Make me. Hey, I met that big bad reporter from New York today."

"Yeah? What're they like?"

"Kinda dorky." *And kinda not.*

"You say that like it's a bad thing."

"Not a bad thing, but not what I expected either. I think I can manage her okay. If I do then I'll probably get to keep my job for a while longer."

"I like it when you're employed." CC's voice was temporarily muffled, as if she was pulling a shirt over her head. "Stop at the grocery on the way home, would you? We're out of ice cream. Even with the A/C going it's an oven above the pizza oven."

"Java Almond and Butter Toffee Brittle coming up."

"I don't care what they all say, you do not suck as a person."

"Nice. Where are you going for dinner?"

"Out. Anything but pizza. I'll be back by ten—I got into a tournament."

"I hope to be home by then. I need an early night because tomorrow the reporter is officially on the job and I am tour guide."

"Good luck with the dork."

Was it about luck? Pepper wondered. She admired the Getty Museum complex at the top of the craggy Crestwood Hills as the freeway wound between Bel Air on the east and wilderness parks on the west. Helene had attended a big gala at the Getty last Saturday for the unveiling of a newly acquired Van Gogh. Art, wine, and music and a cool mountaintop breeze. Maybe it would be her someday.

But not if tomorrow went badly.

It wasn't going to go badly, she promised herself. Alice Paul Cabot would get exactly what she'd come for and not one thing more.

CHAPTER NINE

"Siri, give me directions to Santa Monica."

"Directions to Santa Maria? Okay. Displaying directions—"

"Santa Monica. Mon-i-ca."

"Displaying directions to Monterey—"

Alice punched the phone off and did not throw it into the street. She felt as old and useless as it was. Santa Monica was west, and it couldn't be wrong to head that direction while the slow, clunky GPS built into the car got working.

God, she was tired. That had to be why the outline of Pepper Addington's hypnotic ponytail was swaying back and forth in front of her eyes.

Finally being shown the right directions, Alice put her faith in the guidance, avoided one freeway in favor of surface streets, and finally was situated on I-10 heading due west. She'd driven I-10 through Arizona and New Mexico once on a long road trip that had encompassed the Very Large Array, petroglyphs, and fantastic homemade tacos and burritos at almost every wide spot in the road. In the California promised land, I-10's saguaro and delicate colors had been replaced with vivid greens and swaying palms. In the desert one learned to look for subtle beauty. Here it whacked you between the eyes from every direction.

The car said she was halfway to her destination when she spotted a supermarket off the upcoming ramp. It was a quick and welcome stop. The apartment had a kitchen, and a few supplies were necessary. Back on the freeway she joined the slow progress of too many cars heading west. It felt as if everyone in Los Angeles was going to Santa Monica at the same time.

The concrete walls lining westbound I-10 dropped away and she could suddenly see more sky. Even more palm trees, but also oaks and maples. Pepper had said the drive was scenic—she hadn't lied, but who had the energy for it? Her tired brain almost let her get shunted onto another freeway, but she managed to change lanes in time.

A grinding twenty minutes later the tree-studded landscape was only broken by the soft outline of coastal bluffs to the north. Another ubiquitous shopping mall, a couple of civic buildings—it didn't seem like Santa Monica was much to write home about. She almost missed the marker declaring she was now on the Pacific Coast Highway as the roadway curved into a grimy tunnel.

Out the other side, all at once, wide beaches spread north and south as far as she could see. A sudden sharp wind made her grip the steering wheel more firmly. The arch and boardwalk of the Santa Monica Pier went by in a blur. Beyond the gold-limned sand was a limitless ocean, blue and green at the horizon, with a sharp silver path leading to the early evening sun. Scenic, dear lord yes, but it was brutal. So bright it brought tears to her eyes. She was grateful to turn north out of the glare.

The listing for the apartment proved accurate. A parking space was hers, and it was near the stairs that led to her second-floor door. She put the grocery bag on the counter and her laptop bag on the table. She almost left her suitcases in the car, but she knew if she didn't get them now she'd wake up in the morning in the clothes she was wearing. Two trips later and the door closed and locked behind her, she felt well and truly arrived.

There was nothing particularly remarkable about the decor of the apartment, which made it feel like home. There was a work desk and an efficiency kitchen with a small table. The bedroom had a queen-sized bed and a closet more than big enough for her things once she moved a folding beach chair and two boogie boards aside. A tub in the bathroom was a nice surprise. A soak would take some of the ache out of her airplane-cramped bones. Later, she thought. She should put the groceries away first. Make a drink.

"*By all means,*" Sass snarked at her. "*Whatever it takes to ignore that a blond ponytail made you forget you're here to do a story.*

Sass was silenced by the discovery that the refrigerator had an ice maker. The frozen raspberries and margarita mix with the tequila she'd bought was exactly what she needed. Life got even better when she found the blender. Alas, there was no bar salt to put on the rim of her glass, a fact she would not share with Pepper Addington.

Several large swallows solidified her bones. Even the brain freeze felt good.

She set her phone to play Dave Brubeck and made herself unpack her clothes. With her laptop and notebooks spread across the desk, the apartment was ready for two weeks of living.

The raspberry margarita long gone, she opened the bottle of Buchanan's 12-Year she'd been surprised to find on the grocery store shelf and microwaved the frozen enchilada dinner she no longer wanted.

The sun was a falling disk of orange by the time she scraped the last of the bland white sauce out of the microwave tray. Deep in the second pour of blessed Buchanan's she opened the door to the small balcony where a chaise offered repose under an umbrella that creaked in the ceaseless onshore wind. The steady deep roar that from inside she had thought was traffic turned out to be surf rolling and churning in the distance. Raucous gulls circled as they called to one another in a shrill *my-mine-my-mine*.

It was a bloody, endless cacophony. What had possessed her to rent a place so close to the shore?

Forced back inside to get some peace, she latched the sliding door and pulled the curtain over it for good measure. The living room fell into darkness, and finally she found words for the troubled feeling she'd carried away from her encounter with Pepper.

"She'll see right through me," Alice muttered. "She's no bubblehead blonde and shame on me for thinking she would be."

Pepper seemingly had a brain to go with the curvy, muscled body, but that didn't make her less of a corporate bot. What would Helene Jolie's watchdog see right through, she asked herself. What exactly was she afraid of?

That she'll realize you don't want to be here?

That you're on the verge of losing your job?

That's there's another you—or at least there used to be?

Torn between the desire for a hot bath and the lure of pillows and cool clean sheets, she sat down on the bed to stop the room from spinning. Her last conscious thought was that she ought to set an alarm.

CHAPTER TEN

With her car in the care of the hired valet, a grateful Pepper hurried up the driveway to her parents' Triunfo Canyon home. The swelter was still real, and the large man-made Westlake Lake didn't change that. It only made the mosquitoes more aggressive.

She already knew how the evening would progress. Her father would regale anyone within earshot with the coming year's prospects for the Pepperdine Waves teams, particularly beach volleyball, one of his collegiate letters. She and her parents all shared the alma mater so Pepper would be called upon to show enthusiasm. Her parents had met at the university, and Pepper had been named after it. Her older brother, Steve Junior, had probably been conceived there, but that was not a subject she wanted to dwell on because *eww*.

Before the evening was over her mother would corner her especially to ask about her plans to settle down with a nice, family-oriented woman who wanted kids. Pepper hoped details of her new job and its prospects for advancement in the Simply the Best world would be accepted as a good reason she had zero plans to do so before she was thirty. After the way she-who-shall-not-be-named had jerked her around for a year, she was putting career first for a while.

She wasn't even sure she wanted kids. Steve had taken care of paying the family genes forward and seemed more than happy to follow in the family-church-business footsteps.

She slipped past the front door and circled to the back gate. The backyard had a few scattered clusters of guests, but neither of her parents were among them. Maybe she was going to be able to slide into the party without being noticed. The house proved much more crowded, no doubt because it was twenty degrees cooler inside. The downstairs powder room was empty, and she stopped in and took a few minutes to make repairs. Her bra had of course stretched and sagged a little during the day, and the girls weren't in the same place they'd been this morning. She tightened the straps and bullied her boobages into a higher position and sighed.

Back when she'd surfed competitively it hadn't been hard to figure out that press and videographers were more interested in filming her when she was wearing a bikini. The camera loved her, she was told, and she had gotten a referral to a Hollywood agent. Attractive beach types were a staple in TV, and it was easy money. Even being an extra would open doors, yadda times three.

Turning profile to survey her silhouette, she could still hear the agent's frank assessment. "Honey, you're pretty. Pretty forgettable. If you got a boob job, you'd probably get legit extra and one-liner work for a couple of years, always in a bikini. After that the work you'd get wouldn't include wearing the bikini and I mean exactly what you think I mean."

It had hurt, and yet she was now profoundly grateful for the woman's final, world-weary advice: "Go back to the very nice life you're supposed to have."

Too small for bombshell, too large for perky. Which was okay, in her opinion. Boobages were for fun.

It had been a long time since they, or any other part of her body, had had some fun, however. Since Wilma "Didn't want to hurt you by breaking up with you when I started dating someone else" Nkosi. And no, she was not going to allow her brain to think about the scalding hot look she'd seen Helene give her girlfriend when she'd dropped in recently. Who wouldn't want to melt a seeded tennis pro with legs of steel? That was not a part of Helene's life Pepper thought she should dwell on, of course, and why, oh why, did her brain offer up a squinting Alice Cabot instead?

She retucked and smoothed her blouse, touched up her eyebrows and lashes, and blotted powder on her shiny forehead. Finally, she retied her ponytail and changed lipstick from Barely Rouge to Maniac, both by Your Best Beauty, of course.

A quick foray into the kitchen scored a flute of champagne and an hors d'oeuvre. Using a tray-laden waiter for cover, she managed to pop into the great room with a drink and half-eaten shrimp puff, looking as if she'd been there for some time.

Her mother was easy to spot, hovering near the door where newcomers were sharing enough air kisses to levitate the house. Her father was at the bar, his bald head thrown back with a shout of laughter.

The shrimp puff was crispy and savory. The lemon grass and coconut seasoning woke up her stomach, and she realized she was ravenous. She snagged another and headed in her father's direction.

"Pepper! When did you get here?"

The food and drink in her hands didn't stop him from giving her a bone-crushing hug. "A bit ago." The truth, depending on how one defined "a bit."

"You look terrific. How's the new job?" Her father turned to the man at his elbow. "Bob, this is my one and only daughter Pepper. Pepper, Bob is the newest partner at the agency."

"Pleased to meet you." Pepper lifted her glass and Bob did likewise.

"Now I see that Steve was not exaggerating when he said his daughter had the brightest smile in California."

"Thank you, but he's biased." Bob was probably forty to her father's fifty, complete with a sharply tailored blue suit and wedding band. She knew without being told that Bob and family went to the same church her parents attended. "Not that I mind."

"What's this new job he's so proud of?"

Just like that, Bob had Pepper talking about her work, which led to being introduced to his wife and then to his wife's younger sister. Her mother joined their little cluster a minute later.

Donna Addington had the blended air of a relaxed but still slightly harried hostess. Her curls of short dark hair were smooth and shining, with wisps around her ears suggesting she'd spent perhaps a small amount of time in the kitchen overseeing the delivery of perfect food and drink. Pepper knew once upon a time her mother had been blond, so she accepted that darkening to brunette over the years was probably in her future too.

"When did you sneak in? I love that handbag—what a color. Is that Mark Jacobs? It would really pop with a little black dress."

"It was a hand-me-down from my boss," Pepper confessed as she air kissed her mother's cheek. "And my momma didn't raise no fools."

"What a score." Bob's sister-in-law, Georgi, gave Pepper a cheerful, bright-eyed smile. "Sounds like a great job."

"It could lead to bigger things, I hope."

"What would those be?" Georgi snagged two shrimp puffs from a passing tray and offered one to Pepper. "These are delicious."

Oh, thought Pepper. *Heck.*

"Thanks. They are yummy."

After a bite, she answered, "Ideally, I'd love to work in vendor and product sourcing. We do a lot of work with local producers all over the world, and I think it would be fascinating to learn more about it. Especially what's sustainable and ethical."

As her father launched into a monologue of all things athletic at Pepperdine, Georgi blinked at Pepper slowly enough to convey, "Yes, I had no idea either."

Pepper felt her mother's molten laser gaze on her. As soon her father paused for breath, she did as expected. It was just easier.

"So, Georgi, what brings you to LA?"

"I actually live in Ventura. I'm going to a conference in Burbank and staying the week with Anne and Bob makes a lot of sense. I get to spoil my nephews too."

A nice, employed, family-minded woman, check, check, and check. "What kind of conference?"

"Digital and Distance Learning for Community Colleges. I'm a chemistry prof at Ventura Community College. Don't let me launch into a pedagogical discourse on asynchronous learning and content delivery. I've been doing academic-speak all day."

"Georgi was presenting a paper," Bob volunteered.

Her gaze on the door, Pepper's mother exclaimed, "I thought they couldn't make it." She touched Pepper's forearm. "Don't you leave without us having a chat," she ordered before bustling away to greet the newcomers.

Georgi and Pepper turned toward each other as their conversation circle broke up.

"Sorry," Georgi muttered.

"Don't be. They mean well. Hey, I'm starving, and I saw a cheese platter with what looked like manchego and figs."

"Show me. My paper was today right after lunch and I was so nervous I couldn't eat."

At the buffet they each heaped a plate with slightly more than good party manners allowed and found a corner to talk.

"The thing is," Georgi admitted, "I'm seeing someone, but I haven't told my sister yet."

"Early days?"

"It's been a couple of months and so far, so good. It's a guy, and try as she might, Anne gets totally confused by bisexuality and I'm putting off having another 'No, I'm not going back and forth between being straight and being a lesbian' talk until it's unavoidable. It's exhausting."

"I can imagine."

"There are worse problems to have than family that loves you and wants to understand you. I mean, they have a PFLAG sticker on both cars next to the My Kid's an Honor Student."

"And they are proud of your career." Pepper envied that a little. "My dad lined up an internship at a consulting company after I graduated, but I only lasted about six months. The pandemic hit and that was that. It was for the best, I suppose. Some of the clients were not the people I want to give my energy helping—like there was a big client spending lots of money on a campaign to convince people solar power is dangerous."

"Ugh. Sounds like a lucky escape from a soul-draining grind."

"Other people were happy to do it. Once jobs were opening up again, I started at a nonprofit as a public policy assistant—advocacy and lobbying—but they lost their grant. When I heard about an internship at Simply the Best, I grabbed it. Great products, all about empowering women. I just got hired officially."

"This is my first year as a tenured prof. To getting our dream jobs." They clinked their glasses and proceeded to finish off the cheese and conspired congenially over a second trip to the buffet for spears of pineapple and chocolate-dipped strawberries.

Pepper ended up having the required chat with her mother after the guests had mostly left and her father had retired to the game room to smoke cigars and shoot pool with buddies.

"The caterers will do that," her mother said as Pepper carried a stack of plates into the kitchen.

"I know."

"What did you think of Georgi?"

"She's very nice."

"And...?"

"And that's the whole story."

Her mother pursed her lips, a sure sign of an impending lecture. Pepper quickly asked, "Where did you get that dress, Mom?"

"Soji found it. You should use her too. She's a terrific stylist."

"Maybe someday. It is perfect for you." The bodice of the beige-gray dress was tufted with white polka dots and complemented with a bright yellow and orange infinity scarf of a Mark Rothko print. "That color is *greige*, and it's all the rage."

Her mother's expression softened. "Listen to you, fashion expert."

"I'm fancy now."

"I can tell. What are you doing to your skin? It looks wonderful. Come outside to sit. It's cooler now."

Pepper grabbed a glass of iced tea and followed her mother to the backyard deck where they sat facing the water. Lights from the homes on the island sparkled under a dark sky dotted with a few bright stars and a pale three-quarters moon.

"I get so many freebies now. This handbag. Check out my shoes." She waved her feet. "Skin care products galore. Every single thing we put in the catalog comes across Helene's desk—new fragrances or formulations. She sees and touches everything."

"She certainly seems very hands-on in her Instagram videos. Where does she live?"

"Laurel Canyon. She also has a home on the Upper East Side and at Cremorne Point, which is somewhere in Australia."

"We thought about Laurel Canyon. The estates can be large and still secluded—if you have five million dollars to spend." The note of envy eased as her mother gestured at the lake. "We're bidding on a house on the island."

Pepper was glad the dark hid her surprise. "But you just moved into this one last year."

"Wouldn't you know it? We've wanted to be on the lake for years, so when this house came on the market we grabbed it. But now we might be able to make it into the island itself. The gatehouse is always staffed. There's so many new people in the area these days, you know, and it would feel much safer. Marina privileges. Your father could finally have the boat he's always wanted. They stock the lake with bass."

The idea of either of her parents scaling and cleaning fish was amusing. "And imagine—you could take the boat to the Landing for dinner."

It would be the culmination of her mother's lifelong dream of being with the right people, in the right place, where the world around her would never change. Pepper wished her mother all the best, but it wasn't the life she was after. Of course, it would be great to live without major money worries. Waking up in the morning to something other than the smell of yesterday's pizza would be nice. It didn't have to be huge or lavish. Enough would be enough. "I hope you get it."

"It'll also make a nice inheritance for you and your brother."

"I don't care about that—I fully expect you guys to spend everything, and you deserve to do that."

"I would want your kids to be able to go to college without a lifetime of debt."

"Well, without you and Daddy I'd be carrying around a pile of debt. So I understand that." She realized too late that she'd validated the kids-are-inevitable narrative. "I'm in no rush to do that, though. I want to get firmly settled in my work."

"I hope this job sticks. More time on networking and less time surfing might work out better in the end."

Pepper bit her lip and counted to five. "I haven't been on a board in over a year. Which is a shame—it's great exercise."

"So is swimming laps, and at the gym one meets a different kind of people."

Maybe at the one her mother could afford. "The last time I tried a gym it was full of grunty men doing the full body meat display." She shuddered. "They're happy to strike up a conversation, but what they want is not called 'networking.'"

"If you set the right tone, you can avoid that type." Her mother would have said more, but a clatter inside the kitchen brought her to her feet. "So, Georgi is nice?"

"Yes, Mom. Nice, and going to make someone a great spouse someday, but we don't have much in common."

She followed her mother's sigh into the house and helped collect more scattered plates and glasses. Then she ran downstairs to hug her father goodbye, promised to come to church soon, found her car key that the valet had left after moving her Prius close to the house, and hit the road.

Event survived. Parental units mollified.

Traffic was light and she zoomed through the supermarket for ice cream and was home quickly. CC was already hooked into her game, and from the mutters and grunts of "Die, you asshole, die," it seemed to be going well.

Teeth brushed and finally in a soft, old Surf's Up T-shirt, she contemplated her wardrobe. Tomorrow was a big day and she wanted to set the right tone for her future interactions with Alice Cabot. The dark rose blouse with the pintuck front and fluted sleeves was flattering and professional. That Clarita had said, "That color does something for your eyes," was beside the point. A slimline black skirt and the zebra-striped heels she'd bought while shopping with Beth would complete her outfit.

She held the blouse up to her torso one last time. She caught sight of her determined expression in the mirrored closet door and gave herself a tight nod of approval. Cool, poised, and capable of staying in front of any wave. She straightened her posture.

Bring it, Alice Cabot, she thought. *I'm ready.*

CHAPTER ELEVEN

Alice woke with a gasp. A car honked again.

She had no idea what time it was. She struggled upright. Someone was pounding a sledgehammer on the inside of her skull and she couldn't make it stop.

She was on top of the bed in yesterday's clothes. Bright, hot light shone around the edges of the bedroom curtains—it was definitely morning—and it was enough to set off a nuclear blast in her brain. There was no relief to be found in the bathroom either. She flipped the switch and light bounced off the large mirrors in all directions. If she left the lights off, she couldn't see.

All her glory from three angles. Her face looked and felt like butterscotch pudding left out in a hot room. Her eyes were as red as the inferno burning behind them.

It felt really good to run cold water from the tap over her head. The throbbing eased and didn't return when she stood upright again. If, that is, she didn't swivel her head too quickly in either direction. She realized that among their many suggestions for how to get the perfect start to the perfect day, Simply the Best didn't have a hangover concoction of supplements. She should suggest it to her watchdog.

Sure, that would reflect well on her with Pepper.

"This is ridiculous," she told her wan reflection. "We do not come apart at the seams over a pair of big, beautiful eyes, do we?" Big, beautiful, *observant* eyes.

She was off to a great start on day one of the Assignment from Hell—scared for stupid reasons she could scarcely recall and hungover for very obvious reasons, given the half-empty status of both the tequila and the whiskey bottles.

Her phone said she had an hour and half to get to her appointment with Pepper. Half that would be taken up just driving there. One of the bananas she'd bought yesterday settled her stomach, as did a bagel. Not that any self-respecting New Yorker would call it a bagel. It was as soft as a dinner roll.

By the time she got in the shower she knew she was going to live. Ibuprofen for the headache finally kicked in, and it was easy to get into her tan slacks, men's button-up short sleeve Oxford shirt, and a nondescript medium-weight jacket in a Cape Cod blue. Two more jackets in the same style hung in the closet. One she thought of as Lady Politician red and the other was a heathered green that Bloomingdale's had unfortunately called Green Smoke. She liked the color, but the name made her think of petrochemicals.

She decided on a narrow black leather tie rather than open collar. If ST-Best folks didn't like women in ties, that was tough. She thought of it like a knight's shield—it both protected her and proclaimed her allegiance to something other than How Women Are Supposed to Be.

Once she'd brushed up her hair with a little bit of gel, she took stock. Her eyes were still red, but drops would take care of that. She'd already made who knows what kind of first impression on Pepper.

"Best foot forward," she told her bleary reflection. "Remember who you are." Sass, who loved to speak inconvenient truths, suggested, "*Do you mean a hungover reporter desperately trying to keep a job?*"

"Shut up," she told it before filling her messenger bag with her notebook and laptop.

Direct sunlight brought the return of her headache. Thick sage bushes planted outside the complex's main door made her think of turkey and stuffing, and her stomach did a long, queasy roll. She flinched from the shrill caw of a demon-sent sea gull.

"Who lives here?" she asked herself bitterly. All this sunlight and stuff growing and smelling like nature? Actual birds circling in the sky instead of stalking around on the ground with "I'm walkin' here!" attitude?

Good lord, it was going to be a long day.

She white-knuckled the drive in the stupid convertible. Why was there no suitable mass transit? Why did it seem as if every car had only one occupant? During one prolonged stoppage, she watched the woman in the car next to her apply full foundation and mascara. Behind her a man got out of his car, opened the trunk, and came back carrying a wig on a head stand. For the next mile, as they inched along, she watched him tease out the wig and try it on. It did look fabulous, she had to admit that.

Ahead of her the driver was blasting something very loud that made her brain throb in unison. It was a lot like the subway, except all the spectators and performers were in their own cars. Instead of cussing each other out face-to-face, like you do, Californians leaned on their horns.

The phone said she was ten minutes out when she finally left the clogged freeway behind. The strip malls and gas stations fell away. Old oaks lined the street instead. It seemed as if every other parked car was a Mercedes or a Tesla. An archway leading to a major movie studio was protected by a uniformed guard. A black limousine with dark windows waited to be allowed in while a cluster of kids angled to get a picture of the occupants.

Six women, all in skintight sleeveless blue dresses with necklines ranging from demure to va-va-vixen, and all possessing long, luxurious blond hair, exited the transit bus and stepped off the curb into the slow-moving traffic. All lanes slowed to a halt as they jaywalked the six-lane boulevard. All were young, pretty, and poised as they blew kisses to the cars that had stopped.

A guy leaned out his car window to yell, "Are you famous?" and one yelled back, "Not yet! We're just interns!"

She was in a hellish landscape of blithe ridiculousness, and it was going to suck what soul she had left out of her body.

She longingly eyed a low-key coffee drive-thru, but she didn't have time. Instead she took a right at the Museum of Tolerance and a left at the Center for Outpatient Regenerative Surgery, once again navigated around the back up to get into the country club, and turned into the Simply the Best parking lot.

White buildings, pristine sidewalks, manicured gardens. Whirring golf carts whisking people to and fro. It felt like a scene out of the *Stepford Wives*. A reference P. Addington would be too young to even get. Surrounded by the absurd perfection of it all, she felt wrinkled and old.

There were more assaults on her eyes and nose walking from the parking lot to the lobby of Simply the Best headquarters. The sun was relentless, though the shade from a row of palms gave her respite.

It was time to get her head in the game. Pepper Addington's eyes were of no consequence to her. She needed to put all her effort into not loathing this perfect place, these perfect people, and their perfect lives.

It seemed singularly unfair that the faint herbal scent in the lobby made her head feel better.

CHAPTER TWELVE

Alice's instructions were to walk up to the second floor and turn left toward the pendulum. Another day she'd take the stairs. Today she made her way to the elevator instead. When the doors parted after a quiet *ding* of arrival, she bumped into a woman hurrying out and knew in an instant it was Pepper.

She put out a hand to steady her. Warm skin. Warm eyes, somehow made all the more richly brown by the dark red blouse she was wearing.

They simultaneously said, "Sorry, my fault," then, "I should look where I'm going."

Alice realized she still had one hand on Pepper's arm. She let go.

A tiny wrinkle of concern appeared between Pepper's eyebrows. "Are you okay?"

"I'm fine." *She sees right through me.*

"You still look a little dehydrated. Let's get you some water before we start."

There was nothing to say to that but "Thank you, that would be wonderful." She followed Pepper back to the reception desk.

"Did you go out hiking or something?"

"Or something."

"Are you pleading the Fifth?"

"Maybe."

"Ah, but you just answered a question, so now you have to answer them all."

"Who's the reporter here?"

Pepper slipped behind the receptionist to open a concealed mini-fridge stocked with bottled water. "Role play can be fun."

Don't say it, Alice told herself.

Pepper handed her the bottle, tipped her head as if puzzled by Alice's silence. After a moment, her cheeks stained red. "That sounded so much better in my head."

Glad not to feel as if she was the only one off her game, Alice smiled and shrugged. She did indeed feel better after a long swallow of cold water. Aware of Pepper's scrutiny and unable to think of any other way to change the subject, she asked, "How's the surf these days?"

Pepper gave her a sharp look. "You've been doing research on me?"

"It's a standard practice. You're my point of contact. I want to make the most of that contact and knowing something about you saves time." So much for that famous Cabot charm.

Her expression distant, Pepper answered, "It's been a while since I've been able to get to the beach, let alone gear up to surf. Would you like to leave anything at my desk while we take a campus tour?"

"No, I'll keep it with me."

"Then let's begin, shall we?" She led the way back outside to where several golf carts were parked in a neat row.

"This is very California, I have to say."

"If by that you mean sustainable and reduced carbon footprint, then yes, very California. All electric and recharged by the solar panels that shade the parking lots."

She had been referring to the Hollywood-production values of the Simply the Best Reality Show campus, but sure, sustainability was probably a wise interpretation. "How sustainable is the entire campus?"

"We generate thirty-five percent of our own electricity as a year-round average. The project blew past all the sustainability requirements and then some."

"Impressive."

They settled into the seats, and Pepper steered the cart toward the most distant building. "We'll start with photography, videography, and graphic design. It's the most unusual building we have because it was specifically designed for darkroom and green screen imaging, which requires a lot of heat-producing equipment as well as maximum protection from outdoor light. We'll get a break from the heat, that's for sure."

As they whisked along the path Alice wanted to find something to complain about, even as she kicked herself mentally for her bias. *Shut off the snark and do the job.*

The grounds *were* as lovely as she'd discovered yesterday. The xeriscaping was extensive, and those areas that did require water had small discreet signs warning people it was reclaimed and not to drink it. Overhead solar panels provided shade to brightly painted picnic tables.

Alice indicated her phone. "Can I take a few snaps for my own reference? Not for publication—background only."

"I don't see why not. No people, if you can avoid it." Pepper rushed on, "Not that it's a policy, but it's rude without permission. At least I think so."

"Noted," Alice said. "If I'm intrusive with anyone during the tour just warn me off."

"Hand gesture? Code word?"

Alice laughed. "A simple 'stop that' will suffice."

In addition to the eye-catching picnic groupings at each building, there was art everywhere. Sculptures by local artists in stone and metal ranged from whimsical to meditative solemnity. Two pieces they passed included tubes placed in the prevailing wind to provide quiet, musical notes with the breeze.

Pepper was an excellent guide, which was not a surprise. She answered questions about materials, size, number of employees, and recycling practices with ready statistics. She seemed to know every inch of the campus.

"I interned for quite a while—this is one of my favorite sculptures, it's called 'Upside Up' by an art student at Santa Monica Community College—so I got to know the layout. Mostly in the Laboratory Boutique where small signature items are designed and small lots of exclusives are produced for sale or charity auction. We'll end there."

"So you interned here right out of college?"

"No, there were a few detours after I got my undergrad and master's in a five-year program. I tried a couple of more traditional business internships, then Simply the Best."

That made her twenty-six. Twenty-seven, at the most. "What made you pick Simply the Best?"

Pepper's hands were light on the wheel as she guided them through the central roundabout. "They have a great track record of hiring and promoting from within. My master's thesis was on 'Empowerment, Marketing, and Justice.' It's an ideal place to get hands-on in local and sustainable product sourcing. It's what we do, and I'm interested in it as a focus. Why did you pick Columbia? And MIT?"

"I see I'm not the only one who did research."

Pepper's voice became exceedingly bland. "Google can be our friend. So many interesting things to discover."

She had to have seen the video. Of course, she had. "The congressman really is a douchebag."

"Absolutely."

"I shouldn't have said it."

"Probably not."

Alice allowed herself an ironic nod. The efficient, professional Ms. Addington was fully in charge. "See? We know each other better already."

Pepper gave her a look then that Alice knew she would see in her dreams. Uppermost, there was a veneer of sophistication and determination, yet under it a confused vulnerability. *This isn't her*, Alice thought. Trading barbs and looking for weakness doesn't come naturally. The warmth in her eyes, though, and a smile that flashed as she spoke—that seemed like the real woman.

"What is it to you?" Sass demanded. *"Who cares about what Helene Jolie's watchdog is really like?"*

Alice found herself watching the way Pepper's hand floated in the air as she gestured at an art piece. A tendril of yellow hair had escaped from the ponytail and it coiled against her ear in the breeze. It wasn't hard to picture her on a beach, face to the wind.

It was best not to picture the rest of Pepper in beach wear.

"It's not as hot as it was yesterday," Alice observed. *There you have it, a weak retreat into the weather as a topic.*

"Even cooler tomorrow. It'll finally feel like autumn."

"I didn't think you got seasons here."

"They're subtle, but real. The wisteria will stop blooming."

"In New York each season hits you on the head and takes you prisoner."

"That doesn't sound fun."

"You do feel alive after navigating iced and glazed subway stairs."

Pepper laughed. "I'd say the same thing about the perfect curl off Malibu, but I get to choose them. It's not compulsory."

"I suppose that's one of the differences between NYC and here." Alice eyed the building they were approaching. While it was structurally similar to all the others—two stories, white exterior, blue- and smoke-tinted windows—one corner of the first floor looked as if it had been sliced away, and the missing piece had been stacked to one side in a sand pit along with a giant-sized pail and shovel, as if some superbeing was busy playing at the beach.

"I like starting here because this is probably my favorite lobby. I mean, my favorite is usually the building I'm in—I like them all. But you'll see what I mean. It's the only building with all artificial lighting, and there's a lot of high-tech equipment and a steady drone of fans, which can be desensitizing. The design reflects a special effort to adhere to the Simply the Best philosophy of nature over technology. All of the buildings feature natural forms on every floor to give everyone a piece of the natural world in their direct sphere."

Alice had read similar statements in the media packet. Pepper had it well-memorized. Perhaps there would there be a test later.

She followed Pepper inside and was immediately aware of the transition to artificial light. There were no overhead skylights or cascades of sunbeams. The floor was a cool lake blue under a ceiling painted the color of sky streaked with thin vapor clouds. Long, weighted banners in mottled shades of gold, bronze, and yellow hung overhead and moved slightly in the air conditioning-created breeze, giving the illusion of light streaming down. They also dampened sound.

"Impressive," Alice said as she snapped a picture. "The light tone is blue near the ground and yellow near the ceiling. The windows on the exterior are all for show?"

"There are shields covering the inside that could be removed if needed." Pepper led the way past the reception desk, where various incoming and outgoing pouches were waiting for pick up. "For the sake of consistency, all of the photography for the website is done here."

It was a hive of activity on the other side of the wall of glass architecture blocks separating reception from the rest of the first floor. A tall brunette emerged from a dressing room area and took up position in front of a nearby green screen. She had the kind of ubiquitous beauty and regular features the blue-dressed jaywalkers had possessed. From where they stood, she could see another five similar setups. Two were using live models while the others arranged groupings of products. "Most companies farm out that work."

"I've heard that there was one too many instances of outside work not having the right specifications for the color settings. When the customer swapped out various products against different backgrounds, the same shade of blue looked different, and that was bad. I don't know more about it than that."

"The end user's device would render pants in RBG and the shirt in CMYK, for example."

"You're the scientist."

"My father was the real scientist. I only write about it."

They passed three women in the process of creating an extensive tableau that interwove fall foliage with hats and gloves. A sign dangled from a tripod where several cameras were mounted reading, "Autumn Aspirations-Outerwear" with a string of codes. Behind the scenes, Alice knew, there had to be a large-scale data control and production management scheme, just like any other industry. She looked forward to talking to some of the managers about their span of expertise.

They made a quick walk of the upper floor where a dozen workstations were devoted to photographing small products—watches, desktop sculptures, and more—in green screen boxes. The rest of the floor held the farm of developers and content organizers uploading content to the website. The scale of it was larger than Alice had anticipated. "It would be fascinating to follow one product start to finish through all the steps."

"That would be interesting, I agree."

"What type of product do you think would have the most interesting journey?"

Pepper took her time answering as she led Alice back down the stairs. "I think any of the ones that are designed on site in the Laboratory Boutique. You'd be able to talk with the person who came up with the idea."

"That would add a human element." Alice blinked in the sunlight. Her head began to throb again.

As they toured the building where marketing and vendor sourcing was located Alice appreciated the use of natural textiles in the cubicle walls. The pleasing, clean lines were light years distant from the metal desks and tired linoleum of the newsroom. The air was scented very lightly with a redwood tang instead of the distinct smell of sweaty humanity, hot dog steam, and very old cigars.

She realized the only cussing she'd heard all day was inside her own head. *Freaky.*

Legal, Accounting, and Human Resources were similarly accommodated in a building that was chic yet comfortable, with a lobby that featured a wide spiraling ramp around a water fountain sculpture. The ramp led down to a basement café where employees were already getting lunch.

She immediately noticed some of the women had lanyards that proclaimed they were spa guests. "There's a spa here?"

"There are dozens around the world, featuring Simply the Best products. Like the others, this is licensed with a local company. I understand that they have a four-month wait list. That's why there are two entrances for this building and you have to tap out with your key card to open the doors to the rest of the campus."

The aroma of fresh coffee made Alice realize she was finally feeling hungry.

As if she could read Alice's mind, Pepper said, "Would you like to have lunch now? Or grab some coffee or tea?"

"I'm actually peckish, thank you."

"Never let it be said I didn't fulfill your needs."

Alice blinked.

Pepper's cheeks reddened again. "That also sounded better in my head."

Alice had to laugh at that. Pepper's blush increased. Feeling dizzy and absurdly pleased to again see a facet of Pepper that wasn't perfectly poised, Alice followed her down the gentle ramp. Because of the hillside sloping away, one wall had windows that looked out onto a flagstone paved patio with small tables shaded with umbrellas. Inside were more tables and chairs, many occupied, and several large refrigerator cases, almost like in a grocery store. A coffee and tea station with both hot and iced versions of each was surrounded by employees bearing Simply the Best-branded thermal mugs.

"If you want something to drink or a meal while you're here, feel free to stop in. Lunch choices generally run out around two. The coffee and tea will be freshly stocked until five or six and is free. There's always organic salads, microwavable hot dishes, and sandwiches, one of which will be vegan. Your key card is coded to let you check out gratis."

Generous and useful, Alice thought. "What's your favorite dish?"

"The chicken enchiladas, if they're Christmas-style."

Alice was amused. "Enchiladas with a side of figgy pudding?"

Pepper let out a you're-so-silly laugh. "Christmas style—you get both red and green." At Alice's shake of the head, she went on, "Sauce. Chile sauce. You know, on the enchilada?"

"Oh, I get it." She vaguely remembered the concept from a trip to New Mexico. "I had an enchilada last night. Frozen. It was neither red nor green. Sort of…beige."

"That's tragic. Tragic and pitiful."

"Agreed."

As they chatted, Alice watched employees come and go. A round, placid woman with a handheld device quickly scanned the contents of a tray, and the employee tapped their key card before walking away. It took only moments. Some people then went out the door to the patio. A cluster of women carrying folders all got coffee and sat down at a round table to have a meeting. It was sleek and efficient. "It's nothing like a New York deli. To be fair, probably a lot less food poisoning."

"I would hope so." Pepper gestured at an empty table. "Shall— sorry. My phone."

Alice could vaguely hear a chiming bell as Pepper swiped the screen. "I have to go back Upstairs."

"Upstairs here?"

"No—Upstairs means Helene's office. There's paperwork missing. Please—have lunch and I'll be back for you in a bit."

"Sure thing." Alice watched Pepper's zebra-striped heels disappear up the ramp. She moved with purpose and speed, but not looking as if she was panicked. Yet there had been a note of anxiety in her voice.

When a CEO barks, everybody jumps—that wasn't unusual.

She wandered out to the patio for a few minutes, letting the warmth calm her. The steady buzz of some kind of insect made the air feel almost electric against her skin. It both soothed and irritated. Maybe she should have a spa treatment—no, the idea of being still for any length of time filled her with anticipatory boredom and anxiety. Why didn't she carry a flask? A little Irish in her coffee would take the edge off.

It was, after all, about the time she'd be meeting up with Simon if she were in Manhattan. A drink would help her not think about the fact that she was a forty-year-old queer woman at risk of losing her job in a profession that was downsizing. She could survive without a salary, thanks to the railroad baron life of her mother's grandfather. She doubted she could survive not having work to do.

The Simply the Best campus was exquisitely planned, beautiful in almost any direction you looked, and it was still problematic. All companies are problematic. Just because ST-Best was never going to be her personal bestie didn't mean there weren't positives she could focus on. There was nothing iffy about the science behind the buildings, for example. They used a fraction of the water and power that similarly sized buildings in New York would use.

There was no doubt about it, tomorrow's interview with CEO Helene Jolie would be exceedingly interesting. She claimed a spinach with egg and pomegranate seed salad for herself and chased it with a refreshing iced coffee that still would have been all the better for a shot of whiskey.

Focus on the positives. She'd taken plenty of photos, but it would help to write down some notes while she ate.

Stomach settled, she wrote notes about what she'd seen so far while Sass snarked every time she forced herself to look back at her work and not at the place on the ramp where Pepper would reappear.

CHAPTER THIRTEEN

Clarita gave Pepper a laser beam glare as she whispered intensely, "The new layout for the magazine should have been on Helene's desk."

"It already is," Pepper whispered back. "I put it there before I went down to meet that reporter for her tour."

"Helene can't find it. She asked for it."

Pepper glanced at the phone console. Though she couldn't hear Helene speaking, her line was lit. Using the silent-no-need-to-see-me walk she'd perfected in the last month, she went into Helene's office. Helene's chair was swiveled to face the windows, but Pepper knew she was visible in the reflection. She could see from halfway across the office that the corner of the desk where she'd put the thick oversize yellow envelope was now bare. She couldn't see it anywhere on Helene's desk.

"What do you mean it's not there?" Clarita demanded when Pepper reported back.

"Has anyone been in her office in the last hour?"

Clarita pressed her thin lips together. "Linda picked up the interim financials."

Pepper hotfooted it around the corner and down the hallway to the CFO's office. Linda wasn't at her desk, but the envelope was, under a pile of financial reports. She showed the envelope to Clarita on her way to set it on Helene's desk in the same place she had earlier. In the window reflection she saw Helene's gaze flick to her, then away.

Great, she fumed in the golf cart back to the café. Helene would think she was the one who'd screwed up, and there was no point explaining otherwise. "Oops" was not an excuse Helene wanted to hear. It didn't help that Clarita had simply assumed Pepper hadn't done her job.

She wanted to blame Alice Cabot too, for taking her away from her desk. It seemed like a good idea to blame Alice Cabot for something. *She's not quirky—she's snobby*, Pepper insisted to herself. Not smart, just snarky. Snobby and snarky.

Snobby and snarky Alice seemed deep in thought when Pepper returned to the café. All the while she made herself an iced coffee and downed a mini Simply a Pick Me Up energy bar, Alice's dark head remained bowed over her notebook. A wall of concentration was almost palpable as the point of her pencil moved rapidly across the page without a pause.

Pepper knew she should march over and take control of the day again, but instead she watched Alice tug on one earlobe as she wrote, her lips pursing, then frowning, then flickering with the briefest of smiles. She lingered for much longer than a moment, not hoping, no, absolutely not hoping that Alice would look up.

A slow smile and a disarming sleepy blink said Alice had been perfectly aware that Pepper was there. "It's okay. I've finished my thought."

Pepper tried to use a wry smile to hide the heat rising in her cheeks, but she was doubtful it worked. "Surely I was gone long enough for more than one thought."

"This is page four. And don't call me Shirley."

Puzzled, Pepper asked, "I didn't... Shirley?"

Alice mimed a knife to the chest. "Now I feel ancient. Wow. You haven't seen *Airplane!*, the satire on airplane disaster movies?"

"Should I have?"

Alice twisted the pretend knife in her chest. "Cruel maiden, tell my mother I died well."

Pepper laughed as she sat down. "I don't think I want to have that conversation with *the* Barbara Paul Cabot."

Alice gave her a mocking nod. "You're thorough."

"I try to be. We studied some of her interviews in college. I see the resemblance now."

"There's not much of one."

"Not much, except for the eyebrows, cheekbones, nose, chin. You don't seem as tall, and you have a darker complexion and hair. Otherwise, there's really no doubt who your mother is."

"I'd be my mother's height if I wore heels, which I never do."

Pepper deliberately looked Alice up and down. The tie, the Oxford button-up, the tailored slacks. "I don't know—you could rock heels with that tie."

Their gazes locked and Pepper reminded herself to breathe.

"It would be an unusual fashion statement for a garden-variety butch like myself."

"Are you?"

"Am I what? Butch?"

"Garden-variety?"

"I consider myself on the butch spectrum. Compared to Pride Week in the Village, though, I don't rate much on the genderqueer scale."

Men's slacks, shirt and shoes, a boxy woman's jacket, and those ridiculously full lashes and carved out cheekbones? "Pride Day in West Hollywood you'd still fit in."

Alice's eyes narrowed, and Pepper had little doubt she'd understood Pepper's implied outing of herself. Pepper didn't want to think at all about why it had suddenly seemed important. "Have you had enough of a break?"

"Yes, thank you. The salad was excellent, by the way."

"Our caterers are fantastic."

Alice slid her notebook back into her knapsack. "Where next?"

"Our last stop before we go back to Admin is the Laboratory Boutique where I interned. After that you can spend some time with the archives and you have that three o'clock with Gail Monteif."

"Sounds perfect. Thank you for your planning."

Pepper led the way up the ramp to the building entrance. "I've been thinking about your question—about what product to follow. What about the life cycle of a Simply the Best cashmere scarf? It begins with the weaving of the fabric itself."

"That would be more interesting than the daily pill packets."

"Or nutrition bars. Let's just say that the word 'extruded' does not stimulate the appetite."

"What about jade yoni eggs?"

Pepper blinked at Alice's arch glance. "Yoni eggs?"

"You'll have to look them up."

"I will."

"What was your internship like?"

"A little bit of everything. Visitor and vendor insider tours, a lot of fetch and carry, proofread my boss's reports and memos, chased down missing—well, missing anything. Component supplies, mostly." Pepper slowed the cart as they reached a cluster of walkers. "I learned a lot about the company and people. College can't teach you certain skills."

"Like what?"

Abruptly aware of Alice's interview technique, she navigated past another cart and the pedestrians before answering. "Managing up is a big one. What was abstract in a communications sense becomes concrete." She added before Alice could ask, "Like the importance of figuring out how people take in information. Do they have to be told, or do they want to read it? Or what simply makes them tick—affiliation with certain people, or power to make decisions, or money, or a mix?"

Alice nodded as they rolled to a stop. "Sounds like it was worthwhile."

There was no need to admit it had been a year and lasted longer than it should have. She had to assume everything she said was on the record. "It was. Now I'm working for the CEO, and it's also a learning experience." Alice opened her mouth and Pepper forestalled her with, "No, I'm not going to be more specific."

She waved a hello at Ann, who was chatting with the super cute intern from Legal again.

"Another impressive lobby sculpture," Alice commented. "An alembic. How appropriate for a laboratory setting."

"You say 'impressive' a lot."

"Do I?"

"You do."

"Well, it is impressive."

And yet, Pepper thought, she didn't sound impressed. *Remember, she's snobby and snarky.*

Alice said "impressive" several more times while Pepper showed off the scent room—vanilla again—and the jewelry design workshop. She asked numerous questions about the sourcing of everything. Where did it come from, who had verified the sustainability, how consistent was the supply stream? Pepper disclosed what she knew, which was a lot, but a few times she had to admit she didn't know.

"Don't apologize," Alice said. "You've given me a great deal of information. That you have it all stored in your head is impressive."

This time, Pepper heard that extra note that said Alice really meant *impressive*. Fortunately, Alice was looking at a pattern layout and didn't see the red heat Pepper felt burning in her ears and cheeks.

She panic-babbled, "There are a couple of reasons we do all this design work on site before it's contracted to vendors to produce. One is that we get handmade small batch goods that are premium products and auction items. Another is that the copywriters over in marketing can borrow products, touch them, or smell them. I didn't know the difference between pashmina, cashmere, or viscose, but I learned that here. I can now also tell the difference in aroma between an essence and a parfum of the same botanical."

"Impress—Interesting."

The lopsided smile and again with the sleepy blink. How on earth was she supposed to keep her composure? Why was it so hard to? All at once she was very aware that Alice could be a wave that looked slow and inviting until Pepper was upside down in the water wondering what had happened. "Ready to head to the archives?"

"Sure." Alice tucked away her phone after a few final snaps. "Especially if we can cruise by that lovely iced tea station on the way."

Do not *say her wish is your command.* "Sure."

It was a huge relief to finally guide Alice back to the main building and across the lower floor to the Media and Archives area. Pepper introduced Alice to Gail Monteif's assistant Yesenia, who eyed Alice's tie with a small, knowing smile.

"Yesenia will find materials for you, make copies, etc. If there's any question about access or confidentiality, she'll sort it out for you."

"A pleasure to be of help," Yesenia said. Her trim shirtdress was short enough to show off dark, muscled legs that looked like they knew their way around a dance floor. The smile that went along with the words was warm, Pepper noticed. Then she noticed the amused acknowledgment in Alice's eyes.

Oh please. Then she hoped that she hadn't looked at Alice that way. "Let me know if I can be of further assistance. I'll see you tomorrow at two, Alice?"

"Yes. I'm sure to have some questions, so I'll arrive a little earlier."

"That would be fine."

Without a backward glance Pepper returned to her desk slightly out of breath. That accounted for her inability to focus on anything at all for several minutes. Or at least that's what she told herself.

It felt as if her world had gone sideways the moment she'd seen Alice this morning. Garden-variety butch seemed like an understatement to Pepper. In her particular and deliberate gender-blending choice of attire, Alice looked absolutely comfortable with herself. Which was attractive.

You haven't dated in a while, and you're not going to date her. Recalling Yesenia's overt friendliness, she thought peevishly that she'd let Yesenia cross that line.

She attacked her backlog of messages and phone calls with a furious efficiency. Everything on her immediate To Do list fell before her determination. Vendor Relations sent over a list of names to be verified before new products were uploaded and she was done in record time. Clarita tapped quietly on a bottle of Pellegrino as she carried it into Helene's office. It was a reminder that the supply of cold ones was running low. Pepper was back from moving more into the kitchen refrigerator before Clarita even returned to her desk.

"I can do this all day," she muttered. She was not imagining Alice and Yesenia flirting because that would be stupid.

A ping from her computer announced a new email and of course it was from Alice. It read, "I have some background questions based on what I've learned today. Could we meet before my two o'clock with Jolie tomorrow? Maybe grab some lunch around one?"

She was not going to smile, nope. All business, she sent back a quick note, agreeing. The distraction of food might make conversation easier, and it was also possible she might learn more about Alice's viewpoint for the series—information Helene could use. Which was all that mattered, wasn't it?

With her desk cleared of immediate demands, she found focus to finish the memory card form on Alice that Helene would expect on her desk any minute. The computer form posted the information into Helene's personal contact database, and the space limitations enforced Helene's desire to have only the most important details. In the box for Notable Connections she added the name "Barbara Paul Cabot." Under education she added Amagansett Bayshore, a private school Helene and Alice had in common.

There was no place, really, to put something like, "Called a congressman a douchebag." Perhaps that was best shared in person.

Clarita emerged from Helene's office and paused at Pepper's desk. "Helene's car is due for servicing. The dealer is on the way to collect it. Could you take these keys down and wait until they arrive?"

"Sure. I need to print this for Helene first. It'll only take a minute."

Pepper was reaching for the keys when Helene's voice froze them both in place. "Pepper? Do you have an update on that reporter?"

Clarita looked momentarily vexed. "I'll ask the receptionist downstairs to hold the keys."

Pepper hit the print button and went to Helene's door. "I have an updated memory card for you. It's printing out now."

Helene didn't look up from the thick binder delivered from marketing every day. "Whenever you choose to be ready, then." The sarcasm was audible, and Pepper had no doubt Helene was recalling the missing magazine layout earlier in the day.

Hurry, hurry, hurry, she urged the printer, but it decided to pause halfway through and think about something else. When the blue sheet of card stock finally dropped into the tray, she snatched it up, folded it at the perforations, and tore away the strips.

Deep breath. It was eight steps to Helene's desk, and she moved as quickly as possible without breaking into a run.

She set the card within Helene's reach. "I've updated this with the most useful information. I gave her a thorough tour of the campus. She's in the archives now. Gail's PA is overseeing access."

Helene nodded, her expression distracted as she set aside the binder and picked up the blue card.

Don't be timid, Pepper told herself. "Your interview with her is tomorrow at two. Were you aware that you went to the same prep school as she did, just not at the same time?"

Helene's eyebrows shot up in surprise and she scanned the card. "No, I wasn't."

"Your parents might know her mother."

"Alice Cabot," Helene read from the card. "*Mon Dieu*. Is she related to Barbara Cabot?"

"Barbara Paul Cabot, yes. It's on the back."

Tight lines appeared around Helene's mouth. "How did that not come up in any of the discussions?"

Pepper hadn't been privy to any discussions, so she thought it best to stay silent.

Helene read both sides of the card. "Her mother has enticed a great many people to say things they didn't mean to. I'm going to have to watch every word."

"Yes," Pepper agreed. She quailed inwardly at Helene's sharp glance. "I mean, Alice Cabot is smart. I've found it necessary to be... deliberate and clear."

The card dropped to the desk, and Helene stood up abruptly and began to pace in front of the window, arms wrapped across her waist. Pepper thought her dress was the most flattering one she'd seen to date—a mossy green cotton-silk blend with a starched flared collar and white French cuffs fastened with heavy gold buttons. Pepper imagined herself in just such a dress, strolling fashionably late into a party and laughing while she sipped champagne.

Helene wheeled around to face her. "What is she like? What did you think of her?"

"She asks detailed questions. I think she is a natural skeptic. Her background is in science as well as journalism."

"*Mon Dieu*," Helene said again. "What else?"

Pepper sought for a way to reassure Helene. "If she has an agenda other than what was agreed to, I didn't see any sign of it. She's clearly thinking about her final work. For example, she suggested an angle for part of the series I thought was interesting. Following a single product through its life cycle."

"Hmm." Helene sat down again and swiveled her chair to face the country club. "Not a bad idea. Do you trust her?"

"I tend to, I mean, I trust her to do what she was sent to do. But then," she added honestly, "I'm a trusting person."

Helene turned back to her. "Are you? I don't meet many of those." She looked Pepper up and down as if truly seeing her for the first time.

All Pepper could think was that she hadn't reapplied her lipstick recently and dashing around had probably set wisps of her hair free to do as they liked. Unnerved by Helene's prolonged study of her, Pepper stammered, "I think that's everything for tomorrow that you'll need. The PA in Media is supposed to send me a list of the archives Alice Cabot asked for. I'll let you know if there was anything unexpected."

"Perfect." For the first time Helene seemed to relax. "It sounds as if you have a rapport. That could be very useful. She gestured at the memory card. "Good work, Pepper. I appreciate this."

She had to stop being such a schoolgirl noob about the way Helene said her name—*Peh-pair*. The "good work" was far more important. It was the first sign she'd had from Helene herself that she'd contributed usefully. She realized, then, that she probably ought to have mentioned the douchebag incident with the congressman, but Helene was reassured. What else mattered?

On edge, she sought an outlet for the quivering energy that was running along her spine. She tried to tell herself it had nothing to do with Alice Cabot and her long fingers and sleepy smile, but clearly it did. Thankfully, Helene pointed out the products on her shelves she wanted to change. Pepper jotted down the list of replacements and hightailed it to the Boutique. Along with swapping out a necklace, a scarf, and two belts, she found herself making a swag bag for Alice. She ought to have done so earlier, hadn't she? An assortment of bath products to make living in a hotel more bearable. A sleep mask and aromatherapy candles, too.

She tied the sailcloth shopping bag shut with ribbon, wrote out a gift card, and sealed it in its matching Simply the Best logo envelope. Juggling the other things for Helene's office, she delivered it to Yesenia's desk outside where Alice was now in her meeting with Gail Monteif. "If you'd make sure Ms. Cabot receives this when she leaves?"

"Sure." Yesenia prodded the bag. "Lots of goodies?"

"Traveler hotel relief. Helene always wants visitors to feel welcomed." Pepper told herself that she wasn't lying. Helene always said that. If Yesenia assumed Helene had specified the goodies, that was, well, Yesenia's assumption.

The new items in Helene's office looked good. Pepper couldn't help but glance to see if Helene had taken any notice and found the green, so very green eyes fixed on her as she spoke on the phone. And then the ghost of a smile.

The feeling of an unspent electrical charge was back. It did not get better when Alice texted later, *Thank you for the first aid kit. You have once again met all my needs.*

PART FOUR

A Sky Full of Stars

CHAPTER FOURTEEN

There was a lot to be said about waking up early and without a hangover. Alice didn't hate the seagulls quite as much as the previous day. Last night's long bath, up to her ears in pomegranate-scented suds and followed by a weighted gel sleep mask in bed, had given her the best night's sleep she'd had since getting exiled to Style.

She spent two hours listing out the documents she'd copied from the archives the day before and made notes so she could easily recall why that document had relevant information. She always did it as she went along. She was leaning toward a tried-and-true narrative: Simply the Best, then and now. That would encompass the effect of ever-changing technology, the opportunities and consequences of globalism, adapting to pandemic lockdowns, and how consumer sophistication had changed.

A grocery store bagel and frothy whipped cream cheese they dared to call "shmear" kept her going. It was welcome to discover that traffic did in fact ease later in the morning, and she reached the ST-Best parking lot fifteen minutes earlier than she'd thought she would. Temperatures were cooler than the day before. The campus seemed even more like a park, not a workplace, as she chose to stroll from the parking lot to the building that housed the café. More employees were dining outside at tables, and a Frisbee spun across an open patch of grass.

She'd just reached the doors when a text arrived from Pepper saying she'd be a few minutes late. That gave Alice a chance to wander into the adjacent spa and ask about services. After all of the art and water features she'd seen the previous day, she wasn't surprised to find a river rock-lined stream running through its waiting area. The sound of rippling water was soothing, no doubt about it. The sandalwood, cedar, and sage aromapalooza went perfectly with the beige, sand, taupe, wheat, and tan color spectrum, which in turn suited the beige and heavily tanned clientele.

As she turned to leave, she saw hand-lettered around the door in a beautiful Middle Eastern motif script, "Simple is Beautiful."

Can't argue with that, she thought, even as Sass added, *"For those who can afford it."*

She found a table in the café with an iced tea to keep her company. Once again she told herself not to watch for Pepper, and she had about as much success as she'd had yesterday. Fortunately, Pepper appeared right away, and Alice wasn't forced to examine her unsettling fascination for very long.

"Sorry I'm late."

"No problem." Alice unnecessarily glanced at her watch. "There's plenty of time before I meet with Helene."

"Have you looked at the choices for lunch? I've been told there is avocado everything today."

They went together to examine the refrigerator cases. Pepper enthusiastically seized an open-faced sandwich heaped with avocado, heirloom tomato, and chopped egg.

"There's Christmas enchiladas," Alice pointed out. "I thought that was your favorite."

"They're here off and on all year round. Avocado sandwiches not so much."

"Well, since I had that extremely unsatisfactory frozen enchilada the other night, I think I should erase all memory of it with something fresh and authentic."

"It's all about the sauces—fair warning."

"My treat." Alice made a big show of using her key card to pay for their meals.

"Big spender," Pepper teased.

"That's me."

Alice followed the instructions to warm her enchiladas in one of the café's microwaves. She arrived at the table as Pepper was settling in with a large glass of iced tea. She wasn't sure, but she thought Pepper's turquoise jacket was called bolero style. The short waist made Pepper's legs seem to go on forever, or at least a very, very long way, all the way to floor.

Of course they do, idiot. If she was going to have ridiculous thoughts then best not to look at the woman, she decided. She eyed her plump enchiladas instead. They smelled delicious, very smoky and savory. One was covered with a brownish-red sauce and the other with bright green. There was a container of chunky guacamole and one of sour cream. She carefully tucked a napkin over her shirt and tie. She didn't want to wear lunch to her interview with Helene Jolie. "It smells great."

Pepper made a heartfelt sound of pleasure as she had a large bite of her sandwich.

It was best not to dwell on that sound, nor think of ways to hear it again. And again.

After sampling each of her enchiladas, Alice said, "If wine is sunshine in a glass, then this is sunshine on a plate. The green's hot and the red's not."

"I like to go back and forth. Mild and slow, then spicy hot, then back to mild."

Alice could think of nothing innocent to say to that. She was a filthy-minded lecher—there was no other explanation.

"How did you get on with Yesenia yesterday?"

Pepper's expression was guileless and cheerful, so Alice decided no double entendre was intended. "She was very helpful. Knew her way around the files. The accounting degree probably helps with that."

"She didn't strike me as an accounting type."

Alice had to grin. "You and I have met different accountants. The best kazoo and ukulele band in the country is a group of accountants in Brooklyn called the 'Long-Term Liabilities'."

Pepper blinked. "Maybe I don't want to know more about that."

"You're missing out. Accountants are the life of the party."

Pepper regarded her with suspicion. "Maybe the queer ones are?"

"My general acquaintance is with queer ones, so, yes, my sample of the profession is limited." She continued more seriously, "I was pleased to read the pro-inclusion policy in Simply the Best's employee handbook and policies and procedures manual for workplace complaints."

"We have an A rating from LGBTQ orgs." Pepper nodded at Alice's tie. "I might not be as easy to spot, but I have rainbow socks and I have worn them to my parents' church barbecue."

Alice laughed at that. With an unbruised head and a happy, full stomach, she was better equipped than yesterday to interpret Pepper's expressions. She saw only an open charm. A dangerous, open charm. And still the eyes that saw too much.

She shifted her nearly empty dish to one side and got out her notebook. "The items I have for you are about the interview. This is off the record," she added.

"Okay." Pepper's ponytail bounced slightly as she nodded her head.

Alice wondered how to get her to do that again.

Focus. "I don't expect you to breach confidence. But an interview like this doesn't go well if I walk into minefields because I don't know they're even there. Are there topics where I should tread softly to avoid bruises?"

Pepper sat back in her chair. Alice gave her time to think it over.

"I can tell you things like don't be late," Pepper finally said. "She is on time for any appointment. It's a sign of respect, regardless of who the meeting is with. Everyone's time is valuable so they can do the job they're hired to do. But I think I can say without breaking any confidences that Simply the Best is very personal for her."

Alice gave an encouraging nod as she had the last bite of her red enchilada. "Tell me more about that."

"Everything about it reflects her, and there's a vulnerability that comes with it. Even though she has the most confidence I've ever seen in anyone."

"You haven't met my mother."

"I imagine there might be a similarity. Highly successful, with an image that was self-created."

"She's all that," Alice admitted. "I know what you mean about the vulnerability, in that case. Most criticism rolls right off, but sometimes a remark is taken as personal. I'll try not do that—at least not right off the bat."

The lopsided smile flashed. "Don't be that guy."

It had been hard enough to ignore the eyelash flutter and the bounce of the ponytail, but that smile was going to be the death of her. "Thank you for giving me that perspective."

"You're welcome. You'll be fine."

Not sure at all what her expression was, she stared down into her glass as she swirled the remaining ice. She knew that it was Pepper's job to assist her. But the casual "You'll be fine" was more than that, as if it was in Pepper's nature to help everybody to get what they wanted.

Alice couldn't imagine her backstabbing a colleague to get ahead or gloating over someone else's mistake.

Part of her insisted that nobody was this open and, well, nice. Nice didn't get you much of anywhere in Corporate America. And Pepper didn't seem to see the totality of what Simply the Best sold. Clothes and jewelry were one thing. Cosmetics and cleansers could be ethically murky, but they weren't alone in that. Where ST-Best was raking in the money was with wellness and "vitality" products. Vitamins, supplements, rocks, all of which carefully skirted the law about specious health claims. This was not some late-night-TV huckster selling cheap pillows as mythical cures; this was a widely respected company that stood, in part, on a shaky foundation of truth.

How did P. Addington square that with her conscience? She seemed to possess one.

Not a question she was going to ask, Alice told herself. That wasn't the job she was here to do, and Pepper Addington's conscience was of no consequence to her.

"One last question?"

"Sure."

"Why is the annual event called a Composium?"

"Um... A portmanteau of conference and symposium?"

Alice wanted to point out that conference and symposium were close enough synonyms as to be redundant, but she was too impressed by Pepper's use of *portmanteau* to snark about word choices. "Is that a guess?"

"Maybe." Her voice dripping with solicitousness, Pepper asked, "Is there anything else I can help you with?"

"You've been very thorough, Paddington. Thank you."

"I beg your pardon?"

Alice realized too late what she'd done. Heat suffused her cheeks. "Apologies. It's your email. P period Addington. I kind of read it all in a clump as we corresponded."

Pepper's eyes narrowed. "It sounded like you just called me a bear."

"I wasn't thinking so much bear as a transit hub in London."

"And that's so much better." There was a definite hint of acid in Pepper's voice.

"I am sorry. It was inadvertent."

From the expressions flitting across Pepper's face, it was clear she was trying to figure out if she should be outraged or not. "I will take it that you meant a well-traveled bear. There are worse things to be called." Her lips pressed together but not hard enough to quell a smile. "I do like marmalade. I like it quite a lot. But still, don't make a habit of it."

"Forgive me?" She put on the scruffy puppy big-brown-eye look.

Pepper pursed her lips. "Of course I forgive you, so you can stop that."

She sees right through me, Alice thought again. This time she wasn't sure she minded.

They sorted their compostable dishes and recyclable cups and went out to the patio to shake off the chill of the air conditioning. The broad umbrellas overhead allowed warmth without direct sunlight. Desert sage in planters added a musky, herbal aroma to the air. Again, a perfect ambiance that seemed a world away from Alice's entire life.

Why did all of this make her want a whiskey even more?

She missed what Pepper said. "I'm sorry?"

"I'm going to head back Upstairs—my break is over. When you come out on the second floor—"

"Go around the pendulum."

Pepper nodded. "See you in a few."

Alice watched her go, admiring the slim black trousers with cute buckles at the ankles. Nothing good would come of measuring Pepper with her eyes—the breadth of her shoulders, the sway of her hips— or the fact that Pepper's light and ready laugh was imprinted on her brain in a place that wanted more.

CHAPTER FIFTEEN

The pendulum sculpture was as Pepper had promised—strikingly beautiful. A small plaque in the floor gave its name as "The Water of Light." The bronze bob had enough weight to be heard as a quiet *whoosh* as it made an arc Alice estimated was about ten feet. A skylight of crimson, cobalt, and lemon radiated streaks of color across a black tile floor.

She corrected herself as she looked down. The oval inset into the floor turned out to be several inches of water over a black lining. As if that was not enough to marvel at, the tip of the bob just touched the water's surface at the lowest point of its swing, creating an outward spreading ripple that danced with the colors from the skylight above.

It was a feat of engineering and art that drew her eye rhythmically along the pendulum's path and threatened to mesmerize. She noted the artist's name, hoping to look up more of their work.

She gave herself a shake and glanced at her watch. She was a little bit early, having a care for Pepper's advice not to be late. The pendulum sculpture sat at the junction of two hallways lined with open doors that promised more offices. Beyond the sculpture ahead was a wide, arching entryway to what had to be the CEO's office. Below the arch, smiling in welcome, was Pepper with an armload of files propped on one hip.

Alice joined her, saying, "I was mesmerized for a moment."

"I could watch it for hours."

Alice noticed there were no chairs or benches to allow anyone to do that. "It made me think of the Poe story, but I'm sure that's not the artist's intent."

Pepper mock scowled. "My roommate loves old horror movies, and I've seen that one. Gee, thanks. Now I'll always think of blood and Vincent Price cackling on the way to my desk."

"You're entirely welcome."

"Yeah, right." Pepper's gaze was on the rippling water. "It's amazing to have a Foucault Pendulum right outside where my desk is."

"It's not a Foucault Pendulum. Not even close."

One eyebrow arched as Pepper met Alice's gaze. "Why do you say that?"

"The only thing it has in common with a Foucault Pendulum is the pendulum. Point one, there aren't any compass markings for reference. Point two, it touches the water which will introduce resistance. Point three, its top mounting is fixed, so it can't track rotation."

Her tone dry, so very, very dry, Pepper asked, "Oh, so, I can't prove the earth turns on its axis with it?"

Alice realized she'd been had. "Are you trying to assess how much hooey I can stand?"

Pepper gave her an angelic smile. "Could be."

Don't blush. "Well, then, you've experienced my officious know-it-all voice. I've been told by friends it's annoying."

"You have honest friends."

"Ouch." Alice plucked a pretend dagger out of her heart. "Not the first wound. Which reminds me—thank you for the first aid delivery yesterday. Honest, I had a great bath and slept well."

"That makes me happy. Follow me," was all Pepper said, leaving Alice reeling from a mischievous wink that she might have imagined.

"Alice Cabot, meet Clarita Oatley, Assistant to the CEO."

Alice had read all about Oatley, but pictures had not done the woman's pallor and ice blue eyes justice. She was all cold steel, razor-sharp, and willing to cut if necessary. "Pleased to meet the power behind the throne."

"Welcome to Simply the Best. I hope you've enjoyed your visit so far." Oatley's handshake was firm, her gaze direct and self-assured. This was who she had expected Pepper to be, though not as evolved as Oatley's decades of experience showed.

"I have, thank you. You moved here from New York with the company, yes?"

"I did."

Okay, not the chatty type. "Just making sure I recalled correctly. Would you be willing to answer a few questions about that for me later? About what the transition was like?"

"Of course."

"Thank you."

Pepper glanced at her watch and nodded. "It's two on the dot. One moment."

Alice watched as Pepper put the folders she'd been carrying on her desk, then went to the open inner doors to say, "Your two o'clock is here."

After a moment Pepper gestured, and Alice found herself at last in the inner sanctum of the founder and chief executive officer of Simply the Best.

Her first glimpse of Helene Jolie's office revealed that it continued the sleek, pristine white background present in all other buildings, softened by wooden whitewashed shelves and bleached maple tables, plus woven fabric on the chairs instead of corporate faux leather. The interior walls were covered with a nubby white fabric that, Alice realized, naturally cut down on the ambient drone of electronics and air-conditioning. Beautiful and functional.

This inner sanctum was exactly as pictured in architectural and interior design trade magazine and blogs. The striking, self-assured woman at the desk, rising to her feet, was also as expected. The red hair glistened in the light, and perfect lips were curved in a charming smile.

Helene Jolie was the kind of woman who could tie on a hospital gown and wear it like couture. That was Alice's first reaction, and she itched to jot it down in her notebook. The sheer, casual elegance of a denim jacket over a form-fitting black dress was undeniable. All that style combined with a confidence that would make anyone feel that, in comparison, they were bare-assed and way, way outclassed.

It looked effortless and unconscious, but it would be a mistake to think Jolie did not know the effect she had on people. Alice knew that had she not grown up around people like this, who breathed a magnetic star quality into the air around them, she would likely fall under the woman's spell. Though she tried not to react, her hackles rose in resistance.

Pepper murmured, "Alice Cabot, this is Helene Jolie."

"Alice," Helene Jolie said, using a long *E* so it rhymed with *caprice*. "We grew up within miles of each other, but I don't believe we've ever met."

"*Isn't that special*," Sass cooed. "*You're already old friends on a first-name basis.*"

Alice firmly closed a mental door on all inner voices and gave all focus to the interview. "Neither do I. My mother recalls you, but that was from decades ago."

"I was only a child, but I remember her glasses." The perfect, charming smile was momentarily directed at Pepper. "Could you bring us some water, please?"

In a tone of voice Alice hadn't heard before, Pepper said, "My pleasure."

Alice did a double take. Pepper's eyes were aglow with admiration, her posture one of utmost respect. Of course she was relatively new to her job and eager to do well, but the expression seemed like more than that. Jolie was probably the most dynamic woman she'd met so far in life. She's *young*, she told herself, with a viciousness she didn't understand.

Pepper quickly brought in bottles of mineral water, the epitome of quiet efficiency, like a buck private on inspection with a general. She might not be the alpha watchdog Alice had expected, but at the moment she looked exactly like one of the pack.

"Thank you, Pepper." Helene made her name rhyme with "pear." "Could you close the door on the way out?"

"Certainly."

To Alice Helene said, "Let's sit at the table. It's more comfortable."

"Thank you. I'll be able to take better notes. Let me set up to record."

At the pale, maple conference table Alice let Helene set the stage to her liking, which was Helene in the chair at the head of the table, hands folded in her lap. Alice sat on her right, back to the windows. She put her phone on the table between them and pressed the record button. She gave the date and time and started down her list of prepared questions. She had little doubt that she would receive prepared answers.

She started with a softball—Why move to Los Angeles?

"It's the territory of angels—what could be more perfect for our company? I have personally always loved California air and sunshine. You have to admit, this is a long way from New York."

Not so softball—What was wrong with New York?

"The Knicks? The Mets?" After Alice's appreciative laugh, Helene added, "We were growing madly. Everyone said to outsource, but I wasn't happy with the results. I wanted to keep control of my dream, especially design. As we hired more and more people it was clear we had to expand, but I wanted the company under one roof. Impossible in New York. So we came here. Fresh start for everyone."

Softball—When did she first suspect that the company would not be merely stable and profitable, but wildly successful?

A wave of one hand. "When we sold out tickets for the first Composium in twenty-four hours. It was like Comic Con—long wait lists, black market selling of badges. Vendors who hadn't wanted to work with us were suddenly very eager. I wasn't sure, not completely, what exactly we were doing so right, but I knew if we did more of it there would be no stopping us."

Hardball—How had the company enforced compliance with the agreements made when settling lawsuits over false promises?

No hesitation. "We changed our entire approach to acquisition, vendor due diligence, and creating our own descriptive copy. Previously we had relied on the vendor's representations, but that's not good enough for our customers. Now we start from scratch. I personally read every initial listing so that I can be sure our tone and content is what I expect. We also brought in our own in-house counsel. It was imperative."

Softball—What was her personal favorite product?

Laughter, charmingly self-deprecating. "The rose quartz facial roller. It's ridiculously self-indulgent and I love it."

Softball, but likely unexpected—What had relocation done to her personal life?

For the first time, Helene's answer wasn't immediate. The assured, confident smile faded slightly. She pulled her thick, red hair back into a ponytail, frowning slightly in thought, then let her hair swirl back to her shoulders. She seemed unaware she was doing it—almost. "What CEO of a company this size has much time for a personal life?"

Follow-up—So she had less time for a personal life?

"The company doesn't leave me a lot of time for a personal life, but I manage."

"The entertainment tabloids seem to think so."

Helene's dismissive wave underscored her words. "What can anyone do about that? They specialize in clickbait."

"I can't disagree with that."

It earned her a more comfortable smile, to Alice's relief, and they continued with expected questions and pre-scripted answers for quite some time. Alice looked for any opportunity to turn the stilted Q&A into an open, revealing conversation.

Segue—What was life like before the company? Home life, education?

"Much like yours. I didn't realize until yesterday that you also went to Amagansett Bayshore."

Alice set down her pen to encourage a more casual exchange. "I think I was six or seven years behind you. Do you remember Mrs. Terwilliger?"

"*Mon Dieu*. She terrified me."

"I don't know how she managed to pop out of thin air, right when you were perhaps not where you should be."

Helene leaned forward and whispered, "I think she had superpowers."

"I think you're right. Speaking of superpowers, you have a few of your own."

The ultra-charming smile didn't dim, but there were new guards in the vivid green eyes. "Enlighten me."

Alice didn't miss the fact that while Helene was suspicious of Alice's flattery, she also seemed to like it. "I had no idea how large and wide the company's distribution reach is. No real idea of how skilled the management has been during every turn of the market while leveraging every new technology. It's an admirable success story that few companies this size can claim."

Helene nodded in appreciation for Alice's praise. "It's a matter of pride for me that we balance between trendy and classic, while avoiding stodgy. I don't want young women thinking, 'I can't be caught dead with anything my mother likes.' Or older women put off by fads they see as recycled from their youth. We avoid that by addressing women's inherent needs."

"What do you think those are?"

Helene's eyebrows went up. "I *think* that our research and past success indicate this isn't guesswork."

Alice pushed back on the pushback. "So you *know* what women need?"

The green eyes—surely those were colored contact lenses, Alice thought—narrowed and fine lines appeared around Helene's mouth. Alice could well imagine that the minute change in expression reduced most people to puddles. "I misspoke. We always show how our products can help women with the individual needs all women express. To accomplish a goal for themselves or their family. To be safer, grow stronger. Live happier, heal from the costs of modern life. Each of these has subsets, of course. Some women draw strength from feeling attractive. Others from emotional balance."

"So, a woman your assistant's age could find products that inspire her career planning. But her mother might see that same product as healing?"

"Precisely. You understand—like that. Our descriptions have elements that appeal across ages and needs. That's what I was trying to articulate."

"Your customers seem crystal clear on it." Alice wanted to admire the woman, but there was something off, something manufactured. She was like a picture that appeared to be one thing but was something else—like photographs of melting good ice cream that were in reality tinted shortening. A show for the camera that worked until you got very close.

Or maybe it was the French accent that came and went—it annoyed her. "As I said, I've learned many things so far that surprised me."

"It sounds as if you had preconceived notions about the company. Would you mind sharing them?"

Well, she asked, Alice thought. "That your primary product is the label." Helene nodded but said nothing. "That you sell many products that are straightforward and work as advertised. Clothing adorns. Jewelry sparkles. Moisturizers soften."

"And?"

"There are also products that have no efficacy at all. The good products lend credence to the questionable."

Helene looked annoyed and yet smug. "That's nothing I haven't heard before. Those who don't look outside the ordinary for health and healing often don't understand what we sell, and they are not our market. That's fine by me. I have no desire to be bland and ubiquitous."

"Is 'outside the ordinary' a euphemism for scientifically disproved?"

"Such as?"

"Yoni eggs."

Helene's eyes narrowed. "The need for vaginal health isn't scientific?"

Alice tried to mask her irritation with a stiff smile. "It is. There is a difference between what's healthy for vaginas and rocks stuck into said vaginas."

"I'm not aware of a scientific study."

"Experts in the field—"

"Experts say all sorts of things."

Douchebag. Alice bit down on her tongue not to say it. "The weight of scientific evidence has no validity?"

"I think science needs to prove itself, and in this regard it hasn't."

Alice's hackles rose at Helene's smug expression of having won the argument with her logic, but she had to let it go. She'd brought up the issue of a product like yoni eggs, and she had the official response. Every instinct said to press harder, but that wasn't in the ground rules. This was not an exposé. Her duty was to the assignment she had agreed to do.

She lightened the tension by asking, "What is your favorite thing about Los Angeles?"

Helene's answer was prompt, but wary. "The mix of cultures. Every culture in the world is represented here, just as in New York, but there's also the culture of make-believe and possibilities. A true entrepreneurial sense that opportunity is limitless." Helene seemed to relax. "And the complete lack of humidity."

"I can't fault you for that. The Dog Days were brutal this year."

"It would be wrong for me to say that I moved us here so my hair would no longer frizz from May to September, but I'll admit I did think of it during negotiations. I know it must seem silly." The last was said with a glance through her eyelashes, as if to play an "I'm just an illogical woman" card.

Alice kept her eyeroll to herself. Before she could start another question she realized that Pepper was standing in the doorway.

"I'm sorry to interrupt," Pepper said quietly. "Helene, your three o'clock meeting will start in four minutes."

Alice realized she was stiff with tension. She gave Pepper a grateful look as she switched off the recorder, but Pepper's gaze was fixed on Helene.

"Where did the time go?" Helene rose to her feet. "This has been an illuminating conversation."

"For me as well." She slid her notebook into her satchel.

Pepper picked up a folder left on the conference table and examined it, then handed it to Alice. "Yours, I think."

"Thanks." She saw a question in Pepper's eyes, including a nervous glance at Helene. She tried to smile in a way that told Pepper everything was fine. She wasn't sure it was, but it wasn't Pepper's fault. It dawned on her that Helene might think so, given that Pepper was the watchdog in charge of keeping Alice in her place.

"Um, should I schedule a follow-up?"

Helene's expression was neutral as she looked enquiringly at Alice. "What do you think?"

"I think that would be useful. A week from now, perhaps. I'll have a firm idea of the framework for the series by then, and I would be grateful for your input." She couldn't help but glance at Pepper again, who was watching Helene as she waited for instructions.

"I'd be very interested in discussing that." Helene returned to her desk, clearly skeptical.

"I'll block out an hour." Pepper said to Alice, "You're in luck. The heat wave has broken, and the sea breeze came in about a half hour ago."

"That's great news. It'll make it far easier to explore."

"Given your scientific bent, you might find the La Brea Tar Pits interesting."

"I've actually been there."

Her gaze traveling back and forth between Alice and Pepper, Helene asked, "You're not going back to New York for the weekend?"

"No. I'm not fond enough of airplanes to do that. Not when, apparently, the sea breeze is in."

Helene's gaze went back to Pepper, who hovered, awaiting instructions. "Autumn is a glorious time here, isn't it, Pepper?"

Pepper raised a hand as if to smooth her hair but stopped herself. "I've always loved it."

Alice looked for any sign in Pepper's expression that the way Helene French-ified her name annoyed her the way it already annoyed Alice. With a nod at Helene, she asked, "What highlight of Los Angeles would you recommend I see?"

"The Griffith Observatory or the Getty," Helene answered. "I've got another donors' reception to go to at the Getty this evening. Tomorrow night the Griffith is hosting a…" Distracted, Helene lifted some papers on her desk as if looking for something.

"I'll look into it."

Helene looked up with a suddenly wide smile. "That won't do. Pepper, ask Clarita about the details for the Observatory's event. I had an invite—something about telescopes. You should take Alice. It's the science event of the season."

Pepper stilled, or at least Alice thought she did. "Of course. I haven't been in years."

"Perfect." Helene's beatific smile turned on Alice. "It's all arranged. Pepper is a wonderful guide. You won't regret it."

Clarita appeared in the doorway. "Your three o'clock, Helene."

"Send them in."

Alice found herself at Pepper's desk, wanting to tell her that she was not required to give up time on a weekend to show Alice the sights. With Clarita so near, how could she explain that she found Helene's presumption highhanded?

"I have it right here," Clarita said in answer to Pepper's query. With a bright, curious glance she handed a square card into Pepper's care. "Helene didn't RSVP."

"I'll do so. We're... I'm... Helene would like me to take Alice to the event."

Clarita's expression held the tiniest flicker of skepticism.

"It's the science event of the year, I'm told," Alice added smoothly. "I expressed an interest in the telescopes." Not precisely true, but Alice's hackles were fully up at the insinuation of some kind of impropriety in the arrangement. Even though she herself was disquieted by Helene's manipulation, there was no reason Clarita had to know it was at Helene's instigation.

Pepper turned from the small copier behind her desk and handed Alice a copy of the invitation. "The event is open house style, from seven to eleven p.m."

"I don't know the map well. I'm in Santa Monica, so if you're further inland, would it make sense for me to pick you up?"

Pepper nodded. "Parking is usually extremely congested, so one car would be best. I'll text you my address."

"We can meet here, if you'd prefer." Aware that Clarita was now on the phone, she added in a low voice, "It's not in your job description to give your home address to a stranger."

Their gazes locked and Alice felt the world shift into slow motion. She watched Pepper's chest rise with a deep breath. Her lips parted, but she didn't say anything. Alice's heart beat hard against her ears.

The phone on Pepper's desk rang, breaking the spell.

"It's fine. How about around seven? We'd arrive fashionably late."

"Well after sunset for the best experience." Alice cleared her tight throat. "For using telescopes. I'll text when I'm a few minutes out."

Pepper's cheeks were flushed, but she only nodded as she slipped on her headset and tapped the phone console. "Helene Jolie's office, Pepper Addington speaking."

Alice turned to face Helene's office, not sure what she wanted to say. Something in the vicinity of her heart was really pleased she would spend time with Pepper away from her job, but her brain was dismayed. Social time together created possibilities—distracting, inappropriate, delicious, detailed possibilities. She was looking forward to every minute and equally uncomfortable that it was only possible from Helene's largess.

Pepper was not something to be treated like a gift.

Helene was watching her—rather, watching them. Her gaze was speculative and satisfied before she returned her attention to her visitors.

The penny dropped for Alice. Helene was sending Pepper out with Alice to keep tabs on her. There was nothing creepy about that—it was just business. Pepper seemed okay with that too.

She glanced at the copy of the invitation.

Black tie.

It seemed she was going to need a tuxedo.

CHAPTER SIXTEEN

Pepper recognized the cherry-red convertible and gave Alice a wave indicating she should pull into the loading zone. She made an exasperated face at the white hard top locked firmly in place. Did Alice have a problem with fun?

She leaned down to look in the passenger window as it smoothly lowered. "It's a beautiful evening. Why don't you have the top down?"

Alice's face was in shadow, but her irritation was clear. "Because I'm from New York?"

"Fresh air burns you?" She shook her head in pity. "You're in LA. Come on."

After a long pause there was finally a click and whir. The white top detached from the windshield, retracted, and folded smoothly into a compartment above the trunk. Pepper had never ridden in a convertible, and the idea of it added to the flutter in her stomach she hadn't been able to suppress the entire time she was showering and dressing in her cobbled-together fancy dress gala outfit.

She reached for the handle, but Alice forestalled her.

"No, wait. If we're putting on an LA show, let's do these things properly." Already out of the car, Alice came around to open the passenger door. "Your chariot, milady."

"Thank you," Pepper said smoothly, as if she was used to a woman in a sleek tuxedo opening doors for her. She glanced up at the apartment window that faced the street to see CC feigning a heart attack. *Stay calm*, she told herself but a voice inside was chanting *ohmygod ohmygod ohmygod she's gorgeous* loudly enough to drown out the ringing in her ears.

"Are you sure your hair and outfit can handle the wild wind of the open road?" Alice checked her mirrors and merged into the slow-moving traffic.

It *had* taken a lot of hair product to get her hair to curl smoothly around her shoulders. Still, a ride in a convertible? "I can make repairs, if needed."

Alice gestured at the beaded clutch in Pepper's lap. "That's a Bag of Holding?"

"Yes. I have an entire makeup studio inside."

Alice smiled, as if pleased Pepper had understood the reference. "I wouldn't have pegged you as a D&D aficionado."

"My roommate is a big-time gamer. I know a lot of the lingo, whether I want to or not. For example, I'm sure that your undertaking the adventure of driving in a convertible with the top down adds to your lifetime XP. We'll see the Hollywood sign while doing it, which gives a one-point-five multiplier."

Alice laughed outright, the earlier irritation gone. "Well, when you put it that way, I should probably embrace all things LA."

"Might be good for you."

"Don't hold your breath. You were right, though. It's a beautiful evening."

Pepper sighed at the truth of it and tipped her head back to gaze at the sky. The sun was only a hint of orange at the horizon behind them, and the sky was deepening to indigo. The moon wasn't up yet, and the Evening Star was all by itself at the moment, sparkling above the freeway as if leading them onward to miracles. Wind rushed past her ears and the smell of cars and diesel faded under the tang of salt from the onshore breeze. Mixed into that was a hint of sandalwood and musk she knew was Alice's cologne.

Alice's cologne had nothing to do with feeling as if butterflies were tickling the inside of her ribs.

"The night air this time of year," she volunteered, "is like a cool, light blanket. Nature telling us to chill out."

"Okay," Alice said after a pause. "Convertibles do not suck."

Pepper turned her head to look at her, but Alice's gaze was on the road. The high cheekbones were even more angular in profile. She found herself unable to look away from the lips that seemed full and soft in silhouette. "I'm glad you see it my way."

"Yes, ma'am."

"That's better."

"Than what?"

"Your usual cheeky self."

Alice's laugh was low, sending a shiver down Pepper's spine. "Oh, you have no idea."

Alice's phone was doing a good job directing them from Encino to the Observatory using the slightly longer but faster route that didn't traipse past the Hollywood Bowl. Instead, the vast reaches of Griffith Park came quickly into view, with banks of dusty green eucalyptus and gnarled oaks encrusting the hillsides along the freeway.

The road leading to the promontory rose steeply to where the observatory was perched, and they crested the top to find a short row of cars queued. While they waited Pepper used the visor mirror and her pop-out hairbrush to restore order. "That's better."

"You look terrific," Alice said quietly. "A little windblown, which is quite attractive."

"Thank you." Suddenly she didn't care quite so much about perfection. "I have to say, a tuxedo does wonders for garden-variety butches."

Alice mimed a tip-of-the-hat as Pepper showed their invitation to a security staffer. The car was surrendered to a valet who eyed the convertible with pleasure. In a few moments they were joining others walking slowly along the wide sidewalks to the copper-domed Art Deco building that looked down on the entire Los Angeles basin. Centered in the lawn was the iconic Astronomers Monument, its column circled by the likes of Galileo and Newton.

Alice was gazing up at the armillary sphere with a relaxed, open smile. "The sphere makes me think of the opening credits to *Game of Thrones*, though that one was not marked with our solar system. One of my favorite movies was filmed here—*Bowfinger*."

Pepper was taken by Alice's transformation from snarky reporter to ardent science fan. "I haven't seen it."

"That's a real shame. I never looked at Planetarium-style seating with the 3-D glasses the same way again, after learning that they're all aliens worshiping their false gods. The final scenes were filmed on the lawn right here, featuring the Zeiss telescope dome."

Pepper looked up at the wide opening in the dome through which the telescope was visible. "It's rotated… Southeast, maybe?"

"Roughly," Alice agreed. "I meant to look up what might be of interest in tonight's sky but ran out of time." She lightly touched the small of Pepper's back as she pointed out an uneven patch of concrete and guided them around it.

Pepper gestured to the right as if she couldn't feel the lingering pressure of Alice's fingertips. "There's a terrace that looks toward the Hollywood sign, if you want a closer look at it than we had from the freeway."

"Maybe later, ma'am."

"Don't be a pill."

Alice glanced at her. "Yes'm."

Pepper pursed her lips to quell a smile. "That's better."

"I see."

"What do you see?"

"You like being in charge."

A cold flush spread over Pepper's back and arms followed by a wave of heat in her face. Thank goodness the exterior lighting was low. "Not always."

"Yes'm."

"Knock it off."

"Yes—"

She whacked Alice in the arm just hard enough to make her laugh. "Are you always this obnoxious?"

"You expect me to answer that honestly?"

Pepper opened her mouth to say, "I thought you were a scientist," but startled when a voice to her right spoke almost in her ear.

"Aren't you Helene Jolie's assistant? Is Helene here?"

She recognized the Beverly Hills councilwoman who sometimes dropped in Upstairs after her spa treatments. "Yes, what a great memory you have. Helene wasn't able to make it tonight, but she's such a proud supporter of the Griffith that she sent me instead."

She introduced Alice and contributed little as the councilwoman promptly took advantage of the opportunity to talk to a member of the fourth estate about the marvels of Beverly Hills. Pepper hoped desperately that she looked good enough that the councilwoman would have no reason to mention her to Helene in anything but a positive way. She reminded herself that only she knew that her Little Black Dress was several years old. Nobody else knew that the gold lame wrap was borrowed from Beth and the coiling gold necklace and earrings set had been temporarily liberated—with Helene's permission—from the Boutique before she'd left work yesterday.

When the councilwoman segued into a stump speech on the need for supporting science, as long as science wasn't being politicized with unproven theories like global warming, Pepper stole a glance at Alice and quickly pointed out that the main event was going to start in a few minutes.

Aware that she needed to remember that she was representing Helene and could run into other people who knew her, Pepper was only half joking when she said, "Thank you for not calling her a douchebag."

"I figured out after a few words that I didn't need to listen."

"You looked attentive."

"I practice that in front of a mirror. Shall we go inside?"

She wanted to melt into the returning sensation of Alice's fingertips brushing her back. But what if someone told Helene that her assistant was seemingly quite cozy with that reporter? She increased her pace just enough to feel Alice's hand drop away and shivered at the chill that seemed to have fallen over the evening.

CHAPTER SEVENTEEN

Alice's inner kid was dancing like she was in a candy store.

Just a glimpse of the Zeiss telescope through the open dome had put her in a better mood than she could remember being in for a long while. It didn't hurt that she was in the company of a vivacious, intelligent woman who stopped to marvel at models of comets and gave her a twinkling, teasing smile when she pointed out the working Foucault Pendulum.

The Oschin Planetarium was the venue for the evening's talk by a former commander of the International Space Station. After accepting the 3D glasses which would be needed for one portion of the images to be shown, she and Pepper chose seats on an aisle.

Pepper laughed as hers immediately reclined. She put on her glasses and stared raptly at the ceiling. "I'm worshiping my false gods."

Alice couldn't stop her gaze from tracing the smooth silhouette of Pepper's throat, chin, lips, nose—even the outline of the ridiculous glasses didn't break the spell. "Yes, but are you an alien?"

"Anything is possible, I suppose. I admit I haven't asked my mother about it." After a contemplative pause, Pepper added, "I saw her in a backless gown once, and there was no zipper on her neck."

Alice's bark of laughter turned heads. She reclined into her seat as well and was grateful that dimming of lights made any further comment unnecessary. Pepper's teasing grin had rendered words out of reach.

The opening minutes by the speaker, with his low Slavic-accented voice, were predictably pro-exploration and of course heavy on the passion for Earth's joint endeavor to understand the universe humanity shared. It could have been a press release from any of the world's space agencies.

Alice shushed her cynicism toward rote talking points. Compelled by a deep, wordless instinct, she gave herself over to the confirmation that knowledge for the sake of it was something other people still valued. That thirst was evident in the photographs the speaker had taken himself from the windows of the ISS and on EVAs.

"Here, in the middle of my picture, is this empty zone," the speaker pointed out, circling the area with a laser pointer. "Let's look again at the same area of space with this image from the Hubble telescope."

Alice heard Pepper gasp too when the small grainy picture that scarcely covered the top of the dome was replaced by a massive image that spread from edge to edge. Stellar dust, and so many suns. So much light.

"When we zoom in," the speaker continued, "we see it's not empty at all. The distance between stars is filled with matter, much of which we don't understand and some of which we know is the dust of stars. The distance between the microscopic cells in our own bodies also seems empty, but when we look closer and closer, we see that we're all held together by the stardust that defines our universe."

She smiled as she recalled similar quotes from Carl Sagan, whom she'd met once in her mother's salon. But that hadn't led to her fascination with space. No, that was due to an outsized crush on Lieutenant Uhura with a booster shot from Princess Leia. Maybe humanity finding a way into a better future was all merely a beautiful dream, but she yearned to see and hear the truth of it.

She needed facts to be facts again. For something to be true. Certain.

All at once she was aware of the pale glow of Pepper's arm alongside hers. All she could hear was the murmur of Pepper's surprise at another image of once impossible sights—churning clouds of white and yellow stellar dust, the frozen blue and gray wake of comets, the billowing towers and balloons of nebulae incubating new stars.

Pepper was not the kind of truth that Alice could bring herself to believe in. She forced herself to count the days, four, only four, that she'd even known Pepper.

She desperately wanted a drink.

"That was *so* interesting!" Graceful in high heels in a way that Alice had never tried to master, Pepper bounded up the stairs to the exit. "The images were breathtaking."

"They were impressive. Beyond impressive," she added quickly as Pepper made to swat her arm. "When the Hubble first went up the mirror had been polished incorrectly. The shape was off at one edge by about one-fiftieth the diameter of a human hair and the images were hugely disappointing. Since it had been designed to be maintained by astronauts, they fixed it. And now we know how rapidly the universe is expanding."

"It's hard to fathom that something so powerful is only eight feet long."

"That's just the telescope. It's in a craft that's almost fifty feet long and weighs about twenty-five thousand pounds."

"Look at you with all your fancy statistics." Pepper flashed another of those teasing smiles before excusing herself with a gesture at the ladies' room.

Alice caught sight of the observatory's map, noting the star that indicated where the reception was on the lower level. The event was adjacent to the Leonard Nimoy Theater.

She stood there with tears in her eyes, unable to put words to any of her emotions except that she felt raw and vulnerable. Surrounded by joyful science and all that it inspired with a beguiling, vibrant woman beside her had brought all her emotions right to the surface. One scratch might kill her.

She should have never left New York, never left the safety of the walls that living there required.

"Ready?" Pepper's bright-eyed smile dimmed. "What's wrong?"

"Nothing. I think I'm hungry." *She sees right through me.*

"Me too." She leaned forward conspiratorially. "I spent all day scraping together this outfit."

"I spent time in a tuxedo rental shop."

"Let's hope there's cheese."

"And wine," Alice said fervently. Trying for the same air of gallantry as she'd used to open the car door, she offered her arm, and they went down the wide spiral stairs together.

There was wine, passable, and cheese, excellent. Reminding herself that she had to drive Pepper safely home, Alice limited herself to one small glass of the chardonnay while she watched Pepper chat with another woman who'd recognized her.

Pepper asked after the woman's children by name and picked up a conversation from weeks ago, apparently, as if it had been yesterday. She had a career ahead of her as a people person, if that's what she chose.

She's so young, Alice reminded herself. She pushed the comparison of their age and life experiences out of her mind—there was no purpose to it.

Deciding that Pepper was now in need of rescue, she interrupted smoothly with, "The other person you were hoping to see tonight—I think I spotted him going up to the promenade."

"Really? I don't want to miss him." She excused herself from the older woman and preceded Alice up the stairs again. "Thank you. Do you want a strawberry?"

Alice helped herself to one of the two impossibly ripe, red fruits on Pepper's plate. "Fresh strawberries in October, a wonder. I still have some Jarlsberg."

Pepper used her toothpick to spear the cube Alice indicated and popped it into her mouth with a contented sigh. "I'm finally sated."

There were so many flirtatious ways to answer that remark, and all of them were inappropriate. Lecherous, even. She did not want Pepper to think she was a cougar out for baby chicks.

"There's nothing good about that metaphor," Sass pointed out. *"And you are a lecher."*

The inner argument fell away as they stepped out of the southern doors onto the broad promenade that encircled the back of the observatory with views to the east, south, and west.

Her bones threatened to melt as the cool breeze stole what was left of her breath.

Pepper said quietly, "This is all worth every minute I spent putting product in my hair."

Alice set her glass on the cement balustrade and steadied herself. Seemingly at her feet the world fell away as if a vast jeweler's cloth of velvet night had been spread over the world, and scattered across it were thousands of glittering diamonds of light. Skyscrapers in the distance clustered together in black and gold. In all directions boulevards and highways cut across the landscape, fusing thousands of taillights into sharp lines of red, all pulsing like a beating heart.

The excess, the pollution, the waste.

The order, the chaos, the beauty.

"Look at the stars," Pepper whispered. "Star light, star bright."

"Beautiful." She was not looking at the stars.

If there were people near, Alice didn't see them. Their surroundings faded into the distance and suddenly it was just the two of them. She half expected violins to swoon forth a romantic tune and that if she put her arms around Pepper they would discover they knew how to ballroom dance.

None of this is yours, she tried to tell herself. *This is not your life, not the crystal air, the iridescent landscape, the gloriously alive woman.*

None of this was real, none of it. It was a Hollywood-inspired illusion, make-believe in the land of make-believe. Not real—except the glow in Pepper's eyes.

For as long as it took to breathe it all in and feel her heart beating against her ribs, she realized she was happier than she had been in a very long time.

It was as undeniable as it was terrifying.

Pepper spread her arms and exclaimed, "Have you ever seen anything like it?"

"No," Alice said, still not looking at the stars. "This is a first."

She averted her gaze before Pepper caught her staring. An airplane was lifting into the night and her own spirit rose with it—she was Icarus, suddenly free of the weight of the world.

Icarus flew too close to the sun, she recalled, and fell to his death. What was the point of that myth? A warning not to dream too big? Not to risk too much lest you tempt the gods or your fate? She glanced again at Pepper because she couldn't help herself.

Blond hair tangled again in the wind, far from the coiffed perfection of earlier or the constrained day-to-day ponytail. Cheeks stained red with the rising chill. Body tense and standing on tiptoe, glowing with excitement and awe.

Alice remembered the first time she'd seen the Very Large Array. She'd felt exactly the way Pepper looked right now, on the verge of dancing for joy.

"Let's get in line for the telescope. The woman I was talking to said it was trained on Saturn."

Alice agreed—there was no resistance in her—and they returned their wineglasses and plates to the reception before walking up to the rooftop to join the queue. She regaled Pepper with everything she could remember about Saturn and ended up with a small circle of listeners eagerly asking questions.

She ought to have been pleased by their interest, but a spreading numbness made her a dispassionate observer. The shell threatened to melt when Pepper put her eye to the telescope and leaned into Alice for balance on the platform. Her body was warm, pliant. Trusting. Her own minute gazing at the pebbled rings and planetary shadows was long enough for her to make a stupid wish, as if planets granted wishes.

Finally they reclaimed the car from the valet and began the much less clogged journey back to Pepper's apartment.

"I'm still sorry that Helene made you give up your Saturday night, but I'm glad you enjoyed it."

"I truly did." Pepper had both arms in the air while her hair whipped around her ears. "This car is the cherry on top of a very nice evening."

Alice wanted to ask Pepper if she'd like to stop for a drink or dessert, but she also wanted to escape to the safety of her rental digs, just her and the rest of the whiskey. That was a choice she should probably think about—whiskey versus Pepper. Pepper was unquestionably more dangerous. "It's impractical, but I might miss it, a little, when I'm back in New York."

Pepper made a Munch scream face before clasping her hands to her head in a vain attempt to save her hair. "It's a total mess now."

"Not a problem." *Don't picture it spread out on a pillow in a wild tangle.*

Don't.

Damn.

"So this is awkward," Pepper said quickly. "Helene told me to take you out after, her treat. But it's a little late for that."

It wasn't *that* late, not by New York standards, but Alice already had the feeling that Pepper was an early-to-rise type. "Will you get in trouble?"

"No… Probably not. But I was thinking we could make it true if you're not busy tomorrow. Maybe lunch? I know some terrific spots in Santa Monica. It'll be Sunday—does brunch sound good?"

Say no. "I'm planning on first drafting the history overview."

Pepper turned to face her. "You have to eat any way, and it's free."

"Compelling arguments."

"Let me check on The Sinking Tide. It's kind of a dive, but they get lines out the door for good reason. We used to go there after morning surf." After consulting her phone, Pepper said, "Best time on a Sunday to avoid a long wait is around eleven. Would that work?"

Say no. "Sounds good."

"Meet me there? Or should I pick you up?"

"I can meet you there. The Sinking Tide? Sounds questionable."

"It's *so* questionable. Super casual dress. The getup we have on right now would get us thrown out."

"I'll keep that in mind."

The lack of traffic made the return journey much quicker, though Alice couldn't decide if that was a blessing. She leaned on the hood of the car, legs crossed, while she waited for Pepper to wave from her window. Pepper's cheery "See you tomorrow" had ended the evening after she'd opened the car door for her. Now that she was safely delivered home, Alice's job as an escort was done.

She could still hear an orchestra playing in her head and too easily she could feel Pepper in her arms, their bodies moving together in increasingly urgent rhythm.

Time for her to see herself home as well, with a stop at a liquor store on the way. She needed to be numb again. She needed to put these make-believe feelings out of her mind.

CHAPTER EIGHTEEN

Unused to the alarm going off on a Sunday morning, Pepper slapped it twice before remembering she had to be at the Sinking Tide by eleven. She stumbled from bed to the shower, yawning until the first blast of tepid water woke up every last nerve in her body. When the water warmed, she surrendered to the bliss of shampoo and suds.

Why, at that sublime moment the water became truly hot and her hair felt silky and clean in her hands, did she find herself picturing Alice from the night before? They'd been standing on the promenade, gazing at the skyline and stars. It hadn't even been for very long, but all at once the skeptic and cynic had fallen away and Alice's face had held only wonder as she gazed at the illumination of darkness with light. There was also a blend of joyful awe, a feeling that Pepper understood. It was how she felt when she saw a good wave developing and gave herself over, not to bending the water, but to being bent by it.

She laughed and had to spit out soap. Alice Cabot, science journalist, would likely dispute that surfing and stargazing had something in common. Well, if they ran out of things to talk about over brunch, she could bring it up.

Hair toweled and loose around her shoulders, she wrapped herself in her terrycloth robe and followed the promising aroma of fresh coffee.

CC grunted a good morning as she sipped from her favorite Caffeine Now Loading mug. Her gaze was fixed on a bright yellow box of baking mix. "Do you want pancakes? I feel like making them. Maybe. I need an incentive, like you want some too."

"I'm having lunch out." Pepper filled her Simply the Best mug and took her time with the milk and wiping the counter before turning to see that CC's eyebrows were as high as Pepper had thought they'd be. "It's work."

"Okay."

"I'm supposed to entertain the reporter."

"Okay."

"Helene is buying."

"Okay." CC ran one hand through her hair, making the short red spikes point in all directions.

Time for a distraction. "I heard you hoot last night. Did you win?"

"Won the redemption round at least. Next month's rent is secure." CC hoisted her mug for a toast.

"Great news." Pepper busied herself toasting half of an English muffin. "Is there still marmalade? Oh!"

"What?"

"The reporter—she called me Paddington!"

CC's shout of laughter was very loud. "How on earth did we all miss that in high school? We could have made your life a living hell. And think of the costume opportunities. Though it's not too late."

She regretted sharing the tidbit. "I am *not* a lost bear."

"No, but you are cute, and some people seem to want to cuddle you, from time to time. Where are you going for lunch?"

"The Sinking Tide."

CC rolled her eyes so hard Pepper expected to hear them crack. "Sure, that's where you take a work acquaintance for Sunday brunch. Not the Sheraton Grand, not Mimosa over the Water."

"It's close to where she's staying." She peered into the marmalade jar. "We're going to need more."

"Sure, Paddington. Let's talk about the marmalade—"

Pepper smacked the jar down on the counter. "If you call me Paddington one more time, I will make you sorry. You won't know when."

CC waved off the threat. "Let's talk about marmalade and not the drop-dead gorgeous butch with the convertible."

"It's a rental and she hates it."

"Point in her favor. It's a real blue-haired Bel Air maven sort of car."

"No it's not. It was hecka fun." Peeved, Pepper said, "It was so beautiful out last night so I was happy for the experience."

"Sure, you floated in the front door last night over a car."

"I hadn't been out at night for fun in forever. And someone else was paying for it—winning all the way around."

CC got up to warm her coffee, stepping around the crack in the linoleum where the floor had buckled over time. They believed the pizza oven downstairs was right under it, and chilly mornings they both appreciated it. "I'm glad you had so much fun that you're having a second date right away."

"It's not a date. I'm doing what Helene told me, like she told me to borrow some jewelry if I needed it." Pepper sighed, knowing full well that once CC had an idea she wouldn't let it go. "Those other places are so formal. I didn't want to get dressed up again."

"Okay." CC's way of wrinkling her nose when calling bullshit was hilarious—when someone else was on the receiving end. "It's true they have no dress code. Nothing says business brunch like cutoffs and a bikini halter top."

"She's nice and not as snobby as I thought. Still kind of stuffy but funny." Alice was all those things at once, a unique blend.

"She looked old. Older. In a distinguished sort of way."

"Not old. Fortyish, I think."

CC let out a dramatic sigh. "I guess if I'm not making pancakes and I can't sponge lunch off you, I'll have to make my own fun." Her cell phone chimed at that moment and she wandered into her bedroom as she said, loud enough for Pepper to hear, "Pepper's being mean. Have lunch with me."

She sent the middle finger salute the remark deserved at CC's back and finished her muffin while working out timing for the morning. She needed to figure out clothes posthaste or she'd be late. Sunday traffic on any sunny day could be stop-and-go near the beaches. Lacking time for much dithering, she finally picked out white- and beige-striped beachcombers and a simple cotton V-necked shirt in a pumpkinish orange. She didn't know if they'd go for a walk on the beach after eating, but she kept the possibility open by opting for her water-and-sand sturdy Tevas.

The parking gods smiled on her and she found a spot right in front of the Sinking Tide with a few minutes to spare. The sun was bright and hot, but the sea breeze in the shade reminded her it was October.

She'd be glad of the nubby greige cardigan she'd tucked into her burlap tote with her wallet. It was one of Helene's castoffs and a little narrow in the shoulders, but Maje Paris was Maje Paris.

It had been a few years since her last visit to the Sinking Tide, but nothing had changed. The paint was still faded, the roof still sagged. More vehicles were pulling into the lot, most of them small trucks loaded with surfboards and their owners. Wetsuits were being stripped off and there was a short line of people waiting to rinse saltwater off themselves at the pull shower. Rinsing was one of the few rules the restaurant enforced. That, and abiding by the arrow and sign commanding, "Smoke your weed over here" to keep the scent downwind of the kitchen and dining room.

As she joined the queue for a table she looked out over the pale gold sand to the rolling water, now the murky green that signified an outgoing tide. There were still a number of surfers on the water, but she judged they had a half hour at most before the waves flattened. She ought to have cranked herself out of bed and joined them. Of course that would have meant having brunch with Alice in soggy clothes and water-wrecked hair. It was unthinkable—what would Helene say if she found out how poorly Pepper had represented her? Maintaining a polished and professional appearance was essential.

Next weekend, she promised herself. She'd get her board out, wax it properly, and enjoy the waves. She had to carve out the time—make it a priority.

The smell of sizzling bacon and fresh baked biscuits left her light-headed. At least that's what she told herself was the cause when she saw the top of Alice's tousled head, then the black-framed glasses, and the perpetually half-mocking smile as Alice scanned the line looking for her.

She waved a hand and fought to steady her breath when Alice's smile broadened. She was glad of her sunglasses and wasn't going to name what she hoped to hide behind them.

CHAPTER NINETEEN

The Sinking Tide was a low white building framed in teal-green timbers, none of which were square to each other or the ground. Time and tide had not been kind. Alice guessed it had been built before a moratorium made it impossible to develop anything on the beach side of Highway 1. The 1930s Historic Landmark placard was probably why it hadn't been pulled down or updated.

The crowded parking lot was awash with sand and surfboards, and the morning tide had left a blend of seaweed, fish, and salt in the air to mingle with the mouth-watering smell of baking bread. Alice was instantly, painfully hungry, and regretted last night's post-gala whiskeys, followed by oversleeping this morning.

The sun was hot on her neck, but the steady wind had the edge of winter in it. At least what counted as winter in Santa Monica, Alice thought. Evergreen ivy and juniper bushes covered retaining walls, and palm trees creaked overhead. The beach was dotted with families, sunbathers, and dog walkers. All were wearing swimsuits or shorts and tank tops. Endless summer, under a shimmering intense yellow sun.

Autumn was her favorite season and there was little of it here. She thought of the vivid red and orange trees spreading across Central Park and imagined inhaling the aroma of spiced wine and a smoky fire.

"*Get real*," Sass snarked. "*You haven't gone out for leaf watching and hot toddies in a decade. You're only forty, and you're already living in a mythical past.*"

She wondered if the Sinking Tide sold anything stronger than beer.

Pepper had said the place had a funky vibe. She wasn't wrong, Alice decided. Small packs of scruffy, bearded youths with tanned, rock-solid abs gathered around tables with trays of beer mugs, water still dripping from their board shorts. A gray-haired couple in matching tie-dyed Grateful Dead T-shirts were trading bites from each other's plates—fluffy stacks of pancakes on one and a breakfast burrito the size of her head on the other. A line of waiting diners was already snaked along the side of the building.

She wondered for a moment if she'd arrived before Pepper but caught sight of a Simply the Best parking pass dangling from the rearview mirror of a pale green Prius. She took note of the bumper stickers—a baby Pikachu dressed as Deadpool, flanked by Wonder Woman and Captain Marvel emblems. Mayhem, grace, and power. She did not have a problem with any of that.

Scanning the line, she spotted Pepper most of the way to the front, already smiling at her in welcome.

"You made it."

"I hope you haven't been here long." Alice concentrated on Pepper's face to avoid a long, lingering stare at the curve of shoulders, hips, and thighs as Pepper leaned against the whitewashed wall. Though the daily corporate attire and last night's little black dress had all been worn with aplomb, this Pepper—casual knee-length pants, a simple shirt, hair tied back, and makeup-free face turned like a sunflower to the light—was even more comfortable with herself. Devastatingly comfortable.

"Not at all. The line is growing fast. The host said it'll be ten-fifteen at most for a table. I said outside, I hope that's okay. Inside is a little loud."

Alice gestured at the long line of beach and the distant crashing waves. "With this view? Outside is great."

"I'm fainting at the smell of the biscuits and gravy. It's agonizing."

Alice agreed. "I'm going to admit that I know next to nothing about surfing. Is it a morning thing?"

"Not always. It's a wind and depth of the water thing. This time of year you have to be on the beach at sunrise if you want to get in two-three great hours, but you get another shot in the early afternoon.

The onshore wind makes the waves crumbly, especially later in the afternoon when the wind tends to peak."

"Crumbly?"

"The tops crumble instead of curl." At Alice's lifted eyebrow, Pepper continued, "You won't get long lines of waves breaking because the wind is pushing the tops of the waves over more quickly and erratically. If the wind were blowing out, the waves would take longer to break, which means a nice, long ride."

The way she scrunched her forehead and pursed her lips in thought was adorable, Alice decided.

"Water waves, light waves, sound waves—don't they all follow the same laws of physics?"

Alice blinked. "Of course. Everything does."

"Even with variables." Pepper shrugged. "The athlete is a variable. The wind and weather. The more variables the more…"

"Chaos," Alice supplied with a nod. "A friend of mine covers baseball and he'd probably agree that it's the variables that make the game interesting. And they're why you have to play the game instead of run a simulation."

"Some surfer tech people tried to create a program that would predict best waves. Works great in general locales—like picking between Malibu and Santa Monica any given day. But not for individual choices."

"Your best wave isn't going to be someone else's?"

"Exactly." Pepper beamed at her. "Have you ever tried?"

"I've been windsurfing. Parasailing."

"Thrill-seeker scientist?"

"A long-ago ex was a travel writer. She couldn't get me to jump out of a plane though."

"That's on my bucket list." Pepper glanced over her shoulder at Alice as the gnarled host led them past a dessert case filled with enormous pies, around a corner and out a narrow doorway to the patio. He gestured with a grunt at a small once-white metal table up against the Plexiglas windscreen. A tattered umbrella advertising Amstel gave them enough shade to avoid sunburn.

"You're too young for a bucket list." Alice didn't realize she'd said it aloud until Pepper, seated, looked up, her expression abruptly grave.

"Nobody really knows how long they have. Or how long we'll all be here. The last couple of years made that abundantly clear."

Alice let settling into her wobbly chair take as long as possible. She wasn't sure she could speak without her voice cracking. Her mind was flooded again with the memory of the empty desks back at her office. The funerals that were never held, the colleagues she'd never see again or who were still bowed under the grief of losing family and loved ones.

Tunnel vision sent Pepper's smiling face and beguiling body into a distant well. The babble of voices and caws of gulls faded into a distant roar with the surf.

She wanted a drink. It would help. It would numb. It would put out the remote spark of light in her own head trying to tell her, "You're broken, broken, broken…"

Intellectually she knew she couldn't fix anything by breaking something else, but there was no room in her for logic, not right then.

"Remember," Pepper said. "This is my treat—well, Helene's treat."

Helene.

Helene had to be responsible for what Alice felt—she didn't want to blame Pepper. But Pepper was only here at Helene's behest. Pepper and her natural sensuality and lack of guile. All so attractive. What if Helene knew that and would be happy for Pepper to seduce Alice, and what if that was Pepper's plan? What other explanation could there be for Pepper's warmth and friendliness?

Broken…

She knew she wasn't making sense and had no power to stop herself. It was easier to turn Helene and Pepper into effigies of villainy and set fire to them. Easier to make the world black and white, no gray, no context, no complexity.

You're broken…

This place only served beer, and that wasn't going to do it.

Pepper was another Instagram wannabee like her idol Helene. What a waste.

Broken…

"You feel okay?"

"Yeah—headache. The sun. I'm not used to it."

"They don't have it in New York?"

"Not like this."

"Not even at Coney Island?"

Alice tried to smile. "You got me there. Ever been?"

"No, just seen pictures. My parents always liked to travel to tropical destinations. As an adult I haven't been able to afford much beyond dragging my board to Malibu or Topanga Beach once in a great while."

"Student loans?"

"Thankfully no. I'm lucky. But trying to break into a great company means taking intern gigs."

"Colleagues of mine reported on the Internship Culture. It seems especially prevalent here."

"Well, that could be because of demand—more people want the jobs than there are jobs. So they're willing to work for free to get their foot in."

"You end up with industries built on free labor."

"Which is not right." Pepper gave a philosophical shrug. "I have no solution to offer. I'd like to think, if I ever have the power, that I'd make sure everyone who works for me gets a wage that's enough to live on."

In the back of her mind, Alice was already outlining an article about wage structures at Simply the Best. She wondered what kinds of public filings and disclosures would provide her with wage scale information. She was well aware that, in spite of corporate-wide wage grades, somehow big companies still found ways to pay women less. How did ST-Best's wage practices, for their overwhelmingly female workforce, compare to those in the general region around them? The extensive use of interns she'd noticed throughout some parts of the company said they weren't above making money off free labor. It wasn't a stretch to presume they also underpaid women whenever possible as well. She criticized other corporations for the practice— was the same criticism verboten if the corporation was run by women mostly for women?

Her moral compass declared that it shouldn't be. If anything, it was even more reprehensible.

But that was not what she was here to write about, and she was only here because of her own stupid mouth.

Broken…

She lifted her menu as a distraction. "Any recommendations?"

"Whatever appeals. I'm fond of the Sunday quiche, and their spiced bacon is awesome, if you partake. October is my favorite month. It leads to Halloween, for one thing. And eating delicious things outside." Pepper's glance at her own menu had an anticipatory, predatory gleam that left Alice feeling weak.

She regained some of her composure by studying the choices of diner classics. "Eggs over Cajun-smoked turkey hash—Sunday brunch only," she read aloud. "Cornmeal waffles. Ricotta pancakes with lime-pepper jelly?"

"Those are to die for. The jelly is the whole deal, maybe the kind of thing you can't get at home, if you're looking for something unique."

"Unique isn't a problem at home. I live on a street with a Ukrainian diner, a Greek deli, Indian takeaway, and an Italian sit-down that's been making their own gnocchi for a hundred years. That said, though, the pancakes are not something I've stumbled across anywhere else."

Pepper raised her sunglasses to rest on top of her head. "My roommate has worked in eateries all over the Valley, and she says if it's sweet, rich, sour, and spicy all at once you've found California cuisine."

"Other than the frozen enchilada—"

"So sad."

"—I think everything I've had here has that explosive California quality."

Pepper's gaze flicked to Alice's face before returning to her menu. "Maybe it's the California sun?"

"Could be, though, as you said, we do have sun in New York." It could be the company, Alice thought. *It could be a woman with eyes I feel like I'm going to drown in.* She shook off the image of gasping for air, like Pepper was a wave that could pull her under. "It's the same sun."

Pepper's bright eyes widened with exasperation. "Work with me. Less UV radiation or something."

"It would be roughly same UV radiation, even considering the different longitudes." The brown eyes narrowed, and Alice gave up resisting. "But you're probably right. Something about the UV radiation."

Pepper smiled. "Was that so hard?"

Not a question she was going to answer. "I think I have to have this hash."

"If I got the cornmeal waffle, could we go halfsies?"

"It's a deal."

Their waiter arrived promptly and jotted down their orders and sped away before Alice could ask for a beer.

"Why else is October your favorite month?" It seemed like a natural question to ask, and she needed to say something to hide the low buzz of panic that had started in her gut. She'd been counting on at least a beer to give her distance from the uncertainty of shifting sand under her feet. She wanted more than one beer—she wanted a cool, amber whiskey. And she didn't want Pepper to know.

To know what?

The question scared her, and she wanted nothing to do with the answer.

"And it's the one week a year I get pumpkin spice anything."

She'd heard nothing else of what Pepper had said. Her brain was spinning in circles. "I'm not a pumpkin spice latte kind of gal," Alice admitted, hoping it was the right reaction. Their waiter appeared with the order for the table next to hers. She hoped she seemed casual as she waved and asked for a Corona.

"Make it two," Pepper said. "It's early, but on a day like today..."

Alice's panic subsided. She'd have something to help her get through this. "Thanks for choosing this place. I'm not a morning person—"

"No!"

"This was worth it, smartass," she finished. To her great relief, the waiter reappeared with their beers. She had a large swallow as soon as she thought Pepper wouldn't notice. Fortunately, their food was delivered shortly thereafter, giving them the distraction of the huge portions, the smoky, spicy aromas, and how to work out sharing.

The waffle was like crunchy cornbread with spicy bacon and cinnamon apple all through it and tasted like a gift from truly beneficent gods. Pepper's little whimper of bliss at her first bite made it even better.

"That is incredibly tasty. I could eat six of them."

Pepper nodded, her eyes half-closed with pleasure.

Don't look at her, Alice thought. She focused on her food and was partway through her half of the smoked Cajun turkey hash before she felt on a more even keel, too, and not so much at the mercy of unwanted self-reflection.

"If I eat the rest of this," Pepper said with a gesture at the last third of her hash, "I'm going to be miserable. But I think I'm going to go with miserable. It's so good."

"I'm making the same choice about the rest of my waffle. Well worth the indigestion." Alice's beer was nearly empty, and the buzz of anxiety flickered at her nerves again. *I'll catch up later*, she tried to tell it, as if there was a quota.

Her brain went round and round in circles while she tried to keep up the conversation with Pepper.

"Cosima in *Orphan Black* is the sexiest scientist ever," she said in answer to Pepper's teasing question. "I really, really wish she were real. There's also Science Officer Burnham. And Captain Janeway loves her some science too. Mostly in the form of Seven of Nine, but I digress."

"So you are way into *Star Wars*."

Alice went numb with shock, only to see Pepper laughing at her.

"*Trek, Trek*, I know. And if any of them were real?"

"We'd be the very best of friends." She cleared her throat to underscore her intentions. "Your turn. Sexiest superhero? Remember, too, that scientists are superheroes."

"I haven't seen *Orphan Black* so I can't pick Cosima, even though it's clear I should."

"This is true."

"I have to say that all of the Spocks are attractive."

"Science Officer, plus Spock is an ice king. I get that intellectually."

"Superhero, though. Carol Danvers—Captain Marvel."

Alice recalled the bumper sticker. "Movie version? Leather jacket and Nine-Inch Nails tee? Hates it when men tell her to smile?"

"All of that."

"So she'd be your bestie forever?"

Pepper gave a non-committal head bob as she shook her head.

"What?"

"I don't really do the thirst object thing."

Alice blinked. "Thirst object?"

"My roomie, CC, stans Janelle Monáe on an epic scale. I guess I'm an admire-from-afar type. I like knowing these powerful, interesting, smart women are in their worlds—real or made up—and doing their thing. They're bigger than life. I don't want them to be mortal enough to know the likes of me." Pepper leaned back in her chair and patted her stomach with a moan somewhere between bliss and distress.

"So you put epic women on a pedestal?"

"I guess. Why not? There's precious little to look up to in this world. CC was euphoric when Janelle shared what she likes to sleep in. I love Beyoncé and Jennifer Lamont. But I'm content without that much detail. I'd probably drool on myself if I met any of them."

It was fascinating insight into Pepper's mind. "Where does Helene Jolie fit in the pantheon, then?"

Pepper's smile vanished as her hands tightened around her beer. All warmth fled with, "This. What we're doing right here. Is it off the record?"

Alice realized she couldn't have ruined the mood any better if she'd done it on purpose. Had she? "Of course. It was never—I mean she's larger than life in her own way."

Pepper bit her lower lip but said nothing.

"I'm sorry."

"She is larger than life. She's also my boss. Of course I admire her."

That's how young she is, Alice thought. She believes one unquestionably admired one's boss. "I didn't mean—I'm sorry. Please forget I asked."

"She's not a thirst object."

Part of her wanted to hear Pepper's protest as half-hearted. It would make it easier. She needed everything to be easier. The silence beat at Alice's ears. Was she jealous of Helene? Was it that Pepper looked at Helene with respect and admiration and likely never would look at her that way? Ridiculous, stupid, useless questions to go with her ridiculous, stupid, useless feelings about a woman she'd just met. What was she thinking? What was wrong with her?

"I'm not even sure what a thirst object is."

Still unsmiling, Pepper said, "Pretty much like it sounds."

"Objectification?"

"Yes. But no. You're an ardent fan, and you stalk them online regularly as a fan. It's not loaded with ownership, like you're entitled to the real person. Truthfully, I hadn't thought about it that much."

Like she hadn't thought about Simply the Best and their questionable claims and yoni eggs for sale? *A young, unformed child. Too young for…anything.*

The grumpy waiter dropped checks at several tables, including theirs. Pepper tucked it under her water glass to pay at the register on the way out.

Her expression now nowhere near the sunny openness of earlier, Pepper lifted her sunglasses from the top of her head as she shook back her hair and settled them on her nose. "The sun is killer today."

Back to the weather. Good. Safer than thinking about the precise shades of yellow and gold the sun created as Pepper's hair lifted in the breeze. "Lots of UV."

Pepper's shoulders moved in an almost shrug. "The line is huge now. We really should give up the table."

And that is that, Alice thought. Her offer to leave the tip was refused as Pepper carried the check to the cashier. The smell of pancakes and syrup left her nauseated now. Her stomach was too full, and the conversation had soured the good food afterglow.

Pepper led the way past the now doubled line to the parking lot. She gave a half-hearted wave toward the distant Ferris wheel and promised tourist delights of Santa Monica Pier. "If you're up for a walk, we could make it to the Pier, have a quick tour, and be back here in an hour."

The smile that accompanied the invitation was forced. She'd truly spiked whatever ease she and Pepper had had. Alice glanced at her watch. "I was hoping to get a draft of the first two articles done today. To stay on deadline so they can move along the approval pipeline. It's a long one on this project."

"Of course."

"Thank you for the experience of the Sinking Tide. I enjoyed myself."

"It was my pleasure," Pepper said, clearly on autopilot.

"I'll likely see you tomorrow. I've got two appointments in Admin and two more in Marketing."

"Great."

She waved Pepper goodbye and took long enough to get to her car for Pepper's Prius to disappear into traffic. In her rental car she turned toward the grocery store. The whiskey was gone and there was not enough left of the tequila to last the rest of the day.

PART FIVE

Ice Cold

CHAPTER TWENTY

On the record, off the record. As she drove toward home, Pepper reviewed everything she'd said during lunch and the night before.

It was the one thing Helene had warned her about—make sure when you're on the record. She'd told Helene she was up to the job to keeping a reporter in check, but clearly she wasn't. Had she said anything about work to Alice? Made any kind of offhand comment about anyone or an internal policy or practice?

She'd been a fool. *You work in the big leagues now, and there are people who will use your access for their own purposes.* Was Alice one of those people? She didn't want to think Alice was like that, but what did she really know about Alice's reputation as a journalist?

The pedestal question about Helene had come out of the blue just when Pepper was thinking it had been a perfect lunch. That they'd go for a walk on the beach and be…

Be what?

No. No, they weren't doing some California lesbian postcard.

What had she been thinking would come of spending more time with Alice?

The longer Pepper thought about it the angrier she became—this was Alice's fault. Of course it was. Not that she could say exactly how.

She was too angry for that. It felt like she'd been riding a wave and some asshole surfer cut into her path. She was *not* wiping out because of CabotAliceP.

"Exactly what did she mean about Helene and if she's part of my pantheon of strong women?" Pepper glared at herself in the rearview mirror. "What does she think is going on? Helene is epic in her own way. Why shouldn't I admire her?"

Her worries about whether she'd made an on-the-record misstep wouldn't abate, so it seemed perfectly reasonable for her inner revenge demon to stick Alice Cabot's effigy with skewers. Forget those adorable glasses and the tall, lean warmth, and quiet intelligence. And funny wit.

Alice Cabot was a spy and an interloper and a New Yorker Know-it-all out to prove some point about Simply the Best and Helene Jolie.

"Well, she's not going to get anything juicy to put in her newspaper from me. From here on out it's nothing but business, every interaction." She gritted her teeth as she squeezed her car into her parking space behind the pizzeria. "I'm going to kill her with professionalism."

She stomped up the stairs and pushed open the apartment door. She was greeted by laughter and the aroma of pancakes wafting from the kitchen.

"Hey," CC called. "There's still one left."

"I'm stuffed." She hung her tote on the peg and rounded the corner to find that CC's lunch companion was Val.

She covered her surprise. "Hey you—CC makes great pancakes, doesn't she?"

Val paused with a forkful of pancake glistening with syrup halfway to their mouth. "I feel honored to have been invited to partake after all these years. Who knew? CC says you took some reporter to a dive bar."

"Did not," Pepper protested. "A dive. Not a bar. Well, there was beer."

"With a reporter?"

Pepper explained about the special news series while she got a cup of coffee and joined them at the table. Val seemed to understand it was important in a corporate sense.

That is, until CC added, "You left out that the reporter is totally hot and drives a convertible."

"If you like that sort of thing," Pepper said, as if she didn't. And couldn't. And wouldn't. "And it's a rental. I suppose she owns a car in New York. I mean, her mother lives in the Hamptons."

CC goggled. "How do you know that?"

"It's my job to know things like that." She found herself hacking the last pancake into tiny bits which she ate one by one, successfully drowning out the protests of her already full stomach.

"You're so fancy."

Pepper curled her lip in CC's direction. "Alice and Helene went to the same school, though not at the same time. And get this—Alice suggested that I have put Helene on some kind of pedestal. Like there's something wrong with admiring her."

"I like her more and more."

"As if. She was trying to get some inside juicy scoop for her story." She ignored CC sneezing "bullshit" into her hand. Time for a change of subject. "How's the promotion working out, Val?"

Val shook their swoopy bangs to one side. "Really great, thanks for asking."

"They made their quarterly sales goal with a week to spare." CC got up to take the plates to the sink.

"I think it's the Asian thing," Val said. "Rectal pharmacology is super technical and systemically interdependent. Take something for the lower GI and you could throw off liver, kidney, pancreatic response—it's a long list of interactions. People still expect Asians to be better at anything sciencey." After a philosophical shrug, Val added, "I find myself at peace with leveraging their stereotypes."

Pepper leaned across the table to high five. "You are the Ruler of All Things Rectal."

CC chortled. "Now *that's* a bumper sticker."

"Without working tail pipes we'd all explode." Pepper spread her hands. "Truth."

"Indeed. Everybody has a tail pipe." Val laughed. "I tell my mother that rectal care and treatment is one-hundred percent job security for the rest of my life. Appa wants me to use euphemisms, like 'elimination pharmacology' but I think that—"

"—Sounds like drugs for assassins," CC finished as she returned to the table.

Val beamed at CC. "Exactly."

"Which would actually be very cool on a business card." CC leaned over Val's shoulder for the bottle of syrup.

"Pharmacist to the *Blacklist* cabal?" Val's tiny nose was cute all scrunched up. "Nah. Lots of money but dead by thirty."

"But your life would have a badass soundtrack until the fatal shootout."

"My life already has the soundtrack of my choosing." Val nodded with satisfaction.

Pepper realized Val was probably the right person to ask, since she hadn't bothered yet to look it up. "Do you know what yoni eggs are?"

Val blinked at her and burst out laughing. "Why on earth do you ask?"

"We sell them, and Al—the reporter—seems to think that's silly."

"It totally is."

CC sat down with a fresh cup of coffee and stretched out her legs with a contented sigh. "What are they?"

"Vaginal pseudo-science."

Pepper cocked her head. "Say what?"

"They're egg-shaped rocks—highly polished alabaster or jade or glass. Supposedly—and there is zero and I mean zero evidence to back this up—if you insert them into your vagina, you exercise your vaginal muscles and tighten your vaginal walls."

Pepper stared at Val. "You're kidding."

"Wish I were. We sell a vaginal suppository to quell the damage and irritation the eggs might cause some women." Val launched into a high-speed disclaimer. "Reduced sensitivity may occur but usually returns to normal once course of treatment is concluded."

CC managed to laugh and roll her eyes at Pepper at the same time. "So on top of her face, her skin, her makeup, her weight, her hair, and her clothes, women are also supposed to be worried about whether they have perfect vaginal walls?"

Pepper saw the absurdity of it but said, "It's just one of over two thousand products we sell."

"Simply the Best sells just one product." CC sipped her coffee with her truly annoying I-know-everything air.

Don't ask her, Pepper told herself, but she couldn't help it. "Which is?"

"Insecurity."

Val came to Pepper's rescue. "I sell insecurity, especially when I repped for the dermatology line. Sad, but true, there is no limit to what some women will spend to achieve uniform skin tone. Which is nearly one-hundred percent determined by genetics." Val held up one arm. "Korean-Samoan worked out okay."

"Meanwhile, I got the *I Zombie* genes." CC sighed. "I have to say, Pep, I like your reporter even more. Yoni eggs sound exceedingly stupid."

"She's not *my* reporter." She threw a napkin at CC when she again sneezed "bullshit" into her hand. "Maybe Val can give you something for that cold."

Yes, yoni eggs are stupid, she decided later, as she fell into a fury of closet cleanout to organize her ever-growing accumulation of Helene's castoffs. After a glance at them with the ST-Best shopping app on her phone, she decided they were bought as a gag gift. Ergo, Alice Cabot was wrong to judge a product that was clearly satiric. There were certain things, items, objects, that were perfectly fine to be inserted into various places, and Simply the Best was not the kind of site that sold them.

The kind of sites that did was *not* a subject she was going to broach with Alice Cabot, that was for sure. She folded sweaters and leggings and told herself there was no reason to be tingling as she thought about the kinds of activities consenting adults could do, especially with the proper kind of insertable items. And lubrication.

She slept badly.

Monday morning, after coffee plus toast with marmalade, she managed to return to a more reasonable frame of mind that she carried with her to work.

There was no reason to be angry at Alice for anything. Emotional extremes weren't called for. She didn't care enough about Alice Cabot to feel an emotion, let alone an extreme one.

She didn't immediately glance toward the elevators every time they opened, nor, after being away from her desk, did she ask Clarita if Alice had come by. Whatever and whenever, the possibility of seeing Alice wasn't going to interfere with her day.

Deep in a stack of pages with spelling of people's names to check before they were seen by Helene, she didn't immediately realize Alice was standing in front of her. Her heart beat faster because she was startled, she told herself, not because Alice was dressed very much like she had been on Friday, in slacks and this time a red jacket, but no tie. Her open collar revealed a pronounced notch in her collarbone.

Pepper had to force herself not to caress it with her eyes.

Just like that, her resolve crumbled like wind-crusted sand.

The cool and professional smile she'd practiced in the mirror after her shower was what she hoped was on her face. It was hard to be sure with her skin tingling all over.

"I was wondering if you had more recent contact information for a couple of local politicians. Like the woman we met Saturday night."

Thinking that Alice could have looked them up in public records, Pepper took the list of five names and searched the database she shared with the other assistants. She wrote the information on Alice's list and handed it back without quite making eye contact. "These should be up-to-date."

"Thanks. I have a couple of questions for you. Could I ask you over lunch?"

"I don't have time today, I'm afraid. Could you email them?"

After the slightest of pauses, Alice said, "Sure."

Clarita suddenly got to her feet, and Pepper knew that meant Helene had arrived back from a unit meeting in the building where Legal was located. It was a welcome distraction, and she gave Helene her full attention. Today she was wearing sleek leather pants with a simple silk shell and lace-trimmed jacket, all in black. The emerald green heels looked perfect with a jade pendent and earrings.

Pepper was keenly aware that Alice was watching her, and she did her best to hide her lust for the jacket, which was steampunky with a cutaway front and shiny buttons across the shoulders.

Clarita had already come around to the front of her desk to greet Helene, a folder in her hand. "I have several speaking contracts for the Composium ready for your review," she told Helene. "Mayim will be here in fifteen minutes with that layout you asked about. Nasrallah and Luu are on at three."

Helene nodded and was still facing Clarita when she said, "Ms. Cabot, back so soon?"

"Alice, please. My work continues."

Pepper was caught off guard when Helene pivoted to look directly at her, then at Alice.

"Did you enjoy the Griffith?"

"Yes, very much."

"I was right, wasn't I?" Helene's gaze returned to Pepper. "Pepper is an excellent guide."

Pepper felt her cheeks warm, and she brushed imaginary dust off the sleeve of her jacket.

"Of course." After a slight pause, Alice added, "All of your staff are exceptionally efficient."

It sounded like a compliment but somehow didn't seem like it. Helene's expression was a mask of good humor, but none of it reached her eyes. Pepper wanted to look at Alice, but it didn't feel safe to do so, not with Helene looking at them both so intently.

"I'm pleased that's been your experience." Helene waved a hand as if dismissing her and took several steps toward her office. "Pepper, I have a few things in my office I wanted to change out."

"Of course." She quickly followed. Clarita, who had been poised to follow Helene, retreated to her desk in confusion.

To Pepper's immense surprise, Helene waited for her and tipped her head toward Pepper's as if they were conspirators. "I think it's time to go to the next level."

Flustered, Pepper answered, "I hope I live up to your expectations."

Helene laughed, a full-throated bell of a laugh, leaving Pepper bemused. "I'm sure you will. Over here."

That's when Pepper felt, ever so lightly, Helene's fingertips on the small of her back. Or perhaps she imagined it because hardly a heartbeat later, Helene was in front of her, walking along the display wall.

"I want all of these items updated." She indicated several pieces of jewelry, a belt, scarf, sliced soaps, and a singing bowl set. She gave Pepper a long, considering look. "All from the new Best Bliss layout. You decide."

"You want me to choose them?" Goodness, she hadn't known her voice could get so squeaky.

"Yes. Arrange them how you think they should be. And we'll see."

Was it a test? To prove she could match Helene's flawless aesthetic? Pepper didn't know what to say other than, "Yes, right away, Helene," as she took several pictures with her phone, and began the process of removing the products.

"We'll review what you've done when I get back from San Francisco on Wednesday. I have confidence in you, Pepper."

She felt her face flame with heat, and there was no way to hide it. Helene looked amused, then dismissed her with a wave.

As Pepper juggled the armful of products safely onto her desk, she heard Alice say to Clarita, "I'll see you at ten after four then."

"She's making a big change," Clarita observed.

Pepper pulled the original boxes for the jewelry from the cabinet behind her. "Yes, to Best Bliss. I'm going down to the Boutique to pick out replacements."

"You're picking them out? On your own?" Clarita's voice was unusually tight, and Pepper risked a glance. She looked as surprised as Pepper felt.

"Yes."

"First time for everything," Clarita said slowly.

Helene's voice called out from her office, "Clarita? The Composium speakers?"

Clarita scooped up her folder and a pen and hurried into the inner office, leaving Pepper alone with Alice. She busied herself hooking earrings into their loops inside the matching box.

Every nerve in her body was aware when Alice moved from next to Clarita's desk to in front of hers. She centered a necklace in its black velvet box before looking up. "Did you need something?"

"That looks like a big job."

"All in a day's work."

Alice's face was unreadable, though Pepper didn't try very hard. She had work to do and wanted to do it well, and she was so confused about exactly what Helene wanted. It was hard to think with Alice hovering over her. She coiled the belt and slipped it into a satiny pouch.

"I'll see you later," Alice finally said. "I'll be in the Archives at four to talk to Clarita."

"Of course." Pepper threw a smile in Alice's direction but could not, would not, look at her.

CHAPTER TWENTY-ONE

Wow, Alice thought. That was an icy cold shoulder, and she was being given it. Her mind fixed on the image of Pepper folding a large cashmere scarf as if the future of humanity depended on perfect lines. *That whole scene was theater for my benefit.* Helene Jolie had wanted to be sure Alice was completely aware that she was the boss of all she surveyed, and she'd moved Pepper around on her chessboard to prove it. Alice had not missed the disbelief on Clarita's face when Helene had laughed at something Pepper had said. Clarita hadn't been in the right position to see Helene's hand on Pepper's back, but Alice certainly had been.

The skin on Alice's arms was prickling with anger. Pepper wouldn't see Helene's subtle and skilled manipulation. It wasn't in her nature to see it, and Alice had no doubt that Helene knew when she had an unquestioning acolyte in her grips. A laugh, some attention, oodles of charm, and Pepper had emerged from Helene's office covered in blushes and even colder to Alice.

She had hoped to have lunch with Pepper to make some peace over her clumsy remark about Helene and pedestals. That plan was dust, and she wasn't going to make nice when it was obvious now that she had been right.

One thing was for certain, she wasn't going over to the café to have perfect food in a perfect setting among perfect people. The nearest bar couldn't be *that* far away. Her next appointment, in Product Discovery and Development, was in ninety minutes. There was time.

The noonday sun was bright overhead as she headed for the parking lot. What a difference a few days had made, though. The heat was pronounced, but nothing like that bone-penetrating force she'd felt when she'd arrived.

She tipped her face up to the sun the way Pepper had the first afternoon Alice had spent with her—how could it not be even a week? *You just met her*, she reminded herself. *You're not her friend, not her family, and not responsible for her.* It was entirely possible she was misreading everything because she didn't want to be here and she did want an excuse to drink.

Part of her could remember a time when she hadn't felt this way all day, every day. Had instead felt as if her mission in life was to put the magic of science out into the world so it could shine with the joy of mysteries solved. She had wanted to make people say, "Wow, that's so cool," because the way the world interlocked and worked had always been a symbol of hope to her. All problems can be solved. All it would take is time.

It was reaching back a long way to remember what that had felt like.

A hotel that had hidden itself into the Pico Boulevard landscape had a bar. Two sips of Bushmills 10-year rolled all the stress out of her shoulders. Her mind stilled and she had the moment of peace she craved.

It was only a moment.

From a long way off, somewhere foggy in her brain, she wondered what had happened to the woman who'd paid her own way to be in person at the Jet Propulsion Lab for the Curiosity Rover landing and who had cried because it was so awesome and the engineers who'd designed the craft and its ingenious landing were crying too? Why was she gritting her teeth and wanting to find someone, *anyone*, to call a douchebag?

Why did she want to stay angry? Why did it feel as if anger was the only thing keeping her safe?

She finished the trail mix the bartender had offered her along with the rest of the single malt. Back at Simply the Best she made her way to the café for the undeniably refreshing iced tea. The employees who came and went chattered happily to each other, like they all knew some secret that eluded her, and she was jealous of that. And yes, jealous of

Pepper's clear admiration and respect for Helene. She was going to have to let it go if she wanted to get out of this assignment alive.

After listening to a bubbly and extremely savvy manager explain about the process of discovering and locally sourcing new, unique products from places like Kuala Lumpur and Micronesia, she moved on to a social media specialist—even younger than Pepper—who discussed in very general terms how they listened for suggestions of unmet needs and potential trends.

"I've been okayed to show you this example." The delicate bronze beads at the end of Darla's corn rows clicked softly as she moved.

"Great, it'll be better than in the abstract."

After tapping rapidly at her keyboard, she turned the monitor for Alice to more easily watch a short video of a perky brunette who fervently loved so many things with lemon zest. "This TikTok post had sideways virality. That means it didn't have deep spread in the expected audience, but a broad spread across multiple groupings— age, race, even income levels. We followed up in pockets and found ready acceptance to the idea that fruit zest is perceived to have higher quality, more artisanality, and premium differentiation."

Alice winced. *Artisanality?* "What did that lead to?"

Darla's narrow face lit up. "My suggestion for next spring's line got picked. That's a big deal. When you see "Simply the Zest" and "Zest for the Best" language, think of me."

"I certainly will. Good for you." Like she would have a choice. "I want to switch gears a little, if that's okay?"

"Sure."

"You sound like you're from the Bronx."

"Born, raised, and educated. PS 196, Bronx Community College, and Fordham."

"So the Bronx is in your DNA. What's something you love about living in California?"

Darla frowned in thought. "I didn't think I'd like ballgames here, but they have tacos and barbecue at Angels' games and not plastic American versions—the real thing. Like better than my nona's, but I shouldn't admit that." Almost as if she was afraid to know the answer, Darla asked, "How is it doing? The city?"

"Recovering. We still all hate each other—as you know, that's New Yorker for love."

"Love is the only thing you can count on to see you through hard times." Darla spread her hands in acceptance. "No real difference between New York and California on that one."

Alice walked out of the marketing building musing over what she'd learned.

She took a break at one of the shady picnic tables near the café and reviewed her notes in preparation for interviewing Clarita Oatley. Oatley had joined ST-Best right before it had launched as a national brand with its own product lines. Before that, there were mentions of her in New York trades as a model. She'd have been a natural for any line that put haughty in their haute couture.

When she strolled into Media Relations a few minutes before four, Yesenia's pleased smile was balm to Alice's battered ego.

"You're back."

"Is your archive room available? You said it usually is, and I made an appointment to interview someone. I won't need any materials."

"Yes, no bother at all." She tapped at her computer while treating Alice to a scarlet-lipped smile of pure flirtation. It turned to frustration when her desk phone rang. "The door is unlocked now. Maybe we'll see each other later?"

The woman's sidelong look was so good for Alice's ego that she nodded. Clarita arrived exactly on time, in keeping with ST-Best's corporate practice. Alice knew that being annoyed with it was irrational, but she couldn't help it.

"Thanks for doing this," Alice said as they got settled. "I'm going to record our talk, if that's okay. It keeps me accurate."

"That's fine." Clarita pulled her wheat-blond hair back on top of her head for a moment, then let it fall back to her shoulders in a gesture highly imitative of Helene. "Where shall we start?"

"Your bio says you're originally from New South Wales." The occasional swallowed *R* had made Alice look up her birthplace. "How long have you been living in the US?"

"Thirty years. I moved to New York after school. I spent a couple of years on the runway, trying to break into modeling, but that didn't work out, much as I hoped it would." Her voice held the echoes of relinquished dreams.

Alice shook her head at the inexplicable. "I would have thought you'd be a natural for it."

"Thank you." The ice blue eyes warmed ever so slightly. "I think you actually mean that."

"I do. You have all the ingredients, but there's no rhyme or reason to fame."

"One designer told me I needed to be three inches taller, another said my neck was too long." Her shrug was philosophical.

"How did you end up at Simply the Best?"

"Luck." Her answer was so prompt Alice knew she'd told the story before. "One day during Fashion Week I wandered into a Simply the Best pop-up store. And I loved the clothes. *Loved* them. Modeling gigs were getting rare. I took lessons to lose my accent, business classes at night, and I applied for any job they had open. I started as a PA and moved up." She paused for emphasis, and added, "Helene and I liked each other immediately. My responsibilities expanded rapidly, including primary oversight of the Composium, our most visible event."

After several minutes asking about the biggest changes Clarita had observed in the business, Alice segued to her feelings about their customers' resilience with wide swings in the economy and the effect of a global pandemic. Clarita's answers were guarded, and at every opportunity she credited Helene with the foresight and adaptability that had helped the company survive.

Not having expected less from someone who was a good corporate soldier, Alice felt completely comfortable with Clarita. She was exactly what she appeared to be—ambitious, guarded, career-focused, smart, protective, privileged, and loyal. Clarita used her many skills in the service of Helene Jolie and Simply the Best. She was everything that Pepper wasn't, at least not yet.

Alice stopped the phone recording. "This has been very helpful. I appreciate your candor."

"You're entirely welcome."

Alice added another few words to the notes she'd taken before she packed up her notebook and walked out with Clarita, who turned toward Helene's office. At the elevator Alice paused, telling herself she had no reason at all for going that direction as well.

Instead, she turned back the way she came and found Yesenia at her desk. "I know this is off the cuff, but I was wondering if Gail had a few minutes for a quick question."

A hopeful look faded slightly, but Yesenia's expression was still welcoming as she nodded. "I can see. Five minutes?"

"Not even."

After a short consult on the phone, Yesenia waved her in. Though nowhere near as large as Helene Jolie's, Gail Monteif's office was just as well appointed, with luxurious upholstery on the chairs and a small conference table set up for media displays and video conferencing.

"Thanks for letting me take you up on your open-ended 'if you need anything else.'"

Gail's accent held a hint of Queens. "What can I do for you?"

"I'd like to do a voluntary online survey of employees."

Gail's wariness was obvious in the set of her mouth. "Tell me more."

"Ask the former New Yorkers what they miss most. What they like best about California. What surprised them. And also ask the employees from California what they have learned about New Yorkers and what surprised them. Plus ask everybody what their favorite ST-Best product is. I think our design people would make some great infographics with the results. They'd be good social media postings to promote the series."

As she'd spoken, Gail's expression had lightened. "Very upbeat and positive—sure to cause heated discussions. New Yorkers and Californians do love to dunk on each other."

Her mother had been appalled when Alice said part of her job was thinking about how to attract social media attention to a story. It had never bothered her, though, because if it worked, people were talking about science. It had been a graphic she'd proposed on how to calculate carbon footprint that had gone viral enough to save her job the last time she'd chapped Ed's ass. Of course an unscientific survey wasn't exactly science, but at least it would have something like data behind it. She had to look for the silver lining somewhere.

"It's a sport we all agree is fun."

"That's something we should have thought of, maybe. How people adapt to new things is inherently interesting, and lord knows we've all been adapting the past few years." She nodded once. "I like it. I'll run it up the chain, and if it's a go, we can put a link to an online survey in the next all-employee bulletin. That's on Wednesday."

"Perfect. I'll draft some questions for you to use as examples. All wording will be agreed upon before anything goes live."

"Sounds great."

She paused at Yesenia's desk to thank her for getting her in to see Gail. "I really appreciate it. Let me know if I can repay the favor."

Her voice pitched slightly lower so as not to carry, Yesenia said, "Perhaps you could buy me a drink. If you don't have plans. I'd hate to think of you spending another lonely night in a hotel room." The slow blink through her long lashes, combined with a subtle shift of her shoulders was beyond flirtation. Her lips curved as if to dare Alice to admire them.

Alice had no doubt where any further conversation was going to lead. What had seemed too tiring to negotiate at home had a welcome appeal all at once. Her stomach tightened and the hair on the back of her neck raised in anticipation of a dance with a certain conclusion.

This is real, she told herself. Not some ridiculous fantasy that only happens in movies. She already knew the rules. Why was she hesitating?

Because even if you do remember how to feel good, you'll wake up with the wrong woman? She had taken too long to answer, because Yesenia dismissed her with an elegant shrug of one shoulder. "Or not. Go away with your fine self before I think of something else."

Alice allowed herself to be shooed out of the office. All the way to her car she kicked herself.

"You are such a loser," Sass announced. *"That would have been the most fun you were going to get out of this trip."*

"I'm not here for fun," she muttered. Doing anything that gave her pleasure didn't feel safe. She couldn't let her guard down. The sun, the stars, and a pair of brown eyes—they were all too dangerous.

CHAPTER TWENTY-TWO

Tuesday morning Pepper found six more items dumped on her desk that Helene wanted changed out. Even knowing Helene was out of the office until tomorrow didn't help her anxiety about getting it right. Clarita had also given her a large stack of spring line product descriptions with the assignment to flag any that Helene shouldn't even see yet—typos or misspelled vendor names in particular. That was going to take several hours and limited the amount of time she could spend going back and forth to the Boutique and the samples warehouse.

She worked smarter by going to the website to sift through the newest offerings in Best Bliss for likely candidates. The line was more affordable than most Simply the Best offerings, but of timeless fashion sense and designed for the woman just starting to build a work wardrobe. While the regular line had dozens of black trousers, Best Bliss had only two: lined and unlined. Well-made, tailored, inseams by the inch like men's for a better fit, and easily paired with any color or style accessories from the Best Bliss line. And, Pepper noted from personal experience, they had pockets big enough for her phone.

Though the day felt stressed and busy, it was a welcome distraction from hearing the whoosh of the elevator doors and looking to see if the arrival was heading in their direction, all the while telling herself that she didn't want to see familiar dark-rimmed glasses. She'd received an email with Alice's questions, had answered them, and agreed to a Thursday appointment when Pepper would shepherd Alice and a photographer along the path of a new product through the entire in-house production process.

Clarita frowned but accepted the news that Pepper would be in and out for the remainder of the afternoon getting everything together for Helene's office. Feeling liberated and cheered by the sun and breeze as she whisked between buildings with the golf cart piled high, she coasted to a stop to find Alice awaiting her arrival at the admin building doors. *Remember*, she told herself, *you are a consummate professional.*

"You've been shopping."

"It feels like it," Pepper admitted. "What can I help you with?"

"I'm on my way to Finance before I head to the Beverly Hills store for a tour. Allow me." Alice opened the main door and held it as Pepper juggled four stuffed tote bags with two shoe boxes under one arm.

"Thanks. And thanks," she added as Alice grabbed the shoe boxes that were threatening to fall. "I guess I shouldn't be playing the I-can-do-it-in-one-trip game."

"You nearly had it. Partial XP award, I'm sure."

She allowed herself a cool smile. The elevator doors opened as they walked up. "You got my note about Thursday?"

"Yes. The photographer is lined up. Someone we use from a local pool, so vetted."

The elevator's pace seemed glacial. "I'll have a guest pass waiting."

The doors opened and Pepper said a cheery, "See you then!" as she hustled toward her desk. Congratulating herself on keeping Alice at arm's length, she gave herself over to studying the accessories and especially the shoes she'd chosen, worried that they'd seem clunky next to a delicate infinity scarf and thin silk-wool blend gloves. She moved one belt six times and finally decided that its odd olive shade went with black and black alone. It was the only item in the line that didn't have multiple pairings—at least in her opinion.

The next morning she got to work ten minutes early to take one last look. True, it had taken her two hours to arrange what Helene would have done flawlessly in fifteen minutes. It was her first time, after all.

"Let me see what you've done."

She spun in place with a gasp. Helene was leaning against the doorjamb, stunning in a marled aquamarine cashmere dress, belted loosely with a dark bronze leather belt. The wide collar had slipped off one shoulder. Pepper reminded herself not to stare even as she envied the nonchalance that had never been her own style.

Helene began her review of the display shelves at the end closest to the door, studying the items as a visitor might on the way to Helene's desk. She shifted a candle and smoothed the aubergine blouse Pepper had used as a backdrop for Best Bliss's black leather belt. After a quick glance down the rest of the offerings, she frowned, picked up the belt in the peculiar olive shade from the other end and placed it against the dark purple blouse.

Her frown deepened. "I thought that would work, but it doesn't."

Pepper swallowed once to make sure her voice wouldn't break. "I had a hard time with the color. It only works with black. At least that's what my eye told me in afternoon and evening light. It seems worse in morning light."

Helene plucked the offending belt off the shelf and handed it to Pepper. "Your eye was quite right. Have it moved out of the Best Bliss line."

"Certainly. Right away, Helene." Pepper's heart was pounding.

"You need something else where it was."

"One moment." She sped out to her desk, tossed the belt on to it and grabbed up two of the items she had decided against. Helene was smoothing the line of the scarf that was one of Pepper's favorites—a lovely dark cranberry shade with a subtle pattern of polka dots in a contrasting color just close enough that the pattern was only visible in certain lights. "I started with these pieces, but I thought using both belts was more symmetrical." The Best Bliss gold-drop earrings and companion necklace popped against the black as they were meant to.

"*C'est bon*." Helene made a minor adjustment to the necklace position, brushing so close to Pepper that Pepper could smell bergamot and rosehips, a distinct combination in Simply the Best's most luxurious conditioner. "You continue to surprise me with how…" Helene tipped her head and regarded Pepper with slightly narrowed eyes. "How useful you are."

Her eyes were so very green, Pepper thought. The eyes, the bare shoulder—they were very distracting. Afraid that something inappropriate would show in her face, she turned toward the display to unnecessarily tweak the gold earrings. "Because it's Best Bliss, which is about being able to maximize use of an item, I wanted to juxtapose the colors and styles to show off their flexibility. Except for that belt."

"Have you seen the plans for the New York opening?"

"Only what's come across my desk."

"Why don't you go ahead and read through the design file, if you have time." Helene made as if to touch Pepper's shoulder, then drew back. "You've done something different with your hair. Or perhaps a *soupçon* more eye liner?"

Even as Pepper stammered that she didn't think so, Helene went on, "You seem to have a good grasp of what Best Bliss is all about, and part of the New York store will have Best Bliss on display."

"Except for that belt, I hope." Emboldened by Helene's indulgent smile, she added, "Which we shall not speak of again."

Helene's genuine laugh—a low, rolling bell of pleasure and approval—sent Pepper back to her desk feeling feverish and inordinately pleased.

Clarita observed her for a moment, and said, "I take it Helene likes the new display."

"I think so." Pepper picked up the poor olive-colored belt. "This didn't survive. We're going to remove it from the Best Bliss line. It doesn't go with anything but black."

"Really? What an extraordinary conversation you've had. I'll let them know."

Pepper stammered out, "I should do it." In answer to Clarita's surprised look, she blurted out, "I've observed she doesn't like being told someone else took care of something when she asked me to do it."

"Very well." Clarita gave her one last sharp look.

Pepper let the work of the day help her ignore feeling unsettled, flattered, and relieved all at once.

CHAPTER TWENTY-THREE

It was pure stubbornness that kept Alice from putting the top down on the convertible and also why she generally didn't want to acknowledge that it was a stunning southern California day. The temp was topping out in the mid-seventies with a light offshore breeze that made broad green palm leaves overhead slowly shift against a powder blue sky. She ignored all that and let her blood pressure rise for the nearly thirty minutes it took to travel six miles from the Simply the Best campus over to its Beverly Hills retail store.

The only option was valet parking. She asked if any of the stores validated only to receive an incredulous look from the valet.

"I guess if you shop in Beverly Hills you aren't worried about a mere twenty bucks to park," she muttered. She knew that Manhattan parking prices were certainly no less, but there was a subway line a couple blocks away from even the most posh of Fifth Avenue's shops.

The wide marble steps leading from the clogged street to the pedestrians-only "Walk of Style" were free of bubble gum and trash. If money had a smell, that's what filled the air, and fairness made her admit that there were parts of the Upper West Side that had the same sterile dust smell.

Stores like Tiffany's and Saks gleamed in the sunlight, but she noticed that small spaces where eateries had once been had not yet been filled with new restaurants. The big businesses seemed well recovered from the economic crashes. The small businesses—not so much. A universal reality, she knew that.

Typical of much of California, Rodeo Drive featured a pastiche of styles. Greek columns rose above Victorian streetlights. Venetian arches stood next to Art Deco stained glass along a street dotted with Op Art sculptures.

"Why pick one style, when you could have them all?" Sass snarked. *"Because if you're not having it all, you're doing it wrong."*

Give it a rest, she told herself sharply. Focus on the job. Get it done and get out alive.

Simply the Best did not attempt to match the marble columns and solid bronze door of the designer label across the narrow street. In contrast, Simply the Best's thick glass double doors were flanked by elegant white planters that held thriving azalea bushes bursting with hot pink blossoms. The understated display of autumn accessories was accompanied by a simple white sign in Simply the Best's corporate script: Your Best Fall is Here!

Wind chimes tinkled when she pushed open the left-hand door. Like the Simply the Best campus, the store featured the textured fabric wall coverings and whitewashed pine. Display racks were translucent. Merchandise was spaced so no apparel item touched another. A wide curving staircase to the upper floor was just like the one that led from reception to Helene Jolie's office. The banisters were twined with garlands of autumn leaves.

The light scent in the air of forest moss, with the faint edge of wet leaves and cut cedar, was fantastic. There was no way to deny that, though she childishly wanted to.

Several young women were huddled in the far corner devoted to beauty products. They sniffed bath soaps, body sprays, and hair conditioners, chattering with unfiltered comments of "yum-a-licious," "too old lady," "this is so you," and "I didn't know that's what frankincense smelled like." She was heartened by their spontaneity.

In contrast, an older woman with immaculately groomed platinum and honey I-want-to-speak-to-the-manager hair glared at them as she removed a scarf from its hanger, wrapped it around her wrinkle-free neck, only to discard it on the nearest table with a sigh of dissatisfaction. That was who Alice had thought was Simply the Best's customer base: someone with already so much and ready to blame anyone else for her discontent that she couldn't find more.

She glanced again at the younger women. Their presence defied her expectations about Simply the Best, the same way Pepper and some of the other employees did, while Helene Jolie and Clarita Oatley did not.

Crap-on-a-stick, the company and its wares were a nuanced issue. Right now the last thing she could handle was nuance.

Had the smiling, broad-faced young woman at the register not greeted her, she would have turned on her heel and escaped into the perfect sunlight, perfect day, surrounded by perfect people, all of which was so unfair.

"I have an appointment with Tessa Murphy."

"Tessa is expecting you. All the way from New York?"

She made it sound like the other side of the universe, and she wasn't wrong, Alice thought. "All the way from New York."

After a short conversation on her phone, the young woman cheerily informed Alice that Tessa would be right down. Alice drifted to the display of $30 dollar tights, noting the description included an unprovable claim of energy-enhancing properties. Well, it wasn't as if the five-buck drug store versions didn't claim the same thing.

She was admitting to herself that a pair of dark purple suede ankle boots with zippers down the back of the heel would be very sexy on the right woman when she heard light steps coming down the stairs. Tessa Murphy's gold-brown skin shimmered under the store lights, and her thick afro was caught back with a blue bandeau. They exchanged pleasantries, and Ms. Murphy answered all of Alice's questions about the ups and downs of the economy and the general retail theory behind the store's layout. She also shared insights about the difference between Beverly Hills' location deep inside a wealthy enclave and the store in Barcelona she'd also worked at.

"I was getting my master's at Universidad Autónoma. The store is at the northern end of La Rambla. Tourists, yes, but also career women, rich people, sometimes students looking for a nice gift for a friend or themselves. If you're sharing an apartment with four other people and living on potatoes and oranges, a special bar of soap can make life bearable. So we had all kinds of people there. Here my customer base is much more homogeneous."

After a few more questions she thanked Tessa for her time and went back out into the warm, sunny afternoon. She'd discovered nothing new and met yet another smart, motivated employee who was happy with the gig. More fodder for her series about the wondrous Simply the Best.

She had a few notes to revisit, so she walked in the direction of the Beverly Wilshire, where surely there was a bar with a fine selection.

And there was. She decided on Midleton Very Rare to accompany a sliced California Roll topped with more crab and alongside avocado yuzu soy dipping sauce. It was delicious and she didn't want it to be, even as she savored every bite. The whiskey, served in a heavy lead crystal cocktail glass and chilled with a whiskey stone, was aromatic with smoke and oak.

After a second glass she went over the notes from the day, though the only real truth she knew was that she didn't want to write any articles about Simply the Best. It was too messy now.

She'd expected to find—and mostly had—capitalism on steroids with all its usual trappings. Blind acceptance that if any practice made money it was good—yes. A cult-like reverence for the founder's vision—mostly. Selling insecurity to women and calling it empowerment—definitely.

Then there was the exploited workforce. She'd had to burrow for it, but a disclosure for a tax break application had yielded a summary chart of ST-Best's wage grades from three years ago, covering the entire spectrum from entry-level administrative to executive staff. It hadn't been hard to compare it to county and state reporting on regional wages.

Her takeaway was that in management wages, ST-Best paid ten to thirty percent below normal for the region. Compared to other companies, they hired a lot more women for those jobs, and ST-Best's annual report cheered that fact as well as its nearly all-female executive management team. It left out that they paid them less. All the empowerment aside, Helene Jolie was just another CEO maximizing shareholder value.

There was something off about the woman, too. Alice recalled Jolie's light touch to Pepper's back, the physical proximity, the intimate laughter—and Pepper's confusion. If Jolie were a man, Alice would know exactly what was going on. Was she hesitant to think Jolie might shop among her employees for paramours because she was a woman?

Power was power. Women were not immune to its corruption, even though Alice truly, deeply, wanted them to be. Watching Jolie's practiced charm knock the breath out of a smart, idealistic person had filled her with a despairing belief that the world was as broken as she thought it was.

She wanted to get back to a world where some things were simply black and white. Good or evil—no in-between. Like a Depression-era black-and-white movie where common people worked together to make sure the rich didn't always cut the line. Where congressmen were shamed by Jimmy Stewart for not doing The Right Thing. Where a funny blonde or winsome brunette had a career she loved, the respect of her colleagues, and still got the relationship of her dreams.

She knew those visions of America were part of the Hollywood dream factory, but she'd clung to those ideals long after the lie of it all was obvious. She was the kid who had believed in Santa for years after peers stopped, making the moment of accepting the truth all the more gutting.

She wanted it to stop. The loss, the lies, the callous cruelty from the people who were supposed to be better than that. She wanted a world where believing the vulnerable should get a vaccine before the strong wasn't considered idealistic liberalism instead of committed, common humanity. She did not want to watch the continual mounting evidence that too many people would choose their convenience and comfort over the life of other people every single time.

She wanted the hell out of Beverly fucking Hills. And she did not want to go back to those empty desks and the ghosts of tragedy that stalked her in New York.

The only place left for her, the only place that promised peace, was the bottom of a third round of whiskey.

CHAPTER TWENTY-FOUR

It was almost chilly when Pepper arrived at work Thursday morning, and she was glad of the dusty green jacket she'd paired with slim cut chocolate-brown trousers. She didn't think Alice Cabot had seen any of these apparel choices before—not that she'd dressed for the woman. She wanted to represent Simply the Best as best she could as she took Alice and the photographer around the campus.

She did not spend any time considering that this could be the last time she saw Alice. What did that matter to her? There was no need to dwell on it.

When her phone chirped to remind her it was ten o'clock, she was already halfway down the stairs to the lobby. Alice was talking to the receptionist, and an immaculately tailored man toting a heavy bag of camera equipment stood alongside.

"Pepper Addington, this is Rafael Hernandez. He'll be doing the photos for us today."

"Welcome to Simply the Best." Pepper shook hands and gestured at the door. "Where would you like to go first?"

Alice looked to Rafael for an answer.

"Given the forecast for scattered clouds around three, we should get outdoor shots done as soon as possible. There'll be no golden hour today, so no need to put it off."

Pepper assumed the role of chauffeur. Alice and Rafael spoke in a rapid shorthand, with Alice consistently deferring to Rafael's expertise. Hundreds of shutter clicks later, they ended up back at the administration building. Rafael took his leave, promising a digital array within a few days.

Pepper gave a friendly, final wave. "He really knows his business, doesn't he?"

"I was told I was lucky to get him."

"See you back here at two for your interview with Helene?"

"Sure."

For the first time Pepper let herself look directly at Alice. Her already lean cheeks were hollow. Had she eaten? *Don't do it*, she told herself. Alice Paul Cabot, superior New Yorker, knew where the food was. Though sharing a last meal would be appropriate, wouldn't it?

Her ear recognized the unmistakable, rapid tap of heels on the stairs. Helene was on her way to the lobby. So she said, inanely, "Be safe out there."

Alice glanced over Pepper's shoulder, then back at her before retreating toward the door. "See you at two."

"There you are. Clarita was sure you were still gallivanting with that reporter."

"We just wrapped up the session with the photographer. He seemed very competent, and the staff members who had pictures taken have all signed the necessary releases. I'll make a list of those who are chosen so they're aware and can be certain to get copies and help promote."

"How thorough. I'm hoping we can put this entire exercise behind us."

"The interview today at two is to wrap up."

With the twinkling smile that always left Pepper at a loss for words, Helene asked, "Is my car back yet?"

"Yes. I gave the keys to Clarita."

"You did?" Her gaze now fixed on the door, Helene took Pepper's arm. "Oh yes, I must have forgotten."

"I'll go up and get them," Pepper offered.

"Oh, no. There's no time now." Helene turned them toward the stairs. "I should go back up. But I'd like lunch."

"What can I get for you?"

Helene's laugh was low and intimate and brought a surge of heat to Pepper's face. "Surprise me."

There was no sign of Alice as Pepper hopped into the nearest golf cart and headed for the café. Helene had never told her to pick something out before. She was usually quite explicit and precise. At least Pepper knew how Helene liked her tea.

The seared ahi with tamari-sesame glaze on microgreens was acceptable. At least Pepper hoped that's what the vague wave meant when she set the plated meal—sans the green onions Pepper knew to remove—on Helene's desk. She retreated to her own workspace and tackled the To Do list for the first of the invitation-only soft openings for the New York store. The store manager, Patty O'Neil, had provided two dozen A-list names. For some reason, her own assistant was having trouble verifying availability, and Clarita had passed the responsibility to Pepper.

It was slow going as she juggled making calls to social secretaries and answering incoming calls. Only when Alice quietly cleared her throat did Pepper realize the time.

"How can it be two already?"

"Our current minimal understanding of time suggests that entropy—"

"You know what I mean."

Alice did look wan behind the glasses. *She's a big girl*, Pepper sternly reminded herself. "Helene is on a call that will end in a minute."

"Good. Listen, you've been great. I got so much done a lot more quickly because you gave me so much of what I needed, made appointments... I was wondering if we could maybe get that margarita."

"Oh." It was unexpected, but not, Pepper realized with a flush, unwelcome. *So much for professional distance.* "Tonight is out—having dinner with my parents."

"Tomorrow night then? Before I head back to New York?"

Pepper had been trying not to think about that, but really, how childish not to accept it was inevitable. "That would be great."

"You pick the place—you did say great margaritas were everywhere."

"I did, didn't—"

"Pepper, if Ms. Cabot is ready."

Pepper hadn't realized Helene was standing in her office doorway watching them.

"See you tomor—thank you for your help," Alice said.

"You're welcome," Pepper answered automatically.

She refocused on her work, but it took several minutes to clear her mind of the inevitable reality of Alice's impending departure.

There was no reason for it to matter.

It didn't matter, she told herself. She would look forward to dinner as a pleasant and appropriate way to close the chapter on a work assignment.

She started when Helene emerged almost immediately.

"What is your progress on the soft opening invites for evening one?"

"I'm nearly done. One last confirmation."

"In just a few hours? Patty's assistant was working on it for a week." Helene cocked her head with a glint in her eyes Pepper hoped was never directed at her. "It may be unfortunate for her that you're so competent."

Pepper didn't know what to say to that, but her nervous laugh seemed to be all that was required. Helene returned to her office. She shot a glance at Clarita, who was staring after Helene.

"Well," Pepper muttered, "I guess I'd better go on being competent."

PART SIX

Fireworks

CHAPTER TWENTY-FIVE

"Let's sit at the table again."

Helene gestured in that direction and Alice dutifully resumed the chair she'd used for the first interview not quite a week ago and set out her notebook and phone to record. Helene paused, excused herself, then went back to the outer office.

A moment later Alice heard a nervous laugh from Pepper and Helene returned, her expression silky with satisfaction. Her gaze met Alice's briefly and narrowed.

Helene Jolie knew how to make a person feel like they were in trouble. A subtle purse of the lips with a minute lift of the eyebrow had left Pepper ashen. Fortunately, even before Alice had called a congressman a douchebag she'd been used to people trying to convince her she was making a big mistake. They didn't want her to print that they were buying up energy patents and hiding better tech from the world to keep profiting on fossil fuels as long as possible. Or that research findings benefited the people who'd paid for the research.

Some shouted, but that wasn't Helene's style. She'd deliver a threat with the nonchalance of impunity.

Alice had never worried about reprisals for the truth. Getting fired for telling the truth was a badge of honor. Getting fired for not pleasing the likes of Helene Jolie was something else entirely.

Bad timing for her to realize she should have simply quit. She was capable of writing nothing but happy truths about Simply the Best, but it was not in her nature to ignore the unhappy ones. And here she was, with Helene Jolie looking at her with that practiced, so charming smile.

"I want to thank you for the hospitality and cooperation I've received. Your staff is exceptional and accessible."

"I'm pleased to hear that."

"I have some preliminary observations that form the general structure of the series, which is six print and two digital-only articles. Starting with article one. Opening with the ubiquity of Simply the Best's products and how they're marketed to different kinds of women. Leading to sidebar of corporate stats, with some corporate history." She glanced at her notes. "Product stats, such as number of bars of soap sold in a day. How many women are likely to be wearing something from Simply the Best any given Friday in corporate America. Our stats people say they can be defensibly accurate with the data I've sent them. Close with corporate structure and brief bios of the woman at the helm and some of the women behind the woman."

Helene nodded. She did not look impressed.

"Second article on the marketing of empowerment, to give a small amount of airtime to the critics who say that Simply the Best is like every other company that markets to women based on the desire for perfection."

"We're not like any other company."

"I didn't say you were. Critics say you are. I need to air that before continuing with the ways that Simply the Best is different and how that has turned into a business strategy."

Helene's nod was tight with suspicion.

"Article three will be purely fun and the results of the surveys asking New Yorkers and Californians to talk about each other. I assume Gail ran that by you?"

"Yes." There was an infinitesimal thawing in the hard green eyes. "I agree, it should be very fun and a social media hit."

As Alice continued her outline, she could feel a growing knot in her stomach. Helplessness. A feeling of complicity. She was sliding down a slippery slope and the only way she knew how to quiet it was with whiskey. A lot of whiskey. She should have had a drink at lunch instead of a Simply the Best Café iced tea.

"With all that said, I have a few questions for you for the final article, which gets more personal."

"Go ahead."

Softball question. "Do you spend a lot of time thinking about how many people see you as the embodiment of the modern woman? Poised, graceful, smart, and unapologetically ambitious?"

"I don't spend any time thinking about it."

"Seriously," Alice chided with a smile. "You—your visage, your style—all part of the marketing plan."

"It's not my goal to be the embodiment of anything. I look at myself as I am, and Simply the Best reflects that. I don't believe that I've ever changed myself for the sole reason of being more...marketable. For example, I never hid that I was gay. Some people would have and still do."

Alice nodded, in complete agreement. "I've also noticed your inclusive HR policies and that you are a donor to Pride and LGBTQ groups. But I don't see Pride Month or corporate support celebrated on the site."

"I don't hide my life, but I do try to keep private life and business separate."

Annoyed by the picking and choosing of what was personal and what her company would leverage, Alice observed in as mild a tone as possible, "But you have blogged about the circumference of your vagina."

Helene laughed, though she clearly wasn't amused. "Women's bodies are nothing to be ashamed of. I've blogged about being gay and supporting gay policies. We don't do features about Women's History Month either. Other people are doing that. We don't do what other people do."

"I can't argue with the continuing success of your brand."

"I wish I could say it was hard. It doesn't seem so to me." Helene dripped practiced charm. "We're a business. We learn what our customers want and sell it to them."

"Or convince them they want it." It was out before Alice could stop it.

Sure enough, a sharp, hard line appeared between Helene's eyebrows. "The essential and much lauded iconic American auto industry convinces people they need a new leased car every other year, and they do so to cheers from economists and politicians." Helene tapped her index finger on the table. "Why should my company have a different standard?"

Because... Alice clamped her teeth on her tongue and counted to five. "Because you don't do what other people do? Because your entire ethos is about empowering women?"

"Because women earn less than men, I should charge less for my products?"

"Claiming 'sisterhood' when you charge *more* for your products seems counter-productive, if not co-opting the concept of sisterhood to sell stuff."

Helene moved as if she was going to get up but leaned into the table instead. "Is that what you really wanted to write about all along? How I'm not a feminist if I make a profit off women?"

Alice did her best to keep her posture relaxed. "That's not it at all. You are phenomenally good at what you do. I would love to write about you using your brains, money, and all your charisma to do something that helped women in a permanent and lasting way."

Helene's words were increasingly staccato. "Empowering women to control their work, home, and personal environments helps all women. Encouraging women to believe that their dreams are realistic and valid helps all women."

"It makes women's empowerment an awesome accessory you can buy and not a necessity for survival. You're selling trappings, not change."

"Change is not my responsibility," Helene snapped.

Aware that their voices were rising and helpless to stop herself, Alice snapped back. "Yet you take credit for changing women's lives. You use the word over and over. Lifting women up—at least those who can afford your goods. But what about your employees? Aren't they women too?"

Helene shook her hair back, taking her time to answer. "I don't know what you mean."

"Did you know that your Graphic Design Department is a mind-boggling twenty-five percent intern workforce? Interns who get a stipend once every three months that won't rent a bedroom for month in the entire region?"

"And work experience that will help them land very nicely in their next job."

"There are no interns in Legal or Human Resources, however. Couldn't you say the same thing about their prospects? Or is it that those employees know more about matters such as overtime rules?"

"That's absurd. We're not doing anything that isn't industry standard practice."

"Exploiting them financially is helping them out? Isn't that what men say when they underpay women?"

"I'm not responsible for what men say or do."

"But you'll use the patriarchy's playbook to increase the wealth of a few women and declare it a victory for all women, regardless of the means. Even if it's other women with heel marks in their backs."

The red hair and red, red lips were blots of color in a face frozen with icy rage. "This is not what was agreed upon."

"You're absolutely right. The series I'm writing will make you happy. It will make your friend the managing editor's daughter-in-law happy. Your Manhattan store launch will have a perfect piece to set it up." Alice took a breath to calm her racing heart. "But I thought it was important for us to understand each other. This has been an illuminating discussion, thank you."

"I'm very clear on your opinion and deeply concerned about what will be in your paper." She shook her hair back from her face, and Alice could only see the sharp, feral glint in her eyes.

"We have ground rules about that."

Helene's lips were stiff with outrage. "This interview is over." She stood up so quickly the chair stuttered backward a few inches. "Over."

Helene stalked over to her desk and snatched up a folder. Alice packed up her notebook. From the door she said, "Thank you for your time," and left the seething silence behind her.

Their voices had carried. That was evident from the angry horror on Clarita's face. She risked a glance at Pepper and was met by a frozen gaze of shock and incomprehension.

"What just happened?"

Alice paused long enough to say, "We came to an understanding," before making her way down the curving stairway, through the exquisite shafts of color pouring down onto the pale tile floor and out into the warm, green, impossible—annoyingly impossible—autumn day.

Fuck California, and fuck Helene Jolie.

The convertible was finally paired to her phone, and she cranked Incubus to eleven to silence her brain. The verses battered at the windows while the throb of the heavy metal chorus tested the limits of the speaker's bass.

Without any memory of driving there, she was again at the nearby hotel bar. She tossed back the first shot of Midleton and carried a second to a booth. She was completely untethered from purpose, from knowing what she'd do now.

Other than have another drink.

CHAPTER TWENTY-SIX

"Pepper?"

Ever since Alice had bolted from the interview yesterday, Pepper had expected any summons from Helene to end with her termination. Helene was obviously upset and had vented in a long face-to-face with Gail Monteif. She'd overheard some of what Alice had said. Alice wasn't wrong about the way interns were used when the company was so profitable, but—surely there could have been another way to say it.

Though she'd not heard from Alice, they technically still had dinner plans in a few hours. She was so certain she was going to lose her job that she hadn't even told CC. CC had been out anyway, leaving Pepper to mope and worry in solitude.

She didn't want to go back to borrowing money from her parents. She didn't want to start over somewhere else and with no references.

Her legs were trembling as she presented herself in front of Helene's desk, notebook in hand.

"I've come to a decision."

Pepper felt faint.

"Peggy O'Neil's assistant in New York seems incapable of anticipating a single issue. Though I'm very upset with that reporter's rude and unprofessional behavior, you handled her well." Helene rose from her desk, outlined by the setting sun. "I'm up against the wall in New York, so I'm making you the assistant in charge of the soft openings and gala. You're my only hope that competence can be restored."

She wasn't being fired. The relief rose through her body like a balloon, leaving her euphoric. "I'll do my absolute best."

"Starting tonight. You need to catch up." She gestured at a stack of folders and an ungainly roll of blueprints on the conference table. "I'll walk you through every aspect of my thoughts. Call Pesca's and order dinner. *Pour deux.*" She waved a hand. "Find someone to fetch it."

Clarita observed Pepper's wobbly return to her desk. "And?"

"I'm primary assistant on New York." Pepper realized her voice sounded as terrified as she felt.

Clarita went rigid. "What?"

"We're going to go over absolutely everything tonight."

Sharpness gone, Clarita almost smiled. "Oh. I see."

Too shaken to ask what Clarita saw, Pepper said, "I'm to order dinner from Pesca's and send someone to get it. Who do I ask?"

Clarita shrugged and turned back to her work. "If you can't manage to get dinner here, how will you manage New York?"

Clarita was right—it was time to focus. After a deep breath, she grabbed her phone to text Alice, *I don't know if we were still on for dinner, but I just found out I have to work tonight.*

Her finger hovered over the button for a moment, then pressed Send.

Pesca's was always the choice for Helene's working dinners, and Pepper knew the menu well. She'd never ordered for herself, though. Given that Helene had had carbs with lunch, Pepper thought the duck medallions on a bed of steamed spinach and kale, lemon herb sauce on the side, would be okay. It traveled well. For herself she settled on the much less expensive chicken roulade with quinoa and marinated hearts of palm.

Her phone chirped. Alice had responded, *I understand. Thank you again.*

She dithered over the dinner order and didn't think about the fact that she might never see Alice again. It was ridiculous to feel anything at all about it.

Dinner—order the dinner. She didn't have an assistant to send, and anyone who might have done her a favor in return for first dibs on future swag had probably gone home. A delivery app? It needed to be perfect. The driver had to check it.

She ordered the two meals and added a 50 percent tip on the condition that the driver arrived at Pesca's before the meal was even ready, checked it for correctness, especially the presence of the sauce, and then delivered it right away. Then she called Pesca's and told them which order was Helene's so they knew. Helene had helped bankroll the restaurant, and she and the now celebrity chef went way back. She had to trust that everything would be fine.

Dinner on the way, she quickly took a bio break, then returned to Helene's office, hair tidy, lipstick reapplied. "Dinner should be here in thirty minutes. Would you like a Pellegrino?"

Helene glanced at her watch and pursed her lips. "Very well, if we're waiting that long."

Clarita looked up from her desk as Pepper passed by with the bottle and glass on a tray. "Enjoy your evening."

"There seems to be a lot of work."

"A great deal, I'm sure."

Pepper wished her a pleasant evening and set the water within Helene's reach as she sat at the conference table.

"We're at a crossroads, Pepper." Helene absentmindedly poured water into the glass. "My instinct says this opening is crucial to my hope of elevating the brand and recovering our prestige in New York. Influencers in NYC were very angry when we left. Now Fifth Avenue needs us like never before."

"I understand."

"It's likely that you don't." Helene added a smile to the words, taking out the sting. "But let's see if you can catch up."

Pepper found weights for the blueprints as Helene unrolled them. The centerpiece of the ground floor of the store was Simply Detox Destination, which included new products Pepper hadn't been aware of. There was a dizzying number of people involved in the opening, across the company and several prominent vendors, quadrupling her span of contacts in just a few minutes.

Their dinner was delivered by the time Helene had gone over the blueprints, zone by zone, and explained where she wanted food and bar setups. It had only been twenty-five minutes, and Pepper hurried down to collect the bags from the driver waiting at reception. She verified that Helene's meal was perfect, approved the tip, and sent the driver on her way. In the mini-kitchen she warmed up the containers, then plated the hot food and set out silverware. It was strange to be doing so for herself. The savory aromas sent her stomach into a hunger spasm.

Helene pursed her lips slightly as Pepper set down the tray. "Wine?"

"Of course," she said quickly. "What would you like?"

"It's duck."

The wine choices that Helene kept on hand for dinner meetings were limited. CC had drilled a simple rule into Pepper's head: it was always safe to presume that the darker the meat the darker the wine. So a red wine, and she had a 50/50 chance. "Pinot noir?"

She flooded with relief at Helene's slight nod and fetched a bottle. Once the wine was poured, Pepper followed her mother's coaching for meal etiquette: wait for your host. She picked up her fork moments after Helene did and began with a small bite of her chicken, then a sip of wine. Inside part of her was shouting, "*OMG, you're having dinner with Helene Jolie!*"

"The tricky part," Helene said over the top of her wineglass, "is that we want to embrace the people who matter, embrace them very closely and publicly. The soft opening events and the gala are, first and foremost, to put specific people in our store and get those photographs into media."

"Of course." Get the A-listers in, it made perfect sense. "The first evening is mostly done."

"That's the easy one—they're all our ardent fans and friends. That the assistant couldn't even take care of that didn't bode well for evenings two and three. Evening two is about envy. It needs the kind of people who will make others regret the fervor of their previous condemnation of the brand and me. That's what that assistant in New York couldn't seem to grasp. We can't just move people from one night to another and send the right messages."

Pepper managed to continue eating as she rapidly wrote down names she didn't know how to spell, creating lists: *Must* for the exclusive soft openings two and three, *Invite* for the charity gala where attendance would be in the hundreds instead of the dozens, and *Oops* sorry we overlooked you.

"Everyone is used to a certain amount of incompetence, so if one of the Oopsies calls demanding access, explain that you made an error and the event is full."

"Okay." So she was going to have to lie?

Uncertainty must have been in her voice, because Helene looked up from her forkful of greens. "It comes with the job. Don't be too sincere in your regrets. Most will get the message when you don't offer a Wait List. It's the way it's done."

She reminded herself that this was the job she'd wanted. It wasn't as if she hadn't seen similar machinations in her parents' social circle. Adoration was plentiful, while invitations got "lost in the mail." She was certain that if she ever saw Jasmine again, that would be the explanation for the lack of wedding invites for her old high school chums.

Helene poured them both a second glass of wine. "What is dessert?"

"The small mocha pot de crème. They're chilling in the refrigerator."

"Chef Finn always knows what I like."

Irritation she might have felt for Helene's friend getting the credit for Pepper's choices was lost in the subtle, sensual edge in Helene's voice—almost a purr. The images it conjured in Pepper's brain were disquieting, and it was hard to shake them even when the mature part of herself stamped each and every one with "Inappropriate!"

After the dinner dishes were cleared away, Pepper expected to return to the soft opening plans, but she found Helene standing at the window, gazing across the golf course where the clubhouse was festooned with white lights. The rolling landscape was silhouetted against the nearly full moon.

Uncertain what to do, she paused, leaving Helene to her thoughts.

"*Après le déluge, la lune.*" After perhaps thirty seconds, Helene added, "Success is a lonely business."

When Pepper could find nothing to say, Helene turned to face her. "Don't you think that's true?"

"I don't think I've had enough success to know."

"You will someday, and then you can tell me if you find it lonely too." Helene sighed. "Should you get any questions while making calls to confirm guests, I will be attending solo. I'm single again."

"I'm so sorry," Pepper said. Maybe that was why Helene's manner seemed so odd. "As my friend Beth would say, it's the bitch's loss."

Helene's eyes went wide as Pepper clapped a hand over her mouth, then she laughed, a deep, from-the-gut laugh that went on long enough to hint that tears might not be far behind. Pepper fetched the tissue box from the conference table and Helene dabbed at the corners of her eyes.

"You…" Helene paused to drop the tissue into the trash. "You are quite possibly too sweet for this job, but I suppose New York will rub some of that off of you."

"N-New York?"

"I'll be traveling to New York on my own several times next month, of course. You will join me on the Sunday before the opening. See to your air tickets—business class. You will no doubt need to work on your flight. The staff at the brownstone will prepare a room for you. I'll need reservations at Le Cigare Volant on Monday evening. The theaters are dark on Monday, so see if Harris Telemacher can join me for dinner. Who knows if the newspaper series will happen now, so I will need to be in the spotlight to get positive buzz circulating. You can use Monday to prepare for the last-minute deluge of mistakes other people will of course make. Eight a.m. Tuesday block out a mandatory meeting for all staff who will be on shift during any of the events, followed by a walk-through. Everything must be perfect, without exception, by the time we open the door for our first guests that evening."

Pepper belatedly grabbed her notebook off the conference table, while taking in that she was going to New York the Sunday before the grand opening. She needed an appropriate wardrobe for a week in New York, including their high-end swanky parties.

"Do you have that?"

Pepper nodded. "Yes. I didn't realize I would be traveling to New York as well."

Helene frowned. "The Composium this year is absorbing more of Clarita's time than ever before. I can't count on the assistants in New York, so of course you will be at my side. If you survive that long."

Pepper felt as if her brain was spinning in place. "I'll do my best."

Helene ran her hand slowly through her hair with a tired sigh. "If you're done with your notes, I'd like to go home."

"Yes, I'm done. See you Monday."

Helene was still near the window and Pepper couldn't clearly see her face, but her tone was much warmer as she asked, "Do you have special plans for the weekend?"

"A friend has her first gallery opening tomorrow evening. We're all so excited for her."

"Sounds diverting. You deserve to enjoy yourself."

"It will be fun."

There didn't seem to be anything else to say, so Pepper tucked her notebook into her desk and gathered her things. She could hear the chunk of a printer and the murmur of conversation from the direction where the finance staff seemed to work all hours. Nevertheless, the echo of her footsteps across the deserted lobby was disconcerting.

She gave herself a minute in the car to gather her wits. She'd been given a huge new responsibility, and that came with the real risk of epic failure.

Part of her knew the feeling well. When the perfect wave arrived, you had to choose to ride it. Once the choice was made there were only two outcomes—a glorious ride to the safe shore or a wipe out, with or without a board to the head.

Choosing the risk was not new to her. She knew how to choose, and she knew how to accept the result. But there was more than a wave forming in front of her. It was an ocean of details, all of them of equal importance to Helene.

She was elated, like when she'd first landed the job. Still gut-deep afraid that the slightest misstep would get her unceremoniously canned as another failure. She had to move faster, think better, anticipate, anticipate, anticipate. All the while the waves would keep getting bigger, and bigger, and bigger.

Wasn't it inevitable that eventually she'd get smacked off the board by a wave she never saw coming, suck salt water up her nose, and surface just in time for the board to give her a concussion? In this case, a concussion that wiped out more than a year of her life and left her starting all over again?

There was something else, layered under the rush of the afternoon, dinner, the wine, and the effort it took to give Helene her utter and complete attention. It didn't surface, however, until she saw a red convertible ahead of her in traffic.

For a moment her heart pounded high in her throat. Not the right model to be Alice, but still…

She didn't give herself time to think about it. She pulled into a parking lot and idled long enough to text, *I don't know if you will have left for home, but a friend is having a gallery opening tomorrow night. Maybe we could meet there and have dinner after?* She added a link to the event info and pressed Send.

All the windows down to let in the fresh, cool night air, she cranked K/DA's "Pop/Stars" and sang *loud loud loud loud*. She didn't want to think about Alice for a few minutes, worried that a text would bring her *down down down down*.

It was odd that CC wasn't home and gaming on a Friday night. She wanted to talk about everything but didn't want to all at the same time. She opened a Corona and sat numbly at the table for a very long while, trying not to feel anything when an answer from Alice never came.

CHAPTER TWENTY-SEVEN

When Alice opened her email Friday morning, she expected a message from Ed about yesterday's disastrous interview. Helene Jolie wasn't the type not to use leverage she had, but her mailbox was empty. The hangover headache didn't abate until after a lunch of crackers and peanut butter. Even then, all light felt like bolts of lightning stabbing into her eyes.

More crackers finally settled her stomach. Focusing on work also helped, especially after she outlined deks and ledes for each of the articles. It was a relief to let go of the content and think only about how to organize the presentation of data to the reader. By the time the light suggested the afternoon was waning she was stiff from the chair and thoroughly bleary eyed.

At least she had a pile of work to point at. The lack of communication from Ed suggested that maybe Helene Jolie was taking a wait-and-see approach. Or waiting for the perfect time to make a call to the daughter-in-law of the managing editor.

There was also the matter of dinner with Pepper. After the way the interview had ended, Alice wasn't sure they were still going to dinner. Pepper hadn't texted. But it was getting late to make any plans.

Just as Alice screwed up her courage to ask if they were still on and where should they meet, her phone beep-booped with a text from Pepper. Working late. Very sorry.

Having expected it, Alice told herself she wasn't disappointed. She believed the excuse—she was certain Helene had overheard their plans. Maybe she wouldn't call Alice's editor, yet, but she was making her displeasure plain through Pepper. Pepper was possibly too naive to even realize it.

Or I'm too old and too jaded to accept a coincidence.

Damnitall.

Recalling the Pacific Coast Highway traffic and length of the drive, Alice decided the scant two miles from her digs to the Sinking Tide was a more than doable walk. She walked that far all the time at home, especially when nice weather made a walk infinitely more pleasant than the subway or bus. There was enough sun to get there, and she could always order a ride back.

Earbuds in place, she set off in jeans and a tee with a NASA ball cap to shade her eyes. She paused to catch her breath at the top of the pedestrian walk that crossed over the Pacific Coast Highway. The bumper-to-bumper traffic under her faded to a dull roar. All at once she was lost in the patterns of dark blue water edged in sea foam pouring across and then receding along the miles of flat, tan beaches. There was no wind to speak of, and the ocean surface was an easy, smooth, rise and fall, almost as if it were sleeping.

She was glad she'd chosen a Bach playlist. There was comfort in the logic of Bach—doubles, reverses, upside-downs, and staggers exploded one simple theme into a universe of combinations. The playful humor behind the mathematical rigor seemed very much like the surf. Variations in every wave, but underneath was inexorable nature at work, doing what it does. She could hear the sharp caws of the seagulls above the music, but she didn't mind. Bach and tide made sense at the moment, and it was enough.

Walking on the beach was easier than navigating up, down, and around the Santa Monica Pier complex. Under the pier were gatherings of sea gulls watching her with resentful eyes. She made the mistake of getting between a few and a french fry tossed from above and knew what Tippi Hedren had felt like as they swarmed past her squawking *mine my mine my mine*.

The sand on the still sunny side of the pier radiated warmth into her feet. It made sense to shuck her sneakers and enjoy the fine grit between her toes. Simply the Best's spas sold a special Malaysian sand for buffing skin, along with a questionable history of native cultural worship. It included using "shaman" as a verb.

Screw that. She was getting a foot buff for free. Then she chided herself for thinking about Simply the Best, and Helene Jolie, and Pepper's hair in the wind...

She tapped open her phone. Expecting to go to voice mail, she was surprised when Simon gruffly answered, "You still alive, girl?"

"Not only am I alive, I'm walking on a beach."

"Get out. Is that a sea gull?"

"Yes. Like pigeons, only extroverts. They'll dive bomb people for ice cream." His easy chuckle eased an ache inside her. "I'm not making that up—there's a sign warning about it. How go the playoffs?"

"You caught me between innings. I have about twenty seconds. Any special reason for calling?"

"I'm done here. See you on Monday at McGinty's?"

"You won't see me until probably Halloween. I'm covering the Series too."

"We'll wear costumes, then. Congrats on the gig."

"Thanks. Batter's up, gotta go."

The call ended and Bach resumed. The Sinking Tide was now in sight with only a few more minutes to go. It only took a few taps to book a flight for the next day. People didn't generally choose to fly into New York on a Saturday night, let alone into the pit known as LaGuardia. The ticket still cost more than the paper would reimburse. *Thank you again, dearly departed forebear, for your rapacious capitalism.*

The Sunday brunch crowd in swimsuits streaming salt water everywhere had given way to a slightly more upscale but equally relaxed clientele, all in a festive mood as they cheered a baseball game. Probably the one Simon was covering. She was glad to score a table at a window where she could turn her gaze to the setting sun.

The Sinking Tide even had a sunset menu, and Alice downed a succession of local craft brews while enjoying every bite of an open-faced crab sandwich on grilled sourdough and a spinach and shredded apple salad topped with chunks of a blue cheese made up north. While she savored her meal the sun was fully embraced by the darkening ocean, painting over the sky with smoky crimson and dusty orange.

As much as she wanted to sit there all night, stuck in one moment in time, the past wouldn't stay out of her thoughts. There were ghosts around every corner. Ghosts of the six Metro and Health reporters who'd died in the first wave of the pandemic, before anyone had known how bad it would get. Mad Dog, the line editor she hadn't known was Jamal until she'd read his obituary. Ghosts of her ideals about common cause against ignorance. Ghosts of reason and science and decency. Ghosts of the way she had thought her life would be.

The future clamored too. A future doing a job that no longer called on her to use the skills she had always believed were her contribution to the world. A future full of the loneliness she saw overtaking her mother and without even the memory of a long-ago great love for comfort.

When the waiter delivered the bill instead of asking if she'd like another beer, Alice took the hint and made her way back to the sand. It was still radiating heat, but the night air was cooling quickly. So much for her Friday night. If she could have managed to keep her temper, she might be still looking at Pepper over dinner and margaritas.

She tried to force herself to relax and simply enjoy the bright lights of the Pier's Ferris wheel churning against the sky. The moon was nearly full and rising. She took the stairs up to the Pier in search of a warm drink and found hot cocoa. Why didn't any of it make her happy? Why did she look at the soaring canopy of stars and think again about the warning of Icarus? She wanted a drink. Needed to feel safe. Find her footing again.

Her mother answered on the first ring. "What's all that noise? Where are you?"

"Friday night on the Santa Monica Pier. Hang on." She clambered down the stairs to the beach. "That's better."

"You're still in Los Angeles?"

"Flying home tomorrow."

"How has it gone?"

"I didn't call anyone a douchebag."

"But the tone of your voice says something else may have been said?"

Alice went around a break in the shoreline that let the tide come too close to her bare feet. "I may not have been able to disguise some of my skepticism about their...policies. The final interview ended abruptly."

"I see."

She waited.

"Did you call her a name?"

"No."

"Was it ethical?"

"Yes."

"So what's the problem?"

"It wasn't the assignment. It could get me fired for good."

"There are worse things than being fired for asking ethical questions."

"You think I should have turned down the assignment to begin with?"

"I didn't say that. You chose and now you have to deal."

"I'm not dealing well. The series will be what everyone wants. I won't be particularly proud of it, but I won't be ashamed either. At least not a lot." Alice reached the bottom of the curving concrete stairs of the pedestrian bridge. The highway was still bumper-to-bumper. It suddenly felt like too much to climb and she plunked down on the sand. "The world is so fucked up, Mom. Nothing I do makes it any better."

"The last time you talked like this was after that superbloom incident."

Alice's breath caught at the memory. That was it—that was *exactly* how she felt, though no single incident like it had happened. "I think you're right."

"What got you out of the mood back then?"

She thought about it while studying the moonlit reflection of white foam marking the tide line. "I'm not sure anything did. It all got buried under elections, chunks of the Arctic melting, Siberia turning green, and pandemics, nearly four million dead, vaccine line jumpers, and unending science denial—and all of it. I feel like I haven't had a chance to catch my breath."

"I know what you're feeling, Al. I really do."

"Just modern life?"

"There's nothing modern about it. It's life. I've had more than my share of golden days when peace was inside and out. But they're still an exception. The world is awash with pain and injustice, grief and tragedy. You and I are lucky enough to know it doesn't have to be that way, but far too many people don't know any other reality."

"I know. I can quit my job and still pay the rent. But I don't want to quit. It feels like admitting that science and facts no longer matter."

"You can regroup if you have to. Give yourself a break and find room to catch your breath."

"It's getting late to start over."

"Pish."

Alice cocked her head. "Did you just say 'pish' to me?"

"Don't make me say 'tosh' as well."

"Okay, I won't."

"Al. The world is a shitshow most of the time. The older we get the more we can't not see it. And I am twenty-plus more years along the diminished job opportunities pipeline."

"Can't I whine a little bit?"

"You're having a cheese plate with your whine, and you're whining about what's only an inconvenience to you versus a tragedy."

"I'm not sure I can tell the difference." Alice knew her mother's eagle ear wouldn't miss that her lower lip was out.

"Then you do need a break to get your perspective back."

She pushed her feet down into the sand. "I'm not sure a California beach right out of a Hollywood production is a place to get perspective."

"It's a fake beach?"

"No, it's real—"

"A real beach sounds like a treat."

"I wish—I don't know why I can't let myself enjoy it without resenting it at the same time."

"That sounds like something you should think about."

Adrift in conflicting data that refused to form a coherent picture, Alice was grateful that her mother was a north star. "Thanks for talking."

"I'll always talk, sweetie. Come see me when you're home again."

With her shoes back on she began the climb up the stairs, pausing halfway up to look at the view. The sky had darkened and the moon was so brilliant a white ring of light surrounded it. Venus reflected the sun with a hot white light as well, just above the arc of the neon that outlined the Ferris wheel. The black velvet ocean was dotted with the bobbing red and yellow lights of craft in the distant shipping lane. Much closer to shore a dinner cruise was heading out to sea, leaving raucous music and laughter in its wake.

Perfect lives, perfect view, perfect night. The perfection of it all wasn't a lie—the air was cool and crisp. The stars and moon were lovely, and sailing into the night would be very fun.

It was also the perfect life to fly a helicopter into the middle of wildflowers in rampant bloom due to a once-in-a-decade combination of rain, temperature, and sun. All the Instagram selfies of it said so.

When the National Park Service had announced the first signs of a superbloom several years ago across a wide expanse of California's inland desert, she'd felt very lucky to already be in Phoenix. She'd started out before dawn and arrived at one of the Death Valley vistas before noon. The crowds were sparse—tens of thousands were flocking to poppy fields closer to the coast, parking on the freeway, and going off trail into the flowers.

The desert, though, was not as easy to get to. She had shared the overlook with only a dozen other visitors and one extremely excited park ranger. The broken, ragged hills were a dull and dusty tan that drained color from everything around them, including the sky. In between the barren hills was the desert floor—miles of it—blazing with yellow, purple, and blue.

A gust of wind stirred the flowers into repeating waves that showed the riot of color, the green leaves and shoots underneath, and the chaos of the wind pattern.

Her first comparison had been to the ice fields of Alaska. Bigger than humankind on a scale that stretched her mind's capacity to comprehend. It was an endless sweep of orange and gold poppies, purple phlox, blue salvia. A profusion of beauty that was everything the natural world produced, from the moment a star exploded to the impact of a raindrop on seeds that had held their breath for years, waiting, waiting. They lived and breathed without regard to humankind.

And while they all witnessed that astonishing perfection of nature, some asshole had flown a helicopter into the middle of the valley. People got out, walked around, stomped on the flowers, and took their selfies. Waved happily as they got back on board and flew away leaving behind the clear impressions of the helicopter struts and a circular wave of destruction from the blast of the rotors and their feet.

The park ranger had been apoplectic, yelling the call numbers of the chopper into her radio.

At first she'd been just as angry and then—numb. Disbelieving that this group of people had no filter inside them that said "Leave this alone. Let it live. Let it be pure. Let others take it in."

She stomped up the remaining stairs. The pilot had at least got a suspended license. The passengers hadn't been held accountable at all and had shrugged off the public shaming. No doubt, the women on the helicopter had gone shopping at the Simply the Best website later, looking for natural and pure via retail after ruining it for everyone else.

Who walks into perfection and takes the best of it for themselves and spoils it for others? Her mind leaped from there to climate change denial for profit, to people who told big lies for a living, and she wanted a drink.

These helicopter people—they held their lives up as perfect, and perfection meant they got to have whatever they wanted. "I'm richer than you are, so you can't understand. Mums and Dadums weren't nice, so you can't understand," she ranted. "Excuse my immoral lust for money, my bad ethics, and my venal selfishness because if only you could understand, you'd see it was that or be *inconvenienced*. I authorized my oil company to dump a year's worth of methane into the air in two weeks because shareholder value meant I had no fucking choice!"

She clutched the rail at the top of the stair, consumed with the rage she realized she'd been drowning in for years. They pretended their perfect lives were the default, that they'd earned them somehow, and the suckers who didn't have a perfect life must not be trying, buying, or taking enough.

Simply the Best sold hoo-hoo rocks as if vaginas weren't already perfect. They sold empowerment without empowering the women who worked for them. Profits went to those at the top, where life was perfect and envied by all.

Helicopter people had broken her faith in humanity, and Helene Jolie was another helicopter person. She had cheated her out of time with Pepper, just for spite. There might have been something between her and Pepper, but the chance was gone now, and she was not waiting around for anything to change.

She had to do the job and get back to New York where she belonged. Go home and fight with everything she had to get back to science and get back to herself.

She was most of the way to her condo when the adrenaline of her anger ran out. Shaky and dazed, she reached her room and collapsed onto the couch. A stiff pour of Buchanan's sharpened her wits enough to fetch some crackers. She turned on the TV to quiet the silence and found the baseball game wasn't over yet. She didn't care about the outcome but didn't care enough to change the channel.

After a few minutes a pan of the media booths gave her a glimpse of Simon tapping away at a laptop as he held an animated conversation with the guy next to him. He looked exactly like a happy man who was living his dream.

"Bastard," she pronounced, as she lifted her glass to him.

In the vain hope of slowing down the angry fugue in her head, she muted her phone and dumped several of Simply the Best's products into the tub. Might as well use them up instead of throwing them away when she packed her suitcases tomorrow. A few minutes later she eased her footsore body into aromatic bubbles. Eyes soothed by cucumber gel on a cool washcloth, she listened to Jami Sieber's most ethereal work until the shaky aftermath had finally passed.

She found the willpower not to have another drink, though she wanted one. Navigating airport security with a hangover was not an experience she craved. She didn't have the willpower to leave her phone off, though. It was four a.m. in New York, so she would have been very surprised to have a message from Ed, but maybe she'd missed one earlier.

There was one new message—from Pepper.

A soiree in Beverly Hills? Nothing could have appealed to her less.

Exhausted, drained, and weak from the hot bath, it was not in her to deny that she'd put up with that and more to spend a few hours with Pepper.

It took only a few minutes to change her flight, penalties be damned. Once confirmed, she wrote back, *I'd love to. See you there.*

She tumbled into bed, her mind once again spinning. She had no strength left to silence the orchestra that swelled into a romantic melody. Accompanied by the distant thrum of the surf, suddenly welcome and marvelous, she drifted on possibilities and finally into restless sleep.

CHAPTER TWENTY-EIGHT

Pepper didn't know when CC had come in last night, but she was grateful for the already made coffee. CC must be exhausted—a late night followed by getting up for a four-hour early breakfast shift at the bistro was grueling. Plus they were all going out later to the gallery opening to support Beth. It was a big deal. Pepper had even invited her parents because they took a kind of familial pride in the accomplishments of Pepper's friends, even though her mother still didn't understand how CC made money gaming.

Once the caffeine had worked its magic on her brain, she realized her phone wasn't where it should be on the charger. It wasn't in her bedroom, not on the sink in the bathroom. She'd had it last night—it was here somewhere. When CC got home, she'd have her call the number and wake it up.

She ate a banana and she got out her notebook to go over all the notes from last night. She needed a plan. At work she'd be able to use the corporate event database to manage many of the details, but a lot of steps needed to happen right away and in the right order before she even got to that stage. Like issuing invitations to the right people and in such a way that some people understood they were the first to be asked without others thinking they were afterthoughts.

The front door banged open and sent Pepper's heart into her throat until she realized it was CC carrying a couple of takeout boxes.

"Unsold pastries, it was my turn to take them. Good ones, too, croissant with egg, some spinach and ricotta. Breakfast for a couple of days."

"Nom nom!" Pepper relieved CC of a box and opened it. "Please let that be sausage and Gruyere."

"With apple. And here's your bloody phone! I stuffed my scarf and crap into my bag, and it got bundled up with them. It's been vibrating and beeping the whole time."

"I wondered where it was. Sorry I left it on your gear." She unlocked her phone but wouldn't hope for a message from Alice. When she saw that there was, she braced herself for bad news, though she didn't know right then what response would be "bad."

She read the text and thought, *This could be bad, really bad.*

CC plopped into a kitchen chair. "What are you blushing about?"

"I'm not blushing." Pepper busied herself finding a plate for her croissant.

"Your cloaking device is malfunctioning. I can see you. Out with it."

How much of the truth? "It's just—I invited the reporter to Beth's opening. She said yes."

"Oh."

"Stop it."

"There's no significance to you inviting her? Did Hel*eeee*ne make you do it again?"

"No. It's just that she had asked me out last night to say thank you, and then I had to work late."

CC heaved a heartfelt sigh as she kicked off her shoes. "Why did you have to work late?"

"Well." Pepper pulled her croissant out of the microwave. Her stomach growled in anticipation of salty, savory, cheesy bliss. "I kinda got promoted. I think?" She relayed the gist of her new assignment, hoping CC was suitably impressed.

"So a ton more work for the same pay? Working late, travel?"

"If I do well—"

"That's the same song from being an intern, isn't it? After this challenge there'll be another?"

Pepper hadn't even thought about all the extra work for no change in her pay. Was she supposed to ask? Or would Helene think that was trying to cash in before proving herself? "I actually want to do this, CC. It's not what I want to do forever. I don't want to turn into Clarita. I mean, she makes a ton of money and has a lot of power, but she doesn't seem very happy about it. Anyway, I want to see if I can. For myself. And then see where knowing what I'm capable of can take me."

"So that's why you invited Alice tonight?"

"She and Helene sort of tangled a little at the final interview. It was...tense."

"About what?"

"Several things. Like how many interns there are in parts of the company."

"I think I like your reporter more and more."

"She's not my—anyway, it's not that it wasn't true, but maybe she could have said it in a better way."

"So it's not about *what* she said, but how she said it? Classic response when people speak truth to power."

CC was *not* helping. "I'd like her to have a better final thought about us."

"Us?"

"The company, of course." This time she could feel the heat in her cheeks. "What do you want from me? She's attractive, yes."

"You've blushed more over her in the last five minutes than you ever did over Wilma Nkosi." CC added, as required, "That evil bitch."

"Seriously? You're going to bring up my ex for comparison?"

"She's the only one you dated for more than a few months. It was true love, remember?"

"Until it wasn't, which for her, was right away, and she didn't feel like telling me for a year. And look who's talking? It's not like you're burning up the sheets."

When CC didn't respond, she looked up from her contemplation of the coffee. "Get out! Who are you seeing? Is that why you were out last night?"

CC's cheeks and forehead were mottled with red to match her hair. "It's Val."

"Are you kidding? When did this happen?"

"After their announcement. Val always seemed meek and happy to go along with the flow and suddenly, wow."

"Suddenly she—sorry—they are a brand-new person."

"They turned into this gorgeous, confident person right in front of my eyes. And someone who loves themselves enough to insist on their own worth must be able to love other people with that kind of commitment, you know?"

"And then?"

CC picked at a crack in the table with her thumbnail. "I sent them a note saying I hoped that teasing wasn't over the line. And they wrote back, and we talked a while and then they had a spat with someone at work about how selfish they were being. You know, expecting common courtesy and decency is *so* selfish. And I offered to split a pizza and commiserate with them."

"And then?"

"None of your business."

Pepper was ashamed that she had been so caught up in work that she hadn't noticed such a big change for her BFF. "I hope both of you get good things from it."

"Don't tell anyone yet. We're keeping it low key—they're not ready to tell Umma and Appa just yet."

Pepper recalled the times they'd hung out at Val's house. Val's folks were nice and went to the same church as Pepper's did. "It's not like you're a stranger."

"They've been mostly okay with Val being non-binary, just worried about how other people will treat them, a boss deciding they're no longer a team player, and like that. Val wants to give the parental units some space before breaking the news that they're dating a woman. I wasn't supposed to tell you, but Val's not going to mind. At least I don't think." She picked up her phone. "It's just—kinda early. We already liked each other, but this is different."

Pepper licked a smear of cheese off her thumb after popping the last bite of the croissant into her mouth. "How? I mean other than the between-the-sheets thing."

CC finished tapping out a message before answering. "Like last night, we were going to go the arcade again, but the power was out. We looked for a movie but couldn't find one that was appealing. So we thought we'd window shop and eat cheese fries, but the parking sucked. Four hours later we hadn't done anything, and it was still the best date ever." She smirked suddenly. "I'm glad pharmaceuticals pays so well and they've got their own place. You would not have been happy with the noise."

"Show off."

"You should maybe make some noise with Alice."

"It wouldn't be appropriate."

"That sounds like even more fun."

Pepper frowned her disapproval of the very idea but only said, "We should leave around five thirty if we want to be able to park and not be late."

"You should wear that electric blue halter dress."

"You mean the one I wore for Fifties Night at Pepperdine? I'm not sure it still fits."

"Yeah, the one with the poofy skirt and teeny-tiny waist. You still have it don't you?"

"The dress, yes. The waistline? Not so much."

"I bet you still fit in it, Miss Bikini Body."

"It's been ages since I wore one of those either."

"Yeah, it's not like your body has gone to hell the last couple of years. Wear it. And the zebra shoes." CC punctuated the suggestion by clomping her foot on the floor along with a gusty whinny.

Pepper sent back a one-finger salute. It was too cold for a backless dress, even if she did now possess a chic black wrap that would look perfect with it. Not the heels with the zebra stripes. The aubergine suede ankle boots with the zippers would look much better. They were so cute and such a perfect fit that she hadn't felt even the least bit selfish not offering them to anyone else.

Unwilling to ask herself why she had to sit quietly on her bed for a minute, gather her thoughts, still her fluttering heart, and take several long, cleansing deep breaths in preparation, she finally sent a text back to Alice. *Great! See you there!* was the first draft, but she was unhappy with it even after she took out both exclamation points. Finally, *Glad you can make it!* with a smiley emoji seemed exactly right.

After she sent it, she realized she'd picked the emoji that was blushing. Maybe Alice wouldn't realize that. Was she too old to get emojis? She wasn't *that* old, Pepper told herself. Younger than Helene. But sciencey. And serious. She definitely knew who she was, adorkable glasses and all.

* * *

They left on time and traffic wasn't horrible. The search for a parking space concluded with CC yelling, "Meter! Meter!" and Pepper flooring the Prius to the spot where a black Mercedes was pulling out.

"Only a couple of blocks to walk," Pepper said.

"And the parking just became free. It's a good omen for good things to happen." CC waggled her thin eyebrows.

"For you. I have no such plans."

"The last time you wore that dress you got—"

"I'm perfectly aware of what happened. It was fun, it was over, and I can't even remember what she looked like because then I fell for she-who-shall-not-be-named and lost the memory."

"That evil bitch," CC intoned. "Okay, I'll buy that you're not looking for a quickie tonight."

"Thank you."

CC picked up her yellow patent leather bag and opened the car door. "You want way more than that."

CC had shut the door before Pepper managed to splutter, "As if!"

She gave CC the silent treatment as they walked to the gallery. As usual, CC didn't notice, so Pepper gave it up at the door to the gallery.

They paused to go through their usual ritual for parties.

CC ran a hand over her spiky red hair. "Everything okay?"

"Only you could wear blue and yellow eye makeup and make it work with that handbag and all black."

"Today I decided primary colors only."

"What about me?"

"As usual, you put the va-va-va in the capital-V voom. That dress looks way, way hotter on you now than it did in college."

Pepper tugged at the banded empire waist. "It's a little tighter than I remember."

"Especially the boobs, which is all good. I could be stereotyping, but I'm going to guess that a smoking hot butch lady reporter from New York might be okay with women who have boobs."

"Dear lord, please don't embarrass me."

"Have I ever?" Before Pepper could start listing the occasions, CC's face lit up like she'd just learned that her favorite game was dropping a new version early. "There's Val!"

Pepper watched CC sprint down the street and rolled her eyes as the two of them smooched and giggled. Val was wearing a button-down Oxford shirt with a boxy, nubby oatmeal-colored jacket that suited the asymmetrical swoop to the straight black hair and bangs. When they were close enough, Pepper said, "You two are so cute doing the kissy-face thing."

"Shut up," Val said fondly. "This is why someone wasn't supposed to tell—oh my god, where did you get those boots?"

"Free sample. Perk of the job."

Val sketched an outline of Pepper in the air. "I like the whole fashion thing you have going on."

"It's easy when it's free." Looking through the wide plate glass doors, she could see that the narrow gallery was the usual white marble floors, white walls, and white carpet of upscale Beverly Hills establishments. There were already a dozen people scattered throughout. They were mostly much older people, in dark suits and shades of gray dresses.

She caught sight of her parents talking to a willowy older woman with wisps of blond hair framing a deeply tanned face. All that and mauve lipstick made Pepper think she was probably the gallery owner. Her father's Armani suit and mother's little black dress were overly formal for an early evening art gallery event, and Pepper hoped that meant they had plans for later. This was good. With any luck they'd be long gone before Alice showed up. She knew what conclusion her mother would jump to, and she didn't want to deal with it.

She finally caught sight of Beth, toward the very back of the long space, biting her lip and looking as if she didn't know what to do with her hands. Aside from the art pieces themselves, her brown skin, bushy natural hair, purple jacket, and booty-hugging black jeans were the only genuine color in the place.

"Stop hanging on each other, guys. It's an ocean of white in there, and Beth looks like she's going to faint."

"Time to storm the castle!" Val declared.

CC yanked open the door with a bow. "After you, fine people. Lead the way."

CHAPTER TWENTY-NINE

The three of them swooped down on Beth en masse, congratulating her with big hugs and a raucous set of cheers that some of the more staid patrons of the arts didn't appreciate. Beth shushed the three of them as her face turned ruddy with pleasure and relief. She'd tied her hair with the kente cloth scarf Pepper recognized as the one Beth's grandmother had passed down to her at her high school graduation. The long, woven bronze and copper ST-Best earrings Pepper had given her at their last dinner looked fantastic—she'd been right, they would never look that good on her.

"You look like the artist of the hour," Pepper said. "Is your dad coming?"

"He'll be here soon, and he's bringing Nana. My brother was going to try to make it too."

"Girl, you done good." CC turned to the piece closest to Beth to study it.

"No, no, you start at the beginning." Beth pointed at the door. "There's a progression. If I'm lucky people might buy some of them, which means they'll never be all in one place again. It's now or never."

Val grabbed CC's arm. "Come on, let's do as we're told."

Beth lifted an eyebrow as the two walked away, Val still holding CC's arm. "Are they…?"

"It's adorable that they thought you wouldn't notice."

"That's awesome." Beth cocked her head. "They make sense together, especially now that Val's coming out of their shell, you know?"

The evening became a series of air kisses and incomplete conversations. Beth's art school friends and favorite teacher trickled in and out. Pepper's parents talked happily with Beth's dad while Beth showed her grandmother the exhibit.

CC and Val were in their own world, so Pepper decided to follow the exhibition start to finish on her own. Beth had been working on *Here/Now* all through art school, and there were twenty-four mixed media pieces in all. Her pride in Beth's accomplishment, and that she'd drawn a nice crowd for her first show, helped her not constantly glance at the door for Alice.

She had reached the third piece when a low voice, very close to her ear, said, "You look like someone who could introduce me to the work of this promising young artist."

Pepper gasped and lost her grip on her wrap. She quickly pulled it over her bare shoulders again. "Helene!"

Helene's hair was casually held back with a gold clip covered with glittery clear stones. Her suit was the dark shade of green just before it might be considered black. "The gallery owner and I are old friends. So this is your friend's work?"

"Yes." Pepper made an effort to steady her voice. "Beth's concept is a study in time. She selected the materials, and every piece has all four. Then—I'm not very clear on exactly how it works. But she used an atomic clock down to the micro-second and a math theorem to determine the relative sizes of each media within the piece. Like this one," she said, gesturing at the first piece.

"*Day One*," Helene read from the small wall-mounted placard. "Mixed media of photograph, fabric, glass, and pewter."

"If I remember how she explained it, she wanted to juxtapose time, geometry, and chaos. Time supplies the numbers for the theorem, which determines orderly, though varying visual weights. Chaos is represented by the subject matter of the photograph, which is based on the headline of the *Los Angeles Times* on the first day of given months." She dug down into the deepest recesses of her brain. "Which moves us through time as a predictable force and function of memory."

"I knew you would have all the facts." Helene's eyes were on the narrow black-and-white photograph of a careworn nurse with her face in profile to the camera. A glass-and-pewter lattice reminded Pepper of peering through a pane of safety glass, making the nurse seem far away and all alone. The only color was torn shreds of green medical scrubs fused into the glass in one corner. "Of course, given these past few years, there is much sadness. This is very thoughtful work. The order of nature against the chaos of experience."

"I think that's exactly what Beth wanted it to be." Pepper had a sudden horrible worry that Alice would arrive any minute. What did it mean that she didn't want Helene to know?

"Perhaps you will introduce me to the artist?"

As they walked toward the cluster surrounding Beth, Pepper wasn't surprised that Helene was turning heads. Several people seemed eager to catch her eye, and Pepper was fascinated by how Helene's bearing kept everyone at a distance. It didn't have any effect on her mother, though, who parked herself directly in their path, with the smiling demand, "Pepper, please introduce us!"

Pepper dutifully obeyed, aware that Helene had not eased her aura of distant politeness.

After introductions, her mother said, "We were so excited when Pepper told us she was going to work for you. I'm sure she'll learn a great deal that will help her advance her career."

Thanks, Mom. Her mother made it sound like Pepper was twelve or something.

"*Au contraire.* I have learned from her. She is excellent at her job."

"She gets that from her father." Her mother waved in his direction, but Pepper knew he wouldn't leave his sports catch-up with Beth's father. "Addington Insurance Associates? He handles the major commercial properties in Westlake Village and the surrounding area. So much detail, and of course, so good with people."

Pepper distracted her mother before she launched into name-dropping prominent clients by saying, "Helene wants to meet Beth, so, Mom, if you'll excuse us."

"Of course, sweetie. We'll be leaving soon. Dinner at Lidiot with Jerry Renfro and his wife. His new wife." Her mother glanced at Helene as if hoping that Helene would say she knew them or that she wished she too were having dinner with them.

Helene only said, "Lidiot? How lovely. *Bon appétit.*"

As she steered Helene toward Beth she saw CC off to her left making a Munch Scream face. Pepper mouthed back, "Ohmigod!"

Once introductions were complete, Pepper wasn't sure what to do with herself. If she was nearer the door, she could perhaps waylay Alice before she crossed Helene's path. It didn't seem like she ought to walk away from her boss, though.

The gallery owner joined them moments later. Instead of sharing mere air kisses with Helene, lips and cheeks actually met. "I knew you would be intrigued."

"I am, Lira. When you told me how young the artist was I expected something jejune. But this is truly engaging. I want to add three of them to our campus collection."

Beth made a shocked noise that sounded exactly like Pepper felt.

"Of course. Which three?"

Helene turned to Pepper. "My assistant, in consultation with the artist, will choose." Her lips curved in an indulgent smile. "I look forward to seeing the final result."

Stunned, Pepper stammered, "I hope you're pleased with the choices."

"Of course she will be." Pepper couldn't define the look that passed over Lira's face as she spoke. Comprehension and a touch of amusement? "I'll weigh in if you have any questions about Helene's preferences."

Pepper was spared making a response by a burst of laughter near the doors that made them all turn their heads. Helene fell into conversation with Lira as they moved together to examine *Day Twenty-Three*.

Beth exhaled all at once. "I can't believe it. Three pieces!"

"You have to decide. I don't think I could."

Both hands pressed to her cheeks, Beth managed a deep breath. "I can't even, right now. I really thought none of them would sell and this would be my first and last show."

Pepper shoulder bumped her. "Let's meet up here next week. We've always told you that you were amazing, and you are."

"Your boss is super hot, and yes, I will take her money, even though she's kind of extreme."

"What do you mean?"

Beth wrinkled her wide nose. "Well, yeah—the way she says your name for one thing. *Peh-pair*."

"That's her accent. I kind of like it."

"Well, Lira thinks you're sleeping with her."

Outraged, Pepper gasped, "No way!"

"She just gave you carte blanche to spend at least ten thousand dollars. You've worked for her for what? A month?"

"Longer than that!"

Beth rolled her large, expressive eyes. Pepper had always been impressed by the way they conveyed her skepticism. "Barely."

"There's nothing going on. I got my job because I worked hard."

"I know that. It just seemed like she was heaping it on, but last time we had dinner you didn't know where you stood. It's pretty obvious she thinks you're awesome."

"I think it's an in-public thing," Pepper said with more certainty than she felt. "Helene is dynamic. A powerful personality. Of course she's alluring. That's her thing. Her brand. It doesn't mean anything."

Beth pursed her lips. "She's hot. You have to admit that."

"Well, yes, but I don't think of her that way. No more than I do any celebrity." She remembered arguing with Alice about thirst objects and pedestals. Beth sounded just like Alice, as if it wasn't possible to admire someone who was very attractive and *not* want to jump into bed with them. "I do think she's beautiful. I've got eyes. Sometimes everything she says sounds like a double entendre. But I don't want to know what she wears to bed." The last she hissed at a whisper because Helene and the gallery owner were turning back to them.

"We have a more than generous budget to work with," Lira said with an approving smile for Pepper.

Do not blush. It didn't matter what this woman thought. "Great. Beth and I will sort it out."

Prisms of light flashed across the glass and windows as Helene pulled the clip out of her hair. "I was thinking of the lobby for Marketing. There's the wall on the left—"

Pepper blinked away the dazzle. "Where it's only whitewash pine? I always thought it was one of the few places that seemed bare."

With a practiced twist at the nape of her neck Helene reclipped her hair into its casual, tangled mass. "Yes, exactly. You know the premises almost as well as I do at this point. I'm not sure how I got by before you."

Pepper fought down heat in her cheeks, aware of Beth's eye roll. Bemused but definitely gratified by Helene's fulsome praise, Pepper couldn't help but fall into step as Helene took her leave of Lira with more cheek kisses. Anything she could do to hurry Helene on her way was a good thing. Alice was sure to show up any minute. She didn't know why her heart was beating so fast.

"Thank you, Pepper," Helene said as they reached the doors to the street. "I expected this to be merely a courtesy call, with the possibility of picking up a new piece I liked. But your explanation made a difference to my appreciation."

"You're welcome. I'm pleased to have helped my friend and to do something that will make where we work even more beautiful."

Helene smiled at her, the perfect lips slightly parted. "I find myself at a loose end this evening. I would prevail on you to take pity on me for dinner, but you must be committed to your friends this evening."

It wasn't a question, but Pepper quickly confirmed, "We are." It was a lie, kind of, but she didn't want to explain that she was meeting Alice, which now felt furtive and disloyal. Not that she was going to call it off.

"Of course. As you should." Helene tipped her head as if to examine Pepper's earrings and brushed Pepper's hair back from her ear. "I do like the change to your hair. Very chic."

"Thank you for the suggestion to shorten it a little."

Helene finally stepped back, and Pepper's head cleared. "I'll be off then."

Pepper's main emotion was relief as Helene's car was delivered by a valet and it disappeared into the night. Helene was magnetic, that was all, and it was hard to get free of her pull. People would see what they wanted to see, especially when a celebrity of a sort was involved. Gossip was food in Los Angeles.

Across the alley from the gallery a figure moved out of the dark, and she realized it was Alice, watching her.

Their gazes locked through the thick glass of the gallery's front door. Goose bumps rushed down her chest and arms. Her nipples tightened against the silk of her dress. Muscles that hadn't had a workout in way too long clenched, sending an undeniable wave of bone-melting desire from her pelvis to her fingertips. Equal parts terrifying and challenging, the wave was powerful enough to roll her over and pull her under.

Was it the confident swagger, the retro glasses, or the direct gaze combined with a slightly mocking smile? The tailored slacks, a black shirt and tie, the deep red jacket that squared her shoulders?

She realized she was breathing in short, rapid bursts. *No*, she told herself, *you can't pant. It's unattractive.*

"That was exciting," her mother said from behind her. "Helene Jolie is everything I thought she'd be and more. That hair! They should name a shade of red after her."

Pepper pulled her wrap tightly across her chest. The lack of a bra was abundantly clear. Alice was crossing the street. It was inevitable she would have to introduce her to her mother. Maybe if she played up the work connection her mother wouldn't ask her for the next year, "Whatever happened with that reporter?" when nothing was going to happen. Or should.

That was the truth of the matter, final word, end of story. Done and done. Her palms weren't damp, her ears weren't hot coals against the side of her head, and she was not still panting.

With what she prayed was a neutral smile she opened the door of the gallery just as Alice reached it.

"Hi," Alice said. "It seemed prudent not to cross paths with Helene."

Pepper agreed with her but hesitated to say so because it seemed disloyal to her boss. *There it is*, she thought. *Who am I tonight? Helene's assistant or not?*

"Are we on or off the record tonight?"

Alice froze but didn't answer right away. Then, her voice tight, she said, "I really want to be completely off the record."

They stared at each other long enough for Pepper to tell herself this was a spectacularly bad idea.

CHAPTER THIRTY

Alice watched the subtle contraction of Pepper's throat as she swallowed nervously. She could so easily imagine her lips nuzzling that spot.

"Good. I wasn't expecting to think about work tonight."

Alice had been dismayed to see Helene at the gallery door with Pepper. There was no way Helene didn't know the effect little intimacies like adjusting someone's hair could have on a person so much in awe of her.

She'd nearly left, but her feet had decided against it. She had plain proof of the result of Helene's games in Pepper's flushed cheeks and sparkling eyes.

The desire to kiss Pepper was so strong that she felt a little faint. She had to force herself to look instead at the woman Pepper was introducing her to. Even before Pepper said "mother," Alice knew that was who the attractive older woman had to be. They shared the narrow nose, wide cheekbones, and slightly hooded brown eyes, though the mother's had the faint cast of perpetual dissatisfaction that the daughter's completely lacked. May it stay that way, she thought.

Having a parent present certainly chilled the libido.

"*You say that like it's a bad thing,*" Sass observed.

"I'm enjoying Beverly Hills and my visit very much," she answered in response to the predictable query.

A tall, well-dressed man with wide shoulders and generic sandy blond athletic good looks was bearing down on them. "Donna, we'll miss our reservation." He smiled inquiringly at Alice and held out his hand. "Steve Addington."

"Dad, this is Alice Cabot, a reporter who's doing a series on Simply the Best."

After the requisite pleasantries, Pepper's father said, "A member of the Fourth Estate—Cabot, you say? Any relation to Barb Cabot?"

Alice blinked. "Do you know my mother?"

"We met years ago at a fundraiser. We had a memorable chat, and I tried to convince her to move west."

If her mother recalled anything about this supposed conversation, it would be that some Hail-Fellow-Well-Met man had called her *Barb*. "She loves Long Island too much."

"A pleasure to meet you, Alice. Please give my regards to your mother."

They shook hands again as Donna Addington kissed her daughter on the cheek in parting.

"So that's my parents," Pepper said as the door closed behind them.

She made her eyes stop tracing the silhouette of Pepper's shoulders under the silky wrap covering them. "The Golden Delicious didn't fall far from the tree."

Pepper gave her side-eye. "Is that a good thing or a bad thing?"

"I think it's possible you got the best traits from both."

"Okay, you can stay." Pepper's cheeks were still slightly flushed as she tightened her wrap again around her shoulders. "Would you like to see my friend's work?"

"Yes, I'd love to."

"We're supposed to view them in sequence. Would you like to me tell you about Beth's concept?"

"No. I prefer for art to talk to me. To see if I can hear it."

Pepper heaved a sigh of relief. "Me too, actually. Unless it doesn't talk to me and then I have to ask what it was the artist was trying to tell me that I couldn't hear."

Alice glanced across the group of the first four, seeing uniformity with variance. The photographs were widely divergent, and her eyes cycled between a grieving nurse, a parched riverbed, a Vet in a wheelchair overseeing Latino kids playing chess, and Aretha Franklin's face lifted in high note rapture. There didn't seem to be anything to connect them, not thematically, except perhaps their ability to provoke emotional responses from sorrow to joy.

Alice had been to museums all over the world. Her mother believed that one couldn't say one had truly visited a place without going inside a museum, library, or bake shop while there. Pepper was quiet at her side, a grace Alice appreciated. Janet had chattered all through museums.

"*Great,*" Sass pointed out. "*You're comparing this woman you've hardly known a week to your ex. Good sign.*"

"Sometimes it's all about making sense of the thing for yourself. I see order and uniformity first, then randomness, and I'm thinking about what each of the photographs is about. I could write my own narrative and you could write yours, and neither of us would be right or wrong."

"Beth says that's art for you."

She grinned at Pepper and saw a responsive sparkle in Pepper's eyes. *Don't think about the texture of her lips. Don't think about the breadth of her shoulders.*

When they reached the end of the exhibit Pepper tugged at her arm in the direction of a chatty group that Alice had assumed was Pepper's friends. Their cheerful voices were a welcome break in the growing quiet and chill of the gallery as it slowly emptied and the sky darkened outside.

"Peeps, you have to behave or you'll end up on the front page. Alice Cabot, this is CC, my roommate. She's into gaming and trouble. Val—they know everything about drugs. And the artist, our soon-to-be-famous friend, Beth."

Val shot Pepper a dagger look before saying to Alice, "The *legal* kind of drugs."

CC spluttered, "Trouble? When have I caused trouble?"

Val and Beth broke into a babble of "That time when" examples, making Alice laugh. To Beth she said, "Your work is thought-provoking. I enjoyed the journey."

"Thank you," Beth responded politely.

"She's not an idle flatterer," Pepper said. "Science and truth are a big deal."

Beth gave her friend an odd look as she said to Alice, "Then I really do thank you."

"I try to go to MOMA whenever there's a new artist added, but I'm not as often engaged as I was tonight. The thanks should be from me."

"What a lovely thing to say." Beth's smile widened with pleasure. "Pepper said you were slated for margaritas. She should take you to Mimosa over the Water."

"Epic margaritas," CC agreed.

"It's all the way past Malibu," Pepper protested.

The others went into the same averted gaze—as if reading a map stored behind their eyebrows—that Manhattanites got when asked the efficient way to make stops in Midtown, Tribeca, and the Cloisters.

"It's Saturday," Beth assessed. "Traffic on the One but what else is new? You could try doubling back through Topanga to get home."

"That's if we were ending up in Encino, but my car's here."

"Oh right. Yeah, it's the One both ways, but it's a pretty drive."

Pepper protested the oversell. "The margaritas are not that great."

It might have been the gleaming suggestiveness in CC's eyes that persuaded Alice or simply that she didn't care how long it took to get anywhere as long as Pepper was with her. She said, "I think I have to try them. Local specialties and all that."

"Malibu is north of Santa Monica," Pepper explained, as if that meant something Alice cared about.

"I'll drive."

"Ooo," CC said. "In the convertible?"

"Trouble," Pepper muttered.

"I'll take your car home," CC offered.

"I thought you were coming to my place," Val said, then clapped a hand over their mouth.

Beth crowed, "I knew it! Val and CC sitting in a tree—"

"Shut up," CC and Val said in unison.

"I'll bring you back to your car," Alice said to Pepper. "Is it safe where it is?"

"It's Beverly Hills. If there's any place where a car is safe at the curb it's here."

"The meters are off until Monday," CC added, earning her a hissed, "Trouble!" from Pepper.

"You should head out," Val said. "The bar could sell out of tequila or something. It's getting late."

CC and Beth nodded approvingly.

"They make a good point," Alice agreed, dipping her head to acknowledge Val's contribution.

Pepper rolled her eyes. "Sure they do. A place that specializes in booze can run out of booze in the middle of the booze shift."

CC nodded with mock authority. "I'm glad you understand the precarious nature of the situation."

Alice was happy to have a drink in her future, but if she was driving she'd have to hold back. There was still whiskey at the condo, so not to worry, she reassured herself.

She wouldn't imagine that Pepper would come back to her condo. That was a bad, bad idea, a fantasy. It was one she couldn't shake, though, and if Pepper did, she might see the accumulation of empty bottles in the trash.

A deep warning bell sounded as confusion, desire, and fear made it hard to breathe. Pepper's observant eyes would see who she really was. What she'd become. It wouldn't end well.

"You have done the support bit," Beth said. "You are my hero tonight, Peps—three pieces you sold for me. Have a margarita or two."

Pepper hastily said, "I didn't even know she was going to be here."

"Whatever you said, she bought three pieces." Beth enveloped Pepper in a full body hug that left both women giggling. "Take a picture of where they're supposed to be placed. That will help me decide."

"Will do. Maybe Wednesday night we can get together."

Unable to remember how long it had been since she'd had a friend that hugged so completely and enthusiastically, Alice was charmed, even as the banked anger she felt toward Helene Jolie continued to rise. In addition to standing too close to Pepper and toying with her hair, Helene had dropped a car's worth of money in front of Pepper's friends? *Terrific.*

Out on the street Alice led them to the centralized valet service and handed over her ticket. "Yes, I'll put the top down," she confirmed when the car arrived. "At least until later. It might be too cold for that flimsy wrap you've got."

"So far it's fine. What a beautiful night."

She made a show again of opening the car door for Pepper, giving herself another chance to admire up close the silky dress she was wearing. Alice had yet to see the whole front, but the heart-shaped neckline that curved around Pepper's breasts and the flouncy full skirt had a Doris Day vibe that was confusingly innocent and sexy all at once.

The streetlights cast circles of silver on the sidewalk as they rolled along Rodeo Drive. Pepper's hair and lips were painted with the same shimmer. Alice forced herself to look up as they idled at a stoplight. "You can't see any stars."

"At the beach we should see more, though I think the moon is full, which will cut down on what we can see."

"Have you ever been at high altitude and stargazed?"

"A trip to Hawaii with my folks. We went to see the sunrise from Haleakala. At four a.m. there were so many points of light it felt like there were more stars than there was sky."

Her brain seemed to have no ability to find something to say, so she gestured at the phone resting in the dash mount. "Is that a good route?"

Pepper shrugged. "From here it's the only route. I could have followed you there. Saved you having to come all the way back."

"I truly don't mind." Alice didn't risk a glance at Pepper. They were alone. It might be the last time they saw each other. The possibilities were all dangerous now. "This is fun. I never drive anywhere at night at home."

"What do you do instead?"

"Walk, take the subway, order a ride. My car is at my mother's. I ought to get rid of it or go on a road trip to make the insurance worth it."

"Where would you go?"

"Someplace I could see the stars." *And you*, an inner voice added, leaving Alice shaken with the abrupt and total truth of it.

She was in trouble. Deep, deep trouble.

"I nearly froze to death one summer night on Pike's Peak, but it was worth it for the stars."

"CC and I drove up to Lake Tahoe one summer. Slept in my car and stayed in a campground because we barely had enough for the gas and food. It was nice, though. Quiet—no hum of devices. And my eyes hurt from how dark it was, if you know what I mean. We should do that again."

"You've been friends a long time."

"Met the first day of fourth grade. It was BFFs at first sight." As they glided down the on ramp onto the freeway, Pepper stuck her hands into the rushing slipstream cresting over the top of the windshield. "Thank you for what you said at the gallery."

"For what? Your friend makes good art."

"Yes, that, especially. Beth was so nervous. I think she sold five pieces tonight, which is five more than she ever thought she would for her entire life. But also thank you for getting Val's pronouns right."

"Oh. It's easy enough to do."

Pepper twisted in her seat toward Alice. "We were a gang of five. One of us decided Val's identity was a political attack. After months of hearing from her about menus and honeymoons, we were not invited to her wedding, and she didn't show up tonight though she had promised she would. Not that any of that was wanted if she was going to go on being mean to Val."

"Val seemed like the last person on earth you'd ever be mean to."

"I know, right?"

Alice turned the heat up so at least their feet would stay warm and triggered her playlist of jazz brass bands. The night air whistled past her ears. One moment it felt purifying. The next it was a warning. *Seize the moment. Run for your life.*

Keep her close.

Push her to safety.

The Pacific was a vast expanse of black on their left when Pepper pointed to a high bluff where brightly lit buildings looked down on the coastline. "Looks like there's something going on at my alma mater."

"This is where you went to college?"

"Pepperdine." Counting them off on her fingers, she added, "My father went to Pepperdine. My mother went to Pepperdine. My two uncles went to Pepperdine. There was no way my brother and I weren't going to Pepperdine."

Spectacular view, sea breezes—a perfect location. College for Pepper was only a few years ago, Alice calculated, compared to fifteen for her. "Don't tell me—they named you after the school?"

"My brother got 'Steve.'"

"There are a lot of Steves in the world. Not so many Peppers." *And only one that matters.*

Sass made cat-with-a-hairball noises.

"Were you named for something or someone? The middle name you share with your mother?"

"Yes, her father's mother's family name. It was required at the time. She carried it on—well, subversively." Alice smiled into the night. "The day I was born was the same day Alice Paul died. So my mother named me after her. That it satisfied her family was cosmically coincidental." She didn't want to look at Pepper for fear of confirmation that she hadn't any idea who Alice Paul was.

"Being named for a tough-as-nails suffragette is way better than your parents' alma mater. The more I know about your mother the cooler she is."

"*You did it again,*" Sass scolded. "*Why do you keep trying to convince yourself that she's uninformed? Because she grew up in the land of milk and honey? Or are you trying to make her seem too young, too naive, too unsullied by the world to be suitable for the likes of you?*"

"My mom is cool. Smart, wise, beautiful."

"Is this my turn to say something about apples and trees?"

"You can say it, but only 'smart' truly applies. I got that from both sides."

"What did your father do? I gather he has passed?"

"He died when I was a toddler. He studied lasers before it was super cool. He was raised in foster care, and best as he knew his mother was from Trinidad and his father from the US. My mother met him when he was a research assistant to Charles Kao. A Nobel physicist in fiber optics," she added. It was not a name most people recognized even as their Internet was delivered via his work. "My dad swept her off her feet. They got married after two months. I showed up a couple years later."

"Sounds like a storybook romance."

"Right out of a Hollywood movie. Until it wasn't." She thought of the photograph in her mother's salon, where she gazed adoringly at her husband, and the ring her mother still wore.

"Life is like that," Pepper said quietly.

"Life is like that," Alice echoed.

The Pacific Coast Highway was lined on both sides by one- and two-story apartments that all angled for a beach view. They passed quickly through Malibu itself and turned off the highway onto a narrow steep drive that led to the top of the Malibu Bluffs.

The moon was thirty degrees above the horizon, gloriously full and bright. Even after Alice parked in the restaurant's lot, they sat in the car staring at it.

"The tides have probably been great the last couple of days," Pepper finally said. "Next month we get a supermoon. I have got to get out on the water again."

"Why did you stop?"

"Work. My evil ex surfed sometimes and I didn't want to run into her. And it felt super important to get my job right, so I studied up."

Alice didn't dare look away from the radiant woman in the moon and her beneficent gaze. She wanted to rise up from where she was, escape gravity and reality. Wanted desperately to kiss Pepper, which seemed like the same thing.

Icarus flew too close the sun, but what about the moon?

CHAPTER THIRTY-ONE

After the long minutes studying the moon, so bright and seemingly close overhead, Alice's "Shall we?" and putting the top up on the car had been anticlimactic. Pepper didn't know what she had hoped would happen before they got out of the car, or, at least, she pretended she didn't. She had never before wanted to feel someone's lips against hers so badly.

Fortunately, the entrance to Mimosa Over the Water was flanked by two elaborate tableaus for October involving scarecrows, empty Champagne bottles, pumpkins, and gourds. Alice paused to admire it and Pepper regained some control over her pounding heart.

It was late enough to score seats at a table that faced the water. Minutes later they each had a frosty margarita in front of them. Pepper's was strawberry and mango, blended. Alice had gone traditional—on the rocks, salted rim.

It didn't feel safe to tell Alice how good she looked. She would have easily told CC or anyone else, but Alice's close-fitting shirt and expertly knotted tie were wreaking havoc on Pepper's composure. It seemed best not to say a word about them. She clutched her wrap over her breasts and her unruly nipples.

After they'd agreed on sharing ceviche shrimp street tacos and barbecue chicken nachos Pepper struggled not to blurt out that she was going to be in New York in December. She wanted to make it plain that tonight did not have to be the last time they saw each other, yet why did it matter? They would most certainly be exchanging emails for the next few weeks. There would be follow-ups and questions. She would tell her then.

Alice had fallen silent, her gaze on the view.

"What are you thinking about?"

"If Icarus had a sister. And if Icarus's sister tried to fly to the moon."

Of all the things Pepper had thought Alice might be contemplating, a sad Greek myth wasn't one of them. "It might have been safer."

"Maybe not." Alice gave herself a visible shake.

"Is something wrong?"

Alice turned to face her and finally sampled her drink. "Not now."

"Good." She nodded at the margarita. "Worth the drive?"

An almost unwilling smile curved Alice's lips. "Absolutely worth the drive. Hey, I truly don't want to talk about work, but I'm curious in general terms."

Maybe it was the way Alice asked a question, with careful clarity, that made Pepper wonder if they were on the record again. She asked warily, "About what?"

"I promise, this is just idle curiosity. You said you studied up for work—what did you study?"

"Oh. Well, I wanted to know the product line, especially the small batch items that were sourced outside the US. Ultimately, I'd like to work in vendor relations and product sourcing. To understand the interconnections better. I figured knowledge can never hurt, so I read product descriptions and reviews. Thousands of them. Probably tens of thousands. But I never came across the yoni eggs, I swear."

"You looked them up? What did you think of egg-sized rocks for hoo-hoos?"

She laughed at the euphemism. "Hoo-hoos? Okay."

"Thank my mother. It continues to amuse me."

Trusting that off the record really meant it now, Pepper admitted, "I think they're a gag gift because egg-sized rocks don't belong in vaginas." She would not suggest things that did and saw the same resolve in Alice's barely suppressed smile.

She took refuge in stirring the frozen slush of her drink with the straw to take several large swallows. Moments later she clapped a hand to her forehead. "Brain freeze!"

Her wrap slipped off her shoulders.

She lunged for it, but it was puddled under her chair before she could capture it again. "Sorry," she muttered, but she hadn't a clue what she was sorry for. She twisted around to pick it up, but Alice had already gotten to her feet.

"I'll get it."

Pepper felt completely naked. She blamed the cool air on the chill that ran up her bare back and shoulders. She wanted Alice's warm lips on the nape of her neck. The roar in her ears was so loud she missed what Alice said as she settled the wrap on Pepper's shoulders. Their fingers tangled as Pepper pulled it into place and heat spread down Pepper's arms.

She was sure she made the right responses, but most of her mind was circling around a single thought—she wanted to be in Alice's arms. She wanted her mouth and hands and body. She wanted to try, and try, and try, until they found a connection it was now only beginning to seem real to her. A connection to a place deeper.

"If you were going for the innocent fifties with that dress you mostly failed. For which I and the rest of the world thank you."

Pepper was not going to look at Alice until she felt some of the heat recede from her cheeks. "I learned the jitterbug for a talent night in college. The dress looked different then." She had to clear her throat. "You know, with saddle shoes and ankle socks."

"Sure," Alice said. "It's the shoes that make that dress dangerous."

"CC suggested it. I haven't worn it in ages." She examined the cuticle on her thumb.

"Remind me to thank her."

"Ms. Cabot, are you flirting with me?"

The long silence made Pepper finally look up. She couldn't unwind the mix of emotions flitting across Alice's face. Futility? Longing? Amusement? Regret?

"I'm appreciating you. I'm sorry if I'm making you uncomfortable."

"You don't look sorry."

"Should I actually be sorry?"

She pulled the wrap tighter and blamed the margarita for the waves of heat in the pit of her stomach and places farther south. Hoping she sounded prim, Pepper observed, "I'm not in control of your emotional state."

Alice laughed and some of the spell was broken. "Fair enough. I'm not sorry. You're lovely. This is not an opinion, it's a fact."

"Pretty enough for everyday, but by Beverly Hills and Bel Air standards I'm garden-variety." Something flared in Alice's eyes that made Pepper sit back in her chair. "What did I say? It's the truth."

"Are those the only standards that matter? If you sell yourself short, other people will too."

Pepper didn't know why, but she was certain that Alice was talking about Helene. They were paddling toward dangerous waters. Fortunately their server delivered the tacos and nachos at that point, asked if they wanted another margarita, and sped away when they declined.

She tried to turn back to safer shores by scooping up melted cheese, smoked chicken, and pico de gallo with a thick tortilla chip. "Cheers," she said as she popped it into her mouth.

The food provided a welcome distraction from both Pepper's dangerous feelings and dangerous topics. She made no pretense about how hungry she was and was glad when Alice dug in as well. By the time they finished her fingers were covered in hot sauce and lime. She excused herself to the ladies' room, aware that the evening was naturally reaching its end. A drink had been drunk. Dinner had been eaten. Time to say goodbye and turn the page.

She was resolved until a flyer taped to the back of the restroom door caught her eye. She took in all the details and returned to their table with a bounce.

"How would you like a unique California experience?"

Alice gestured at the restaurant. "This isn't enough?"

"There's a bonfire on Amarillo Beach tonight, until one a.m. A DJ, lip syncing. To benefit Queer Youth Advocacy. A perfect night for it."

"I've never wanted to dance on a beach and howl at the moon." Alice broke into the lopsided grin that melted Pepper from the inside out. "Until this very moment. Of course I didn't know that was a thing one did, which I can see exposes a personal lack of imagination on my part. Sounds like experience points I need."

"You definitely need the XP. I wish I'd known—CC would have loved it too." Her heart was pounding with relief. It was only relief, and if she lied to herself over and over, she might believe it.

Alice settled the check, and they left the restaurant. The wind was considerably sharper as Pepper walked to the bluff's edge. "I was hoping to see where the event is from here, but I don't. I know roughly where it is, though. We'll find it."

"Are you going to be warm enough?"

"Bonfire, remember? I believe they produce heat." Pepper clamped her mouth shut before she added, "And that's not the only thing."

CHAPTER THIRTY-TWO

Pepper eagerly pointed the way once they reached the highway again. Alice was still worried she wouldn't be warm enough—that breathtaking dress covered next to nothing. Her palms were damp on the steering wheel as she recalled the line of Pepper's spine leading to the small strip of fabric that held the halter top in place. Definitely more Marilyn Monroe than Doris Day.

After several westward turns they rolled up to a long parking lot that separated the broad beach from windswept dunes and a wooded park. A tap of her phone to the security guard's scanner gained them wristbands and a parking place. The party was further up the beach, in the lee of towering bluffs that reflected the dancing light from the stage and bonfire. She eased the convertible between a bona fide 1960s VW van and a nondescript black sedan with a ride-hailing company emblem on the dash. After she switched off the car the thump of music was unmistakable.

After squeezing out between the vehicles, Pepper balanced effortlessly at the back of the car to pull off first one boot, then the other. "Pop the trunk. What are you waiting for?"

"I—"

"No way am I getting sand on these boots."

The gleam of moonlight on Pepper's shoulders was beguiling. "I'm thinking a shirt and tie might be overdressed."

"What other choice do you have?"

"I'm wearing a black tee under the shirt." She folded her jacket into the trunk and unbuttoned her cuffs.

With a shimmy so quick Alice hardly knew what was happening Pepper's pantyhose followed the boots into the trunk.

All the blood in her body drained into her pelvis. Her fingers fumbled with her tie clasp.

"Need help?"

"I usually have a mirror." An inane excuse, but it was all she could come up with.

The top of Pepper's head was level with Alice's nose. A matter of inches separated her lips from the tendrils framing the starlight-painted forehead. The flutter of fingertips against her collar tightened her throat as Pepper pulled the tie free and coiled it neatly on top of Alice's jacket.

They both reached for the shirt's top button. Alice pulled her hands away, but not until after an electrical charge sent a dancing spark down both arms. She pulled the shirt out of her slacks as Pepper reached the button at her waist.

From far away, as if from inside a wonderful dream that someone else was having, she heard a low purr as Pepper ran her palms over the thin tee where it covered Alice's ribs. "This will do just fine."

She realized Pepper was looking up at her.

She sees right into me. It wasn't terror that suffused her, but a jolt of raw desire unlike anything she'd ever felt before. *I would let her do anything to me.*

Her voice high and breathy, Pepper asked, "You got it from here?"

"Yeah."

Her socks and shoes had no sooner joined Pepper's in the trunk when Pepper seized her hand, and they ran across the flat sand toward the fire and the music. Pepper's hair streamed out behind her, silver in the moonlight. Rolling shimmers of orange and red reflected off the tide line, and smoke drifted in the air.

The venue was surrounded with temporary fencing festooned with rainbow ribbons. Handwritten signs were staked into the sand on both sides of the entrance. *So many*, Alice thought. Black Lives Matter, Stop the Murders of Transwomen, Climate Change is Real, Like It Or Not We're In This Together, Love Our Mother Earth, Silence is Complicity, AIDS is Not a Death Sentence, Say Her Name, Say His

Name, Say Their Name, I Can't Breathe. The classic Rainbow Pride flag snapped overhead in the offshore wind, flanked by a dozen more. Alice recognized the Progress, Trans, Bi, and Genderqueer flags, but some of the others were new to her.

As they rounded the stage and the rave of dancers came into sight, Alice could see the crowd was mostly twenty-somethings, like Pepper. Her own simple brushed-up spikes were bland compared to the array of neon Mohawks, masses of locs, buzz cuts, and shaved heads. She might have been the oldest person there, but all at once it didn't matter. Pepper threw her arms in the air with a whoop, and they were dancing in the throng to the beat of "Stayin' Alive" as the circling purple and yellow stage lights lit up the DJ and speakers.

"I love Lizzo!" Pepper yelled, and Alice laughed at the marvel of old and new mixed. It didn't matter that she'd been clubbing to the original since Pepper was in grade school. She spun in a circle as the song changed to a galloping thunder of "Born to be Wild." Everything old could be new again, it seemed.

The bonfire flared red against the dark ocean and brilliant silver moon, turning Pepper's skin to crimson as she swirled. The smoke of the fire, the thrum of the surf, the raucous singing of the crowd—it all filled Alice's senses with a high that had nothing to do with the cloud of marijuana smoke or even the margarita.

She couldn't remember the last time she'd been this sober this late at night.

Was that why the moon had never seemed so bright? And Pepper, dear god, her heart ached just looking at her. She was something from myth—a glow of light, her skirt a whirl of purple against the golden sand, on her tiptoes reaching toward the stars, hips rocking, and shoulders swaying.

The heartbeat of the twisting flames matched the rise and fall of the shifting crowd. They were a collective mass of humans every color of the rainbow, Alice thought, thriving and healing in common experience. No different than millions of women in pink pussy hats covering miles of streets or a room full of engineers cheering and weeping as Curiosity touched Mars' surface.

Dance together, grieve together, rise up together. She would not think of helicopters and crushed flowers, not when she was surrounded by people who celebrated life in spite of the pain in the world.

They danced and lifted each other up.

As the minutes passed and the songs changed, she willed herself to accept that, right now, it was enough to breathe, move, and watch

Pepper dance. There would be plenty of time tomorrow to go back to falling into the depths of another bottle of whiskey.

"People like us, we've gotta stick together," Pepper was singing. Alice realized she was singing too, fists in the air, feeling the anthem of misfits all the way into her bones.

Her shirt was drenched by the time she cheered and whooped as a lip sync drag queen mic dropped with "Bitch, I'm Beyoncé." Her energy level drooped, but then Billy Porter made it sound so easy to love yourself that she lost herself in the music again.

Pepper's dress was a purple skin across the swells of her breasts, and the damp waist had loosened to show the hollow at the small of her back. *I'm admiring her because she's art*, Alice told herself, even as she envisioned using her teeth to lower the zipper that was the only apparent device that kept the dress in place.

She was so lost in her fantasy that she missed what Pepper shouted.

She leaned closer, one hand to her ear.

"Having fun?"

She answered truthfully, "I can do this all night."

"So can I!" Pepper threw her arms in the air with delight and then her arms were around Alice's neck and she kissed Alice, laughing. Then not laughing.

Fireworks exploded across Alice's skin with sparkles of gold and green behind her eyes. The heat of Pepper's back was under Alice's palms. Hunger took over, and Alice pulled Pepper hard against her, tasting her mouth and inhaling the smell of her hair and skin. Too late, much too late to think of a way to survive this kiss. It was beyond her to stop.

Maybe, she told herself, they could have tonight. Maybe it would only burn her.

The moon turned to gold. Her wings were melting and she was falling, like she had known she would. She was no longer holding Pepper, Pepper was holding her, tight and close, only their soaked clothing separating their bodies.

"I'm sorry," Pepper said against her lips.

"I can do this all night," Alice repeated, and they kissed again, this time with smiles. The taste of her was intoxicating. The sweet welcome of her lips and sensuous invitation of her tongue left Alice weightless. She wasn't falling after all. She'd been caught by Pepper's magic.

I have no right to this. I can't do this to her.

But it seemed she could. The music finally stopped, the lights went out, and the remnants of the bonfire was doused with sea water and sand. They lingered under the moon, breathless and hungry for the taste of each other. Finally, when the wind sharpened, they strolled across the sand to the car. It was Pepper who clambered onto the hood of the car and pulled Alice to her so they could kiss again. Her hair fell around Alice's face and the sky full of stars disappeared into the glow of Pepper's eyes.

She kissed Pepper until the world was out of air.

Finally, Pepper murmured, "It's only twenty minutes to Santa Monica."

Time began again. "Are you sure?"

"Yes."

She almost offered to put the top down on the car, in spite of the cold. The cocoon of darkness was better, though. Better to escape the stars and the moon, to hoard all of Pepper's light while she could. Their hands were clasped as the miles flew by. The swirling lights of the Ferris wheel on the pier made the night seem even darker.

Shoes in hand, they crept up the stairs, and dropped everything once the door to the apartment was closed behind them.

Alice pulled Pepper close only to realize she was covered in goose pimples. "You're shivering."

"It was warm in the car. My dress is soaked."

"I guess you'll have to get out of it."

Pepper turned her back to Alice. "Undo me?"

She eased the zipper down and the waist of the dress parted. Alice couldn't stop her hands from moving under the dress, along Pepper's hips, then up the swoop of her stomach to her breasts. Pepper gasped and steadied herself with both hands on the wall. Alice covered Pepper's breasts with her warm hands and finally brushed her lips across the beckoning tenderness of Pepper's shoulders.

"Please." Pepper braced herself on one hand and captured and held one of Alice's against her breast with the other. "Touch me before I faint."

Her cold shirt against Pepper's warm back shocked her nipples into rocks. She began to pull up the flounces of Pepper's skirt, but Pepper forestalled her with, "Let me." She grasped the fabric at the nape of her neck and Alice stepped back far enough to let Pepper lift it over her head.

The dress fell around their ankles. The remaining wisps of black silky lace that curved around Pepper's backside delighted Alice's fingertips as she traced them to where they met between Pepper's legs. She covered Pepper with her body and let Pepper guide her other hand back to her breast.

"Here?"

"Yes."

Her fingers found the paths through silky ripples, in awe of the shape of women and the sensuous welcome that invited her deeper. She teased at the responsive nerves and muscles, then cupped her hand over all the wetness and heat as their hips found a mutual rhythm.

She tried to stay right there, in the throb of anticipation. The present was all that mattered until Pepper's whimper of need broke open her own desire. Her fingers slipped inside, and she reached as deep as she could and was rewarded with Pepper's long, guttural moan.

Her tears were hidden in Pepper's hair as she gave herself to the pleasure of sensation. The ache between her own legs and the fire running across her skin threatened to drown out Pepper's pleas. She gathered her closer to whisper, "I've got you. Just feel it."

Pepper nodded frantically, all the muscles of her back tense.

"I can do this all night."

A strangled laugh relaxed them both, but only for a few shared heartbeats. Pepper cried out as her knees buckled.

"I've got you." The orchestra that had been playing in her head from the moment she'd seen Pepper's face under the observatory stars swelled as she scooped Pepper into her arms, carried her into the bedroom, and lowered her to the sheets. Pepper's hand was in her hair, but she knocked it away so she could strip off her shirt finally and get her pants undone. Naked at last, on her knees beside the bed, she pulled Pepper to her mouth and opened her again with her tongue.

Pepper's hand came back to her hair, while her calves crushed against Alice's shoulder blades. A dizzying pleasure filled her when Pepper's cry of release was followed by rippling shivers as she kissed her way up Pepper's body to her mouth. Then they were both limp on the bed in a coil of arms and legs.

Alice kept her palm on Pepper's chest, feeling her heartbeat and the rise and fall as she took one long deep breath after another. Even as she told herself one moment was perfect, the next was as well. She tried to stay there, to stop time again, and delay the inevitable.

"I could use a shower," Pepper finally said.

"Mmm." Time moved forward again. "So could I."

Hot water sluicing sweat and salt off her body felt divine. They were covered in shampoo and suds, and their bodies slipped easily past each other as they took turns rinsing. She ran an appreciative hand over Pepper's breast only to have Pepper shift out of reach.

"I'm too shaky." It was said with a smile as she tipped her head back to rinse soap off her eyelids. Moments later one eye opened, then the other. "You, on the other hand…"

"Which hand?" Alice pulled Pepper close for a laughing kiss, then groaned as Pepper ran her nails down her back.

"Does it matter?"

"No." There weren't any layers left to hide behind. "Whatever you want."

Pepper rubbed her lips against Alice's. "I want to not break my neck in the shower while attempting gymnastics."

"Now that you mention it, I want that too."

They both wrapped up in towels and Alice led the way to the kitchen. "Would you like a drink?"

"Water. Or juice." Peering over Alice's shoulder into the almost empty refrigerator she asked, "Is that banana still good?"

"I think so." She was relieved Pepper didn't want a drink. Alice knew if she started drinking she wouldn't stop and she wasn't ready to destroy the light in Pepper's eyes. "And there's some peanut butter."

"Food of the gods."

They perched side by side on the counter, sharing bites of banana and spoonfuls of peanut butter.

"Less shaky?" Alice drained her second glass of water.

"Yes." Pepper slid off the counter and took the glass out of Alice's hand. She loosened Alice's towel enough for one fingertip to trace a circle around Alice's nipple. "Let's go back to bed."

The muscles along Alice's ribs flexed as she struggled to breathe. She luxuriated in the drape of Pepper's hair across her shoulders and the rising tide of new arousal. Pepper's lips and tongue toyed at one nipple, then she tugged at it with her teeth. She paused and looked up at Alice with a knowing smile.

"Yes, I like that." She leaned down to kiss Pepper and couldn't hide a shiver when Pepper bit gently at her bottom lip. She stretched into the pillows and wrapped her hands around the headboard as she lifted her hips to Pepper's touch. "I love that."

All the warnings of her head to keep something to herself went away. They stayed away during fevered kisses and needy words. She was peeled open and there was no stopping her surrender.

PART SEVEN

Only Happy When It Rains

CHAPTER THIRTY-THREE

The whisper of Pepper's breath was steady against Alice's neck. Even though she had wanted to savor every precious minute, the rise and fall of Pepper's belly under her hand had lulled her into sleep. When she woke a few hours later daylight peeked around the curtains.

Pepper's hair was a soft spill of gold against the white pillows. Her body was utterly relaxed, all except her lips, which curved slightly in a smile as if her dreams were pleasing. Like a field of early spring flowers—delicate and precious. Not to be spoiled.

Don't be the helicopter, don't trample the flowers, she told herself, even though she knew it was too late.

She slithered out of the bed, found a clean tee in her half-packed suitcase, and went to the kitchen for water. The sight of their clothes at the door flooded her with memories of the night. The cool sand, the smell of smoke, the strength of Pepper's muscles, the throbbing beat of music. The taste of Pepper. The feel of Pepper's mouth on her.

Rescuing their clothes, she shook them out and draped them over a chair. The yards of fabric in Pepper's skirt that had given it such lovely flounces last night were still damp and had lost their form. There was no sign of her tie—it was probably still in the trunk.

Standing at the counter she was glad that Pepper hadn't seemed to notice the empty bottles on the floor. The trash under the sink had been full for several days. She hid the empties in the dishwasher and some of her panic that Pepper would figure out how much she drank subsided. It took all of her will not to open the Buchanan's and toss back a shot.

Quiet noises from the bedroom told her Pepper was awake. Panic tightened her heart, but it dissolved at the sight of the tousled hair and sleepy smile. Pepper had wrapped herself in one of last night's towels. Framed in the bedroom doorway where daylight didn't quite reach, she woke all the memories of last night's surrender.

She snapped the dishwasher closed. "Hey."

"Please say there's coffee. Or that there will be coffee. Or that there could be coffee."

"There are pods."

"Yes, please." Pepper gestured at her towel as she slipped onto one of the two barstools. "I was going to raid your suitcase for a T-shirt…"

"You're welcome to, but what you have on is quite attractive."

"Ditto." She slumped onto the counter, head resting on her forearm. "Okay, that's stupid, but I haven't had coffee. Did we eat the last of the food?"

"The banana was the last of the fresh food. There's still peanut butter. I have crackers. And these."

Pepper laughed as Alice unearthed an assortment of Power through Your Morning Bars. "Do you like them?"

"They're great with peanut butter. I may have helped myself whenever I saw a bowl on someone's desk. Hotel life." She waved a hand at the jar of peanut butter, the knife, and the assortment of nutrition bars in their gold, orange, and red wrappers. "In my life, this is a buffet."

Pepper half-choked on a swallow and laughed with a snorting chortle. The joy of it penetrated the chill building in Alice's stomach. For a moment, a blink of time, she thought she could stay right where she was and spend the rest of her days finding ways to hear that laugh again.

Pepper waved a hand at the table covered with notebooks and her laptop. "So this is where all the magic has been happening."

"At the risk of sounding like a Hollywood script, the magic was last night."

Pepper slow blinked at her. "That's a very nice line."

"Thank you. I try." Surprised that her hands weren't shaking when her insides were shivering with the collision of reckless desire and impending disaster, Alice handed over the mug of coffee as soon as the machine beeped and popped in another pod. "There's various tiny hermetically sealed dairy-like flavorings here."

"Yes, please."

"Vanilla, hazelnut, or plain?"

"Yes, please."

Alice grinned as she scooped up her accumulated spoils from fast food and diners in the area. "Take your choice. I also have ketchup, hot sauce, and mustard if you're feeling truly adventurous."

"Ha ha. No thank you, these will do." Pepper opened two hazelnut and one plain in rapid succession, stirred, and sipped her coffee with a deep sigh of pleasure.

"You're making me jealous of the coffee."

She sipped again. "Five minutes out of every day I am Faust, and coffee is my welcome devil. As you can see, the coffee is already working because I am suddenly able to tap my liberal arts brain cells."

Alice slid onto the barstool next to Pepper and doctored her own coffee. "It's early in the day for Faustian references, but I can deal. I get the feeling you're a morning person."

"Maybe. A little." Pepper hooked one bare foot on the rung of Alice's chair. "I am curiously tired this morning."

"I can offer an explanation. Or two. Or four."

Pepper's cheeks turned delightfully rosy. "Nobody has ever given..."

"You think I was giving? Believe me, it felt like I was taking." In ways Pepper couldn't understand.

"I want to say a lot of words that don't have any meaning anymore. Amazing. Awesome. Wow."

"Exquisite," Alice supplied, even as she told herself not to say it.

The silence that followed was fragile with words that could be said and shouldn't be. Pepper unwrapped one of the nutrition bars and smeared it with peanut butter. She broke it in half and Alice accepted the offered bite.

Finally Pepper said, "At least it's not pomegranate."

Her knee brushed Pepper's. The warmth was welcome. "Not your favorite?"

"Used to be. I lived on them for a while."

"While you were an intern?"

Pepper nodded. "My parents kept me from starving. And CC, of course."

"It wouldn't even blip the income statement to pay the interns minimum wage, you know. Let alone something they can live on in LA's housing market." *Stop*, she told herself.

Pepper swallowed hard. "I don't—can we not talk about my work? I know you have some questions."

Why stop? She'd known all along this was how they were going to end. "There aren't questions about any of that. They're facts."

Pepper shook her head. "I'm trying to talk about your work for a change. Like, are you excited by what you're going to be able to get into print?"

No, Alice thought, she wasn't excited. Not something she could explain to Pepper without opening the taps on all the feelings that dancing under the moon and a night in Pepper's arms had pushed so far away.

It was too late, though. The feelings were back, all at once. The despair, the anger, the helplessness. "Excited is not the right word."

"What's the right word?"

She has no idea. "Compromised."

The soft, satisfied light in Pepper's eyes dimmed. "I don't understand."

"It's not my usual work," she evaded.

"I know that. But—is it because it's not about science? Not your usual?"

"In part."

"Why did you agree to it then?"

"It was that or be fired. For the douchebag incident." She tried to smile.

Pepper put down her coffee and gazed into the cup as if there were answers in it. Their knees lost contact. It was a small shift, but the chill added to the pain in Alice's deep and empty places. "Otherwise you wouldn't be interested in anything to do with it."

"Not with Simply the Best or someone like Helene Jolie, no."

"Why do you hate her?" Pepper finally looked up, her face a mix of confusion and anger.

"It's not hate."

"What is it then?"

"Despair. Because of everything she could be and isn't." Same reason she hated herself, Alice realized.

"You mean what *you* think she ought to be. Look at everything she's accomplished."

"Record sales, enduring popularity, millions of Insta followers. While you ate free samples to get by."

"It's not right, I know that. But what choice did I have?"

"It's not on you." Alice swallowed to get control of her voice. "The right question is what choice did *she* have? When how much other people's labor is worth is based on how little you can value them instead of how much, it's not about business necessity. It's about the CEO's and stockholders' money being more important than anyone else's life." She choked to a stop, her ears full of the sound of helicopter rotors.

"Why are you telling me this?"

"I'm sorry."

The color in Pepper's cheeks had deepened, but not with shyness. "No, you're not."

She wasn't. She'd been afraid from the beginning that Pepper would see right through her. *Now I've made it impossible for her not to.*

"She gives millions and millions of dollars in product away every year. We auctioned off a necklace and earrings for twenty-five thousand dollars. This quarter's charity was local artists."

"Is that how she's buying your friend's art pieces?"

Pepper's chin quivered. "A local collective that needed a new roof on their workspace. Jump to conclusions much?"

"I'm sorry. That was unwarranted."

"No, you're not sorry." Pepper spun away from her, her back stiff with outrage. "I suppose you think all the women who want to have cleaner, less toxic lives are wrong?"

"No, if that's what they're buying. But let's be clear about it. Buying a crystal for a perfection altar doesn't clean a single cubic inch of air."

"Do you really think intention means nothing?"

"The road to hell and all that. Helene makes a nice profit on empty intentions."

"I bet you make fun of metal straws. Of course getting rid of plastic drinking straws isn't going to save the planet. Not on its own. But single drops of water, enough of them, bring down mountains, don't they?"

Her voice rising, Alice snapped back. "Sure. But we don't have a hundred million years. What we have is a huge self-care, self-actualization, selfishness movement that says doing the bare minimum makes you a good, even godly person. Especially if doing more is inconvenient to your own desires. Simply the Best doesn't ask anyone to *be* better people. Being best only goes as far as your credit limit."

"Of course intentions aren't the end of change. They're a start, and better than nothing. I can intend to call my friend Val the name they want me to use. I can intend to use they and them for Val's pronouns. But unless I finally start remembering to do it consistently, my intentions are hollow. But at least the intention is there, versus the person who refuses to even try. Who decides to disrespect someone instead of being supportive?"

Whatever bonds of intimacy had still wrapped around them were fading away in the light. "That's not what I'm talking about."

Hands flat on the counter as if she would push herself away at any moment, Pepper snapped back, "Yes, it is, based on what *you* think is the typical Simply the Best customer. You're not wrong about some of them. My example is from my life, and I'm not wrong about a lot of people choosing to be kind and inclusive though their intentions sometimes fall short. But doesn't the science of our brains say that if we *think* consistently about doing a thing, our brain begins to train itself to do it?"

"You still have to do it. In the end, there is no substitute for action."

"Isn't that what I said?" Pepper shivered and slid off the barstool. The towel dropped, but there was no invitation to follow in the quick steps she took to the chair where Alice had draped their clothes. "So you're a good person. And everyone else is selfish?"

"I am *not* a good person." She was shaking but managed to stand up. The last whisper telling her to shut up faded away. "I'm a bitch who drinks too much. Who's all kinds of toxic you can't even understand. Who can't wait to get away from the fakery and cheap imitations."

"Your wish is granted." Pepper pulled on the wisp of underwear that had been such a delightful discovery only a few hours ago. "But for your information, I'm not the only one who's cheap."

"I didn't mean you."

"Yes. Yes, you did. Maybe Helene is not all angel, but I do admire her. I wish I were more like her."

Aghast, Alice staggered against the counter. "Don't say that."

"Now you think you're in charge of who I get to be?"

"That's not what I said." *Just let her think it*, she told herself. *Let her go.* A despairing, distant thought edged around the blackened corners of her heart, that somehow, when Pepper looked at her again, Pepper would know the way out of this place she'd taken them to.

There was no rescue in Pepper's face, no panacea in those beautiful eyes. There was only flinty resolve and open bitterness.

I did that to her, Alice thought. *I'm a black hole sucking her down into the bottomless gravity well of my hopelessness.*

She did the only thing she could do to save Pepper from falling all the way. She cut her loose. "You go on enjoying the pretty life. Being half in love with her, trusting her beautiful vision, and that it can't possibly be built on commonplace, everyday, banal greed. As long as you get to dance, right?"

Pepper stepped into her dress, zipped on her boots, and slung her wrap around her bare shoulders. Bit-by-bit, Pepper disappeared from sight, and there was only an angry, disillusioned young woman in her place.

Who said nothing as she walked out the door.

Alice bolted after her. "I'll take you back to your car."

Without turning around, Pepper waved her phone. "I know how to get a ride."

She turned the corner to the stairs. The sharp tap of her heels faded away.

Alice shut her ears to the beat of helicopter blades and closed her eyes against the memory of bright, laughing faces so happy with their selfies as they destroyed what was rare, undisturbed, and beautiful.

Who's the helicopter now?

CHAPTER THIRTY-FOUR

Even before she unlocked the door, Pepper knew CC was home and she was gaming. She tottered at the threshold and struggled out of her boots. There was a chance she could sneak to her bedroom unseen. She quietly closed the door with her shaking hand and willed herself to keep moving when she wanted to dissolve onto the floor and scream.

"Who's a good little destroyer of souls? You are, yes you are—no way!"

CC's ire was good cover for her tiptoed steps.

"That kill was yours, sorry. I should have gotten an assist."

"It's okay, babe. We're working on your KDR, not mine."

Terrific, Val was here. Pepper doubly didn't want to be seen.

The commotion from CC's room suddenly muted. "There's always a breeze when the front door opens. Peps, is that you?"

She couldn't make her throat cooperate with her voice.

CC appeared in the doorway of her room. "Well, well, well. Look who's doing the Walk of Shame."

Val peered over CC's shoulder. "She's a liberated human being and there's no shame—"

The gulping sobs Pepper had been holding in all through the ride to her car and then the entire drive home burst out of her.

CC's and Val's voices became a babble of concern as CC wrapped her in a gentle hug.

"Are you hurt? Do you need to go to the ER? What happened? Do you want pancakes?"

The idea of pancakes made her laugh in between choking, ugly sobs. "I'm okay. I don't know what happened. Everything was fine. Then it wasn't. And she was m-mean. And I want so many pancakes."

"That bitch! Pancake Patrol is on the job." CC held her at arm's length to study her face. "I did laundry. There's clean pajamas and everything. You need pajamas."

"Take a shower," Val said. "Get lots of steam into your sinuses. You'll feel better."

She gulped out her thanks and retreated to the bathroom. She never wanted to see this dress again. Never wanted to see these boots again. Never wanted to see Alice Paul Cabot again. Never, ever, ever.

"You can fuck off, Alice Paul Cabot. Go fuck off. Fuck off all the way around the world until you are right back here and then fuck off again!"

She spit shampoo out of her mouth. That was her entire allotment of F-bombs for a year, and Alice Paul Cabot could fuck off for using up all of her fucks.

In between ravenous bites of hot fluffy pancakes slathered with marmalade—Alice Paul Cabot was *not* ruining marmalade for her—she tried to explain to Val and CC how it had all gone wrong. "And then after we danced for hours and she said she had fun, she had the nerve to tell me that I should go back to partics, that was all I cared about."

"I knew she was trouble."

Val gave CC side-eye. "Pretty sure you said you liked her."

"She's right about interns getting ripped off, but she is *clearly* a straight-up villain."

"And she said I was cheap. And—and—and fake."

"That bitch! You want to join us and shoot bad guys?"

Pepper shook her head.

"I know what you need." Val fetched Pepper's hairbrush and gently pulled it through Pepper's post-shower tangles. "My umma always does this when I'm upset. I think it's soothing."

"That's really nice." Pepper gave a long sniff and wiped her nose on her pajama sleeve.

"Girl, you are going to need some major rehab. Want more pancakes?"

"I'll be fine. And yes. I may have to have pizza for dinner."

"I already assumed that." CC hopped up to pour two more ladles of batter onto the griddle.

The slow, gentle brush through her hair did feel very comforting. "Thank you, Val."

"Maybe I could braid your hair. I learned a couple ways when I went through my whole wish-my-hair-was-anything-else phase."

"You have great hair," Pepper protested. "You can grow it way longer than I can, and it's straight and thick and—" she blew her nose on the tissue CC handed her "—it's all rich and black and silky. Not wispy and can't make up its mind what color it is and won't ever stay tidy."

"Oh, honey, you need a makeover." CC was nodding sagely. "I will fetch the Utensils of Transformation."

"I don't want to dye my hair," she called after CC. She leaned her head into Val's hands. "Don't let her dye my hair."

"I will not let her dye your hair."

"Do you know how to French braid?"

"Sure."

"That's what I want. No more Ponytail Girl. She gets d-dumped and has to call her own ride." She gulped and blew her nose again.

"Nobody is going to mess with French Braid Woman," Val assured her.

She let CC and Val fuss and pretended they were making it all better because they were being very kind, and why not let them? It did help drown out the echo of Alice's cruel words. How dare Alice dump on Helene's character when Alice was so mean? How could Alice think all Pepper wanted to do was party in the good life?

The French braid made her look older. More serious. Less wounded. She knew she was never going to see Alice again, but let the mean, cynical, rude, user people of the world be forewarned she would not be messed with.

"You know what I really want to do now?" She recalled her promise to herself, made only a week ago.

CC regarded her handiwork around Pepper's eyes. "Face plant in pizza?"

"That woman does not get to put more carbs on my hips. I'm going surfing. There's an onshore wind." She'd walked a block toward the nearest place with shops while ordering her ride and been chilled to the bone. She'd need her wetsuit.

"Beach?" Val perked up. "Babe, I know we want to up my game rank, but it is kind of a nice day outside. Let's take my car."

"Good idea." Val's mini-SUV was much wider and longer than the Prius. "I can only take one passenger in mine if I have my board."

Pepper was glad the route to the nearest beach didn't take them through Santa Monica. Her suggestion to stop at Topanga Beach avoided going anywhere near Malibu. It turned out to be fortuitous. The day was cold and sharp enough to keep casual beachgoers away. She was heartened to see boards on the water, some paddling out, others riding in.

"I don't know why I don't do this every weekend," Pepper told CC and Val as she quickly yanked off her T-shirt and pulled her wetsuit up over her shoulders.

"Work makes everybody dull." Val was swaddled in sweats but shook their hair in the wind. "Those are brain cobwebs floating away."

CC took charge of the cooler where they'd tossed in a few beers and day-old scones for later. Pepper was glad to see her white and aqua board out in the sunlight. Her spirits lifted in spite of the still uncomprehending ache in her heart. "It needs wax, but another day. I just want to be on the water."

She left CC and Val to spread an old navy blanket over the sand and ran across the waves toward the surf. After a minute to assess the flow of the other surfers, she attached her leash to her ankle, faced the first shock of the cold water, and threw herself across the board for the paddle out.

The exertion felt good. It had been too long. Saltwater on her lips was better than tears. Whatever else she wanted to be in her life, she was still this—stretched atop the board she loved with the sun on the soles of her feet and back of her head. She'd feel the strain in her pecs and shoulders tomorrow, but she didn't care. Keeping to the general area other surfers had already proved was a good spot, she followed the rise of developing waves. Looking for the wave that was perfect for her took time.

Finally she picked a green wave about three meters out. She aligned her board to match its path and paddled madly to pick up momentum. When it began to swell under her she curled her toes to grip the board and lifted her body into push-up position. Balance was good. In the fluid motion that her muscles remembered she planted her back foot, front foot, and popped upright.

Exultation made her whoop with delight. She was on top of the wave, left hip pointed at shore, arms in the air with a nice run ahead of her.

Until a side current caught her unprepared. Her core muscles didn't respond as quickly as they had years earlier and that was all it took to unbalance her. Spluttering and forcing water out of her nose she surfaced and used the leash to pull the board back to her.

First attempt and a wipeout. She spit out salt water. *You are clearly out of practice.* At least she hadn't knocked herself silly. She ought to have seen the challenge coming.

There was a lot she should have seen coming. Alice Cabot was the last board to the head she was going to allow.

Belly against the board again, she reoriented herself into the flow of the waves and picked another. This time she stayed on top.

CHAPTER THIRTY-FIVE

Pepper walked across the first-floor lobby Monday morning with her head held high. Her aching shoulders and ribs had been subdued with ibuprofen. Her puffy eyes were hidden with eye drops and the generous application of concealer. She'd duplicated Val's French braid and very much liked the way it made her feel—like wearing a cloak of confidence.

Helene needed perfection for the New York opening. Carefully balanced guest lists, kid glove treatment for VIP egos, and flawless cooperation with the New York staff. Perfection was exactly what Helene was going to get.

Her desk still held remnants of Friday night's multitude of lists. How could that have only been three days ago? She took care of her morning routine first. Refrigerator stocked to accommodate Helene's schedule and guests, check. Print out memory cards for tomorrow's visitors, check. Restock any gifted items from Helene's shelves, check. Set timer to pick up lunch, check. Make sure today's product for Helene's off-the-cuff *Quickly the Best* Instagram video was on the way, check.

Clarita arrived at her desk as Pepper returned from the kitchen. "You've changed your hair."

"Do you like it?"

"I'm sure Helene will approve."

That wasn't what Pepper had asked, but she knew by now that asking another way wouldn't get an opinion out of Clarita. "There's so much to do for New York. I might need a little coaching on the event software. I mostly know it, but there are so many VIPs and VIBs and people who can't be there the same night and others who have to be there the same night. I've never used the Never/Always feature. I know it interfaces with the Contact database."

"When you're ready, I'll show you." Clarita looked her up and down again. "It's simple to use, but it's only as good as what you put in."

"I'm working on that. Some people have a half dozen other people they should never be near."

"Those lists will only get longer. Helene holds it all in her head."

Which was amazing, Pepper thought. She rolled up her mental sleeves, congratulated herself for not thinking about Alice for a few minutes, and pulled out multiple colors of paper to color code each night. Markers could create subsets. She reminded herself it was much the same as the seating chart for her parents' 25th wedding anniversary party, only on a bigger scale. With much, much higher stakes.

When Helene arrived on schedule at a quarter to eleven, Pepper was printing her third revision of her notes. Clarita immediately launched into her daily updates on materials due for review and a succinct list of newly confirmed premiere vendors for the Composium.

Pepper was aware of Helene's gaze on her hair as she asked, "And what updates do you have for me on New York?"

"I would like two minutes at your convenience to verify some notes that don't make sense to me."

"We'll work through lunch."

"Of course." When Helene didn't immediately proceed to her office, Pepper asked, "Is there anything else you need?"

"You've changed your hair. Keep it."

"Thank you. I'm planning too." "Keep it" was probably a compliment, though Pepper wasn't sure.

"I want to change the product for today's video. The Cult Gaia hair clip today instead of Thursday."

"I'll see to it."

She was more certain at lunch time that Helene's, "How clever," in response to Pepper's initial organizational scheme was a real compliment, though it was hard to believe no one else had thought of it. Project coordination wasn't difficult. It took a step-by-step focus. "This will all be put in the event software so the printouts will be what we're all used to. But I thought, well, architects do rough sketches before anything gets to a computer, so the colors and highlighters are my rough sketch, trying to get the ground floor right before going any higher."

"I'm feeling much better about New York." With her usual mercurial change of subject, Helene asked, "Why did you change your hair?"

Pepper was not about to say, "Alice Cabot was a mean bitch to me," though that was most of the truth. "A friend knows how and she taught me."

"How useful. Has the new product for today's video arrived yet? I don't understand why it's not here."

"It arrived while I was picking up lunch. I'll have it in the room when we're done."

To her surprise, Helene pushed away what was left of her spinach salad. "You're getting along so well on New York that this has taken less time than I thought it would. Let's do the video now and clear that slot later for another check-in on New York."

"Sure." Pepper scooped up her papers and what was left of her lunch and carried it out to her desk. She unwrapped the gold wooden box the Club Gaia hair clip came in—part of what justified the nearly $200 price tag—and removed extraneous papers so the box held only the clip and the velvet bag it could be carried in. She hurried into the small side room off the conference area in Helene's office. It was little more than a closet, but thoroughly sound proofed and fitted out with diffused lighting and a green screen.

"Stay," Helene ordered as Pepper made for the door. "I'm going to need you."

Pepper froze, not sure what Helene meant.

Without a pause, Helene flipped on the camera, tapped to put product and Simply the Best logos in place of the green screen, and checked the monitor. After adjusting the camera minutely downward, she pressed Record.

"What could be in this delightful box? We already know Club Gaia is genius for accessories and this one is exclusive to Simply the Best." She opened the box and showed the contents to the camera. "Here's why it's genius. You've got to go from work to a special dinner. Of course you touch up your makeup, but how do you show you've made an effort when you can't change your outfit? Accessories, of course—Modern Life Coping Skills 101, right? And we have here a compact, hinged hair clip that can always be in your handbag. My assistant Pepper is going to show you what it does."

Helene deftly pulled the barstool she sometimes used into camera range and waved Pepper forward.

Heart pounding at the thought that thousands of women would within hours see her on their phones, Pepper gave what she hoped was a self-assured wave and let Helene arrange her on the stool, back to the camera.

"The teeth unfold from each side. It's made of a special alloy that is naturally flexible with rose gold and rhinestone decoration in three patterns. Just choose your favorite."

Pepper felt the comb teeth sinking into the coils of her hair where the braid began at the crown of her head. Helene's touch was deft. Once done her warm fingertips lifted Pepper's chin and turned her head slowly and side to side.

"It takes three seconds. It's formal and classy. It's simply perfect and simply radiant. Exclusive today at Simply the Best."

Pepper stayed where she was until Helene had clearly relaxed. She let out the breath she'd been holding.

"You did well."

She began to take the clip out of her hair, but Helene forestalled her by handing her the box it had come in. "Keep it."

The clip wasn't a sample discard, prototype, or an item Helene had worn to promote that couldn't be resealed and returned to the warehouse stock. It was brand new. "I couldn't possibly."

"You'll need it in New York. I expect every aspect of the events to go perfectly and that includes being adequately represented by you."

"Thank you." Pepper couldn't get up without bumping into Helene, so she remained on the stool, not sure what to do. She was vividly aware of the proximity of her nose to the underside of Helene's breast and didn't want to make contact.

Her worry about making inadvertent contact became irrelevant when Helene leaned across her to replay the video, surrounding Pepper with the dusky rose cologne Pepper knew Helene brushed through her hair. She'd watched many of these promotional clips. In them, Helene always seemed more than a little unworldly. Now there she was in one too, looking better than she knew she did, courtesy of good lighting and preset filters. Her wave seemed natural. She hadn't embarrassed herself or Helene.

"Perfect in one take." Helene tapped at the computer screen. "And upload. Thank you for your help."

"My mother will be thrilled."

"I'm sure she will." Tendrils of Helene's hair tickled Pepper's cheek.

"Let me get out of your way," Pepper offered.

"No, we're done." Helene snapped off the extra lights and camera power as she straightened up. "I used to send them over to the social media people to upload, but after a new manager seemed to think it was her job to give me notes I decided having that level of review was a waste of everyone's time."

Finally Helene stepped back enough for Pepper to slither around her toward the door.

"I'll get to work and have an update for you at three."

"Excellent. Oh, and Pepper?"

She turned back to find Helene right behind her.

Helene's gaze slowly traveled the length of Pepper's body. "You'll be in the public eye in New York. Things you already have in your closet might be acceptable here at work, but you'll need to upgrade to avoid getting on the radar in the wrong way."

"I understand completely," Pepper assured her, even as she wondered how she would pull it off. Weekends haunting the thrift stores, possibly.

"Tell Clarita to assign you a standard event clothing allowance."

"That's very generous."

Helene's lips curved in a satisfied smile. "I know. I will enjoy the result."

At her desk she took what seemed like her first deep breath in an hour. She put a hand to her throat to quell a tremor at her collarbone and felt her heart hammering. Being so close to Helene was unsettling. She could hear the echoes of Alice's dislike and suspicion of Helene and pushed them away. Helene's charisma went on for days, and it wasn't as if she could turn it on and off at will.

"Is a clothing allowance for an event a standard thing?" she asked Clarita when she had the chance.

"Yes, when Helene decides it is."

"I'm to have one for New York."

Clarita's face froze in that smile that Pepper found disquieting, like she knew something Pepper didn't. "I'll double-check and let you know the particulars. You'll be in photographs with her, on video, and the like, I suppose. Her standards are quite high."

It made sense, Pepper thought. While they were in New York she'd be wearing a necessary kind of costume. Adventuring gear, CC would call it. Expensive, charity gala adventuring gear, and so the company was paying for it. Like the hair clip. She put her hand to it. She wasn't used to this kind of thing—hundreds of dollars in her hair. That probably explained why she was discomfited by Helene's generosity.

CHAPTER THIRTY-SIX

"Ed, you're not serious." Realizing the skies outside had grown even darker since the last time she'd lifted her gaze from her laptop screen, Alice stretched across her childhood desk to switch on the desk lamp. She reclaimed the lap blanket that had fallen off and tucked it around her legs again.

Damn California and its weather. She hadn't felt warm since she'd walked out of LaGuardia into an unseasonal rainstorm. Autumn was over, at least for her. The overcast skies were predicted all the way through Thanksgiving next week, along with sleet and snow. She'd picked up a cold and it had lingered, prompting her to drag her sorry ass out to her mother's for pampering.

The last thing she was in a mood for was a call from Ed and confirmation of the edict she had suspected was coming.

"I am quite serious. Management is very happy with the STB series. They think you're a natural for more Style pieces. Your analytic take is fresh, authoritative, and unbiased."

So much praise. So little that meant anything of value to her. Ed had no idea what writing the articles had cost.

"Finalize your photograph recommendations. That should have already been done," he continued, "as well as the data for the social media pieces on coastal comparisons. Be sure the California desk gets a heads-up that a special piece they can feature is coming. Ticktock, Al. We're less than two weeks out from the first run date and there's still a lot of T crossing and I dotting left. But good work."

She numbly agreed to everything Ed said and dropped her phone onto her desk.

She wasn't going back to the Science and Tech beat.

Style—always supported with ad revenue. Highest click-throughs past the paywall. She'd have to go to the kind of parties that made her want to drink her way to oblivion, and she didn't need more reasons to do that.

Maybe her New Year's Resolution would be quitting her job. It wasn't as if the need for a paycheck determined her choices. *Meanwhile, finish up the damn series and get it out of your life.*

She fought down a cough with another lozenge and decided it was past time for lunch and time to get out of her room. The photographs—she could look them over on the table in the library where the gas logs in the fireplace would crackle like real ones and help her feel warmer. First, a shower. One could have breakfast in pajamas, but not lunch.

"How is your cough today, Alice?" Sophia bustled across the kitchen to swipe the contents of her cutting board into the sauce bubbling on the stove. "There are sandwiches for lunch. Egg salad with extra mustard, the way you like it."

"You are the best medicine there is." She watched Sophia drizzle olive oil into a bowl of sliced carrots and mix them around with a lazy hand. "What's for dinner?"

"You'll find out at dinner." In the quick succession that Alice had watched for more than half her life, Sophia rinsed her hands, dried them on her apron, then smoothed her thick hair as if it had dared to become untidy.

Alice peered into the saucepan for clues, wondering what the caramelized onions, mushrooms, and herbs would end up as. She reached in for a mushroom, which got her hand slapped.

"There's a sandwich. Leave my dinner prep alone."

She tried her best flattery. "Olive oil makes you smell like Sophia Loren."

Sophia's lined face eased into a smile which undercut the severity of her order for Alice to get out of her kitchen. She retreated with a sandwich on a plate and the welcome reassurance that some things would never change.

She found her mother was already in the library, half done with her sandwich, and apparently reading two books at once. Her feet were close to the fire. Alice envied them.

"Not reading," her mother said in response to Alice's question. "I'm fact-checking one with the other, which I trust as authoritative. Do *not* tell me again I could be using a device of some kind to do this. I know I could. I don't want to." She glanced up as Alice set the packet of photographs and her laptop on the table. "What's happened?"

"Why do you think something has happened?"

"You're angry."

She took a large bite of the sandwich and gave herself a moment to appreciate the mustard, black pepper, and pickle. "I'm going to have to quit my job. They want me in Style permanently. I can't."

Her mother removed her glasses and rubbed the bridge of her nose. "What will you do with your mind and time instead?"

"I don't know. But I think I have to make a clean break. Once this series is put to bed." She prodded the heavy envelope full of prints. "I've got photographs to review."

"Seems like the kind of thing you could use a device for."

"You funny."

"Kiss kiss."

"Love you, mean it." Alice opened the heavy envelope and peered inside, then set it down with a sigh. "I want to put color and black-and-white versions of each side by side. Print and digital use. The photographer did a great job, plus I have some from our own archives."

"Move the standing lamp over to the table if you need the light."

The view from the library included an expanse of the flat, gray water of Peconic Bay. Another dreary day. She did not think of California beaches or blond hair in the wind.

Sass blew a big raspberry. "*Sure, you're not thinking about the warm sand and even warmer body.*"

After warming her backside for a few minutes in front of the fire, Alice settled in at the square table that had held many school projects over the years. She plugged in her laptop and dumped the contents of the envelope with several hundred prints on the table. They spilled across the surface and she was back at the Simply the Best campus, surrounded by warm air, endless sunshine, art, and graceful architecture.

In the middle was Pepper.

Tendrils of gold had escaped from her ponytail and coiled against her cheeks. Her brow was furrowed in the way that meant she was sifting through her brain for details about a piece of art or the water reclamation system. She was looking directly into the lens. Right into Alice's heart.

She must have made a sound because her mother joined her at the table.

"Hmm. I see." Her mother slapped her hand much as Sophia had when Alice moved to push other photos on top of Pepper's beautiful, living, breathing, stunning face. "Who's that?"

"Helene Jolie's assistant."

"She has no name?"

"Paddington." *Damn.* "P. Addington on her email. Pepper."

"She's lovely."

She tried to breathe normally and failed. "Yes."

Her mother lifted the photo out of the stack, revealing the next, and Alice saw her own face. Rather, it looked like her face, but there were only hints of lines around her smiling mouth. Her eyes were wide with indulgence. One hand was ruffling her hair, almost in bemusement, as she gazed at some wonder just out of sight.

"Oh, Al. What a great photo of you. What are you looking at?"

She knew perfectly well what—rather, who—she'd been looking at. "It doesn't look like me."

"Logic would say that these were taken moments apart, so if this looks like your Paddington, then this looks like you."

"You can't blind me with your logic. And she's not my—"

"Please. And what have we here?" A third photograph, this time of the sculpture of huge sandbox toys with both of them in the shot. There it was: Pepper, aglow with her serious charm, and Alice gazing at her like every question she'd ever had in the world had been answered.

Had she been wandering all over Los Angeles with that look on her face? "She's not mine. And won't ever be."

Her mother sighed. "What did you do?"

"What makes you think I did something?"

"I have eyes. You still look like a cat dragged you in. You love your place, but you're here instead. You're not drinking much—wine with dinner. Comparatively, for you, that's next to nothing. Something has turned you upside down."

She was a coward for not having found a way to bring up her decision to limit alcohol. She had trusted that sooner or later her mother would notice.

"I had to do something about the booze. I was lying about it, and letting it plan my day too often. I had the worst hangover of my life in LA. Plus, it was more than a little hypocritical, all the judging I did about women who drop fifteen dollars on vitamins before breakfast to have a perfect day when I was dropping twice that at McGinty's for an hour of numb."

Her mother made a little humming noise that Alice knew well. "Do you want advice, or do you need me to sit with you and listen?"

"Advice please. It's your superpower."

She received a beneficent smile. "Clever child."

"Kiss kiss."

"If you think you *might* have a problem, then you already have a problem."

Alice spread her hands in agreement, then tried to cover up the pictures, but her mother took her hand.

"You're shaking at the sight of this woman?"

"It'll stop."

"What a pity."

"She's living the life she wants. I helped push her down that path."

Her mother sighed and went back to her chair, feet again toasting close to the fire.

"Are you proud of how the series turned out?"

"I did the job I was sent there to do, and I think I did it well." She broke the hypnotic effect of Pepper's picture by studying the gloomy sky. The sunlight was nothing but gray and leeched all the color from the trees and water. "If it's going to look like this, it might as well rain."

"Easily said for someone who is inside and dry."

"True that." She buried the photographs of her and Pepper under the stack. "I'm proud of the series. I'm not proud of myself. I should have turned it down and quit."

"But you wouldn't have met your Paddington, would you?"

"She's not my Pad—"

"Don't lie to your mother."

"She can't be. She's... Too young, too unspoiled. She thought I was attractive. We had fun." A gross understatement of what they'd shared. "But no way am I going to foist my life on her."

"Tell me about this horrible life of yours."

"I'm now a Style reporter, which takes many skills that I don't have and hijacks the skills I do have to make opinions seem like facts. So I have to find some other way to make myself miserable. Misery is *my* superpower."

"What does that lovely young woman have to do with it?"

"Like I said, she's the wrong person for my train wreck of a life. She'd... She'd want to help me fix it."

"God forbid you accept help from someone."

"Some things have to start with me. Why would I saddle her with that job? It's not the life she's supposed to have."

"Are you in charge of that? What other people's lives are supposed to be?"

Pepper had said nearly the same thing, and Alice shook off her annoyance. "Of course not. But I am in control of me. I'm not drinking for my own good. I'm not doing it for her."

After a thoughtful nod, her mother asked, "Does it bother you if I drink?"

"No. The urge is resistible," she added. "It's not a one sip and I can't stop physical impulse. It's deciding I *have* to drink to survive emotionally some days. It's emotional. I lie to myself in clever ways about it. Like I can be science-minded enough to know that the hair of the dog that bit you doesn't prevent rabies and still use that myth to justify drinking at breakfast because I think I can't get through my day without numbing up first."

"Why do you want to be numb? What's the pain?" It was helpful that her mother was looking into the fire and not at her.

Alice finally moved away from the beguiling and maddening snapshots of perfect, green, warm, sunny California. With her backside to the heat from the fireplace, she studied the framed enlargement of what young Alice had called "The Owl Lady" but was actually her mother's *New Yorker* caricature. "I don't even know where to begin. The world is a mess. I'm not making it any better. Which is what I thought I was going to do with my life. Like my father, like you. Make it better."

Her mother's chuckle was annoying. "How did we do that?"

"Knowledge. Decency. Curiosity. Compassion. They're all dead."

That brought her mother's eyebrows down hard into a scowl. "Pish tosh. Al, if that's what you think, you haven't been paying attention. Resistance is not futile."

"It hasn't worked."

"What is your basis for that statement? You have no way of measuring what any one refusal to be part of even the most mundane of evils achieves."

"But I know I'm not saving anyone. Including myself."

"You're standing right here. Every day you save yourself. That is the great leap of faith, after all." Her mother's voice deepened with conviction. "We're civilians caught up in a war. A cold war on knowledge and decency and on the concept of greater good."

"And gaslighted the whole time that what we can see with our own eyes isn't happening."

"It feels like a new war to you. But I was fifteen when the National Guard killed four students at Kent State. I'm sorry if it sounded like I didn't understand wanting to be numb. I get it."

"When the booze wears off everything is as bad as it was when I numbed up."

Her mother's sigh was heartfelt. "Tomorrow morning I'll still wake up in a world where some meat packing plant supervisors bet on how many employees would die from a deadly virus. I could drink all night and it wouldn't change that we share the same world, the same country, with people so damaged that they could do that."

"Human beings are so shitty, Mom. So shitty."

"They can be. Mentally we can be ready for the deep oceans of grief, but not so much for the shallows of it that spread on and on without an end. We can so easily drown in our history."

"Then what's the point—" Alice forced herself to lower her voice. "What's the point of any of it?"

"You're scaring me."

She finally met her mother's gaze and was sorry to see true alarm in her mother's eyes. "I am not entertaining those kinds of thoughts. But flirting hard with an alcohol problem was maybe the same thing. I realize that now."

Her mother rose to take her hands, and Alice was frozen in the owlish stare that always seemed to understand her. "When you get old enough to see the patterns of humanity, you realize most of them bring despair. You also see the one thing that has no pattern. It simply is, and it's inexplicable. It confounds despair. It is the point. You know what it is."

Alice stared at her mother, her mind a blank. What could possibly be left to believe in?

Her mother squeezed her hands again. "Love cuts across all the patterns. You see love in tears, love in grief. Love in an egg salad sandwich or a nurse's bracing smile."

Dumbfounded, Alice felt tears sting her eyes. "That's so simplistic it's almost facile."

Her mother shrugged and returned to her chair. "Occam's Razor. It's the simplest answer that explains everything. Human beings can be incredibly shitty, as you say. Love is the only reason we survive ourselves."

"I can't..." She didn't even know what she couldn't do—believe in it? Feel it? Act on it?

"There's your first and foremost problem."

She glanced out the window. It was raining now, which felt like a relief. Water ran down the panes and reflected back the shimmering glow of the fire. For a moment she was spinning under the moon turned gold, sand under her feet. "What?"

"You think love is a choice."

"Isn't it?"

"We're born knowing how to love, and love keeps us alive long enough to delude ourselves into thinking it's a choice. Count yourself lucky it took forty years to understand how dark the world can be."

"Lucky?" She closed her eyes to the gray and remembered the searing joy when fireworks had filled her soul with vibrant color. When Pepper had kissed her.

"Hundreds of millions of children around the world are where you are now before they can talk. And they still look up for the love."

The bing-bong of the mantel clock chime eased away Alice's desire to cry. She returned to the table and lost herself in an orderly sorting process. The revealing photographs went back into the big envelope with the other rejects.

Her mother finally stretched in her chair. "I'm going to get a brandy and some tea. Do you want tea?"

"Yes, please."

Alone she couldn't help herself. She opened the envelope and got the pictures from the bottom of the stack where, she realized, she had put them to make them easy to find again. Pepper's lovely face side by side with her own unrecognizable one.

She wanted to denounce her mother's surprisingly sentimental take on the world—love conquers all? It didn't.

Those kids dancing on the beach—not kids, she corrected herself. Adults in a revolution to claim the world they'd been left and on their terms. They danced, laughed, and sang. Enjoyed and savored the pleasures of life, even as they struggled and fought and dealt with fear and loss.

Her mother hadn't said love conquered all, had she? She'd said love was there, in spite of it all.

Alongside its fellow travelers, Alice thought. Alongside trust and hope.

CHAPTER THIRTY-SEVEN

Pepper was almost too exhausted to take in the panorama of New York City as the Gulfstream's wing dipped in the final turn toward Teterboro airport.

Almost. The setting sun, peeking under the cloud cover from the west, turned the Empire State Building brilliant orange. The rivers that divided Manhattan from the other boroughs were black in the shadows.

The luxury of flying in a private jet hadn't worn off either, even after spending nearly the entire six hours of the flight going over last-minute arrangements for the four events. And that was on top of working straight through weekends for what seemed like forever. The first soft opening kicked off in less than twenty-four hours and Helene was reeling off checklists to be reviewed at the all-hands morning meeting and combing over the guest list RSVPs and cancellations.

"Tell Micas that there was clearly an error in her not receiving an invitation, that I noticed her absence. You're calling to make sure she attends. She'll say yes and that makes up for Brianna canceling at the last minute."

"She did break her ankle," Pepper reminded her.

"I know. Did we send flowers?"

"Yes. I also thought a rosemary and lemongrass aromatherapy candle would be appreciated. She had ordered a similar fragrance in bath salts."

"Excellent." Helene glanced out the window. "We're about to land. We'll be at the brownstone in forty-five minutes. Just long enough for me to get ready for my dinner."

The trim aircraft lightly touched down. After a brief taxi they gathered their belongings and descended the short stairs to the tarmac. Their luggage was already being unloaded.

As they splashed through shallow puddles on the tarmac, Pepper was grateful it had stopped raining before they'd arrived. The rest of the week was supposed to be better, with low temps but clear skies. A few steps later the wood-paneled terminal echoed with the clack of her heels on the concrete floor. Pepper scarcely had time to take note of the luxurious chairs, a sign pointing the way to the private movie theater, and the entrance to a day spa before they emerged out the other side to a town car idling at the curb.

She'd expected to be flying on her own into one of the public airports, but Helene had had to come back from New York to see to an issue at her house in Laurel Canyon. The Gulfstream and its pilot had been borrowed from a friend, who understood the emergency need for a round-trip from New York on Sunday and back on Monday so Helene could resume her wall-to-wall schedule. Helene had texted for Pepper to cancel her own Sunday flight and join her on Monday instead.

She had thought there would be a few other people, but the two of them had shared the eight-person cabin and catered lunch. Pepper had ended up sitting on the floor using empty seats to hold notes relevant to each of the four evening events as Helene reviewed every timeline in excruciating detail.

It was lavish and amazing, and she felt like someone playing a part in a movie. She was already exhausted at the beginning of an exhausting week. Helene was probably worn out too, but she didn't look it. Still, the change in flight plans had meant instead of arriving on Sunday evening and having maybe a few hours to ground herself, it was already Monday afternoon. She couldn't help but feel she was already running late.

It seemed an impossibly short time later that they alighted on East 69th Street in front of a half-flight of stairs leading to what Helene called simply "the brownstone." Only the steps were brown, however. The rest of the building was ivory, with black and gold wrought iron railings framing the flower boxes at four floors of windows as well as the gated barrier to the building's secrets.

The double doors beyond the gate swung open as Helene swept up the stairs. Pepper kept up, though it was hard not to feel as if she were scurrying. Scurrying was not a flattering look, she thought, and she'd taken such pains with her appearance. Wool slacks and a belted aquamarine trench coat from Michael Kors had been great for traveling.

A thin, very tall man, perhaps her father's age, stood next to the door. His black suit was trim and tailored and was accented with a red bow tie. Next to him, an equally rail-thin woman, also in black but with pearls at her collar, stood back to let them both enter.

"Hill, Amanda, this is Ms. Addington, my assistant. You've made arrangements for her room?"

"Yes, ma'am." Hill took Helene's jacket and gloves and gestured to a pale young man, who immediately joined the chauffeur in removing their luggage from the car and carrying it inside.

"Amanda, tell Rafael I'll be ready for him in ten minutes. And ask him to stay and do something for Ms. Addington as well."

They both observed Pepper through their glasses, leaving her feeling like a new specimen of some kind. *Who was Rafael?*

"Your bags will be brought up in a few minutes. If you'll follow me, miss." Amanda turned toward the interior of the house and Pepper got her first look at the white and gold marble inlay floor, ice blue walls with gold filigree etchings, and the wide curved staircase that led upstairs. Hoping not to need much help finding her way around, she'd scoured the web for information about the house. Somewhere there was a two-story library and a pool. The roof held an expansive green garden. The kitchen was on the first floor, near the salon, and across from the ballroom.

Don't look agog, that's as unattractive as scurrying. They went up two flights at a brisk pace and she was shown into a bedroom suite that was bigger than the entire apartment she shared with CC.

After turning down assistance with unpacking her bags, she plunked down on a beautiful chair that turned out to be hard as a rock. Rubbing her backside, she hopped to her feet again at the knock on the door heralding the arrival of her luggage.

The task of unpacking was mostly completed when a rap on the door proved to be Hill with a card that he handed to her with a grave smile. "Details about the house, miss. Wi-Fi code, mealtimes and protocols, and how to use the staff phone should you wish anything, cleaning and pressing clothes, and so forth. Dinner is *en suite* this evening."

"Thank you. I was feeling overwhelmed," she admitted.

He smiled with understanding. "This is a grand building. Should you have time at some point, I would be delighted to give you a tour." He spoke as if he'd done so many times and enjoyed it.

"I don't know if I will, but I hope that works out." He turned away, but she called him back. "Mr. Hill?"

"Just Hill, miss."

"How do I get to the nearest subway? Or a bus stop?"

He gave her a forbearing smile. "You need only lift the staff phone and ask for a car to take you anywhere you like, miss."

"Thank you."

She wandered the length of the suite, running one hand lightly over the furnishings. She needed to get onto the calls Helene had told her to make. One more minute, she thought, as she gazed around the sitting room and bedroom. The cold marble floors were warmed by thick carpets with Asian designs. A mahogany desk with cubbyholes would be a delightful place to work. The bedroom armoire, now filled with her clothes, was also mahogany, with an elaborate inlay pattern of roses on the doors. The ceiling over the canopied bed was decorated with an elaborate pattern of gold leaf and paint in brown and soft blue. It was all like something out of a princess dream, and it was merely a guest room in this palatial house.

Another tap at the door brought her out of her reverie. This time it was Amanda.

"If you're ready, miss. Rafael has finished with Ms. Jolie."

"Rafael?"

"This way please."

At the other end of the hallway a door was open to another bedroom. She could hear someone humming as Amanda ushered her in.

"Ms. Addington."

A wisp of a man with blond hair longer than Pepper's stood at a dressing table. "I see, I see," he said, coming forward to take Pepper's hand and evaluate her face and hair. "I see, I see."

"Excuse me?"

"You have good genes. You're doing some things right."

"My roommate—"

"But let's fix—" He waved a hand. "All of this."

Bemused, Pepper found herself seated in front of the vanity mirror with Rafael tsking and shaking his head as he undid her braid and combed out her hair. "Make more of what you have for cheekbones with wide plaits. Lift up directly to elongate the line of your skull and neck."

His hands were moving as quickly as a street magician conjuring a playing card out of someone's ear. The result was a tighter and higher braid that made her neck seem longer. The hair clip that Helene had given her would be perfect for evenings. Before she could ask any questions, he flung open a sample case with a wide range of Simply the Best makeup. "You've matched your skin tone well, but my dear, you need contrast on your cheeks, bronzer on your brow, and please put some effort into curling those lashes. Nature gave you enough of them that you won't need any augmentation for a few more years. And a black eyebrow pencil?"

He gave her a pitying sigh as he filled her hands with an array of jars and compacts, two shades of eyebrow pencils—neither of them black—and spent several minutes explaining all the things she was doing to make the absolute worst of her eyes. After she'd wiped her face clean with a series of towelettes, he went to work with deft application of all the new products. Finally he stepped away, looking satisfied.

Pepper almost didn't recognize herself. The everyday brown of her eyes glimmered like smoky topaz. In spite of her weariness, her skin was glowing. Her lips, in a shade darker than she normally chose for daytime, were sexy and full.

Though she had handled relations with the New York staff well, she had been worried about holding her ground with them in person. In video calls they were all effortlessly stylish with the same aplomb that Helene had. Spending the clothing allowance had helped somewhat with her raging case of insecurity.

Now she looked like one of them. She was going to get through this week and ride the wild wave all the way to shore.

Rafael shooed her away and she went back to her room to make her phone calls and send selfies to CC along with a couple of pictures of her room. After consulting the card Hill had given her, she picked up the staff phone and asked for dinner to be brought up and pretended she understood the difference between the two different preparations of branzino. It turned out she'd chosen a delicious, lightly grilled fish topped with chutney and accompanied by al dente broccoli.

Sated and head spinning with the impossible luxury of it all, she decided the best thing she could do for herself was a hot shower and an early night. Sleep, as so many Simply the Best Blog articles stated, was the best beauty treatment there was. Refreshed, she gobbled down the slice of gingerbread that had been brought along with her dinner, brushed her teeth, and tumbled into bed.

The layers of comforters were warm and the pillows soft. The sheets felt like silk against her skin—she could get used to the feel of them. It was hard to still her mind, so she thought about waves and sunsets.

It took an effort not to let her drowsy thoughts turn to dancing under the moon. Alice Cabot did not deserve her thoughts. She had not let herself imagine that they might cross paths. Smiling into the dark, she contemplated her accumulated high fashion gear and now a perfect New York makeover. If she did encounter Alice, she was darned sure going to make Alice regret every word she'd said.

CHAPTER THIRTY-EIGHT

Following the instructions on the card Hill had given her, Pepper went down to breakfast at seven and found a buffet with sliced mango and kiwi and fresh-baked English muffins. The jam selection included marmalade. Of course there was, she thought. This is a civilized house.

Her request for one egg over easy was promptly filled by a young woman with a lilting islander accent. No one else joined her before she'd finished a second helping of the perfectly ripe mango, so she headed up to her room to gather her things for the day.

As she reached the elegant, curving stairs, Hill appeared from a side door. "Ms. Addington, Ms. Jolie asked me to relay that she will be leaving for the store in five minutes."

"Perfect!" She ran up the stairs, glad she'd set her alarm extra early and already taken the time to apply makeup the way Rafael had shown her, using the daytime alternates of blush and lipstick.

Her new leather messenger bag was as organized and sleek as Simply the Best's website promised. It held the tablet the IT folks had given her, its keyboard and charger, and her bulging notebook with ease. She made sure she had her scarf and gloves, threw her trench coat over her arm, and was back downstairs before Helene was there.

She was prepared for this day. She lifted her chin. As CC would say, it was time for Captain Pepper to show her quality.

Quick steps descending the stairs made her look up. Helene had chosen a close-fitting turquoise suit with an open collar. Her hair was around her shoulders, tangling with a red and purple Givenchy scarf tied loosely around her neck. Oversized gold hoops dangled from her ears.

"Good morning."

"I trust you're being taken care of?"

"Yes." Pepper was aware that Helene was inspecting her wardrobe choices of high-waisted nubby slate gray trousers against a cranberry red blouse, both from the STB catalog, and belted with an off-center black belt from Yves St. Laurent she had found in a thrift store. The boxy Madden boots were low-heeled but would serve well for what was sure to be a day with a lot of walking and standing.

Helene said nothing, which Pepper took to mean she had passed muster. The town car waited at the curb and moved into traffic as soon as they were seated.

Helene rattled off questions about the tasks she'd given Pepper on the flight. Gratified that she could say all of them were done, Pepper resisted the urge to press her nose to the window of the car as they glided down Fifth Avenue along Central Park.

"Is this your first visit to New York?"

"No, but I was a child last time. I remember thinking it was nothing but boring museums and crowded theaters."

"You weren't wrong." Helene's smile was slightly indulgent. "But there is so much more. We're just a few blocks from the store now."

The car turned to circle the block. St. Patrick's Cathedral came into view, but Pepper was distracted as Helene took a small box from her bag. "Your earrings are a trifle conservative."

Pepper opened the box to find STB's iconic Balance earrings. Oval gold disks etched with triangles pointed up on one earring and down on the other. She couldn't afford the copper ones, let alone the eighteen-karat versions she held in her hand. "They're—they're beautiful."

"You've earned a *petit gâterie*." Helene glanced out the window as the car slowed. "A small gift to finish your look."

Pepper hurriedly unhooked her classic gold studs and replaced them with the new ones. She was intent on remaining balanced regardless of what this week threw at her and the earrings were a lovely reminder of her goal. It was more than a little intimidating to be wearing a $1,500 pair of earrings. Helene called it a small gift— maybe to her it was.

The driver opened Helene's door. Once Helene was clear of the car Pepper slid out behind her. She sucked in a deep breath against the sharp cold as she followed Helene toward the wide doors of the store.

She was glad to see that the long runners of green and red that hung from the third story windows had been anchored in place after she'd passed on to the vendor that they were blowing across the façade of the adjacent store. The exterior now looked like a three-story gift-wrapped package. Two rows of eight-foot potted blue spruce, flocked with gold and white, flanked the doors as ordered, creating a pathway. On Friday for the gala a red carpet would cover the sidewalk in between them. Helene broke stride and began to point at one spruce that was considerably browner than all the others, but Pepper took out her tablet and forestalled her with, "I'll see to it."

"I should have known I didn't even need to point it out. You read my mind so well."

Then they were into the whirlwind of the day. Pepper was greeted with air kisses by people she'd already met on video calls and ran out of mnemonics to remember all the new faces after the first dozen. Helene delivered curt instructions to the assembled staff about the necessity for every last element of the store interior being completed and ready for final review at five. Caterers would arrive then, and the first guests at six. The assembled employees dispersed to their units, and Pepper was able to get her first glimpse of the expansive interior.

Not even the Beverly Hills store had this much space and so many different product groupings. Like everywhere else in Simply the Best world, the walls were whitewashed pine. The displays created a wide center aisle, so the customer was drawn deep into the store to reach the featured Simply Detox Destination. Its U-shaped counter was gray slate. Though all the items could be found in their category elsewhere in the store, this was a one-stop shop for supplement blends, facial masks and scrubs, brush-in scalp treatments, water purifiers, bath salts, and more. There was also a scanner station that analyzed skin elasticity and tone and recommended a matching regimen.

A glittering array of beauty products was on the left side of the wide center aisle, arranged with and around the gold ornaments that were featured for the season. On the right were essential oils and Simply Scents featuring the new autumn unisex cologne. The very rear of the ground floor was occupied by jewelry and handbags. Clothing was upstairs, along with footwear. The top floor held administrative offices and private consultation shopping.

The store manager, Patty O'Neil, was posh in a mix of Simply the Best and Chanel. In contrast to Helene, her red hair was a vibrant dark orange that Pepper found charming with the spray of freckles across her cheeks. She shook Pepper's hand with an expression of mild surprise that left Pepper puzzled. "Is Clarita not here?"

"Not until Thursday," Helene answered. "Pepper is the Go-To."

Why did Patty think Clarita would be here? She reminded Patty of their conversation yesterday morning by asking, "The permit people say they have sent it. Have you seen it?" Pepper followed Helene and Patty up the spiral ramp to the second floor. "The one for the modular building on Friday to serve as a cloakroom?"

"It hasn't arrived here."

"I was afraid of that. Without it the modular people won't do the set up. It was mailed Friday. Let's cross our fingers that it arrives today, or I'll be spending tomorrow morning at the permit office."

"Did you call Susan Marshall?" Helene frowned at the table with rolls of belts just off the top of the stairs. "I don't know what is intended here. Is it a pattern? I don't understand why it isn't attractive."

Patty gestured at an employee who looked as if she wanted to melt into the floor. "Fix this."

"A call to Marshall is how I was able to find out the permit was even mailed."

"Half that," Helene told the employee. "Tie them with ribbons. Anything is better than this."

Pepper jotted a note on her tablet to circle back and check the display when the employee was done. It was the first of dozens of notes before the hour was out.

By the time the catering staff arrived, Pepper was on fumes. If any of the fig with pecan and goat cheese fell on the floor she would five-second rule it in a heartbeat. Once she and the caterer were on the same page—tables were as specified on the layout Pepper had drawn, covered with red drapes, not black, and she had confirmed the quantities prepared for the forty guests—she met with the bartenders who were chilling champagne and white wine and opening reds to breathe. That left her a few scant minutes to transition her makeup to evening shades. The earrings Helene had given her were perfect. When she added the beautiful hair clip, she felt prepared to stand quietly behind Helene and anticipate anything that might be needed to make the night a success.

She'd been paddling all day and it was time to ride the wave.

At five minutes to six the string quartet was tuning up, and Helene returned from a rushed round trip to the brownstone to change. Her emerald suit was splashed with sequins that reflected the twinkling of long icicles of holiday lights that dangled from the ceiling.

Helene immediately walked the tables of food and examined the bar. Her bracelets jangled as she lifted one of the bottles of red and set it down without comment. She glanced to where Pepper waited for any instructions. "Well done."

"Yes, well done." Patty O'Neil had joined them. She sounded impressed, which was flattering, and surprised, which wasn't.

"Thank you."

Helene slowly turned to take in every angle of the store. "We're ready. Light the exterior."

Pepper held her breath. Her watch said it was exactly six. She had reminded ten of the guests that Helene would appreciate their arrival promptly at six. She'd even sent handwritten notes last week. But what if no one showed for fifteen minutes? Helene was looking at the door expectantly. Any moment she would ask Pepper where the guests were.

The door opened. Pepper didn't know who the roly-poly man with a page boy haircut was, but Helene did. They greeted each other as old friends. The door opened again.

Four hours later Pepper collapsed on her bed. When Helene had left to have dinner with several local Very Important Besties and Patty O'Neil, she'd told Pepper the evening had been flawless. Flawless! Once the exterior lights were out, she and the remaining staff had descended on what was left of the catered food, which wasn't much. One of the bartenders had saved her a glass of champagne and now she was a little tipsy. She was a little sorry for him as he'd flirted with her and it wasn't going to get him anywhere.

It was vexing that an image popped into her head of Alice dancing with the firelight reflecting off her adorable glasses. She kicked off her boots in annoyance and then curled her toes with the recollection of Alice in that thin T-shirt.

It was just hot sex, Pepper told herself for the umpteenth time. It felt good, and then Alice proved herself—what had CC said? A straight-up villain. That's what she was.

She sat up, head spinning a little. She had left the bed tidy, but it was now expertly made. The soft, faded Wonder Woman T-shirt she slept in was neatly folded under her pillow. Time for sleep. If she sat here any longer she'd think about the straight-up villain again.

She opened the armoire to hang up her jacket and found a garment bag she didn't recognize hanging alongside her own clothes. As soon as she pulled it out, she spotted the logo of a Manhattan designer that STB had newly partnered with.

It must be her dress for the gala. Helene had had Pepper send her measurements to a stylist who was to arrange something to borrow for the evening. She unzipped the bag and found a calf-length black velvet dress. The skirt was stamped with iridescent shades of blue and green with some of the same on the sleeves as well.

She was being loaned actual haute couture. *Wowie zowie.* It was a good thing she'd found Mischka pumps at a resale shop—none of her other shoes were even close to being worthy of the dress. This was very fine adventuring gear indeed.

She clasped the dress to her body and spun in a circle. After today she was more hopeful that the week would go well. By Saturday she would have proved to herself—and Helene—that she was capable. Competent. Worthy of responsibility.

It was her time to shine, and no straight-up villain would take that away.

CHAPTER THIRTY-NINE

"End of the month, then?" Ed's bushy eyebrows eased from a disbelieving scowl.

Alice had not held any false hope that Ed would try to convince her to stay. It was good to have a conversation with him where he wasn't throwing his pencils. "Makes it clean for Human Resources."

"Can I count on you for any follow-ups needed until then?"

She nodded. "Sure. Of course. There could be some. I hope it's not for the Simply the Best series. I admit I was taken aback by the social media cycle after every article landed. When the New York versus California infographic hits tomorrow it'll be quantifiably insane."

"You hit the nail square for tone, and there's a lot of euphoria upstairs. But I understand why you don't want the assignment permanently. I wish I had something else to offer, but the decision to partner Science and Tech reporting with the wire services won't be changed for at least six months, when someone realizes it was a spectacularly bad idea."

"I thought about waiting it out, but I think the assignment would kill me." She said it lightly, but it wasn't a jest. She did not want a job that helped her drown in her own despair and depression. "I reported over the summer on a quantum computing breakthrough. Their first trial has been a complete success. They broke the quintillion floating point operations per second barrier—obliterated the previous record. I'd love to do a follow-up. This is the ground floor of faster-than-human-thought artificial intelligence, with all the worms in cans that could be set free by the tech."

"Sounds good." He rolled a pencil across his blotter. "Let your geek nerd flag fly high."

She grinned at that. "May it ever be so."

He stood up to shake her hand. "Don't lose touch. I'll always have an open ear for your perspective."

She was pleased with Ed's parting words. No bridges burned. It wasn't her final walk across the once yellow linoleum, but it felt like it. Not like walking away from a tragedy but crossing a graduation stage with a future waiting. She made herself look at the empty desks. The ghosts of people and livelihoods still misted in the air. Today, at least, they could travel with her, and she could bear the journey.

"Al!"

Startled, she turned back to Ed, who stood in the doorway to his office.

"I forgot about this."

She went back for the small envelope. "What is it?"

"Someone upstairs couldn't use it."

Because she expected fate to have its laughs, she suspected what it was. At her desk she confirmed it. A ticket to Friday night's Simply the Best grand opening gala fundraiser for restaurant and theater recovery. It was the social launch of the holiday season, and her articles had helped make it so.

Her first instinct was to toss it, but it was short-lived. She had certainly not expected to be invited—both Pepper and Helene Jolie surely had no wish to see her again. She was surprised by the pang of fear she felt at seeing either of them, for very different reasons. Pepper it was understandable—she didn't want to see how well Pepper had moved on. Or to be treated to the invective she deserved.

But why on earth was she afraid to face the likes of Helene Jolie? It wasn't as if she'd lost out somehow to Jolie. It annoyed her that Jolie was enjoying all the benefits of Alice's work, according to all the plans, and probably enjoyed the thought of how much that had galled Alice in the end. No, she wasn't afraid of Jolie.

Was she?

Fate had handed her a challenge, and maybe it was one she had to take up, then. She needed to prove to herself that her future wasn't stuck in the mire of her history. All it would take was getting her tuxedo pressed.

With the ticket tucked into her messenger bag alongside her laptop, she wrapped a scarf around her neck, pulled a knit cap firmly onto her head, and went out to the slushy street. It had rained earlier, but the skies were supposed to clear starting tomorrow and the temperatures would fall. She paused to defog her glasses with the end of her scarf, which worked about as well as it never did, and jaywalked to the Puerto Rocko food truck she'd been happy to spot from her window.

The piping hot chicken pastelito warmed her hands as she walked down Eighth Avenue to McGinty's. She got mayuketchu all over her fingers, but it wasn't the first time.

Simon was ahead of her. He looked warm and snug and was accepting another G&T from the bartender.

She stripped off her frozen tundra gear and slid onto the barstool. "That your second?"

"It is—I'm celebrating."

"You got the national gig?" At his nod she gave him a hearty hug.

"It's only the streaming broadcast at this point, but the contract is for a year."

"You dog!" She accepted the two fingers of Buchanan's from the bartender and raised it to Simon in a toast. "I was saving this drink for later, but you're worth it."

He regarded her with affection and concern. "We can meet somewhere else, if that would be easier."

She sipped at the liquid amber and appreciated the warmth that spread to her ears. "This is fine. I can limit myself. If I can't, or don't want to, then I know I'm in trouble."

"Send up a flare and I'll come running." The kind concern in his eyes was one of the reasons she hoped she didn't lose touch with him. Once her gig at the paper ended, making a daily stop here made little sense.

"Thanks. Besides, I'm celebrating too."

"You did it?"

"I'm a free woman for the new year."

They tinked their glasses again and sipped in companionable silence.

Simon's inevitable question was one that had been plaguing Alice since she'd made her decision. "What are you going to do?"

"Don't know. Well, not long-term. Short-term I'm going to get my old Subaru out of my mom's garage and go look at cool stuff."

Ever helpful, Simon suggested, "You could visit every baseball stadium."

"That's your gig. I could start right here with MoMath and Brookhaven, then go gaze at the Holmdel Horn across the river."

"Stop it. Looking at cool stuff does not include Jersey. That's just pitiful."

Mostly to annoy him, she said, "There's plenty to see in Boston."

"There's no reason for anyone to go to Boston except to watch the Yankees beat the Sox."

"Or to see the building where your father researched optics."

"Sure, play the dead father card."

She had another sip from her glass, rolling the oaky gold across her tongue. "The Very Large Array."

"All the way to New Mexico?"

"It would revisit the source of my Jodie Foster crush." She could have enchiladas Christmas style and not think about Pepper.

"Now you're talking. That I can understand." Simon grabbed a bar napkin and jotted down locations. In no time at all they had a list that stretched from New York to Cape Canaveral, Toronto to Chichén-Itzá, and circled around the Southwest. "If you're going to Chichén-Itzá for one of the world's oldest observatories, you should see a modern one. Symmetry."

She wasn't going to go to the Griffith Observatory again, but it didn't make sense to avoid all of California. "Palomar, in San Diego."

Simon wrote it down with a flourish. "A trip to reclaim your cool. That'll take a couple of weeks."

"Months, if I do it right."

He took a picture of the napkin before handing it to her with a flourish. "I'm going to hold you to it."

She tucked it safely in her trouser pocket. "When do you start on national broadcasts?"

"Spring training."

"Travel?"

"A lot of studio work, but sometimes. Like to go to Boston to watch—"

"—the Yankees beat the Sox."

They touched their glasses in solidarity.

When she got home, she magnetted the napkin to the refrigerator where she would see it every day. It would take months and she would recharge her science love batteries. A better use of time than moping for something that might have been and screaming at the darkness until she lost her voice.

Her mind flicked through memories of other places that had lifted her out of herself. Places full of the darkest moments of humanity. The Coliseum in Rome, where slaves were forced to kill each other for the circuses of capricious overlords. Dachau, with its unspeakable efficiency of genocide. Canyon de Chelley in Arizona, where thousands upon thousands of years people had lived, where children still played in the river today, and where sanctioned massacres had nearly wiped out a way of life.

Everywhere she looked there was horror, a tsunami of it. In her despair, she'd been unable to see the people who struggled to stay afloat and the ones throwing life preservers. Grief and atrocity transcend time and borders, she thought. But so does the hope of seeing another sunrise, embracing loved ones, and sleeping safely. So, too, her own transcendent awe of a vast desert valley awash in flowers that had waited years for a few brief days in the sun.

She'd only been looking at the worst of it. Seeing only the soldiers on the rim of the canyon with rifles aimed at children and families. Emperors presiding over death matches and still killing the winners. Hate and brutality for ego and profit.

For every one of those things there were people who knew it wasn't right. The victors, with their caprice, greed, and cruelty, had had their version of truth for too long, and she had given them too much of herself. Maybe there were other stories she could tell, however small, to add some balance to the scale.

She ran her finger down her Cool Science Road Trip list. It was a start.

PART EIGHT

People Like Us

CHAPTER FORTY

It was a different kind of exhaustion that gripped Pepper by the time she pulled the luxurious velvet dress out of its garment bag. Her body was begging her to get more than five hours sleep and to get out into the open air. Central Park was not even a block from the brownstone and she'd yet to set foot in it.

She loved the thrill of success, though. The adrenaline from watching all her efforts come together had been enough to keep her going. Helene's praise had been fulsome, and Pepper had been invited to join Helene for dinner after last night's third of three soft openings had ended without a single mishap. It had been a long, extremely interesting meal with a Broadway producer and his husband, the co-chairs of NYC's largest youth foundation, and, of course, Helene. A lengthy discussion about how to train a cat had been one of the funniest and most earnest exchanges of the night. All that and a delicious dinner with lovely wine and post-dinner brandy.

They'd left the restaurant and waded through the throngs in Shubert Alley to meet their car, which had whisked Helene and her back to the brownstone. Helene had told a funny story about being caught in a compromising position by a maître d' at that very restaurant some years ago. In response to Helene's question, Pepper had admitted she had no such adventurous stories to tell.

"None yet." Helene had patted her hand. "I think that part of your life is only beginning."

Helene stopped to answer a question from Hill, leaving Pepper to float up the stairs to her room and fall asleep within minutes of pulling the wonderful sheets up to her ears just as the delicate mantel clock chimed twice.

Waking up had been hard, and her phone pinged nonstop with messages about flowers, balloons, red carpeting, and a kerfuffle about the mobile cloakroom because nobody could find the permit even though Pepper had taped it to the back of the store manager's door and told a dozen people that's where it was, right alongside the capacity waiver and one-night permit for the event.

Hours at the store had been spent assuring people that, yes, they were supposed to remove merchandise from any free-standing displays and reposition them for the grand opening according to the layout plan to create gathering points that viewed the wall displays designed by the same engineer MOMA used for art installations, but with STB products.

Yes, the event permit included an open-flame station for serving Bananas Foster and cherry crêpes flambé.

Yes, there was an open bar for standard drinks on one side of the floor, and yes, the slate counter at the front of the Simply Detox Destination was for the unfettered use of the celebrity mixologist who required four electrical outlets, a tap-to-pay station to collect donations, a steady supply of ice and cut fruit from the caterers, and no interference.

Yes, there was literally going to be a dance floor on the second floor, and yes, all the register equipment had to be cleared out to make room for the DJ.

And on and on.

She'd finally been able to leave the store, but a half hour later than she'd planned. Back at the brownstone she'd devoured a sandwich and started the process of getting dressed for the evening. Her spirits lifted as she smoothed the black velvet dress and thought about feeling it against her skin.

Though she wanted a luxurious hot shower, she kept it short and decided to skip washing her hair. Wrapped in a towel she sat down at the vanity, turned on the lights for night-time makeup, and dabbed skin toner around her eyes. She rebraided her hair and set the sparkly hair clip in exactly the right place at the crown of her head. By the time she was done with her hair her revived eyes were ready for makeup.

The lighting made it easier to get the liner right and to declump the mascara.

Finally she was shrugging into a demi-bra and long slip and coaxing sheer black hose up her thighs. The black velvet dress fit beautifully, shaping around her breasts, tailoring in at her waist, and falling to just above the curve of her calf. The weight of the fabric made it coil and *shush* around her hips and thighs when she moved. The square neckline showed off the Simply the Best necklace her parents had given her, which looked great with Helene's gifted earrings.

"Well, look at you, you gorgeous thing." She smiled at herself in the full-length mirror, twirling several times in her sleek Mischka high heels to get her balance. "Everybody looks so pretty here, and now so do you. It only took a makeover, a haute couture dress, and ninety minutes doing hair and makeup."

"This is what Alice Cabot didn't want any more of," she told the mirror. She took a selfie and sent it to CC saying, *Ready for my gala adventuring quest!* and giggled when CC texted back, *You are a natural Twenty and your mods are off the hook!*

It was almost time to meet downstairs. If she went down a little early she might be able to get some iced tea in the dining room. A fresh-brewed pitcher and a thermal carafe of fresh coffee were always there.

As she stepped into the hallway she realized that Helene— breathtaking in a form-fitting silver and white knee-length duster with a burnout pattern of snowflakes—had just emerged from the suite of rooms at the other end of the floor. Even from this distance Pepper was dazzled by the shimmer of light off the diamonds at her neck and ears.

Pepper waited where she was as Helene approached. She really hoped that she lived up to the dress.

"I was just going to knock on your door," Helene said. "*Por vous.*"

She handed Pepper a square jeweler's case with the name of a Fifth Avenue store discreetly stamped in one corner. Heart abruptly pounding, she opened it to find a necklace and earrings of green-streaked malachite set in eighteen-karat gold. The pendant also had an inlay of a single stripe of a pink stone she didn't recognize. "It's beautiful. I'll take good care of it."

"It is a gift. A thank-you. And because you will need it to go with the dress whenever you wear it."

It took Pepper several seconds to shut her mouth. The dress was hers? And now the stunning jewelry? "I thought—"

"You are worthy of both." She gestured at Pepper's still open door. "Let me help you put the necklace on. Jean-Pierre uses a double catch so there's no chance the necklace will slip off."

They went back into Pepper's room, making Pepper aware that the desk was a mess of papers with more on the floor. At least the rest of the room was tidy.

She unhooked her necklace and earrings and set them on the vanity and joined Helene at the mirror. Feeling shy and unsettled, she lifted the new earrings out of the box when Helene offered them to her. She was aware of Helene's study while she fastened the gold studs and let the long rectangle of stone swing freely. They were heavy. She would have to turn her head slowly.

"Lovely." Helene lifted the necklace over Pepper's head and settled the long, narrow pendant on Pepper's chest before circling Pepper's throat with the thick gold chain. All at once Pepper was aware of the light brush of cool fingertips at the nape of her neck. Helene's breath sent a cold flush down Pepper's spine.

Of course Helene was standing so close to see the clasp. That's all it was. There was no reason to feel weird about it. She avoided Helene's gaze in the mirror and instead lifted the pendant gently. "It's beautiful. Thank you."

"It flatters you, and you flatter it." Helene's hands were on Pepper's shoulders as she studied the pendant in the mirror.

Pepper finally glanced at her and forced a smile. "Thank you," she felt compelled to say again.

Helene's lips were so close that Pepper could feel the heat from them against her ear lobe. Her breath caught as she felt Helene's lips at the nape of her neck—or thought she did.

Helene stepped back, saying, "I'm sure the car is ready for us by now."

Of course Helene hadn't kissed her, what had she been thinking? Her hands were chilled as she struggled to unknot the coil of panic in her stomach. She was being a child. It didn't mean anything.

In the car Helene talked of nothing but the last-minute details to be checked. As they pulled up, Pepper could see that the red carpet between the row of flocked spruce was wrinkle-free and clean. There was already a crowd of photographers and onlookers with cameras all craning to see who was arriving. A small crowd clustered at the scanners checking the tickets. Perhaps ten people, by design. Zero waiting was embarrassing, Helene had said, but ten created an aura of anticipation. Their guests would not be patient for a longer line than that.

The moment the town car's door swung open the burst of light from the combined flashes was temporarily blinding. Pepper flinched and blinked, remembering just in time not to wipe at her heavily made-up eyes. Helene never paused as she rose gracefully from the car, smiling at the driver who had come around to open the door and offer his hand. He waited for Pepper and she alighted with what she hoped was aplomb as flashes continued to pop.

A reporter had lured Helene over to give a statement. Pepper tried to move past them so she could start her checklist, but the bright-eyed woman gestured at her as well.

"This is my assistant Pepper Addington," Helene explained. "She has carried out to perfection all of my instructions for this event and my vision for this entire triumphant week of our return."

Poised, cosmopolitan women don't blush. Nevertheless, Pepper felt her cheeks heat with pleasure at the praise. She didn't hear the rest of what Helene said as she answered another reporter's question about what designer she was wearing and turned toward the doors as Helene continued her walk along the red carpet with nods and smiles.

Pepper glanced at the small mobile building that was, thankfully, open for business as the cloakroom, and confirmed that the stairs had been replaced with an accessible ramp as Pepper had originally ordered.

A tall, slender figure turned from the counter and light reflected off black-rimmed glasses.

Pepper lifted her chin and met Alice's gaze square on. Cool. In her element. High on the wave. After a moment she turned her head to put her attention back on Helene, but not before she saw Alice's mocking nod of recognition.

You got your wish, she told herself. Alice got to see what she's missing.

Except it didn't feel anything like Pepper had thought it would.

CHAPTER FORTY-ONE

Alice was in no hurry to go inside after that glimpse of Pepper on the red carpet with Helene. She'd been wrong to think LA was the exclusive home of make-believe. A gushing line of press, gaggles of onlookers—bright lights, pretty people.

The image was seared into her mind alongside all the photos of Helene and her many watchdogs. Pepper was their clone—perfect hair, perfect skin, perfect dress, perfect jewelry. Perfect for Fifth Avenue and a New York gala of all the perfect celebrity and influencer glitterati. Not only a perfect advertisement for Simply the Best, Pepper was now a cold, razor-edged star that was both adornment and foil for Helene Jolie's fiery, flawless beauty.

Was this her penance? Reliving Pepper's declaration that she wanted to be more like Helene and seeing the reality of it?

"*Get over yourself,*" Sass answered. "*She's a grown-ass woman. She's smart, she's ambitious, and you're just mad that you still want her so much you can't breathe.*"

No longer certain that anything other than regret and pain would come of it, she decided to go inside. The store interior was everything she expected from having visited the one in Beverly Hills. Wood on the walls and stone underfoot, textured fabrics in backdrops, and all with clean, straight lines. The real wow was the three-story atrium and spiral chandelier of tear-drop lights and the long drops of icicle lights for the holidays. Space on Fifth Avenue was limited and expensive—it was a show of confidence to waste any of it on open air.

She got a club soda at the bar and sampled a stuffed fig, but she had no real appetite after seeing Pepper. Had she really thought she'd be unscathed by the defiant dismissal in her eyes?

It was impossible not to know where Helene Jolie was at any moment. She glanced up, half-expecting to see a follow spotlight trained on the woman as she worked the crowd. Pepper wasn't with her, though. Even as she told herself stalking was not acceptable, she caught sight of Pepper in a corner consulting the tablet in her hand and pointing at something only she and a caterer could see. After a short exchange, the caterer nodded.

Alice's gaze followed Pepper as she paused at the bar. Between the braided hair, the long, smooth dress, and heels that screamed, "you'll like it when I walk on you" she moved with a flowing, mesmerizing grace. At her word, the perky bartender rearranged the bottles behind her. Pepper asked a couple of questions and jotted the answers into her tablet. Next she paused at the mixologist's display, where a round-faced black woman with a brick house body was showing off a dazzling high pour into a cocktail shaker.

However Helene Jolie may have dressed her, Pepper was doing her job and making it look effortless. Given the turnout and funds raised and the crowd's celebratory mood, the party was going to be all over social media as a raging success. No doubt Helene had tightly controlled everything from food choices to layout, but Pepper had clearly done a great job making it happen.

She'd arrived too early, Alice decided. If her goal was to have a few words with Helene Jolie, she was going to have to wait. Habit reminded her that all the nearby hotels had a bar, but she flicked the idea away—she needed neither courage nor numbing. She wanted to be very much in the moment if she got a chance to tell Helene Jolie what she thought of her Price Tag Empowerment. There was absolutely nothing Helene Jolie could do to her now.

For lack of any other way to pass the time, she decided to see what was on the second floor. Halfway up the curving ramp she stepped around a cluster of people looking down at the mixologist's performance and came face-to-face with Clarita Oatley. After sincerely complimenting her on her gown—snow white, silky, and outlining a figure a runway model half her age would envy—she added, "A pleasure to see you again."

"Likewise," she responded with a polite chill that left Alice in no doubt as to her status with Helene Jolie's staff.

With a gesture at the party on the floor below them, Alice said, "Great event. Is any of this your handiwork?"

"Oh no, I only arrived this afternoon. I'm not responsible for this."

It was an interesting choice of words, but Alice didn't get a chance to pursue it in the middle of the already crowded ramp. Clarita treated her to a regal parting nod and Alice continued upward. The lighting on the second floor was darker. Vertical bar lights on the walls were lit, but the overheads were off. Spotlights cast snowflakes in gold and white across the ceiling, sparkling in time with the beat of disco music. A small parquet dance floor had been laid out in the center with another bar on one side and a DJ on the other.

Two women in tight-fitting black-tie tuxedos were expertly tangoing to "Don't Let Me Be Misunderstood." She watched them coil arms and legs with sharp gestures and averted faces and applauded with others when the dance ended. The music segued into something more recent, but equally rapid paced. It was familiar, and she hesitated, trying to recall it.

Then the memory unfurled, from the glowing, beneficent moon and crisp night air to the shimmering heat of the bonfire and the feeling of her soaked T-shirt against her back.

The number of people dancing had multiplied with the music change. Through the swaying bodies she saw Pepper on the other side of the parquet squares, also rooted in place. For Alice there was only the sand and moon and the memory of her fists in the air and feeling alive and connected to something that was thriving in a struggling world. In the weeks since, she hadn't been able to touch that memory without flinching, but it was soaked into every part of her now.

She had no idea what Pepper was thinking, but the brown eyes remained on her as the beat of "People Like Us" intensified. Her brain presented the reel from the Hollywood movie of this moment. The dance floor parted. They moved toward each other but stopped just as their bodies almost touched. Feather-light snowflakes bejeweled Pepper's hair as synthesizer strings transformed into orchestral violins. A full gospel choir sang, "This is the life that we choose" and she spun Pepper into her arms like they'd practiced for that moment all their lives and would dance together, never tiring, until forever.

None of it was real. She desperately, achingly, wanted it to be.

Instead, a bartender caught Pepper's attention and shouted something in her ear that made her shake her head. She turned away and the moment was broken.

It was Pepper's last, lingering look across the dance floor that brought Alice back from the pain behind her ribs as she struggled to breathe. Though filled with fire, it wasn't hate, disdain, or even regret. What it was, however, eluded her.

CHAPTER FORTY-TWO

Close your ears to the music, Pepper told herself. *Ignore it, ignore Alice, and focus.*

A prickle of electricity ran up and down her body and it wouldn't stop.

She'd nearly started across the dance floor. Thank goodness a small crisis had pulled her out of the fantasy of removing Alice's tie and undoing the buttons on her tuxedo-bibbed shirt. There would be no repeats of previous mistakes—not if she had an ounce of pride.

She followed the bartender down to the first floor at a pace that wouldn't attract attention but fast enough to make her ears ache from the heavy earrings. She didn't understand why the celebrity mixologist was packing up when there was still another two hours on the contract.

She was surprised to see Clarita behind the counter in a whispered but clearly heated exchange with the mixologist. Hiring Penny Nickel had been Pepper's idea. Her earlier check of the proceeds raised so far, and the persistent circle of happy onlookers, had been gratifying. She was like a DJ with all the flashy moves, though her props were cocktail shakers and bottles of top shelf. Her whole body got into the groove of flipping fruit and ice into the shakers and high pouring the liquor. The rings on her fingers and beads at the ends of her corn rows sparkled in the light. Pepper could have watched her all night.

Penny was not happy, though she wasn't openly scowling. There was no magic mixology underway, which meant there were no $50-suggested-donation drinks being made.

"What's the problem?"

"This setup is not acceptable," Clarita said. "Bar stations do not put bottles on the front counter. It's a hazard. It fronts the alcohol and not the service. Helene has always been adamant about it."

Pepper turned her head to speak to Penny. "I'm sorry about this…this confusion. Please go back to exactly what you were doing, arranged exactly how you want it."

She took Clarita by the arm, and with a grip she hadn't known she possessed, marched her into the small, curtained area where the caterers were plating.

"What do you think you're doing?" Clarita demanded.

"That's my question to you," Pepper snapped back. "You have no authority to make any changes to anything tonight."

"I'm saving you from the embarrassment of having Helene point out your mistake."

"There is nothing wrong with it."

Clarita treated her to a distant smile, the one that had always left Pepper feeling like she didn't understand something basic. "Let's ask Helene, shall we?"

"Let's not."

"I beg your pardon?"

"Helene has duties and she's busy doing them. This is below her pay grade. She had an opportunity to comment on the setup and didn't. Probably because that woman is going to raise another ten thousand tonight, and she can't do that if any of her layout is changed. Every bottle, shaker, blender, ice bucket, and glass is where it needs to be, and I'm not going to disrespect her by thinking I know better than she does how to do her job."

Clarita shook her head in something like pity. "Don't let all this go to your head, my dear. Helene collects pretty things, but she rarely keeps them for long."

And then she had the nerve to walk away, almost laughing.

Shaking with anger and confusion, Pepper followed her, but she couldn't think of how to waylay Clarita before she interrupted Helene's circulation among the guests. It had been Pepper's goal not to ask Helene about a single detail all night, leaving her boss free to do what she did so well.

Clarita wasn't making a beeline for Helene, however, who was currently near the open bar chatting with two men Pepper thought were from the mayor's office. She kept a watchful eye on Clarita as she stopped to apologize to Penny Nickel again.

"Don't worry about it. There's always one diva who has to speak to the manager." Penny shrugged. "Thanks for having my back."

"You're fantastic. Who wouldn't back you?"

"Thank you for saying that. I'm a little ahead of projection on the take, so I don't know why she was messing with success. I do a lot of these events, and you have a lot of not-so-used-to-rocking people really rocking." She pointed around the room. "You got fire. You got celebrities. You got music. Your social media person has your Insta lit. You got TikTokkers uploading on your hashtag. And you got performance," she added, indicating herself. "What agency do you work for again?"

"I work for Simply the Best. I'm the CEO's assistant."

"Oh—that's right." Penny surveyed her layout and adjusted the distance between the bowls of cut strawberries and oranges. She held up a finger to ask the guest at the front of the line for one more minute. "Before we wrap up tonight could I get your number to give as a reference?"

"Sure. Though I don't know what weight my opinion will have."

"You're the person who actually did the work and in event planning world everybody knows the top dog takes the credit, but there's always the people who made it happen. Usually it's a disaster when companies keep the planning in-house. This is a success—you are trending. Don't let the diva tell you otherwise."

"She's not my boss, so I think I'm good."

At least Pepper hoped it was true. Clarita had edged closer to Helene.

Fine, Pepper thought. *Helene does not respect timidity, remember?*

She caught Helene's eye by walking directly toward her with clear purpose. Helene ended her chat with the two men. A cluster of women who'd been slowly moving into position to be next to talk to Helene immediately took over the conversation. Pepper flicked through the contact cards in her mind and came up with two board members from a theater foundation and an actor from one of the crime shows filmed in New York.

"That's very interesting, and I'm so glad you're having a wonderful time," Helene was saying. "Let me introduce you to my assistant. She's the person responsible for executing my vision for this evening. And she's achieved nothing short of a miracle given where we were eight weeks ago."

After air kisses with the actor—who confessed to having eaten more than her fair share of the prosciutto-wrapped scallops—Pepper made a slight gesture toward the tablet tucked under her arm.

"One moment, I think Pepper has a question for me."

"Just a mid-event update," she said brightly. "I could give you details, but the executive summary is that food, beverage, entertainment, and flow is going as projected."

"And there you see why I'm so relaxed," Helene said to the group. "Pepper has everything under control."

Clarita was close enough to have heard the pronouncement and Pepper gave her a look she hoped conveyed "Bitch, I'm Beyoncé."

Her flush of triumph was disrupted by the lightest of touches of Helene's fingertips at the small of her back. Pepper accepted it as a gesture of confidence, but she didn't miss the exchange of meaningful glances between the two women from the theater foundation. Were they like Beth's gallery owner, presuming a relationship was behind Helene's favor? She'd worked so hard and done so well. It was frustrating—beyond frustrating—that anyone would think something else had contributed to her success.

Maybe Helene didn't understand how other people would interpret a gesture like that. Pepper scolded herself for not having realized that some people would presume the dress and jewelry were gifts—which, of course, they were. Rewards for a job well done, Helene had said.

Very expensive, intimate, personally selected rewards. On top of that, there was the makeover and the clothing allowance—all given at Helene's express instruction. They had a business purpose, Pepper reminded herself. Nevertheless, why wouldn't other people think she was a doll Helene enjoyed dressing up?

She caught herself before she called attention to the pendant by touching it. Helene was more than capable of giving a reward and an enticement with the same gesture. Is that what she'd been doing ever since she'd decided Pepper was smart enough to handle the New York parties?

Had she imagined or actually felt Helene's lips on the back on her neck?

Her world tilted sideways.

Stay on the board, she warned herself. *This is only a cross-current. Adapt.*

Indicating the tablet, she said, "I'll get back to it." She nodded to the group and made her way to the caterer's area on autopilot. *Helene wasn't…wouldn't…* What other people thought was going on didn't matter, did it? She was above petty gossip, or she ought to be.

It didn't help that it was harder and harder to ignore that seeing Alice had dissolved all her resolutions. That her first thought now was to ask Alice if she was being a silly little fool about gifts and—and silly stuff, like standing too close, and imagining kisses, and misinterpreting the little touches and intimate evaluation of her body. Alice would always tell her the objective truth.

No—it didn't mean anything. It couldn't mean anything. She was being stupid.

"Congratulations, Pepper! You've done an amazing job."

Startled, she realized that Patty O'Neil had stopped to talk to her. "Thank you. It was so much work, but I think it all came off well in the end."

"Better than well."

Pepper was reminded that Patty had seemed surprised that Clarita wasn't in charge. "I'm flattered that Helene trusted me with so much responsibility."

"You really were thrown in the deep end, weren't you? Well, you've proven you know what you're doing."

"That's good to hear." She breathed easier.

"Will I see much of you next week?"

"Next week?"

"Helene mentioned something about finally getting to do a few things for fun. Theater, other people's parties. I got the impression you wouldn't go back until she did."

Hoping her expression was nonchalant, Pepper said, "As far as I know I'll be back in the office next week. I have a mountain of thank-you notes to send and invoices to go over."

Patty shook her head in a not-very-convincing show of confusion. "Of course. I must have misunderstood. Don't let on I said anything."

She wasn't sure where she found the lighthearted laugh. "I didn't hear a thing you said."

The caterer's point person gave her a little wave and she excused herself. She jotted the update that the supplies were good if they wanted to extend the service time at all. She confirmed that the timetable for signaling the end of the event was unchanged and decided to go upstairs, though she didn't know why.

To see if Alice was still there?

Halfway up the ramp an attractive brunette touched her arm. "Are you Pepper?"

"Yes. Can I help you?"

"I'm Jean—I used to have your job, well, about five years ago."

Pepper now vaguely recalled her from an event photograph—about her height, with thick, dark gold hair, very fine bones, and a pointed chin. "A pleasure to meet you."

"I was talking to Helene a bit ago, and wow, you are totally on your way. Good for you! When she sings your praises, it's like a magic wand. I was only there six months, but every time I apply for a job or promotion, I drop Helene's name or they call to get a rec and, *bam*, I'm in."

It was a relief to hear that the hard work did lead to opportunities. "Paying dues turns out to be the way to go."

"Well. It's not like it was hard."

Jean's sidelong look down the length of Pepper's body settled an icy rock in the pit of her stomach. With a nod at the party, she said, "Trust me, this was hard. I can't remember my last day off."

Jean lifted an eyebrow. "Then maybe you're not doing it right."

The insinuation was plain. She should pretend she didn't understand, she told herself. Or did she want to do that because it was easier? "I'm doing it the way that matters to me."

"You're missing out on a lot of fun. I had a week in the brownstone—theater every night, dancing, shopping. Good times. Lots of *good* times."

"What if you'd said no?" The question was out before she could stop herself.

Jean studied Pepper's face in surprise. "Why would I have said no? She'd just had a breakup and there were no strings… Now I get why she said you and I should have a chat. You've missed your cues."

Was she supposed to make the first move? Did that mean there was nothing wrong with it, then? It was too late to pretend she didn't know they were talking about an affair, about sex, but she tried anyway. "I don't know what you mean."

"Don't be a blonde about it. A few months from now you get to write your own golden ticket." Jean's lips pulled to one side in an almost sneer. "Unless you're some kind of goody two-shoes."

"That's not it. I'm not a prude." She stopped talking because she realized it would sound crazy if she said she had zero interest in the beautiful, powerful, lusciously sensual Helene Jolie. Her taste, apparently, ran more to angular, scruffy, bespectacled science nerds. Or at least one of them.

"If you say so." Jean's flick of her fingers and parting roll of her eyes screamed, "Ya basic."

Dazed, Pepper found a dark corner behind the dance floor bar and closed her eyes. Even if she thought she could handle a casual fling or whatever with Helene, being afraid to say no was not the same as saying yes.

There was no way around that. Even if her body wanted to, it still wouldn't feel right in her head. Having seen how quickly people fell out of Helene's favor after making work mistakes, how could she ever believe that there would never be any consequences if she disappointed Helene in a much more personal way?

"Are you all right?"

Of course, she thought, before opening her eyes. Who could it be except the person she'd told herself she never wanted to talk to again and the voice she wanted most to hear at that moment?

"I'll be okay."

"Can I help?"

She opened her eyes at that. It was beyond her how she could want to kiss Alice, except she knew that Alice's kisses made the rest of the world go away. She failed at summoning a smile to assuage the concern on Alice's face. Raising her voice over the music, she said, "Yes, you probably could. But I have to do it myself."

Alice leaned closer to be heard. "I'll take your word for it, then. But if it should change…"

Pepper could only look her gratitude for the support, but then she remembered she was supposed to be mad. She was still mad, actually. "It's about the party life. The one I want so badly."

Alice pursed her lips. "I deserve that. Listen, I—you can say no. But there are a few things I'd like to say, if you'll let me. Not here," she added quickly. "Later, or maybe a cup of coffee tomorrow. It won't take long."

She hesitated, wanting to immediately say yes but not wanting to appear unable to resist, which was the truth and she didn't want Alice to know that. It was hard enough admitting it to herself.

Alice seemed to take her hesitation as a refusal. "The short version, then. I'm sorry. I was out of line—wrong."

"Then why?"

"Not here." She waved a hand at the DJ. "I don't want to shout it, and whispering in your ear is a really bad idea."

Her eyes half-shut of their own accord at the memory of Alice's breasts against her back. "Later. But I don't know when I'll actually be done." Helene would possibly want her to go out again. Had last night been a cue she'd missed? She realized she didn't want to be alone with Helene, not tonight.

"I'll be around. Outside if it's after the guests are kicked out."

"It's freezing out there. Literally."

The lopsided, mocking smile flashed. "We have garments here of calculated thickness designed for that eventuality."

"Show off," Pepper muttered. "Did you expect to be out in the cold?"

There was the barest trace of irony in her voice. "Yes. I'm glad I was wrong."

How did Alice make all the air in the room go away like that? It was like Alice's superpower or something, and she shouldn't like it. "Well, okay then."

"Good."

"Later."

"Fine."

"I have things I need to do." She held up the tablet which was now actually vibrating with a reminder. "A great many things."

Alice nodded, saying, "Of course," with a lift of her eyebrows.

She managed to walk away then, before she felt any more ridiculous.

CHAPTER FORTY-THREE

The evening was not going as planned, Alice thought. Maybe, however, it was going as she had hoped—a hope she'd silenced as undeserved.

It no longer seemed important to confront Helene Jolie about anything. Her priority was Pepper. If nothing else, maybe she could make some peace for letting her inner bitch say cruel and stupid things. Another hour with her would be one more hour when hope didn't seem like an act of self-delusion.

With perhaps two hours to kill, she prowled the corners of the store and found a stool tucked under a counter. No one seemed to notice as she scooted it into a narrow gap between display cases. A minute later she had a paper on ultrafast laser spectroscopy open on her phone and the party faded into white noise. As far as she was concerned, the only thing here more fascinating than superconducting metamaterials was Pepper. She would wait all night if she had to.

The relative quiet of the corner she'd found—between jewelry and essential oils—attracted other people who wanted to be able to converse, albeit still at a near-shout. She easily overheard a planned assignation between two people whom she gathered were hoping to keep it a secret. Plenty of opinions were shared about the attire, age, weight, and makeup of numerous women present. Several people remarked that they hadn't expected to enjoy themselves, but the food was good and watching both the flambé and bartenders were fun, as was the dancing. The tango dancers she'd seen earlier were apparently professionals hired to both entertain and encourage dancing—one person loved the genderbending duo while the other decried it as cliché.

At first she thought the latest pair of women huddling together to chat was more of the same, but the mention of Helene Jolie perked up her ears.

"Who knew that Helene's latest would actually pull this off?"

The second voice, all nasal, said, "I know, right? I had assumed that since this one was passably pretty and inexperienced that as usual Clarita did most of the work or farmed it out."

"I was a nervous wreck at first asking her to do anything. But every time I asked she said yes, and then she did it. Permits! Good lord, she navigated getting the permits." After a shared, knowing laugh, the first voice went on, "I asked her to do it because it never works out and I didn't want the blame."

Nasal opined that a woman passing them could not possibly be using the Simply the Best anti-aging products correctly, then said, "Do you suppose you could keep asking her to do the crappy work?"

"I'd give it a try. But they never last for long. You know, once all the fun has been had."

There was a meaningful silence. That, or they drifted away. It was hard to tell over the ringing in her ears. She'd been right that Helene was very comfortable using her riches and beauty to bemuse and dazzle. Certainly those women thought assistants were hired for their attractive qualities and not their skill. She was willing to bet that if she looked into the background of Helene's assistants over the years, most would be relative neophytes, eager to get a foot in and work long hours on a small paycheck, which only increased the desire to be rewarded, eventually, in whatever way Helene Jolie felt like dispensing.

Less experienced women, like Pepper, would also be far less likely see the wolf in the all-natural cotton-cashmere clothing because the wolf was a woman. If they showed alarm or resistance, Helene could gaslight them and move on.

Just like men did.

She wished Simply the Best made Helene Jolie dolls. It would be the only money they'd ever get from her—she'd buy one to turn into a red-headed shish kebab. Her familiar and constant friend Anger suggested she set fire to something. Or better yet, Sharpie over "Best" wherever it appeared and turn this entire store into Simply the Douchebag.

The flash of rage abated before she'd decided if any of the food could be used for graffiti. She needed to back up. What she'd overheard was gossip, and from sources who indulged in casually spiteful comments about other people. Just because she could see how it could be true and had witnessed the way Helene unleashed her charms didn't mean Helene had actually seduced anyone. Gossip flourishes even in barren fields.

Pepper was all that mattered. And Pepper had told her that whatever it was that had upset her—most likely something about the party—she didn't need Alice to fix it. She had to respect that.

"*You thought she was a bubblehead,*" Sass announced. "*You, however, are a total nitwit.*"

She had to move around, if only to get rid of some of her tension. As she stood up, she realized too late that she'd done so right in the path of another woman who'd been using the narrow back aisle to quickly get around the crowded center of the floor.

Helene reared back as if she was unused to impediments—and she probably was, Alice thought. People got out of her way.

"I beg your pardon. I didn't see you," Alice said honestly.

Surprise was replaced with icy displeasure. "I wasn't aware you were on the guest list."

"The ticket was handed down from management. This is a great party."

"Of course it is." One eyebrow indicated that she wished to be on her way.

Alice was disinclined to step aside.

It was the only moment she was going to get. She'd come here intending to say her piece, she reminded herself, but did she really have any expectation that she'd change a single business practice at Simply the Best by telling Helene what she thought about them?

But wasn't that the point? Wasn't that what Pepper had meant about intentions? Not following through because she thought it would fail was hollow.

"I'm glad to run into you, actually. There's something that I need to clear the air about."

Helene's eyes were full of green daggers. "Your little stories are all done, so why should I care?"

"Yes, those stories are done."

"You're wasting my time."

"The ethics and economics of empowerment. That's where my mind is these days. Simply the Best could be the centerpiece of a discussion about companies that makes much of empowering a group—women, for example—to find their full potential, yet fails to equally compensate their own employees. You may not know this, but paying women more money is a sure-fire way to empower them."

"Are you back on that tired subject?"

"It's a standard practice of most corporations to pay what they can get away with. Plain and simple. And here you are selling empowerment to women and at the same time paying the women who work for you what you can get away with. How little, not how much."

Helene swept her long white jacket back to put one hand on her hip. It was impressive and intimidating, Alice had to give her that. "You can kiss your job goodbye."

It felt wonderful to say, "I already did. You can't threaten me."

"Are you threatening me?"

Feeling more like her mother's daughter than she had in years, Alice answered, "That depends entirely on you."

"You wouldn't be talking to me like this if I were a man."

"The point is you're not a man. This is an ethical question about wage policy in a company for women owned and run by women."

Helene's laughter was genuinely merry. "How naive. Fortune 500 CEOs do not care about ethics. Ethics are what they use to keep other people—including women—in their place. I do not subscribe to patriarchal restrictions."

"But you're willing to use them to make yourself and your circle richer while not giving your own employees parity with male counterparts in the industry and region. I crunched the numbers. Those are the inconvenient facts."

Helene's eyes narrowed. "They're free to go elsewhere. That's the point of the marketplace."

"You've never been powerless in your entire life, have you?" Alice realized that they hadn't been interrupted because only a few people would dare to do so.

Helene dismissed her with a flick of her hand. "Is this how you think you'll get even because I won?"

Momentarily puzzled, Alice asked, "Was there a contest?"

Helene's expression became so smug that Alice had to put her hands behind her back to hide her clenched fists.

Clearly gloating, Helene said, "You know exactly what I'm talking about. She is everything I thought she'd be, during—and after—work."

Something surged in Alice that felt absurdly like she'd discovered how to fly or a radioactive spider bite had given her enhanced senses. Lord, yes, she was indeed her mother's daughter. She evaluated Helene's practiced, icy, superior smile, her hooded, accusing eyes, and her looming-bully stance.

What do you know? Alice thought. *I can see right through her.*

"And that's the first time you've lied to me. Why would you lie about a thing like that?" *Because the gossip is true*, she answered herself. And what's more, Helene Jolie is so insulated from consequences that she'd alluded to a workplace impropriety in the age of MeToo without a flicker of guilt.

Helene turned to go back the way she'd come, but Alice stopped her by saying, "You can take all my power away in an instant."

A quick flip of her hair and pointed glare made it plain to anyone watching that she was not amused. "Enlighten me."

"Make it not true."

"What are you talking about?"

Alice decided not to get distracted by mentioning how completely Helene's French-ish accent had disappeared. "You could neuter me permanently on the subject of your economic exploitation of the women who work for you by making it not true. You truly have all the power here."

"I should hand out bonuses? That would shut you up?"

It was her turn to glare. "Enough with the *noblesse oblige*. Bonuses would be voluntary, and you would expect people to be grateful for them because it's a gift, not something they're owed. Raise your entire wage structure, starting from the bottom with the interns. You have a recession- and pandemic-proof business. Profits have only gotten larger. The world burns and you get richer. You wouldn't even miss it." She did sound hopelessly naive, but it appeared she could still be a dreamer. "You have all the power. Make some use of it."

Rescue was on the way in the form of Clarita Oatley, one of the few who would interrupt Helene mid-conversation. Other people had also clearly interpreted Helene's irate body language and were making no attempt to hide the fact that they were trying to listen in.

"Your watchdog is here." Why not be overheard? She raised her voice to say, "One last thing. You and I both know that vaginas are perfect. Selling a rock to purify them implies they're dirty. Criticizing vaginas is a tool of the patriarchy."

With that she stepped aside. It was a good thing those green eyes didn't have directed-energy particle beams. Helene stalked away with an equally hostile and glaring Clarita in her wake.

Alice checked her watch. The evening was going so much better than she had thought it would, and in a short while she'd see Pepper again. And she hadn't called anyone a douchebag.

CHAPTER FORTY-FOUR

Pepper made the rounds of the bar and catering to check quantities again. It kept her moving throughout the building and was a great excuse not to do more than share a few words with anyone. She tried to give the party her entire focus, but her brain was running two other programs. One was undeniable delight at the prospect of seeing Alice later.

The other was how to avoid any conversation with Helene that could open the door to a proposition Pepper did not want to hear. What if there was more jewelry? More clothes? More stories about sexual peccadilloes? She would have to plainly say no. It was a conversation she didn't want to have.

She suspected the conversation was inevitable—she just didn't want to have it tonight. Couldn't tonight be perfect for a little while longer? Until she saw Alice again?

As she updated her checklist she tuned out the other voices in her head telling her she was overreacting to something that hadn't even happened. Which meant it was not wise to be thinking that seeing Alice later would be the perfect end to the night. Even if Alice was sorry about what she'd said that morning, she could have sent an email or a text to say she was sorry. *Remember what happened to Ponytail Girl and why French Braid Woman is in charge?*

The party finally wound down with the aroma of hot coffee, lack of food, and closed bars having their intended effect. People disappeared into the street to seek out more fun elsewhere or to head to their warm beds. It looked really cold outside, and Pepper hoped Alice would be okay.

When the doors were locked behind the last guest there was a collective round of applause. It was on the event plan for Helene to make a few closing remarks with a toast, and Pepper accepted a flute of champagne knowing she wouldn't drink much of it. She was off balance enough as it was.

Helene took several steps up the ramp and raised her glass. After conversations fell silent, she said, "You have all exceeded my expectations. Simply the Best is back, baby! We are the new jewel of Fifth Avenue. Each of you played a part and I salute all of you."

Pepper lifted her glass along with everyone else and took an obligatory sip.

"There is one person who has worked tirelessly to make this week an unquestioned success. I could not have done it without her. Pepper Addington, where are you? Take a bow."

Gratified and anxious all at once, she stayed where she was next to the caterers and mimed a bow to scattered applause.

"Thank you so much, Pepper." Helene pushed her hair away from her face, and Pepper realized she looked tired and yet wound up. It had been a grueling week—it was absurd to think Helene was planning some kind of seduction. "We are off to a great beginning, and I hope that over the rest of the season we'll show sales to match the investment in the beautiful space. The hardest part of our return to New York is just beginning."

After another round of applause everyone began moving in all directions as the clatter of dishes and glassware filled the air. Pepper started down her wrap-up checklist. Her signature went next to the caterer's to accompany the never unwrapped food to the nearest hunger project. She closed out the pay station as Penny Nickle packed up her supplies and noted that they'd exceeded their fundraising goal. She visited each bar and confirmed the empty bottles of liquor and wine. Something dark had spilled on the second-floor carpet, and she dashed off an email to the cleaning crew that was arriving at dawn to bring supplies and equipment to deal with it. Thank goodness she wasn't the one to have to let them in.

When she finally felt she'd done all she could, she took a deep breath and thought of exactly how she would let Helene know she was leaving for the night. She hadn't been this nervous speaking to

Helene for weeks, and it was a different kind of nervous. Her heart wasn't beating hard because of a forthcoming challenge and hoping she'd succeed.

It was dread that her fears would come true.

Clarita had been hovering in the background as Pepper had made her final rounds, but as far as Pepper knew she'd said nothing about their earlier disagreement to Helene. Still, it seemed as if Clarita was listening in on Pepper's decisions, possibly hoping to find a mistake. Did she see Pepper as some kind of rival?

As Helene finished saying good night to Patty O'Neil, Pepper stepped into view. With a bright smile, she handed Helene the tablet which detailed the totals by bullet point. "I think we're over budget on income and under budget on expenses. There's an open issue about a fine because a permit wasn't posted in exactly the right place, but the crew chief on the mobile unit said every single site ends up with a fine of some kind. It's a feature, not a bug."

Helene scrolled the list. "You were right about asking for donations on the mixologist."

"That tip was from Patty—it was a great idea."

Without interrupting her study of the data, Helene asked, "Did you and Jean have a good chat? I happened to see you speaking with her."

She wants to see if the message was delivered. "Yes, though we had only a moment."

"Jean understood me so well. I think you do too."

How she kept smiling she didn't know. "I have tried. I think tonight's success shows we work well together. It was a goal of mine to prove that."

"You truly have. On an almost impossible scale." Helene handed the tablet back with a beneficent smile. "I think you're due for some rest and relaxation. Take the next week off and hang out at the brownstone. I've decided to linger here until after Christmas. There's so much going on, and I can cement relationships that have been established."

Helene tipped her head the way she always did when staring at Pepper's face. One hand brushed an imaginary speck from Pepper's shoulder.

It took all she had not to shrink away from her touch. "That sounds lovely, but I'm expected home next week. The time off would, in fact, really help. My parents are moving." It was the truth, but her mother hardly required Pepper's assistance beyond moral support. "My flight is tomorrow evening. Just enough time to visit Ground Zero—I was too young the first time," she babbled on. "And have pizza at a place under the Brooklyn Bridge that's in all the walking guides."

Helene's face was an unreadable mask. "Are you sure? I don't understand why your mother would require assistance with something so tedious. We could have such... Such *fun* together."

"I'm sure." Pepper blinked and hoped her smile was still bright and open and even slightly stupid.

After a long, almost disbelieving silence Helene squared her shoulders. "By all means, take a few days off. Of course the thank-yous will need to go out as planned."

"Of course," Pepper said. The offer of a week off was now a few days, and work was expected to happen first. She'd probably get texts and notes from Helene all day Sunday. *Message received*, she thought. Jean was right, having "a week at the brownstone" would be easier. The very idea was making her skin crawl.

A gleam returned to Helene's eyes as well as the intimate purr to her voice. "Let's celebrate, however, *ma chérie*. Some friends are planning to club hop. We could join them. Or go back to the brownstone and celebrate, just the two of us."

"That sounds fun—but so exhausting. I'm about to collapse. When I'm this tired, I'm horrible company." Pepper took back the tablet and did her best to make eye contact though she felt as if she were fighting for balance, with a cross-wave possible from any direction. "Don't worry about me. I've already ordered a ride. I'll see you in the morning, perhaps, before I leave for the airport. And back at the office, of course."

She walked away on shaking legs, awash with conflicting and mutually exclusive desires. Hoping that Helene thought that she was too naive to understand what Helene was offering. Hoping at the same time that Helene knew that Pepper knew *exactly* what the offer had been about and had turned it down, allowing Helene the opportunity to pretend it had never happened. And to make sure that it would never happen again.

The only issue that mattered was whether *she* could pretend it hadn't happened. Her challenging, exciting job was compromised, and it didn't feel anything like the time a photographer had gotten handsy or when men persisted at hitting on her when she'd flat-out told them to go away. Pepper had always known all about being on her guard with boys, with men. Like every woman she knew, she'd grown up layering on armor with each passing year. She could shake off a guy calling her a bitch because she wouldn't smile for him without breaking stride.

This felt like the same thing and much worse.

She hadn't seen it coming. There was no armor for it.

"Pepper!"

She turned to find out what Clarita had to say.

"Are you a fool?"

"What do you mean?"

"Helene just offered you a wonderful time." Clarita's gaze flowed up and down Pepper's dress and focused on the pendant. "And has already given you so much."

"They were gifts for…" She was suddenly so angry she couldn't help herself. "For services *already* rendered."

Clarita seemed nonplussed. "She can give you the world."

"Like she did you?" It was a shot in the dark. From Clarita's gasp of outrage it seemed to find its mark.

"You know how good I am at what I do."

"But doesn't it totally suck that I'd assume maybe you're not because Helene—how did you put it? Gave you the world? I don't want people assuming that about me."

"You'd have lasted much longer than Jean did, and she's an ad executive with major accounts now." Clarita's lips barely moved. "You're competent, above and beyond certainly my expectations. But don't think playing hard-to-get will ever have you moving into my job. You're not *that* kind of good."

"The last thing I want is your job," Pepper protested. "Especially if it includes—" she couldn't help the distaste she knew showed on her face. "Especially if it includes procuring."

Like Jean, Clarita seemed surprised and disdainful all at once. "Helene will realize now that you're not as savvy and willing to do what it takes to move to the head of the line. She admires women who seize opportunity, after all. But she has many other choices and won't hold it against you. You'll be promoted and forgotten." With a last contemptuous look at Pepper, she finished with, "But I will make sure you don't land well. I'm a much worse enemy."

Pepper watched her walk away—there was nothing more to say. Did it matter whether the consequences of turning down a proposition came from the boss or the boss's henchwoman?

No, she thought. *No, it did not.*

She took one last look at the scene of her triumph. All three soft opens and the gala had been spectacular. *Be proud—you rode that wave all the way in.* Except now it looked like the beach was a brick wall.

Torn between anger and tears, she escaped onto the street. The cold air stabbed into her lungs and she was sorry for every minute she'd wasted trying to make Helene happy—and for what? To be given a so-called prize she absolutely did not want and robbed of what she'd earned?

There was no denying how much she longed for the sight of Alice's spiky hair or lopsided smile. In spite of what had just happened and her hoped-for future crumbling away, seeing Alice now would be simply perfect.

CHAPTER FORTY-FIVE

Alice hadn't lied to Pepper about having a warm coat. Her problem was a lack of hat and gloves. Her turned-up collar only reached the bottom of her ears. She guessed it was around thirty degrees—as warm as could be expected this time of year at midnight. The doors had been locked a few minutes ago. She kept one hand on her phone in her pocket in case of a new message and the other slipped in the front of her coat like Napoleon, keeping it warm against her stomach. There was no hope for her ears.

Most of the crowd waiting for cars had dissipated while Alice paced up and down to keep her feet limber. She was so glad to see Pepper emerge from the doors that she didn't immediately realize Pepper had no coat. A tiny handbag dangled from her shoulder and she carried only a tablet, clutched against her stomach. There was no one else with her, which was a relief.

Pepper spotted her the moment she stepped away from the now-closed up cloakroom. Her relief was plain in the sharp exhale—or it might have been the impact of the cold. Right now, Alice thought, she wasn't going to worry about the difference.

"Did you forget your coat?"

"I left it at the brownstone. I was worried about crushing my dress and keeping a wrap on my shoulders while using a tablet all night—oh, you don't have to do that."

Alice slipped off her overcoat and held it so Pepper could get her arms into the sleeves. "I have my suit jacket. Hurry, don't lose the precious body heat I gave to warm it."

"Is there somewhere we can be inside?" Pepper pulled the coat tighter around her and continued walking at a brisk pace toward 52nd Street.

"It's only just midnight—half the town is open for business. What do you feel like?"

"Hot chocolate. Any kind of chocolate. Lots of chocolate. Or cake. We could have cake. A lot of cake."

Pepper turned at the next block toward Madison. Alice let her put a half-block between them and Fifth Avenue before pulling her to a stop. "What's wrong?"

"I don't want Helene to see me. I told her I had a car waiting."

"I figured you didn't want to be seen. But what's really wrong?"

Pepper buried her chin in the coat's collar. "I think I may have cost myself my job."

Incredulous, Alice shook her head at the impossibility. "After pulling off all of that?"

Pepper finally looked up with a sniff. "It has nothing to do with my work. I didn't realize that my idea of a reward for a job well done is completely different from Helene's."

"What was her idea?" Alice had a sick feeling in the pit of her stomach.

"An affair. A fling. Gifts and her unlimited goodwill."

The gossips had been telling the truth, while Helene had indeed been lying when she'd implied she'd already seduced Pepper. "I take it this wasn't agreeable to you?"

Pepper momentarily looked so angry that Alice raised her hands in peace. "It was not. I can't make myself do something I don't feel."

"I'm sorry for asking. I wanted to be sure there was no misunderstanding between us. You shouldn't have to do anything you don't want to."

"I have a choice in the matter, and I choose not to. So—it's clear that if Helene doesn't get rid of me, Clarita will find a way. She thinks I'm after a more permanent gig in Helene's life."

The abstract satisfaction of being right about Helene didn't matter. "What do you need from me right now? How can I help?"

Pepper's ferocity faded and all at once she looked exhausted and unutterably sad. "A hug would be great."

It was exactly what she wanted to do, and she gently pulled Pepper close and wrapped her tight in her arms. She resisted the urge to bury her face in Pepper's hair and contented herself with a long inhale of the deeply remembered scent of shampoo and skin.

"You're shivering." Pepper's voice was muffled, and Alice could feel the vibration of it against her heart.

"Not really."

"I don't want to go back to the brownstone tonight."

"The brownstone?"

"Helene's house. Somewhere off Central Park."

"Of course it is."

"It's stunning. There's a manservant and everything. Even a pool somewhere." Pepper sniffled. "I could stay there all next week if I wanted."

"There are tissues in the left inside pocket. You don't have to go back. I have a day bed in my home office. There's a lock on the door." She thought about it and added, "There could be a package or two of Swiss Miss. No milk, though."

"Did you steal those from a breakfast buffet at some hotel?"

"I plead the Fifth. Even if I have a vast collection of salsa and ketchup packets and little cups of hermetically sealed coffee creamer, I resent the implication that I am a thief."

Pepper squeezed her, which Alice took to mean she was amused but too tired to laugh. "We can put the creamers in the watery hot chocolate."

Alice chuckled. "That would be more cooking in my kitchen than I've done in a year."

Pepper finally let go of her. Her eyes were rimmed in red. "Crashing at your place is a crazy lot to ask of you. Considering."

"I haven't even really said sorry about the stupid things I said. Not properly."

"Enough for now. I'm so tired. Tired and scared. Starting over somewhere else. My mother will want to know what I did wrong to lose my job."

"You did nothing wrong."

"She'll be certain I could have handled it better and somehow kept my job when the only way to handle it better was to say yes."

Alice slid her phone out of her pocket to order a ride. Siri said there was one about two minutes out. "It's not far, not at this time of night."

Pepper sniffled again and fished out a tissue. "It's unfair how great pockets are on men's clothes. Did you know she would do that?"

"Try to seduce you?"

Pepper nodded, gaze on the sidewalk.

"She's very alluring, knows it, and uses it. I didn't like that she used it on you. You were already a loyal and devoted employee."

"You didn't say anything about that when you were so angry. You know, after we… The morning after."

"I wasn't sure if I was seeing her as a predator because…"

"Because?"

There was nothing for it but honesty. "Because of how I was beginning to feel about you."

"Oh." After dabbing her nose, she gave Alice an accusing look. "But you said I was cheap."

She wanted to hug her again, but it seemed a very good idea to wait for Pepper's invitation for any further physical contact. "That wasn't my intention, and I'm sorry it hurt you. I meant Beverly Hills and that whole cult of youth and beauty. The make-believe. Simply the Best and the price tag they put on perfection. Impossible dreams and… Fairy tales that aren't ever true." She gulped to a stop. Her face felt hot.

Pepper scuffed the toe of one shoe at a cigarette butt. "But all you talked about was business and Helene."

"I'd rather you thought me a judgmental know-it-all than a jealous nitwit."

"You are a judgmental know-it-all."

Alice laughed—every minute that didn't include Pepper walking away was a minute her soul shed more of its darkness. "I'm working on the judgmental part, but I will never, ever stop trying to be a know-it-all. It's hardwired all through my DNA."

"I don't think you could be a nitwit if you tried." She locked gazes with Alice as she said it. "Well, except of course that morning—"

"I was a nitwit." Alice nearly lost herself in the welcome she thought she saw in the shimmer. "You're tired. The ride's here."

She had to rouse Pepper when the car stopped in front of her building. She didn't want to—Pepper had dozed off against her shoulder, and the dark of the car had allowed her to fill her mind with fantasies and fairy tales. While it was still easy to imagine nothing but a shriveled husk where her heart ought to be, there was finally a glimmer inside her of other possibilities.

A groggy Pepper gave up the overcoat once they were inside Alice's apartment and nodded gratefully when Alice pointed the way to the bathroom. Alice flipped on the hot water pot and dug into the back of the cupboard for the Swiss Miss packets. Miracle of miracles, they had a month to expiration.

When Pepper returned, she seemed a little more awake. She'd taken off her jewelry and her face was ruddy, as if she'd splashed water on it. "My ears were aching. This will sound stupid, but I had no idea rocks were heavy."

"It's not stupid—some rocks aren't heavy." She tapped the tablespoon against the top of one thoroughly stirred mug of hot chocolate. "Hazelnut or French vanilla?"

"Hazelnut. There's nothing French about that vanilla."

"Just like Helene's accent. Sorry," she said in mock horror. "Did I say that aloud?"

There was an affectionate curve to the wan smile on Pepper's face. "You're not sorry."

She saw no reason not to admit the truth she'd known all along. "You see right through me."

Pepper accepted the mug and sipped with a grateful sigh. "Thank you. You're a lifesaver."

"I'm sorry it's cold in here. The heat isn't set to come on this late. But I've got a throw if you'd like to sit for a while. Unless you want to crash now."

"Sit for a while. It's quiet. On top of everything else I think I'm on sensory overload. Shouting all night—the music. I feel like I've been shouting for a week."

When Pepper didn't move, Alice gently pulled her toward the living room sofa. "Come on. Take off those lovely but painful-looking shoes."

"That will be a relief." After another sip of hot chocolate, she perched on the middle cushion and fumbled with the clasps at the back of her heel.

Alice considered offering to help her with them, but a flutter of caution stopped her. The moment was so fragile. She didn't want the possibilities of the future to be caught in Pepper's emotional overload or Helene's poisonous machinations. Tomorrow, when Pepper would surely go away, there would be no escape from the memory of how her voice floated between the living room and kitchen or the graceful curve of her body against what had been—until now—a very forgettable sofa. Or the way the highland plaid throw draped over their legs as she leaned into Alice's shoulder and drank her hot chocolate.

Alice related her earlier skirmish with Helene. "So I'm big time *persona non grata*."

"You really quit your job?"

"I'll find another. Something. I don't know what." Alice would have shrugged, but she didn't want to dislodge Pepper's head from her shoulder. "It'll involve science. I'm surprisingly lacking in anxiety about it."

"I know you'll find what you want. You're like a wave that knows where it's going. The wind, the temperature, the moon all do their thing, but you keep going where you mean to." In an increasingly drowsy voice, Pepper added, "And I thought you were too cynical for jostling at windmills." She stifled a yawn. "Jostling? That's not right. Whatever."

Alice grinned to herself. The hot chocolate was not why she felt warm as she rested her chin momentarily on the top of Pepper's head. "So did I."

"Why did you yell at me, then? Not like I could do anything. I thought I'd get a promotion and be able to make things better—" This time the yawn broke through.

"I was driving you away, for your sake." Not at all sure Pepper had even heard her, she reached for the almost empty mug that tipped dangerously toward their laps. "Do you want me to take that?"

"Mm-hmm." Relieved of the mug, Pepper slid down until her head was on Alice's thigh, which she prodded once or twice as if it were a pillow not quite in the right place. Alice imagined that a haute couture dress that clung to every curve was probably not all that comfortable to sleep in, especially with all the undergarments on as well, but there was no power in the universe that could make her disturb Pepper now.

She managed to get her bow tie off and unfasten the cummerbund and toss them both onto the coffee table. Cuff links off, shirt studs out, and collar finally loosened, she rested her hand on Pepper's hip and heard the impossible rise of an orchestra, all violins and sunlit oceans. Thousands of miles away from Hollywood, in her chilly, dull apartment, she gazed down at the peacefully sleeping Pepper and saw a sky full of stars.

CHAPTER FORTY-SIX

The fabric under her cheek was wet. Pepper tried to lift her head, but her neck screamed at her not to move. She waited a moment and tried again. Bit by bit she took stock. She was in New York. She was in Alice's apartment. Her bra was super tight and poking her in one underarm. She had drooled on Alice's tuxedo pants. She was willing to bet that what makeup she hadn't been able to mop off the night before was now smeared, crusty, or both.

This was the glamorous life, all right.

Alice's head had lolled into the corner of the sofa at an angle that exposed her throat. Pepper entertained a vivid fantasy of waking her up by nuzzling at the hollow of it, but she promptly discovered her right shoulder was sound asleep and that a pantyhose wedgie had caught various folds of skin that were protesting the indignity of such treatment.

The light from the kitchen provided enough glow to get her bearings. She'd not noticed a thing about Alice's apartment last night. In the soft light it seemed all dark wood and forest colors, with splashes of orange and purple from art prints on the wall. Sitting up she spotted a digital display on the side table that read 5:13. Too early to be awake. There was no way she could get back to sleep.

Alice made a squeaky noise.

Pepper leaned closer.

"Oil can." Alice made a helpless gesture.

Laughing made her neck hurt. "I don't know how but it feels like my dress is now on backward."

Alice was flicking her fingers and moving her elbows as if she was testing that they still worked. "Why is my leg wet?"

"I drooled on you. Sorry."

"Normally I would say something suave like 'you missed,' but that is not happening right now."

Pepper's laugh turned into a groan as sensation tickled and needled into her shoulder. There was nothing for it. She gritted her teeth and lifted both arms to pull the hair clip and ties free so she could undo her braid. "I want a shower so much."

"I can understand that."

"You're going to join me."

The very spot where Pepper wanted to kiss Alice's throat flexed with a sharp swallow. "If you meant to make my entire body warm you succeeded."

Alice's hard swallow and nipples now visible through her shirt sent a thrill of power through Pepper. It was absurd to feel like a sexy seductress as she wiped one eye and so-called twenty-four-hour mascara came off against her fingers. She did feel it, though, like a fire she could turn up and down at will in both of them. "That was part of the plan."

Alice finally raised her head so she could look at Pepper. Without her glasses she was more vulnerable, though the sardonic twist to her mouth was still there. "Only part?"

Pepper enjoyed an instant replay of their panting kisses during their previous shower. "I figured between the two of us we have one working body."

"I'm pretty sure my legs will never wake up."

Pepper gave her head a shake as the last of her hair unwound. She was feeling more alive by the moment. She could rotate her shoulder now, and the creak in her back subsided. Arousal lubricated more than the usual places, who knew?

Well, she thought. *In that case…*

She managed to get somewhat gracefully to her feet and pull the zipper on her dress down, all without wincing. The dress was awkward to get out of, with a second zipper under one arm, but after a squirm she was able to pull it over her head and fold it onto the coffee table. Reaching under her slip she unhooked her bra and sighed with relief.

Alice was watching her every move, her breathing shallow and hands held stiffly as if she was keeping them still by willpower alone.

Dangling her lacy black bra from one hand, she smoothed the black slip over her body with the other. "Such a pity you can't move."

"I think I have all the incentive I need to try."

"We're still going to have that shower."

"I have no objection. You can leave the slip on if you want. That could be fun for a bit."

The thought of Alice's hands molding her breasts through wet silky fabric left her light-headed. "First this."

She discarded her bra on top of her dress and straddled Alice's legs so she could slide the length of their bodies together. Finally she could kiss Alice's throat and run her tongue over the notch in her collarbone. Pressing her cheek against Alice's jaw she bit softly at her earlobe and felt the race of Alice's heartbeat against her mouth.

"Pepper," Alice said softly. "What's this about?"

"It's not about talking."

The soft sound might have been a laugh. "It seemed like a good question to ask, but honestly, right now, I don't care what the answer is."

She unbuttoned Alice's shirt and found a supple close-fitting tee that was warm against Pepper's lips. Alice groaned as her mouth closed around one taut nipple. She bit gently and felt the swell of Alice's body under her. Aware that every touch was finding a response, she moved to the other nipple while her fingers toyed with the first and felt the shiver of Alice's body against her own tingling skin.

Alice's voice was a thread of desire. "May I touch you?"

Pepper looked up to find such naked desire in Alice's eyes that she gasped. They stared at each other for a long moment. Not knowing where she found the confidence, Pepper finally put her lips to Alice's ear and whispered, "In a minute."

Alice's body tightened under her and now Pepper was dizzy as she unfastened the buttons and zipper on Alice's trousers. After the wild night of abandon that had proved their attraction, she wanted something deeper to bind them. An exchange layered in pleasure, with the kind of fulfillment that felt both ending and beginning.

She shifted so one leg was between Alice's and smiled to herself as Alice lifted to meet her thigh. They were both beyond teasing. Her fingers followed the swoop and plane of Alice's pelvis and glided through ripples and wet until she was inside, and against the quiver of muscles that jumped at the flutter of her fingertips.

For a moment Alice seemed to dissolve under her, then she thrust back and lifted her hips in a desperate twist to push her pants farther down.

"More?"

"Yes. Please, yes."

"You can touch me now."

Alice's hands were immediately in her hair, holding coils of it to her face, then slid down to cup her breasts through the slip.

"More?" With a shift of her weight, she moved her thigh behind her hand.

"Harder. I won't break."

Pepper gasped at Alice's tug on her nipples. "You're going to make me forget what I'm doing," she warned.

"Really?"

Their gazes locked again. There was no looking away, only a twining spiral of now that lasted until Alice threw her head back with a cry and her hands fell limply to her sides. Pepper pressed her ear to Alice's chest, listening to her pounding heart while her fingers teased out another, weaker cry.

Finally, a sighing, mutual laugh.

Kisses were sublime, especially after she'd made use of a freshly unwrapped toothbrush from a local dentist. The shower was the bliss she had thought it would be, including a tingly massage of her back with Alice's front. The faded, soft T-shirt Alice lent her was decorated with an equation showing that a velociraptor was equal to a distanceraptor divided by a timeraptor, which was beyond adorkable.

They curled together in Alice's bed, sharing drowsy, featherlight kisses.

"I don't want to waste time sleeping," Alice murmured.

"We have to sleep so we can wake up and have a different kind of morning than last time."

"Yes, please." Alice kissed the side of her mouth. "I know you have things—"

Pepper moved her mouth to silence Alice with a deeper kiss. Part of her was wringing her hands and worried about references and the rent and all the long list of choices and consequences of adulting. It was easy to ignore as she burrowed deeper into Alice's embrace. It would all still be there after a few hours' sleep.

The drone of cars and occasional murmur of neighbors' voices faded away until there was only the sound of Alice's steady breathing.

CHAPTER FORTY-SEVEN

Alice returned to the kitchen with the delivery bag in hand. Pepper was frowning at her phone. Exhausted as she was by last night's and this morning's wakeup amorous sexy times, she still wanted to devour Pepper whole. How could anyone make her old T-shirt and too long sweatpants look so damned sexy?

She set the bag on the table. "Breakfast is served."

Pepper put her phone down and pounced on the bag. "I should offer to help find plates and forks, shouldn't I?" She tore the bag open. "That smells so good I'm going to faint."

"I usually eat these animal style. Bare hands and all."

They bit into the Taiwanese breakfast crepes at the same moment and shared a long, mutual sigh of relief.

"There's a dipping sauce," Alice said after a swallow. "Tangy, kind of plum and soy sauce."

Pepper rifled through the bag, scattering thin napkins across the table. "This?"

"That. Gimme."

"Find your own." Pepper popped the lid off and dunked the end of her rolled egg crepe in it.

"So that's how it's going to be?" She watched Pepper bite off the end with obvious relish. "Now I know where I stand."

"You're the one who is out of coffee and I had to wait fifteen whole minutes for you to acquire some. Payback's a bitch."

"If you should ever be a guest again, I promise there will be coffee."

Pepper paused in mid-chew as a slow, shy smile spread across her face. "Good," she finally said.

Alice was certain she had the same look on her face. "Anything unexpected in your messages?"

"Helene expressed concern that I hadn't returned to the brownstone. I let her know I was fine. A friend had waylaid me—"

Alice let out an adolescent chortle that earned her a disapproving look.

"And offered a place to crash so we could have early breakfast together and catch up before I had to leave." Pepper took another bite of her crepe, then finally set it down. "She replied that if I returned by nine—" She glanced meaningfully at the wall clock displaying 8:37. "If I did, I could join her for the weekend at Martha's Vineyard."

"It's a beautiful place."

"Is it possible it's platonic? She's never—mostly it's other people who make me think she means sex."

Hell yes, she meant sex, Alice wanted to shout. She began on the second crepe and found the other container of dipping sauce since Pepper was clearly not going to share. "Feelings are their own truth. How does she make you feel?"

"There were a couple of times before this week I felt uncomfortable. I told myself I was seeing something that wasn't there. It was Helene being Helene and she doesn't know the effect she has on people."

Alice snorted.

"But now—I don't think she's going to stop until the ugly truth of it is plain. I won't be able to pretend it didn't happen. I already can't." In a rush, she pleaded, "Don't ask me what I'm going to do next. I don't know. I don't have a plan. Except to go home and assess the damage. See what I can salvage."

Alice hadn't expected Pepper to stay. It would be the easy solution, until they both figured out that being an escape route wasn't a solid foundation for any kind of future. She glanced at Cool Science Road Trip list still on the fridge. She had made a promise to herself to fix herself.

"I won't ask then, Paddington."

Pepper shook her head. "There is no marmalade in this apartment, so nope. You can't call me that."

"I didn't know that was the rule."

Her expression serious, Pepper put her hand midway across the table, palm up. Alice wiped her fingers and clasped it. Warm, soft, relaxed.

"What happened last time? When we could have had this?"

"I was being a bitch?"

"Too easy." Pepper squeezed her hand. "You just told me that feelings have their own truth. Tell me the truth."

Denying it felt like giving the dark another chance to have power over her. "I didn't believe in you."

"But I'm right here."

"Yes, you are. I can't find a way to explain you, which means you're some kind of magic. I didn't think I could survive believing in magic. Not after—" She swallowed hard. "Not after the past couple of years. Not after millions dead, and so many people deciding science was irrelevant to keeping people alive. How can magic exist? I don't know how you do it."

Pepper tipped her head to one side in confusion. "Do what?"

With a helpless gesture at the vision that was Pepper sitting cross-legged on a kitchen chair, she said, "Be you—I thought you were another person living a pretty life of denial about everything that's broken right now. I was wrong about that. You are so much more resilient than I am."

"I don't feel very resilient at the moment. I have no plan."

"You have the intention to make one. And that matters. My entire plan for a long while was to drink and be angry. You were right in the middle of that failure, being all impossible and magical."

"And you stopped? Changed?"

"I stopped most of the drinking. I'm still angry but it's—it's not in charge anymore." That was the truth, she realized. Anger was a tool, not a goal.

"So why didn't you text me or send an email saying you were sorry?"

That was easy to answer. "Because you might have forgiven me."

"Honestly, Alice." Pepper squeezed her hand and let go. "Maybe you are a nitwit after all. Would my forgiving you be so bad?"

"My heart—my life—was in a bad place, and I didn't want you in that place."

"Don't I get to have a say?"

"I thought I could get over you." Alice's voice softened with wonder. "But you're a seed that waits for its moment to bloom."

Pepper opened her mouth and closed it again. "Okay. I mean, I don't know what to do with that, but I can tell it's a compliment."

"It is." There are no helicopters now, she wanted to say, but how to explain any of that with the morning sun in Pepper's tousled hair? What about when the all-take-and-ruin-it-for-everyone-else people came back? They'd never left, had they? The world was not going to be fixed any time soon.

"*Nitwit*," Sass accused. "*A fixed world as a prerequisite to happiness guarantees you'll never be happy.*"

"Why did you think I don't see the world for what it is?"

"A lens on reality is not what Beverly Hills is known for."

"I only work there."

"I knew I was wrong about you the moment we met. Almost. Nevertheless, I thought I had the only path to truth."

Pepper finished her crepe and sat back with a sigh. "I feel like I flounder around trying to find it, but you're always headed to Truth Beach. There's more than one ride to get there, though."

"Well..."

"Don't scientists come to the same conclusions along completely different lines of inquiry, like, literally all the time? That's one of the ways they prove something must be true, right?"

Alice was forced to nod and didn't hide that it made her peevish. "Did you take debate?"

"It got me out of Philosophy and Metaphysics. Truth is a lie. Lie is a truth. It all gives me a headache. Why?"

"I sometimes find it inconvenient that you're smart." She cocked her head. "Did you just paraphrase Captain Janeway?"

One eyebrow went up. "I might have. Stop changing the subject because you know you're wrong."

The woman was all magic.

"*Occam's Razor,*" Sass offered. "*It's the simplest explanation, nitwit.*"

"You know, I'm well aware that we could be permanently screwed out of a planet to inhabit," Pepper continued. "And that too many people believe the one with the most toys wins in the end. I did just have my very own brush with a one-percenter who thought she could put me in her shopping cart. That doesn't stop me from trusting in people or believing that the future is worth being in. CC says the world is a crappy place to live, but the other option is worse."

"I lost sight of the fact that other people cared too. I felt very alone, and old, and cranky."

"You're not old." Pepper blinked innocently. "Cranky, well..."

"Thirty-nine and I parted ways last summer," she added in answer to Pepper's inquiring look. "You're what? Twenty-seven?"

"I'll be twenty-eight soon."

"That's quite a diff—"

"Age is just a number." As Alice opened her mouth, Pepper held up a warning finger. "Arguing about that is not going to get you anything you want."

"You're scary. And by the way, that entire hair thing you had last night—intimidating."

"I had on all the gear for my special quest."

"The black slip was very effective." Alice didn't fight the shiver the memory sent down her spine.

"What is it about unbuttoning a tuxedo shirt? It's yummy." Pepper waggled her eyebrows. "Maybe it's because I'm a Pisces. Into revelations and mysteries. You're a Virgo? Leo?"

"You did not just bring up astrology."

"Yes, I did. Cancer? Oh yeah." Pepper's nod was knowing. "You're a Cancer."

"There is nothing scientific—" The warning finger came up. "Okay, I get it. Arguing will not get me what I want. That's not going to always work, by the way. I might, after all, want the argument for the sake of it."

"Admit it, you're a Cancer."

"Okay, I'm a Cancer. It proves nothing."

"It does—" Pepper's phone chimed again, and she sighed. "I would like to stop time for a while."

"I'm familiar with the feeling. But it doesn't work that way."

"If we had an Infinity Stone…"

"Now you're just being nerdy to turn me on."

"Could be." Her smile was flirtatious for a moment, then her phone chimed again. "My flight is at six."

She wanted to ask Pepper to stay. Stay as long as she wanted. But it would only postpone the inevitable. It made these feelings, whatever they were, all about right now, when neither of them was ready to decide anything. Instead, it seemed wiser to let something grow from what was only a crazy, impossible hope for a future worth keeping. "Is there anything I can do to make it easier?"

"If I asked, could I stay here?"

Alice nodded. She didn't have it in her to say no.

"I can't use you to hide from facing—" She gestured at her phone.

"I know. This will sound weird coming from me, the nitwit loner, but you don't have to do it alone. You can lean on me. You have my number. Occasionally I'm right or even smart. No pressure."

Pepper blinked rapidly for a moment. "And if I asked you to have pizza with me under the Brooklyn Bridge?"

"I know the very place."

"Helene is gone by now, I hope. I'll pack up and come back here. You'll have to tell me where here is. And lend me your coat again."

Pepper was a sight getting into a ride with her hair clipped back by that fancy, sparkly clip and swaddled in Alice's overcoat. It didn't entirely hide the sweatpants. The fantastic walk-on-me-please heels were offset by a shopping bag that held her clothes from last night.

She'd almost asked to keep the slip, but it was better to imagine it on Pepper or on the floor next to her bed. Definitely better.

Trust her, Alice told herself. *She will come back. This isn't the end, it's the beginning.*

CHAPTER FORTY-EIGHT

Pepper's surprise Monday morning was learning that Clarita, as well as Helene, wouldn't return to the office until the day after Christmas—a week from tomorrow. Clarita was obviously filling the loneliness gap for Helene.

Whatever made them happy, Pepper thought. The pre-holidays pace, now that the New York open was behind them, was slow enough that she could keep it together. Urgent documents were forwarded overnight guaranteed to the brownstone. Product deliveries were stacked on Clarita's desk. Some mail she dealt with herself.

While Clarita's messages and calls were as curt as Pepper expected, she rolled with it. Helene sent an absolute tsunami of reminders about post-event follow-ups. None of them were tasks Pepper didn't already have on her list. She kept her workday to eight hours and had dinner with CC. Wednesday she arrived at her mother's with dinner from the nearby restaurant her father liked and spent the night agreeing with her mother that moving was such a mess, but worth it for a house right on the lake, with the best people. Thursday night she, CC, and Val went out for dim sum.

If her job could have continued that way, she might have been able to go on. But she dreaded Helene's return and the physical force of Clarita's animosity. She would expect to be fired for almost any mistake. The tension had been bearable before because she thought she was paying dues that would be rewarded. Even if Helene did offer her a promotion now, it would be tainted in the eyes of her colleagues. She'd spend the rest of her Simply the Best career with a notorious reputation that she couldn't use the way Jean so clearly had.

It did help that her days were broken up with messages from Alice. Over pizza at a wildly busy place that had been in the shadow of the Brooklyn Bridge for a century, she'd heard all about the road trip Alice was planning to see cool science stuff all over North America. Some other year she'd do the same thing in Europe, Africa, and Asia. Antarctica wasn't out of the question.

Finally they'd been standing on the platform with Pepper's train to the airport pulling in. Thanking Alice for a lovely afternoon had seemed inadequate. "Not just today, but thank you—for last night. Not just for...you know. For being there."

Alice had pulled her close for a tender kiss. "I just realized," she'd said, "that I forgot to say my road trip is ending in Malibu."

Not knowing what to think, Pepper had asked, "What's sciencey in Malibu?"

"I'm hoping a surfer I know will explain crumbly waves and onshore winds to me in more detail."

"Oh." Relieved, pleased, and a somewhat giddy, she'd thrown her arms around Alice and kissed her soundly. "Explaining will take a while. Hours. Days."

"Longer?"

"That's a distinct possibility."

Alice's face was as flushed with delight as Pepper hoped hers was. "We'll—see. See how it goes."

The train doors had opened, and Alice had helped her move her cases inside. "I take it I'll be welcome, then," she'd whispered, with a parting nuzzle at Pepper's neck.

"Be sure to keep me posted on the itinerary." Bold and shy all at once, she'd added, "I want to count the days."

It had only been a few words, but it seemed to set in motion some kind of future. A future that was ninety days from today if Alice's latest plan hadn't changed again. She kept finding new things to see. Her last email had mentioned—with great excitement—a site in Idaho where you could role play a nuclear meltdown.

Alice was such a geeky nerdy dork, and Pepper wished the road trip was already over. The time would pass quickly, she told herself.

There was the distraction of the holidays, and she'd be job-hunting. Ninety days would pass in a flash.

CC and she kept to their traditional Christmas Eve—appetizers in the air fryer and watching *The Long Kiss Goodnight*, their favorite mutual Christmas movie. CC's parents had taken off for some tropical destination, which was good. It left CC free to go to Val's parents' instead, seeing them for the first time as Val's official girlfriend.

"How was Christmas Day with Val's family?" Pepper emerged from her bedroom in post-holiday meal sweatpants and found CC in the kitchen unpacking a takeout bag. "Whatcha got?"

"It was great. Val's folks are so nice. I have here leftovers—some of Judith's bulgogi and sweet potato noodles."

"You're calling her Judith now?"

"She insisted, and I couldn't call her Umma. Maybe someday. One of Val's uncles makes pecan tea cakes. They melt in your mouth."

"Do I get some?"

"Depends on what you brought back from your family shindig." CC peered into Pepper's bag.

"Sliced ham and turkey and some apple-cinnamon cake. A bunch of Brussels sprouts because I was the only one who liked the balsamic glaze."

"Who doesn't like balsamic glaze on Brussels?"

"I know, right?" Pepper finished stacking CC's containers in the refrigerator. No cooking for a couple of days, hallelujah. She remembered the mail she'd stuffed in her coat pocket when she'd gotten home and fetched it. She handed it off to CC. "We forgot to get it on Saturday."

CC gave it the once-over. "Catalog, catalog. How was your day?"

"The service was great. I will never tire of 'I Wonder as I Wander' by a full choir in an echoing church. The sermon was on making room in our lives for good to happen."

"Sounds like Sunday service at Pepperdine."

"They would have said make good happen and there will be room in everyone's life for it. That whole emphasis on deeds over talk thing."

"I proved it today," CC said. "Everyone made a feast, and there was room in my stomach for it. You were right about taking flowers. Judith liked them—I earned points."

"Excellent."

"Look at this." She held out what Pepper had thought was an advertising circular.

"Isn't that—"

"Yes, Jasmine's new hubby."

"Are you kidding me? He's running for office?"

"Apparently she *does* have our address."

"We will be on this mailing list for the rest of our lives." Pepper unfolded it and scanned the bullet points. "Oh gross. He's running on a dual platform of 'traditional values' and 'keeping our children safe.'"

CC wandered into the living room with one hand on her bulging stomach. "That means get the wimmins back in the kitchen, erase the existence of the queers—especially those gender fakers—and definitely do not do anything about assault weapons."

"Remind me to give some cash to whomever is running against him." Pepper collapsed into the saggy depths of the sofa and checked her phone. No email from Alice, but she usually sent one later in the evening.

"So did you tell your folks you're going to quit?"

"I decided not to."

"Chicken."

"It wasn't that—stop it," she said in answer to CC's bauk-bauking. "My sister-in-law went to a ton of trouble. First time at their house and all that. I didn't want to derail her day. After the fact will be better, because instead of advice on all the reasons I shouldn't, it'll be advice on how to salvage my life." If anything, her resolve to quit had grown even stronger. Every time her mother dropped a name and her brother brought up talking points that sounded a lot like Jasmine's husband's candidate statement, she'd realized how much she didn't want their lives.

She loved them and wished them happiness. She didn't regret her blood, sweat, and tears investment into Simply the Best. The dreams she'd had weren't ones she truly wanted.

"You're going to stick to the plan?"

"Yes. Helene can only say no."

"It would be better if she said yes—you'd be gold to that headhunter Beth knows."

Pepper sighed. "Beth's pieces look so good where we placed them in the marketing building. I'll be sorry not to visit them."

* * *

Helene can only say no, Pepper reminded herself as she settled in at her desk the next morning. She was nowhere near as nervous as she thought she'd be. She thought about how Alice was like a rock that simply wouldn't move.

Helene could not move her.

She made her way through her morning checklist. When Clarita arrived a few minutes later, she greeted her cheerily and got an unemotional response as usual. At Clarita's desk, she explained the piles she'd made during the previous week.

"All of the deliveries that were held are here. This stack is Composium-related, and this stack is all the rest. Layouts and product additions are here. Accounting summaries from New York are in this folder. I think that's everything."

She went back to her desk but hadn't sat down when Helene arrived. She waited until Helene was well into her office before picking up the slender orange folder on her desk. It was about seven minutes before the first call of day was scheduled.

Helene did not respect timidity. There was no point in waiting.

She didn't care what Clarita thought when she went into Helene's office and closed the door behind her.

"I need a few minutes of your time."

Helene reclined into her chair. "Something urgent left over from New York?"

"No." The woman was beautiful, there was no denying that. It was as if sunlight bent to find her hair. The brilliant blue jumpsuit and jacket were iconic and daring at the same time. "This is personal."

Helene's gaze went to the small stack of papers on her desk. "I hardly think it can be important first thing in the day."

Pepper sat down in the chair across from Helene and settled back. "I think an honest conversation is essential."

One eyebrow lifted in doubt.

"From your comments, from what Clarita said, from the message that you sent Jean to give me, and the rampant gossip that finally reached my ears in New York, it's plain that you expected our work relationship to become sexual. That was the purpose of your offers to stay in New York and have *fun*."

Helene's face spasmed with distaste. "Clarita was right. You have no sense of reality."

"It also seems clear that you believed I would be the one to initiate it, and if I did, there was therefore nothing wrong with it. Fun would be had, it would end, and all would be well. No consequences, only benefits."

The bangles on Helene's wrist clattered as she waved a hand. "There would have been no consequences."

It was an admission and any doubt Pepper had about her plans went away. "For you, of course not. Only for me. Most of the people

I worked with in New York thought it was already true. They were surprised I was good at my job. That kind of stigma you can't outrun, and I have no desire to learn to live with it, let alone leverage it."

"I had no idea you were so wrapped up in what other people think."

"You mean the only thing that matters is what you think. You'd have been fine with it all. Meanwhile, I'd spend the rest of my life wondering if an opportunity was a gift from you. Or if a missed opportunity was a reprisal."

"You will never have that much of my attention." She flicked her fingers in dismissal.

Pepper didn't budge. "What you don't know is that Clarita explicitly threatened my job."

Helene's gaze was narrowed, but Pepper couldn't tell if she was surprised.

"Before you ask for proof—I don't have any. She might say it never happened. I'm going to give you the power to make all this go away. You can have my conditional silence and my departure from your company in return for what I have earned."

Helene ran one hand through her curls, almost smiling. "Oh, do tell me what you think that is."

"A bonus of a month's salary to compensate for two months of event planning during eighty-hour workweeks on an entry-level personal assistant's salary. A signed letter of recommendation. And a week off with pay as you offered earlier, which will count toward my two weeks' notice."

She set documents out on Helene's desk. The authorization for a bonus and summary of employment termination were in ST-Best standard memorandum form. The recommendation was not.

Helene glared at them, then looked back at Pepper, clearly undecided.

"This is the solution that lets me respect myself. I'm asking for my worth, and I know you respect that."

Helene pursed her lips. She was angry, but Pepper wasn't entirely sure it was all with her. "What did you mean by *conditional* silence?"

Alice was right—Helene's French accent was completely absent. "This personal matter will only be disclosed if you force me to do so."

"And how would I do that?"

"By doing it again. Here's what you don't know and nobody else will tell you. Your habit of shopping for lovers with your assistants is widely known in the company. It is *common* gossip." Helene winced at the word, and Pepper rushed on. "Sooner or later, you will pick the wrong person, and there will be proof. If that happens, I won't be silent. So maybe—maybe you should stop." Pepper took a deep breath, all run out of words.

The phone on her desk chirped. Clarita said, "Your call is ready."

Helene picked up her pen, signed the bonus, made a change to one word on the termination document, then paused over the letter of recommendation. "'You will not regret hiring Pepper Addington.' That's it?"

"Do I need more? Do you regret hiring me?"

Helene almost smiled. "No. And no."

"That's good to hear."

She signed the letter and pushed the three papers toward Pepper. The green, so very green eyes dismissed her. "Get out. For good."

Pepper ignored Clarita's furious look when she opened the door. Behind her Helene was already on her call. She glanced down at the pages, making certain it was actually Helene's official signature. It was. And on the termination agreement she'd changed one week's paid vacation to two and initialed it.

It only took a moment to amend the email she'd already composed to her connected contacts. She thanked them for their support and friendship and expressed her hope for their good wishes as she took her life in another direction. Effective immediately.

Clarita watched Pepper pack her things in a box with a satisfied glare that dissolved into confusion when Pepper picked up the box and said, quite sincerely, "Thank you for everything."

Her calm lasted about half the drive home. The rush of tears and bout of the shakes was post-adrenaline letdown, she told herself. Pulled over into a strip mall lot, she sent CC a text saying it went even better than she had hoped, then tapped open her phone app. The call went to Alice's voice mail, which was good because she was blubbering.

"It went okay. It was just like you said. I showed her how it could be a win for her." She paused to gulp in air. "So now I'm just—it's just letdown. Ignore me. I'm a mess. Promise me you'll still end your road trip here. I don't mean—just don't change your mind, okay? I'm counting the days."

She disconnected. Reconnected with a tap on Alice's picture. "Sorry about that. I'm not desperate. It's just—" Her thumb accidentally brushed the end call button.

She made herself take three deep breaths before trying again.

"Sorry about that. Sorry. No pressure, I just really want to see if—if there's an us. Eighty-six days I can make it. I have a life to get together. It'll be fine. I'll hardly miss you. I didn't tell you, but the mixologist from the gala referred an event planner to me who left a message that might be something to pursue, but I didn't call back yet because I didn't know what would happen today and now I do and it's okay. I'm going to be fine. Just don't change your mind." She sniffled. "Sorry, that was probably loud. I lied before, I will miss you, like a lot." Even as she screamed at herself not to be any more stupid, she tacked on, "No pressure. Just circling back and checking in. See you. No worries. And you were right all along—rocks shouldn't be anywhere near hoo-hoos. Hoo-hoos are already perfect."

She threw her phone on the seat. No more calling Alice. It was too pathetic.

A scant hour later, changed into her wetsuit and hair caught back in a ponytail, she pulled her board out of the Prius, tucked it under her arm, and headed for the surf at Topanga. No matter how the conversation with Helene had gone, she'd promised herself time on her board before the day was out, even if it was floating with her feet in the water.

SurfsUp app said Topanga was today's best bet with middling offshore winds. There was fifty percent chance of finding a good wave or two. Tomorrow it predicted Malibu might be even better, though the best waves were likely two hours north, above Santa Barbara. For the first time in ages she would have a whole day to herself, no plans. Why not go for a drive and blow away some cobwebs to start this new phase of her life? She could surf every day until a new job was found.

She walked her board into the surf until it was easy to settle on it, belly down. Paddling out felt good, as if she was leaving everything Helene Jolie behind. She was headed toward her own definition of "best."

The quiet of the ocean, combined with the habitual scanning of the waves, freed up her mind to think about the future. It was full of unknowns, and that included Alice and whatever future they could make. Now that she no longer had anything to fear from Helene, however, the deeper fear that Alice might never make it to California after all surfaced.

She desperately hoped that Alice had seen her text first, telling her the first voice mail was the only one worth listening to and to please delete the other two. Alice had plans, and they would make Alice very happy. Whining and sniveling was not attractive—why would Alice want that? They'd talk later. She'd convince Alice that all was well. They both needed time to roam—so many beaches, so little time, she'd say.

The sun bouncing off the water made her tear up. Yeah, that was why.

A forming wave looked promising but flattened a few seconds after she positioned to ride it. She paddled out a little more and went back to watching the ocean roll. The water was bracing, there was salt spray on her face, and the sun was warm on her shoulders. How could she be wasting this moment on foolish worries that would still be there when she got back to shore?

Today, Topanga. Tomorrow, Santa Barbara? The day after…who knew? Soothed, there was nothing more in her mind than finding the best wave. It would come to her. She just had to be patient.

CHAPTER FORTY-NINE

Alice shaded her eyes as she once again scanned the waves off Malibu. All the surfers wore wetsuits. From this distance most of them looked alike. Could Pepper be the one on a turquoise board, hunched low to eke a few more seconds before the wave crumbled? Or the one surging gracefully to a full stand atop an aqua and white board as a wave reached its peak?

She watched the second surfer trace a delicate line along the wave for a minute, then cut right and left as if dancing with the water as it sloped toward the shore.

This was her third beach since leaving the airport after a thankfully uneventful red-eye. She'd even managed an hour's sleep.

Discouraged, she glanced at the nearest parking lot again. There were eight Priuses. Three were pale green. None of them had the Wonder Woman, Baby Pikachu, and Captain Marvel stickers she was looking for. That didn't mean Pepper wasn't there. Some beaches, like this one, had street parking in all directions.

Every time she told herself this was a stupid, impetuous plan, she played Pepper's voice mails from yesterday again in her head. In her attempt to give Pepper space and time to deal with her job in her own way, she hadn't convinced Pepper that nothing would keep her from ending her road trip right here.

As soon as she'd heard the voice mails, she'd called Pepper back, only to go to voice mail. When they'd finally connected, Pepper had laughed it off—she'd been overwrought. It was all reaction to quitting. Alice should ignore her temporary insecurities. She would be very busy making up for lost time at the beach, not to worry. Alice was to take her time roaming the continent and have as much fun as possible.

Alice hadn't believed a word of it. The sound of Pepper sniffling in the voice mails—loud, human, and adorable—had made her realize it was stupid to end her road trip in LA when she could begin it there instead. All the items she'd gathered to pack in her car went into suitcases instead. Anything else she could buy. Then she had called her mother to explain why she'd miss New Year's Eve because she was getting on a red-eye.

Her mother hadn't sounded the least bit upset. "You may have dodged a bullet."

"Why would you say that?"

"I've decided to have a salon in the spring. You were going to help me plan the guest list."

"That's a great idea. I'd have been happy to help. What made you decide to do it?"

"I asked around, here and there, and it seems people are hungry for interesting conversation, and in person. Tell me why you're abandoning me."

"I'm California dreaming, I guess you could call it."

"Is this about your Paddington?"

"She's not my—"

"You want her to be."

"Yes. I might not have been plain enough about that, and she's afraid I'm going to ghost her."

"You should correct that assumption."

"She's a lot younger than I am. What if this is a midlife crisis of some kind?"

"Oh, Al." Her mother had laughed. "Whatever crises you have started long before now. Wanting a future with your Paddington is not one of them."

Her mother was right, of course. Even if this impetuous plan was a crisis, she wasn't going to fight it. She could fight the urge to drown her uncertainty in whiskey, but she wasn't going to fight love.

Arriving on Pepper's doorstep as a surprise was the plan. But Pepper hadn't been there and hadn't yet answered a casual text asking what her plans were for her first full day of unemployment.

Blinking away sleep, CC had told her Pepper had gone surfing. "She went out on her board yesterday and said last night maybe Santa Barbara for today, but look at SurfsUp. It's an app. It's not great surfing this time of year as a rule, so she'd go where the waves were predicted the best."

Alice had thanked her and turned to leave when CC had asked, "Did she know you were coming?"

"No. Please don't tell her I'm here."

"Dude. I knew I liked you." She had stifled a yawn and closed the door.

The downloaded app had said Malibu was best today, at a spot nicknamed Heaven. But it didn't say if Heaven was at Malibu State Beach, Malibu Lagoon Beach North, Malibu Lagoon Beach South, Malibu Surfrider Beach—

"You're eighty-five days early."

And there she was, standing to her left, with the California sun turning her wet hair the color of wheat. This square of pale, satiny sand, under an impossibly blue sky, with raucous gulls declaring everything was *mine-my-mine-my*—it was Heaven.

She was impossibly there, water still dripping from her wetsuit, with a white patch of sunblock on her nose. Close enough to touch.

Close enough to kiss.

Pepper dropped her aqua and white board and Alice pulled her close.

"You'll get wet."

"That's the idea."

Pepper laughed until Alice kissed laughter away. The salt on Pepper's mouth made Alice thirsty for all of her, every inch.

She only stopped when Pepper put a hand on her chest and pushed her away. "Why—how are you here?"

"A cab ride, an airplane, and a rental car. CC told me you'd gone surfing."

"I left super early. I was thinking Santa Barbara—"

Alice waved her phone. "But it was better here, at Heaven."

Pepper's smile pulled hard to the side. "Clever woman."

"We could still go there, if you want. Or stay here and you pick some more waves. I have a picnic."

"But why did you come?" Pepper's smile went away. "Because I was stupid and pathetic on the phone?"

"No—because I was stupid and pathetic."

Pepper's gaze narrowed as if she suspected a trick. "Could you explain more about that?"

Alice lifted Pepper's hands to her lips, kissing first one, then the other. "I drove you away the first time for your sake, at least that's what I told myself. This time I didn't push you away, but I didn't pull you close. I believed that if you knew me better, you'd love me less."

The frown had slowly left Pepper's face. "I thought I was giving you space to roam and recover your bliss. Then I quit my job and this crazy fog lifted off my brain. I could see clearly for the first time in a long while that if I kept going the direction I was headed, I'd end up where I didn't want to be."

How had she ever thought Pepper was a bubblehead?

"Wait." Pepper looked up through her eyelashes. "You think maybe I love you?"

"I'm not going to find out one way or the other from the other side of the country."

"Do you think maybe you love me?"

"It's impossible that I do, but I think—" Alice's gaze swept over the golden sand, the sparkling surf, the pattern the surfers drew on the water, and back to the soft wonder in Pepper's eyes. "I didn't know I could believe in impossible things, but I do."

Pepper's lips parted with a soft sigh. "Is it hard to do that?"

"Not with you close to me. And keep looking at me like that and we're going to get arrested."

Pepper's shout of laughter scared away a gull stalking them. "Do you have any idea how hard it is to get out of a wetsuit? Underneath I'm covered in salt water. Parts of me are sandy, and there are places where I do not want that sand to go." She went on tiptoe to kiss Alice softly on the lips. "But I am naked underneath."

Alice shivered in spite of the warm sun. "That's not helping my composure."

"What makes you think I care about your composure?"

"Well, when you put it that way, composure is clearly overrated." She brushed her lips over Pepper's forehead. "When you realized what direction you didn't want your life to go, did you think about where you did want it to go?"

She felt Pepper's nod against her shoulder. "Time with you. Time to learn you. Of course that whole sexy thing we do—"

"—so well." Alice nodded vigorously. "We do it so well."

"But more than that. I think we can have more than that."

"Me too." Her heart settled into a solid, steady beat for what felt like the first time since their kiss under the moon. "Want to start with a picnic? I tried not to buy too much, but there was an insane selection of cheese and gorgeous strawberries."

Pepper picked up her board and let Alice pull her toward the parking lot. "I am starved now. That was my last run."

"I'm glad to be able to take care of one hunger at least."

Pepper stumbled to a stop at the Alice's rental car. "Is that a convertible?"

"Your powers of observation astound me."

"You are such a snark. Why did you rent a convertible?"

"I thought you'd like it." Alice watched the hard top fold in half and slide into its storage compartment, revealing the ice chest she'd bought at a drug store and two shopping bags on the backseat.

"You're not wrong, but, well, how long are you planning on being here before you take off for the wonders of science?"

Alice blinked in surprise at the question. *You think you're so smart, but honest-to-god you're dumb.* She'd left out the most important part.

"I don't think I was clear."

Pepper looked up from her gleeful anticipation of what might be in the ice chest. "About what?"

"About why I'm here, Paddington." Alice forestalled the protest by pointing at the shopping bags. "Marmalade is right there. I have two jars."

"That's a lot for a picnic."

"Probably not enough for a road trip, though."

Pepper's mouth parted. "Are you suggesting... That I come with you?"

"I don't want to start on a road trip without you. Let's explore together. Science. Local artisan crafts. Mexican beaches. You name it."

"But what about New Year's Day being the big launch, leaving from your mother's?"

"That doesn't matter. It's not where or when we go, it's the journey." She let herself fall into the warm invitation of Pepper's brown eyes—eyes full of stars. "If we're lucky, the journey's never finished."

"I like the sound of that." She leaned into Alice's hungry kiss with a sound of surrender.

"I'm going to take that as a yes."

"Yes. Yes to a road trip and yes to a journey that's the best we can make it. Every night and every day." Pepper's gaze slid toward the driver's seat. "Can I drive?"

Alice wasn't used to her stomach dropping into her pelvis, but she liked the sensation. "I think I made it clear I'm okay with you taking charge sometimes."

Pepper blew out a hard breath. "This wetsuit just got really tight."

"Then I'll help you out of it. There was more than one motel on the highway."

"We could picnic indoors?"

"Brilliant idea."

She pulled Pepper close for another kiss, one that was as satisfying as it was promising. The world was still broken in so many ways. Now, it seemed, her heart was finally brave enough to be happy anyway.